"You do not recognize the pin I am wearing? It is yours."

She raised her hand to remove the diamond from the headdress of ostrich feathers fixed in her hair, but he took her wrist and arrested it.

"Please, don't. I never want it back. To my memory, it is full of ill luck." He brought her wrist down between them within the firm band of his fingers. "If you don't want the thing either, you may throw it in the sea."

"I don't think that's necessary." Her voice sounded odd. "You really did not notice it?"

"No. I was too aware of the feathers. With the slightest movement of air, the tip of one floats down and just brushes your face. Here." His fingers let go of her wrist and followed his glance, to touch her temple with the lightest caress.

An incredible impulse overcame her to turn her lips into his palm and lean her whole body into the warmth of his. All the resistance she could summon was to close her eyes for an instant, and he withdrew his fingers, but only to place both hands over her shoulders. She felt his breath soft on her face. "Look at me. Ever since that night I have wanted to obliterate the piece of madness and misfortune we forged between us."

She opened her eyes and felt as though she were spinning into the blackness of his. "But how?"

She knew the answer. She wanted the answer.

Once again his lips spoke to her alone . . . .

Siren

Cheryl Sawyer

A SIGNET ECLIPSE BOOK

SIGNET ECLIPSE
Published by New American Library, a division of
Penguin Group (USA) Inc., 375 Hudson Street,
New York, New York 10014, USA
Penguin Group (Canada), 10 Alcorn Avenue, Toronto,
Ontario M4V 3B2, Canada (a division of Pearson Penguin Canada Inc.)
Penguin Books Ltd., 80 Strand, London WC2R 0RL, England
Penguin Ireland, 25 St. Stephen's Green, Dublin 2,
Ireland (a division of Penguin Books Ltd.)
Penguin Group (Australia), 250 Camberwell Road, Camberwell, Victoria 3124,
Australia (a division of Pearson Australia Group Pty. Ltd.)
Penguin Books India Pvt. Ltd., 11 Community Centre, Panchsheel Park,
New Delhi - 110 017, India
Penguin Group (NZ), Cnr Airborne and Rosedale Roads, Albany,
Auckland 1310, New Zealand (a division of Pearson New Zealand Ltd.)
Penguin Books (South Africa) (Pty.) Ltd., 24 Sturdee Avenue,
Rosebank, Johannesburg 2196, South Africa

Penguin Books Ltd., Registered Offices:
80 Strand, London WC2R 0RL, England

First published by Signet Eclipse, an imprint of New American Library,
a division of Penguin Group (USA) Inc.

First Printing, January 2005
10 9 8 7 6 5 4 3 2 1

PUBLISHER'S NOTE
This is a work of fiction. Names, characters, places, and incidents either are
the product of the author's imagination or are used fictitiously, and any resemblance to actual persons, living or dead, business establishments, events, or
locales is entirely coincidental.

To my beloved
Benjamin, Gabriel and Catherine

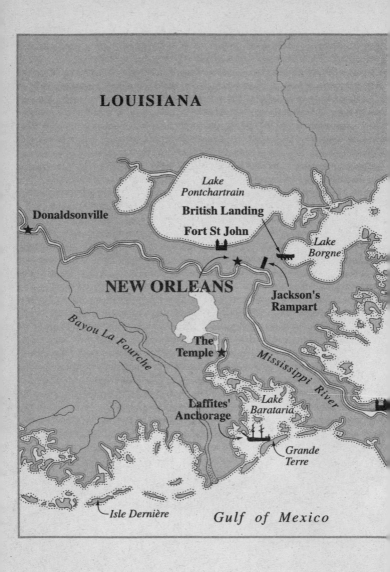

LOUISIANA

Donaldsonville

Lake Pontchartrain

British Landing

Fort St John

Lake Borgne

NEW ORLEANS

Jackson's Rampart

Bayou La Fourche

The Temple

Mississippi River

Laffites' Anchorage

Lake Barataria

Grande Terre

Isle Dernière

Gulf of Mexico

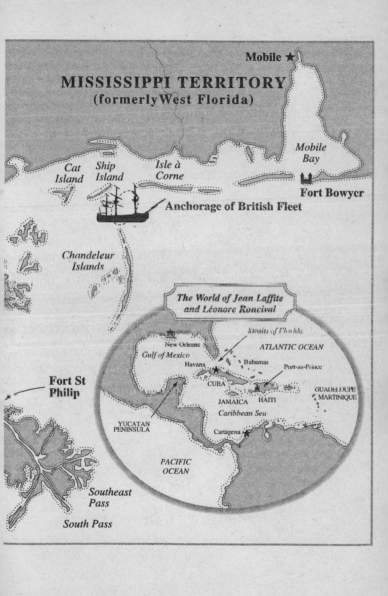

MISSISSIPPI TERRITORY
(formerly West Florida)

Mobile ★

Cat Island

Ship Island

Isle à Corne

Mobile Bay

Fort Bowyer

➤ Anchorage of British Fleet

Chandeleur Islands

The World of Jean Laffite and Léonore Roncival

New Orleans

Gulf of Mexico

Straits of Florida

ATLANTIC OCEAN

Havana

Bahamas

Port-au-Prince

CUBA

JAMAICA

HAITI

GUADELOUPE
MARTINIQUE

YUCATAN PENINSULA

Caribbean Sea

Fort St Philip

PACIFIC OCEAN

Cartagena

Southeast Pass

South Pass

Yes, it was love—unchangeable—unchanged.

Byron, "The Corsair"

CHAPTER ONE

Whore

"The Whore of San Stefan is recruiting."

The word was out from the Antilles to the Floridas when it reached the ears of Jean Laffite, but he caught it only in passing from a conversation in the street and did not bring it up until nightfall, when he sat in a harborside tavern on Haiti with the captain of one of his ships, the *Raleigh*.

Curtis looked uneasy jammed in the corner before him, but he was a surly rogue at the smoothest of times and unready to meet the eye. Curtis was prompt in action, so he saw no profit in being pleasant in the bargain. The crewmen on the *Raleigh* had always remarked that there was a deal of oil in him, which put an odd sheen on his dark, greasy locks and the olive-green eyes that were moving continually just now as he took in the crowded barroom.

Jean Laffite, with his back to the crowd, was well placed to observe the captain's face.

"I heard tell of the Whore of San Stefan today. That wouldn't be Roncival's daughter by any chance?"

Curtis nodded.

"So she's abroad. With what, a press-gang?"

Curtis shrugged.

His leader caught and held the swiveling gaze. "She was in Port-au-Prince three days ago. So were you. What was she up to?"

"Hiring. She came in a cutter and held court at the Amiral de Grasse."

In the succeeding pause, Jean's patience gave out, though his voice was even as he said, "And what was she offering?"

Curtis started. "The usual, I suppose: no pay without a prize."

"That's not what the bosun said. He told me she was handpicking and offering retainers to the most likely. How did that sound to you? Serious?"

Curtis shook his head and shifted on the chair so that it scraped on the lime-washed wall. "No doubt she's run short of staff on the island. The father's been dead a while—she'll have lost a few who have gone to seek work elsewhere."

Jean took a sip of rum, dissatisfied with the shadowy picture in his mind that the captain, from inattention or dubious motives, had done nothing to clarify the mistress of an island coming out of seclusion and sailing sixty leagues or more to personally interview a servant or two.

"Seamen, gunners, carpenters, what of them?"

Curtis shrugged again. "Can't see what she would want them for—Roncival's brigantine has not been seen for a year, and the cutter was fully manned when she sailed in. She hired a mason, though."

"Rebuilding the fortifications," Jean said thoughtfully. They said that San Stefan had an enviable little harbor and the Roncival headquarters was a veritable fortress. "Whence comes this Whore of San Stefan business? I never heard her called so before. Nor anything, come to think of it, besides Madame Ch'ing." At Curtis's puzzled frown he said, "It's in jest, man. You've surely heard of Madame Ch'ing—she rules the South China Sea, with tens of thousands of pirates under her command. There's competition for you! Whereas Roncival would seldom have led more than two hundred tars and landsmen together, and only the dregs of them would be left on San Stefan now. Explain this talk of whores."

Curtis took a swallow of ale and licked his lips. "It

seems the father took her education in hand when she was a slip of a girl. Her first bedfellow he chose for her out of the finest bucks in the crew. From then on she singled out her own. They say there's nothing even a doxy from Havana could teach her."

"Enough of that." Jean shifted his chair closer to the table and Curtis sat up straight in alarm. "Name what she offered you. Then tell me everything you know about San Stefan."

It was marked on few charts, and those mariners who had sighted it would have been puzzled to state whether the solitary coral cay was rightly in the Jamaica Channel or the Windward Passage. Even for the rare navigators who knew it, finding it in that confluence of currents was like snatching one sapphire from a cascade of aquamarines, for they reckoned it a jewel of price. It might have been formed by volcanic eruption, but it had a near-perfect ring of coral around it, and was high enough to give vantage to a fortified mansion, built of the greenish lava that was the bedrock of the island. Behind that the home farm flourished on a sheltered plain, watered by a stream that ran from the peak down to the palm-fringed lagoon. It might be tiny, but it had a harbor and means of subsistence, and it was positioned in one of the busiest sea lanes in the Caribbean.

On their morsel of land, roughly equidistant from the hammerhead shark of Cuba, seal-shaped Jamaica and the crab claws of Haiti, previously Santo Domingo, the inhabitants of San Stefan had always maintained circumspect relations with the colonial administrations of Spain, England and France. All of these had fitfully argued over the sovereignty of the island, but none of them had rejected any trade and tribute that came their way from the families who had lived there over the last two centuries. For nine years, since 1800, the island had been more or less accorded to France, and Edouard Roncival of San Stefan had operated as a privateer with letters of marque from the governor of Guadeloupe. But now the letters of marque had expired, Roncival's ships had not been sighted for a year, and the master himself was dead. San Stefan, hard to locate and even harder to define, was adrift again in her expanse of blue ocean.

Though their haven had seen no traffic for many months, the islanders kept a sea eye out; and one fine afternoon, some time after Jean Laffite's conversation in Haiti, the lookouts and guards had been faithfully posted while Roncival's daughter took a dip in the little bay they called Anse des Lianes—or, in the unmelodious English also spoken on San Stefan, Creeper Cove.

Here the reef lay closest to the island's white sand, and a few strong strokes through the turquoise water brought a swimmer over its clustered coral and luminous fish. Alone, half-naked in the bay, the young woman glided with the gentle wash of the tide back and forth across the coral. Clad only in a piece of white cloth knotted around her hips, she opened her eyes wide in the warm, clear water to watch the sunlight ripple over the treasures of the reef.

Her ears were filled with the tingling, electric sizzle of the coral organisms around her, the peppery sound of small fish feeding amongst the sea urchins, the louder concussions as bigger fish crunched into the outcrops, sending bright fragments drifting to the sea floor. She lingered, looking seaward each time she took a gulp of air, opening her eyes again the moment her face plunged into the water, her mind expanding to take in this other world, this paradise garden that always greeted her with the unfamiliar—a yellow fish with an orange-striped tail that she had never noticed before, a chartreuse sea anemone with arms like pygmy grass snakes and, barely visible at the bottom of a dim coral canyon, the blue-painted zigzag in the sand that was all she could discern of a giant clam.

She followed a depression in the reef that guided her back to the beach, taking a last look at a shoal of blue-and-green fish that were going the same way. Then, when the outcrops grew scarce and lost their color, she drifted in on her back, eyes shut, letting her hair slide off her shoulders and undulate like weed tendrils in the waves.

Lazily scooping the water with her hands, she turned on the surface so that her toes pointed to the beach, then lowered them to the sand. When she stood, eyes closed and head tilted back, her hair tugged at her temples and clung to her skin, the ends curling into the small of her back with a wet caress.

She opened her eyes—and looked straight into those of a man.

He was a few feet away, his tall figure stark as a totem on the deserted beach. The shock drove the breath from her lungs, but she held his gaze, seized with something beyond fear, as though he had come there by magic.

He was a total stranger, for if she had ever seen those eyes before she would remember them: black and hard as jet. The thick lashes did not soften the stare, which was shamelessly aggressive. But the sensuous bathe in the sea had roused her responses so that she was aware of each fraction of movement that occurred: though her body was rigid, her eyes and mind had already followed, with minute attention, the split second reactions in his own. She had seen his pupils open like midnight flowers with desire. She saw the flicker of the eyelids that registered an assault on his senses that he had not predicted, even though he might have been watching her for several minutes, waiting for this very particular fish to swim into his trap. She caught the tremor under the tanned skin where his white shirt opened at the neck, and she knew the sight of her had taken him by the throat and reversed for one uncontrollable instant his game of hunter and hunted.

"Damn you," she lashed out. "Turn your back."

The stare became one of rude surprise. "A fine welcome, madame, to civilized company."

She was breathless. Anger and defiance stopped her from the instinctive, maidenly gesture of trying to cover her breasts with her hands or from shrinking down into the limpid water. Her exposed body blazed at him in outrage while she fought to hold his gaze and at the same time see beyond him to the fringe of palms behind the beach where her people had been keeping guard.

"You deserve a dog's welcome for an approach like this. If you claim to be a gentleman, turn your back."

He turned thoughtfully around, which gave him, too, the opportunity to scan the beach. Then his head pivoted so that she could see his profile and he could give her a sidelong glance if he chose. "And what do you do to dogs, madame? Throw stones? Unless you are standing on one, there are none to be had."

He made "madame" sound an insult.

"Mademoiselle," she hissed, then stopped. Fear began to take over from shock. As he pointed out, she had no weapon. She examined him quickly: neither did he, unless he had a knife down the side of one boot.

Soft sea boots: he had come ashore in haste. An invader. The cotton shirt he wore was of an expensive, almost transparent weave; she could see his finely muscled shoulders and back underneath it, and he wore no sword or pistol at the belt. But the fringe of the cove was silent and empty: someone lately had held weapons, and used them to overpower all her people while she swam.

"Dogs like you? We shove a grenade up their backside."

He gave a quick laugh.

Before he could speak again, she said, "Step away."

Her shawl lay just behind his right heel. It was rumpled, so she knew he had lifted it to see what might be hidden underneath. Nothing: her lack of preparedness swamped her mind like a deluge. He could have spun on his heel and grabbed her, but she had time to pick up the shawl, fling it around her and move back to the water margin before he turned and examined her again. Who was he? She was not going to give him the satisfaction of a question.

"This is my island. No one lands here without invitation."

"If it were yours," he said in his flawless French, "I should make humble obeisance and beg your pardon for trespass." He bowed to her: the graceful movement

shook his sleek black hair over his cheeks, but when he
rose the locks fell neatly behind his ears again, revealing
long sideburns. His white teeth flashed at her as he said
mockingly, "But tell me: exactly how does San Stefan
belong to you?"

"By my family's right of occupation." She was drenched;
the fringes of the long shawl clung to her shins while he
stood before her, impeccable in manner and dress, and
his every word implied contempt for her person—but
she cared nothing for what he thought of her. It was
what he did in the next few minutes that mattered, for
he was a killer and her life depended on his whim.

"No deeds, no perpetual leases, not a scrap of paper
to show?" he said. "But I am standing in your way—
please precede me, mademoiselle." He stepped aside
and gestured for her to walk by him.

She padded up the sand, the shawl twisted under her
upper arms, feeling on her shoulders the heat of the
afternoon sun and the hard gaze of the man who followed her. She lifted the shawl high across her shoulder
blades and shook her hair so it fanned down to her
waist: he would read no more from her back than she
permitted him to.

Ahead was silence: Adélaïde, who had been resting in
the palm grove, did not appear, and there was no sight
or sound of Bernard, who had also been detailed to wait,
armed, farther over the rocks as usual.

All the precautions that belonged to her island life
had been taken today, but they had not been enough
against this man and whomever he had brought with
him. She dreaded to find Adélaïde stretched on the
ground amongst the palm trees. But there was no one
there, and her own clothes were gone. Yet she had heard
no shot, no sound from the beach or from the other side
of the high, wooded ridge of rock that divided the cove
from the lagoon. The hammock in the grove hung motionless, empty except for a flat-brimmed black hat, and
nothing stirred in the palm fronds around the clearing.

She faced him. "Where is the woman who was waiting
for me?"

"I sent her home. With your guard, under escort."

The tone was calm, and he stood there looking so perfectly at his ease that there was something almost languid about his posture: one well-turned leg was a little advanced beyond the other, giving a slight tilt to his hips, his arms were balanced at his sides, and there was not a tense line in his body.

"Insults from a cur like you cannot touch me. But if you have harmed any of my people, that is another matter. For which you will pay."

The black eyes snapped open to their largest, revealing for a second white lines below the irises. "Insults? I never in my life offered a lady anything but the utmost courtesy."

The rude implication, that *she* was no lady, enraged her. "Courtesy, you call it, to dismiss my people, steal my clothes and invade my privacy? You may take those manners back to the gutter where you came from."

His left eyelid came over his eye in a slow wink and stayed there, giving him a deceptively humorous look. He said softly, "Would you have preferred that I lurk here in the bushes? Spy on you as you came up from the beach? Watch you as you dried yourself and put on your clothes, while I savored each movement from my hiding place? No, I came to meet you openly, and ensured that no one else should see you thus. Your dignity is intact, mademoiselle; on that you have my word."

Her lip curled. "*Your* word!" To her left was a tall palm tree. She took one step back. "I want nothing from you." Two steps. "Least of all your words." Another palm. Three steps and there, within arm's reach, was the mimosa sapling, in the fork of which Adélaïde always left the paring knife that she used to peel fruit when she lounged in the shade, whiling away the hot hours. "And your actions are beneath contempt."

The fourth step was sideways: she flung out her arm and her fingers just touched the handle of the knife—but he was there before her, swift as a snake striking. He thrust her left arm high and took her right wrist in the other hand. Her shawl, unsupported, began to slip down between them, and his gaze dropped to her breasts. His breathing changed, but his hold did not slacken. She took the chance, however, and drew back one knee to swing it up hard between his—but once again he forestalled her. Twisting, he deflected the thrust with his thigh and crushed her chest against his.

She was off balance in his arms, whereas in that split second he moved to strengthen his stance, wrapping his long hands around hers to clamp them in the small of her back. She strained away, averting her eyes.

Neither said a word. She was trembling, and she knew he could feel it. The warmth of his chest invaded her breasts and ascended in a wave to her throat, robbing her of speech. Her shoulders and back hurt as she arched away, and the front of her body felt the touch of his skin beneath the open shirt, his firm stomach and the contour of his thighs alongside hers.

He bent as though to kiss her neck. "You would kill me? What a waste, for both of us." It was a mere whisper, his breath caressing her bare skin.

She gasped, her body moved against him and she felt his response with an intimate knowledge that only this hot, stifling contact could give her—and with that knowledge came a lava flow of rage so powerful that it seemed to come from outside herself, sweeping her along in its path.

She cried out, twisted in his grasp, rammed her knees against his in a frenzy of protest, and lunged forward to sink her teeth into his collarbone.

She drew blood. She tasted it, warm and salty, before he flung her from him. She staggered back and regained her balance, then snatched the shawl higher again.

He was motionless, so still he seemed not to breathe. The black eyes were wide on hers, not with the naked stare of their meeting, nor the lazy, sensuous contemplation of a few moments before. He made no move to staunch the drops of blood that welled out to soak the soft, absorbent shirt. He had an open, almost questioning look, as though he were seeing her for the first time. To break the gaze, she swung round and walked away.

She went on through the grove to the short, steep slope that led to the top of the ridge, picking her way among the rocks. Without turning, she knew he followed. Out of the corner of her eye, just as she stepped out of the shade of the palms, she had seen him take the hat from the hammock and the knife from the fork of the tree. Thereafter she did not deign to look behind, and he trod so smoothly she could not hear him. But she could feel him, several paces back, stepping like a panther, weighing the pointed knife in his hand.

Over the knoll, onto the forest path along the ridge. The mansion and the lagoon would be in view when she turned at the end to go downhill. If she lived to see them. If the man to whom she had surrendered her knife did not decide to use it.

She reached the giant candlenut tree at the turn, and all at once the knife flashed by her, inches away, and thudded deep into the bark. She faltered and put out one hand towards the ivory hilt. The man behind her stopped. She felt his tension, as though the blood thundered in his veins to the same rhythm as her own. He had given her back the knife: she had only to snatch it out and turn it on him. For a split second she was tempted to try. Then she straightened her shoulders and walked on.

Dominique You was amused and concerned. The entry into San Stefan had gone as smoothly as a hand sliding into a kid glove, and all seemed secure. But he disliked the unexpected, and he had not been prepared for this being an island of women. He had had a long briefing with Jean Laffite, yet it had not been made quite clear that the person who held precedence on San Stefan was Roncival's young daughter, nor that the queen of the house was the splendid woman who was at present glowering at him from the other end of the terrace. Jean must have been attracted by this intriguing situation—hence Dominique You's private amusement. But, as he sat on the terrace waiting for the daughter's return to the house, he felt uneasy.

Women predominated amongst the rest of the inhabitants too, who had been herded into the half-empty storehouse by the waterfront and locked in. Piles of firewood had been propped against the timber building, and he had six men placed around it with rifles. He had sent Curtis along with the crew of the *Raleigh* to check inland for signs of any others about the island, so there were only five sailors left on the brig, which rode in the lagoon below. To begin with they had stood the *Raleigh* broadside on so her cannon could command the shoreline and the fort itself, but now that the velvet assault was over she swung idly on a single anchor, her drooping foresail reflected in the turquoise water. There was plenty of time to check on the rest of the island and gather up the booty—they could not sail out again until the next tide.

Dominique settled his broad, powerful body in a big cane chair on the terrace and glanced over at the woman, indifferent to her resentful stare, and wondered whether it was this majestic creature who interested Jean, or Roncival's daughter. Perhaps neither. Dominique had good reason to know the differences that could exist among members of the same family, and it intrigued him that Pierre Laffite, older than Jean by a year, was notoriously susceptible to women, while Jean was just as famously discreet. Pierre always had a household companion, but Jean could live in solitude or in a crowd with perfect equanimity, and no woman's name had ever been reliably linked with his own. When the brothers attended the Quadroon Balls, Pierre's hooded eyes would gladden to see the most beautiful and richly dressed mulatto women in New Orleans gathered to tempt his patronage, and he would pass amongst them with his full red mouth half-open in appreciation. Jean, meanwhile, liked to stand in a group and talk, his smile flashing in his tanned face as the young women replied to his adroit compliments, his black eyes sparkling while each one tried to guess whether his celebrated charm would ever be directed at her alone. Pierre was a much more likely catch. But if they danced, it was always with Jean.

"Maître!" One of his men pointed towards the screen of rocks that cut off the view of the ocean to the east. Two figures were descending: a fair-haired female in front, clad in some kind of drapery, and Jean Laffite a few yards behind her, strolling easily, his hat tipped up a little to give him a clear look at the lagoon, the fort and the beach.

Unable to guess whether "the bos" was happy with what he saw or not, Dominique stood up and waited. It was only when they drew closer, and he saw the blood, that his unease began to creep back.

CHAPTER TWO

Bos

Jean Laffite possessed a faculty that as a child he had feared as a kind of failing, but which in his later career had often proved useful: his mind could absorb shock before his body reacted. When he was ten and an earthquake struck his hometown, his ragged little companions ran from the street howling for their mothers, but he stood motionless, the tremors shuddering through his brain, seeking with steady eyes the place where they might be safest. He was walking along the levee in New Orleans one day with his old friend General Humbert when a barrel of gunpowder, unloaded onto the docks behind them, was touched off by a spark from a brazier: the shattering roar made the general stumble on the pavement, while Jean simply smiled and bent to help him up before he even troubled to turn his head towards the explosion.

Others admired this miraculous control, this Olympian armor against panic. But it occurred to him that it was, perhaps, just a weird bafflement of the senses. They believed he could never be startled—but they did not know what happened after the shock, behind the impassive features. The reverberations lasted longer, went deeper: like a burn, which bites into the flesh at a brief, stupefying interval after heat has been applied to the skin.

He felt it now. He took in the lagoon and the fort, swiftly scanning the disposition of his men, and all the while the picture before him was dominated by one luminous figure, seared into his vision.

The fall of hair, curling in glossy waves as it dried, spilling like molten gold down her back. He had trapped the wet tips in his fingers as he hauled her to him.

The long, pure lines of her body, revealed when the dampened shawl clung now and then to her slender hips or a sleek thigh, before it was freed by her undulating stride.

He thrust his mind back to the moment before she had risen like a goddess from the sea, watched her again as she drifted across the reef, rapt and oblivious in the translucent water. In that shimmering interval he could have jettisoned every rumor he had heard about her, undone all his analyses, laid aside his strategy—so that when they came face-to-face, nothing would have hovered between them except the bright salt air of the bay.

But in that blinding moment he had clung to his defenses and come out with words so mechanical he could not recall them now. He remembered hers, however, including the opening curse that still hung, barbed, in his flesh.

Even then, he might have given her the consideration he showed to all women, anywhere, in the street, salon, ballroom, bedchamber—for he never made distinction. But the encounter had altered all his responses: he had never before known the unreasoning lust that shook him after she attacked, nor did he recognize the man who had laid rough hands on her, lunging at her like a drunken sailor with a dockside tart. He had become an unknown being in that incandescent moment of desire. Somehow, reaching for her, he had leaped, fallen, and landed in another world.

He was obliged, however, to cope with this one.

When the *Raleigh* had sailed into the lagoon and he first had a good look at the mansion, he had wondered why the holders of San Stefan had not built it farther up the slope for greater vantage and protection. Studying it now, he revised his view. The stone tower on the flank of rock above commanded at least 250 degrees of ocean and another man could always be placed on the peak

itself, in a direct signal line to the tower. A walkway cut
into the rock and protected by a parapet led from the
tower to the flat roof of the mansion, which was surrounded by crenellations. The story under that housed
all the living quarters, sheltered on three sides by deep
colonnades and terraces.

He glanced up towards the center of the balustrade in
front, and Dominique You, with a lieutenant on the alert
next to him, raised a leisurely hand to indicate the all
clear. Directly below the iron gate was a flight of stone
stairs leading diagonally from the terrace to the rocky
ground. The wall it traversed exceeded the height of two
men and was unadorned by window, cornice, arch or
greenery. Anyone approaching from the shore must
cross to it without a stick of cover in any direction. Anyone mounting to the mansion could be enfiladed from
above and would be exposed in the rear to the ornamen-
tal stone aerie that jutted out from the far corner of
the terrace.

The masters of San Stefan had built their elegant
blockhouse close to the lagoon, the ships, their stores
and their men, who were housed in low timber huts
thatched with palmetto that clustered around the warehouse and refectory at the other end of the beautiful
white curve of the beach.

He slowed his pace and drew a long breath, dispelling
a sharp, ridiculous feeling of dread. Nothing, now, could
occur that he had not foreseen.

At the foot of the stairs she turned like a creature at
bay: he would not have been surprised if she had snarled
at him. Instead she stood erect, watchful, ignoring Dominique and the other man leaning over the gate, and her
lips were set in a way that reminded him, despite her
golden fairness, of the firmly chiseled mouths of certain
African women he knew, which could stop up emotion
at will, and whose feelings, when they did choose to
reveal them, were exclusively those of contempt.

"I presume I may enter my own house?"

"Mademoiselle."

She turned from the correct bow and generous gesture
and went up the stairs. She did not see the flick of his

hand that made Dominique unlatch the gate and then retreat out of view.

He mounted behind her, watching her every step. Her bare shoulders were very straight, and the fine bones at the tips were squared almost like a boy's. Yet there was othing boyish about the fluid movements, the spindrift of hair, the hand she put out to the wall, brushing the stone as though in a secret caress. His eyes followed the pink ovals of her fingertips on the rough surface and the insane idea lanced through him that he had just brutalized a child.

When she reached the top she stepped through the gateway and out of view, so he did not see whether she turned to survey from above what he had wrought in her harbor. By the time he reached the terrace her attention was elsewhere as the black woman rose from a chair at the far end and glided towards her.

Ignoring Dominique and his other three men for a moment, Jean observed the women. The younger, seeing the alarm and anxiety in the elder, allowed the greeting to become an embrace. The black woman's wide sleeves, threaded and clustered with ribbons, fell back from her elbows as the two figures melted together within a gold and ebony enlacement of arms. In the perfect oval of the dark face, pressed to the other's ear, Jean discerned a quality of relief that was hidden from the younger woman by her own abundant hair.

Adélaïde Maselari, mistress of Edouard Roncival for—how long? three or four years perhaps?—was seeking to obliterate in a torrent of half-uttered endearments her failure to convey any warning to Roncival's daughter as she had swum naked and defenseless in the cove over the hill. Jean shrugged: the ambush had been only partly her fault, for they had found the sentry asleep before surprising her. But as the women drew away from him, enveloped in their swift, murmured flow of talk, he saw wariness in the taut lines of the daughter's body.

They retreated to stand by one of the columns, and Jean saw the daughter's eyes flick to the armed guards about them, the *Raleigh* on the lagoon, his men disposed on the beach. Not to him.

Dominique, at his side, gave a low, breathy whistle. In reply Jean merely said, "Curtis?"

"No word."

"He's taking his time."

"It's not easy terrain to traverse, and he's to reconnoiter the peak as well."

Jean nodded towards the swivel gun mounted in the half-moon balcony at the other end of the terrace. "What does that cover?"

"Everything except the slope behind us."

"Where's their magazine?"

Dominique, who had turned towards the women again, dragged his gaze down and looked at his buffalo-hide boots solidly planted on the marble tiles.

Jean gave an incredulous laugh. "You're not going to tell me we're standing on Mount Pelée!"

Dominique continued the contemplation of his brass toe caps. "No. We haven't found the magazine yet. Nor the brigantine. Nor the treasure. So it'll be interesting to see what the tall fellow says next. He's in the cellar, at your disposal."

"The Spanish dug mines on San Stefan last century. If there's one in the hill up there, my guess is it's become the magazine." He looked along the bay to the careening wharf, where the island's cutter, dismasted, lay pinned amongst ropes and pulleys. "The brigantine's God knows where. The treasure's a myth."

Dominique lifted his head, his dark brown hair drifting back off his broad brow. "Until we find it."

Jean made no comment as the lieutenant, Maurice, stepped up and gave him back his sword belt. He had handed it and a pistol to the little troupe that went with him to the cove; at the time, it had seemed best to confront the daughter unarmed.

Dominique looked sidelong at him as he buckled on the sword. To accompany his dryer comments, the older man produced a habitual smile that was simply a downward pucker at one side of his mouth. It threw into sinister relief the old black traces of powder scars on the same cheek. "What did she have, a knife?"

"Yes. But she used her teeth."

The smile spread and Dominique let out a delighted snort. The young woman looked over at once, then gave a challenging stare that did nothing to dim the appreciative light in Dominique's narrow eyes. "Wildcat!" he said under his breath. "When are we going to question *her*?"

"When she's clothed. Where are the household staff?"

"Below."

"Good. Start them working in the kitchen, with a man at each door. We'll be six at table here tonight. Maurice! Get over to the warehouse, haul out their cooks and keep them under surveillance while they prepare a meal."

"For how many, Bos?"

"Their own people, ours, and Curtis when he and his idlers get back—a hundred. They're not to stir from the cookhouse; convey any food they request from the stores or the cellars, but no one goes to the gardens. Keep your eyes on them: anyone raising a hand to do more than slice a melon goes back in with the women. With buckshot in him if necessary."

"And drink, Bos?"

Jean said nothing and, when he judged the silence had gone on long enough, asked softly, "You need it before you can move?"

Maurice stammered out, "Yes, Bos. I mean no. I mean—" Dismissed by a flick of the head from Dominique, he escaped down the stairs at a run.

With Dominique at his side, Jean approached the women. There was no fear in either of their faces, but at the base of the fair throat, below the twin accents of her collarbones, there was a shiver in the smooth skin as though she had just managed to quell a movement of alarm.

He spoke first to Adélaïde Maselari. "Madame, will you have the indulgence to go with Monsieur You and give instructions for supper? I would suggest we eat in two hours: besides your good selves there will be four other covers. Until then you'll no doubt prefer to keep to your quarters."

He could not read her expression, but he saw a surprising depth of calculation in her eyes, dark coils of thoughts that flashed nothing from their surfaces except maybe amusement. "You consider two hours sufficient? I would not have them stint on the meal."

"Yes," she said calmly.

He bowed and smiled at her as Dominique moved forward, then watched the two walk away into the shadows under the colonnade. Next to the statuesque woman, Dominique's slight swagger and the set of his square shoulders somehow accentuated his lack of height, but there was no doubt about the quiet menace of his strength.

"A moment." They both turned. "Let us first accompany Mademoiselle Roncival to her quarters."

The woman in front of him looked up with instant suspicion, but he took a step back, inclined his head, and after the briefest pause she walked in under the colonnade. In her swift, raking glance beyond his shoulder he had seen the opalescent blue of the bay and its crescent of sand flash by in bright miniature on the clear whites and deeper turquoise of her extraordinary eyes. She was on the watch.

She passed the others and walked with dignified lack of haste into the cool depths of the house. He snapped his fingers so that a guard followed, and made his way after her in silence. He took a last look at the lithe form that he had seen naked in the sea, and a wrench of temptation seized him so profoundly that he was barely aware of where he placed his feet. The air between his pulsing body and hers was so charged that it seemed impossible the others were not conscious of what was happening to him. Or that they did not await another snap of the fingers, the slam of a door, that would leave him once more alone with the woman who drifted tantalizingly before them, like a shade returning to some mysterious underworld of desire.

Mastering his breathing, he slowed so that he had Dominique at his shoulder and the black woman a little in front with the guard. Today must hold no more of the unforeseen, the unwitnessed. Those present were assembled for his purpose, and he had chosen years ago the path on which the personal was forever bound up with the strategic. Which included the manner in which he was known. He had been called, to his knowledge and with his ironical concurrence, a great many names in his time, but there were some that no man or woman had ever said to his face and that even at a distance no one, he made sure, joined with his. As far as he was concerned, Jean Laffite's reputation for rape had begun and ended in the palm grove over the hill.

The interior of the house was built on classic lines, with square, ample rooms linked by corridors faced with marble. He spread the floor plan out in his mind as they penetrated and realized when they came to a stop in a handsome doorway that the master's bedchamber was hers. It hinted at the recent shifts in status that must have occurred between Roncival's daughter, mistress and company.

He turned and ran his eye over four faces, taking in veiled curiosity, stony indifference, amusement and loathing.

"Alas, mademoiselle, before you enter this room I must in all prudence examine what it contains. I beg your forgiveness for the intrusion." Conjuring up a smile of seraphic sincerity, he continued. "And you have my assurance that this is the last, the very last, outrage that will be visited upon you."

Then he walked into her bedchamber and closed the door.

CHAPTER THREE

❦

Maître

The rage when she was left alone was like a white fire behind her eyes. She could see nothing for a moment, as though the man had swept her whole world out to sea and marooned her on bare rock under a blinding sun.

When the room came back into focus, her eyes scoured it for a weapon so she could smash the door back and launch herself at him, strike him down and render him gasping, beaten, powerless. But there was nothing here she could use, as his efficient survey had shown.

Everything was in place, but he must have seen and fingered it all. With wild anger she flung open the door of one of the armoires. He would have run one hand along this line of gowns to ensure that her French silks and fine muslins did not conceal any less feminine accoutrements. She opened the next. He would have plunged his arms in amongst her dresses from New Orleans, deep into the riot of expensive satins, brilliantly sewn and decorated, with their triple sleeves and flounces, their frills and lace, cascades of beads and ribbons.

He had seen and bruised her naked flesh. He had touched everything she might wear, and he had his hands on her every possession.

She went to sit by the dressing table, with her back to the mirror. As always, despite the turmoil, her gaze went across the dim interior, towards the sky. She looked out and up, beyond the carved frame that divided

the chamber from her sitting room, through the wide
wooden casement that opened onto the western colonnade and terrace. There the sky shone like a piece of
rare porcelain between the columns, its blue glaze reflected in the gleaming floor under her bare feet, at the
edges of the thick, scattered rugs, in fragments under
tables and chairs.

She began to think, and the trembling eased. She was
to emerge when she was dressed. She had not demanded
that he send up her maid, for she wanted no one around
her. She needed quiet and time to gather her resources
and, heedless, he was allowing her both.

She got up, let the shawl slip to the floor and went to
the other side of the room where the big copper dish
full of fresh water awaited her return from bathing. On
the table beside it were towels, soap and a sponge. It
was out of sight of the casement and terrace, so there
was no sky-blue in the dark reflections she disturbed on
stepping into it, and the water was as sleek and cool as
if it welled from the bedrock of a cave.

She bent, filled the sponge and then raised her arm to
let the spring water run over her face and throat, slide
in rivulets down over her breasts, drip into the ankle-
deep pool with a sound like raindrops shaken from the
tips of leaves. She rinsed all the salt from her skin and
hair, and her mind slipped away from him into realms
where he could not follow. No crude gestures, no breaking down of doors, no pillage in the wide rooms of her
house could yield him the key to what she yet held.

Draped in the towels, she trailed water over the rugs
and pulled across the fretted Moorish screen. Jean Laffite. The worst name that Adélaïde could have told her.

Rubbing her hair dry, she padded about in the half-
light, opening drawers and doors, spreading garments
out on the bed, considering. The lieutenant was Dominique You, second only to Pierre Laffite who, it appeared, was not with them. She selected a pair of finely
worked, supple indoor slippers. There was also the captain, Curtis, who had gone inland with fifty men and
would return at any moment.

She would not pay a band of cutthroats the compli-

ment of appearing before them in an elegant gown, least
of all one in the latest imperial fashion, straight from
Paris. One of her New Orleans dresses would be more
than enough to dazzle Jean Laffite's henchmen, to out-
shine the bandit himself at her own table where he had
had the effrontery to summon her. Enough to subtly
mock him—for who knew the origins of that black-eyed
sea gypsy? The tall tales canceled one another out—he
was the offspring of a baron from some port in southern
France, the son of a fisherman from Martinique, a tavern
keeper's bastard from a Mississippi backwater . . . or he
might have been raised in a New Orleans slum, his only
respite from servitude having been to sing and dance
with the other mulattos and Negroes in Congo Square
on Sundays.

She could not care less where he came from. But she
did not mind if, in the encounter to come, the past that
he concealed under the gaudy tissue of his exploits
should slip back into his mind's eye and turn to parody
the civilized meal that he seemed intent on organizing.

She chose a blue dress. Struggling with the fastenings
as she stood before the cheval glass, she remembered
the day when Adélaïde, back from a trip to New Orleans, had shown her the satin, rolling it out like a wave
around their feet. It was turquoise, not the clear brightness of the lagoon under a high sun, but the color of the
water when clouds were gathering out to sea and the
surface took on a miraculous blue, gone in a moment as
the storm swept over.

"You can't cut that up!"

Adélaïde had put her hands on her hips. "What else
would you do? Buy enough to make sails for a ship?"

"Oh! Imagine. The hull would have to be as light as
a cigar box and—"

Adélaïde had given a crow of exasperation. "Out of
this room. Out of this room if you can't stand the sight
of scissors. I'm not even unpacking the rest if them's
your notions."

The rest had gone on to it nonetheless, tricking it out
in swathes and festoons of vibrant colors. Unlike Adélaïde, she thought it crazy to wear jewelry with such a

confection, and nor did she add ribbons to her thick hair when she coiled it up from her neck. With the aid of a smaller mirror she inspected the result in the cheval glass, then moved into better light.

Holding the mirror at shoulder level, she looked out of the casement. Laffite had a sentry on the parapet against the hill and another in the half-moon battery, but from this angle no one could see into her room unless they paced by outside. Colonnade and terrace were empty.

From here she had an unimpeded view to the west: the bay, the careening wharf, the village, the fringe of palms beyond and, in the background, the lofty treetops of the densest piece of forest on the island.

She glanced into the mirror where the sun, beaming in from its vantage point above the trees, planted a golden kiss on one cheek.

Laffite turned up with uncanny timing when she stepped out of her room. A stillness in the firm features told her that he was not about to betray any interest in her concerns or her person, and there was nothing conciliatory about his voice.

"Mademoiselle, you will have the indulgence to accompany me downstairs." He turned at once and with a flick of the fingers signaled for the guard outside her door to accompany them.

She knew what awaited her in the cellar, for she had overheard most of the exchange between Laffite and You on the terrace. What she would do about it was the gigantic imponderable of this catastrophic afternoon.

Baptiste Baudard, second in command to her father for more than a decade, her own steward since her father's death, shaggy as a sheep in wolf's clothing but unmarked by violence as far as she could see from the tanned skin visible beneath his black, curly fleece, was crouched on a low chair in the middle of the vegetable storeroom. Baskets of legumes had been pushed back to make a bare space about him, and his long legs, folded awkwardly under him, were tied to the back legs of the chair with the same kind of twine that held the bags of

onions to the beam over his head. His hands too were
lashed behind.

He was facing her, and she registered with a small
shock the fear in his eyes, without being quite certain
when it had sprung there: before or after she entered
the room. There was sufficient cause for it in the cutlass
blade that hovered over his jugular.

He spoke at once: "Mademoiselle Léonore!"

"Maître." It was like a whiplash: he must not be allowed to call her by the name they all used before her
father died. She saw him go pale in surprise. Then with
a growl under his breath he gave her the title of master.
Something in the expression of the mouth beneath the
thicket of mustache and beard made her withhold her
own greeting. She had known ever since she took over
the island that Baptiste Baudard thought no woman
could ever run San Stefan. She had felt his own doubts
and the murmurings of the others gather around her like
a squall over a darkening sea, and she had formed some
ideas about what might happen when the clouds opened
upon her. Now the storm had come with Jean Laffite,
and found her defenseless.

Laffite, watching, still said nothing, so she ignored him
and the young ruffian wielding the cutlass. The guard
took a position in the doorway.

"How did this happen, Monsieur Baudard?" When he
hesitated, she went on. "I didn't hear a thing from the
Anse des Lianes. No warning from the tower. No shot
across the bows of that brig when it approached the
reef."

"Forgive me, Maître. The mistake over the lookout
was mine. I gave orders for young Rieux to be sent up,
but there was a misunderstanding. The last man came
down with the all clear and after that there was no
one posted."

She stared at him. "The entrance." They kept two
sentries on the point at all times to man a sixteen-
pounder concealed amongst bushes, which she refrained
just in time from mentioning before Laffite. If the cursed
cannon had not been used he might not know of it.

But it was Laffite who answered. "We were greeted

by muskets, mademoiselle, but so far out of range I am not surprised you failed to hear them. They caused some confusion ashore, for we moored unopposed."

She ground her teeth. Wonderful: the sixteen-pounder must have been out of action, and the men, desperate to give warning by whatever means, had resorted to the very signal used to spell friendly company.

"Nonsense," she spat at Baudard. "How many shots did you hear?"

"We were so taken by surprise, Maître, that no one used their heads to count. And someone said they recognized the brig. It was Boursier's, they said."

"Boursier? Whom we've not seen for three years? In a black-painted shell with not a mark or a flag on her to announce friend or foe? You can do better than that." She took a breath to banish the shudder in her voice. "How many did we lose when the boats hit the beach?"

Once again Laffite interposed. "It will gladden you to learn, mademoiselle, that the landing was swift enough to spare everyone onshore. Aside from a few cuts and bruises, no harm has been done."

She rounded on him, fists clenched. "Then why do you have the man tied like this, when he has just lain down and let you walk right over him? You needed no arms to sack my stronghold, so why keep that dolt there playacting with a cutlass? You have what you came for."

Laffite stood in lithe repose, his body relaxed but his senses fully on the alert, his glance probing hers, as though he could see through her fury to her quivering heart. She tried to keep the challenge in her stance, to goad him into releasing her from the penetration of his dark gaze, but it was Baudard who answered her.

"God have mercy, Maître, never think there was no struggle! They took us by surprise, but we fought them. These rogues are my witnesses—they'd have paid dearly if we had not been so outnumbered." His brown eyes, wide and desperate, caught hers. "And they'll get nothing more out of me. I'm as loyal to the Roncivals as ever I was."

When she turned to Laffite again she just caught an ironic smile on his face. He said, "Indeed, the flow of information does seem to be drying up. We are interested, mademoiselle, in the magazine, your father's vessel and his treasure. So I would appreciate a few words from one of you. Now."

The young man opposite brought his blade delicately down. When he raised it, beads of blood began to form along a fine red line at the junction of Baudard's neck and shoulder.

Léonore tensed. So they had not yet found the magazine. As for the rest . . . She turned to Laffite again. "For someone who has just marched scatheless onto my land and into my house, you give a very flattering picture of your opponents! A magazine? You have withstood all our weapons, so you've seen how few they are. We were wealthy once, but my father's last years were not fortunate. All I own is on full view—would that we had something left to hide from thieves like you! The brigantine was traded long ago, and the cutter is in want of repair. Do what you will; this man cannot help you."

Baudard went pale under the woolly beard. Laffite raised the black bar of one eyebrow and said to him, "Is this true?"

At that moment the sentry stood aside and Dominique You entered. Laffite's look at Baudard had been contemptuous, but when his eyes turned to his lieutenant she saw a spark of impatience in them. Dominique You pulled down the corners of his mouth and gave a slight shake of the head, and Laffite spoke again, his voice cold.

"This charade has gone on long enough."

Baudard burst out, "Let me go!" He looked from the men to Léonore, as though they were joined in persecuting him. "What do you expect of me? I don't know a cursed thing more!" His eyes slid sideways to the hovering blade. "Is this the way to treat me, after . . . ?" The last word trailed away into a charged silence.

Laffite gave a short laugh and said, "Very well. You have an hour to sort this out between you." He nodded to Léonore. "At supper, mademoiselle, I shall be grateful for some answers." To the man with the cutlass, he said, "Leave him. Report to the storehouse." To the sentry: "On guard, outside. Come hell or high water, no one opens this door until I get back."

The heavy door thudded behind them, shutting out the light from two large tallow candles that burned in the wine cellar beyond. The storeroom had no windows, so the fading daylight penetrated only through narrow air vents fashioned high in the stone walls. A smaller candle, stuck on a tin dish on one of the benches, looked as though it would last half an hour at most.

Baudard let his head hang, in relief, pain or exhaustion. Seeing the blood renew its course over his skin, Léonore shuddered and her stomach twisted. She went to lean against a bench near him, her hands behind her gripping the worn wooden edge.

She kept her unsteady voice just above a whisper. "What have they done to you? Are you badly hurt?"

He looked at her cautiously under his bushy brows. "Thank you, Maître, no."

"We lost no one in the raid? Not a man or woman injured?"

"No." He sat straighter. "Can you untie the bonds?"

She went behind him in the half-dark and investigated them with her fingers. "They're too tight for me. We need a knife." She walked round so that she could see his face. "Do you have one?"

He shook his head, and she turned away at once to hide her expression. Tall, big-voiced Baudard, who had kept her father's men in order like a bear with unruly cubs, his snarl always followed by a blow if the master's commands were not promptly carried out. Admiring him from afar when she was younger, sure of his respect though not the indulgence she received from some other members of the crew, she had taken years to see that the men obeyed him simply because of his total dedication to Roncival. They expected no mercy if they stepped out of line, and they feared Baudard's violent temper and his expertise with weapons. Like her, they could see no other gifts for leadership in him, but these were not needed while Roncival lived.

Baudard, whose long, purposeful stride was always accompanied by the percussive concert of his private arse-

nal. Even on the rare occasions when he appeared
unarmed, in an instant he could bring his sharpest dag-
ger glittering to his hand.

Baudard, who for the first time had walked San Stefan
today without weapons. Whose readiness against Laffite's deadly strike had been as thin as air.

Her throat hurt, and tears threatened, but she quelled
them. Propped against the bench as before, she asked
him about the raid: the ship, its firepower, the disposition of Laffite's men, the state of her own. It grew dark
outside, and she did not move the candle nearer, so the
interrogation took place in dim light, but she could see
enough to observe his limbs slowly relaxing as they
talked. By the time she asked for a closer assessment of
Curtis and his crew, he was breathing easily.

She said with a note of approval, "You seem to know
a lot about them. I suppose you picked it up at the
Croix d'Or?"

A tremor went through his bearded cheek. "What do
you mean?"

"I mean the day the *Raleigh* put in to Port-au-Prince.
When you went drinking with their bosun."

"Never. I went out only with the mates on Haiti. I
never knew Curtis was in town."

"Listen. You know why I went to Port-au-Prince: to
look about me. So I kept an eye on everything that
happened in the harbor. Within half an hour of their
arrival I knew the name of the ship and her captain, for
by God they knew mine. I held a discreet chat with one
or two—I'll be interested to see if they're of the party
tonight. But I told no one a thing about San Stefan. And
although I knew you'd talked to them, I believed you
hadn't told them anything either. I was so sure, I never
even questioned you on the way home."

He did not speak or meet her eye, and overcoming a
catch in her throat she went on. "But two weeks ago,
when I sent you to Guadeloupe, something transpired,
did it not?"

The look that sprang into his eyes pushed her over
into an anger that held a bitter core of grief.

With an effort, she kept her voice as low as before.

"That was when the plan was laid. Who thought it up: Curtis? You picked a time of day when the tide was high, to let them over the reef. You picked the hour when I went to the cove for their approach. You spiked the cannon on the point and placed no lookouts on the peak. You stood on the beach and allowed that black hell ship to sail in, the vessel you already knew as well as the back of your filthy hand. I recognized it the second I came over the hill, and you know what it told me? That there was no use fighting or scheming or trying to regain the slightest foothold, because I was already betrayed."

He went to speak then, but she forestalled him, standing up so suddenly she made him jump. She hissed the words as she paced around him. "I should have guessed when you came back from Guadeloupe, but how could I? No one could second-guess a fool as benighted as you. They promised you a share of the prize, I suppose. And a position of rank amongst them. They'd never have offered you command of this island, not since you were already incapable of seizing it yourself—from a woman!" She stopped in front of him and gazed down into his smoldering eyes. "No: you ruled my men, but they would not follow you into mutiny. Not yet, at any rate. You were tender in case they despised you, though. Afraid of revenge. So you struck a bargain with Laffite—"

"I had no truck with Laffite! I swear I never laid eyes on the bastard until today."

"With Curtis, then. You were to be overpowered like all the rest. And thrown belowdecks on the *Raleigh,* perhaps? So none of us would know you had stabbed us in the back until you were out of range of our curses and contempt. But you can see who despises you the most— Laffite. He has used you this once and will never take you up again. And he has handed you back to me like a knife with a broken blade."

"You're wrong, by *Jésu.* You saw me stand up to them—who else would keep your secrets with a cutlass at their throat? Why would I stay mute if it was me as brought them here?"

If he had not blustered, the wild anger that had been

seething in her all afternoon might not have swept to the surface, but she rounded on him: "Keep your voice down. They've learned nothing from you yet because you didn't like the treatment they gave you when they stepped ashore. You kept your sullen mouth shut because the game turned sour and you'd no idea where your advantage lay after that. I've news for you—you have none."

"Maître: there's still time. There's still a way. Set me free and I'll help you. You're wrong about me, I swear. Untie me and you'll see."

She turned away, and the hoarse whisper went on and on behind her. She closed her mind to the lies, pressed her upper arms to her sides to stifle the ache under her ribs, kept her gaze on the stacks of bagged and bundled produce in front of her.

She was still facing away from him, but her voice cut through his like acid. "I trusted you. Never again." The pain threatened to become a sob, and she had to bend over to contain it. "As for your silence—"

She swung with all the force of her body. Aghast, he took the full weight of the loaded sack on the side of his head, and with a crack like an explosion pitched to the ground with the chair and collapsed into stillness. The candle flame, fanned by her whirlwind movement, guttered and went out.

Léonore sank to the stone flags and listened: she could not detect his breathing. She heard a footstep, an uncertain pause outside the door, then the scrape of shoes taking up their position again. The sentry was set to ignore hell or high water.

Hell had come. Now all she could do was wait in the dark for the flood.

CHAPTER FOUR

Pirate

The dining room had the same simple elegance as the rest of the Roncival mansion. To Jean Laffite's eye it seemed best suited to a leisurely meal in the early afternoon, when the expanse of marble tiles, the lofty walls plastered in white and the ample ceiling would create a giant cube of cool air, a haven from the tropical heat.

Tonight, other qualities came into relief. The casements, which faced east towards the ridge and north onto the lagoon, admitted a subtle breeze that had begun to blow in from the sea, freshening the air along the strand and stirring the palm trees against the hill. The whisper and clack of their leaves drifted in through the windows, punctuated by the more distant sounds of his men taking their meal at the refectory on the sand. He was a trifle irritated that Curtis and the other party had not yet returned, but they had apparently found one of the Spanish mines, high on the peak, and were investigating the galleries for treasure. The captain had conveyed as much in a misspelled note sent down to Dominique with one of the slaves. Curtis was gifted at sea but impulsive onshore—witness the risky plan for the raid that he had concocted with Baudard.

The furniture, beautifully crafted and some of it brassbound in the new Empire mode, was from France and Spain. Wide gilt frames held a collection of tiny, dim landscapes, all European. There were a few engravings of scenes nearer home, but no family portraits, except for the slender watercolor of a golden-haired child, which hung near the head of the table and which he refrained from looking at.

The servants moved around them with practiced lack of haste, responding like sleepwalkers to the invisible promptings of their young mistress. Meanwhile she matched her manners to the effortless quality of the meal—not surprisingly, for the pleasanter the supper, the later he might be expected to postpone the next interrogation.

When they first sat down, Dominique exchanged a long, eloquent glance with him from the foot of the table. The perfume the women brought into the room was as refreshing as the breath of flowers on the evening air. As they took their places within the blaze of candlelight, the gleaming fabrics they wore and the colors of their hair and skin seduced the eye like the rich tones of an old painting.

Adélaïde Maselari on his left wore scarlet, as intense as flamingo flowers, cut wide to reveal the ebony smoothness of her sloping shoulders and set off the proud column of her neck and unmoving face. A mysterious smile, directed at no one, seemed as though carved on her features.

Earlier in the day, he had registered with a shock of pleasure that Léonore Roncival had clothed herself in the exact turquoise of her astonishing eyes. Now, in the light from the candelabra, the dress turned to aquamarine while her irises seemed to draw in shadow from the margins of the room, darkening to a more somber blue.

He could sail tonight if he wished, as soon as the tide was high enough to let him out over the reef, taking with him everything of value on San Stefan. But she couldn't know what he was about to do; she had to sit there and wonder if his men were here for good. He could see how it tormented her. She was like a beautiful beast in a cage, but she was too proud as yet to admit that she could see the bars.

She did not refuse to talk, and they spoke of wine at first. He had made a selection from the cellar when the old black man who ran the household informed him, with dignified distaste, what they were eating for supper. Spanish rosado to accompany the crab, and a Bordeaux for later, decanted and waiting on the sideboard. She allowed herself to discuss the vintages and to mention San Stefan's various legitimate sources of wine. She did not touch on the much more likely route by which the rosado had arrived in the cellar.

The cellar! He looked at her while a young mulatto circled the table serving the first course and relived the scene he had come upon when he opened the door downstairs: the big man sprawled on the floor amongst the crooked remains of the chair and a chaos of produce. Baudard was speechless and groggy, only just regaining consciousness, while she stood unmoving nearby, indifferent as to whether the tremendous blow she had dealt might have killed him.

Jean had not been able to suppress a short burst of laughter and, gripped by bemused admiration, he scarcely said a word as he ushered her out of the cellar and up the stairs. She was a young lioness—the very creature she was named for. Léonore.

Yet at that same moment there was something more powerful than laughter that shook him, as it did now when she looked at him across the corner of the table. Unlike Adélaïde Maselari's, her face was never a mask. It was not always possible to guess what she was thinking, but in its clear, beautiful contours one could often see what she felt. There was, evidently, much about this meal that she disliked. No doubt she objected to the company, though Dominique was perfectly polite, Maurice was too stunned by the honor to contribute and Curtis's chair was, perhaps thankfully, empty. And she hated being forced to sit at his right hand like a guest instead of at the head of her own table.

Unlike her, he felt this meal suited him nicely, for he had much to think about. Now that he had San Stefan, what would he do with it? In the beginning he had planned a straight-out raid—swoop in, plunder the place, take the ships and treasure and sail off. Teach the Whore of San Stefan a sharp lesson, so she would take

care never to get in his way. Charming though the island
was, he did not want to keep it—it could not rival his
own headquarters in the Mexican Gulf, so there was no
point in occupying it, and if he garrisoned it he would
tie up men. Nonetheless, with safe harbors scarcer and
scarcer in the Caribbean, it might be handy to have San
Stefan as a victualing port, even though the lagoon was
tiny. And as for its mistress . . .

He said, "I should have liked to ask your advice about
the Bordeaux before it was opened. But I hope you will
approve the choice."

"Of course—since you have taken everything else,
why not have my advice on my own wines as well? The
rosado is always a bit of a risk, however: it often travels
badly. Rosado is a tradition on San Stefan, otherwise I
should not keep it. My mother used to like it."

He considered this, his fingers idly twisting the stem
of his glass so that a candle flame quivered in the midst
of the blushing wine. Why mention the mother? Was
she trying to make him feel guilty for sacking the family
home? It was not a subject he intended to pursue.

Dominique, however, chose that moment to address
her. "When did you lose your mother, mademoiselle?"

Jean gave him a glare, but her reply came at once.
"You may well talk of loss. When I was eight years old
her ship disappeared in a storm, on the way to Martinique."

Dominique murmured something and Jean took the
chance to turn the conversation. "Are you familiar with
Martinique yourself?"

She shook her head and picked up her fork again, her
eyes lowered. A trace of sadness lingered on her face.
All at once he felt absurdly sorry for her, and on the
heels of that came the guilt that he had suspected her
of trying to inspire. He cursed inwardly: her company at
the table, which he found piquant in its own tantalizing
way, was also unpredictable.

Then she went on, as though the pause had not occurred. "I have traveled a great deal, but not to Martinique. My mother turned her back on her family to
marry my father, and they never set foot there again.

Yes, I have been to a great many places in the Caribbean and the Gulf. But none of them compares with San Stefan."

"Even New Orleans?" Dominique was frankly amazed.

Her answer proved that she knew the city, and the two of them began a discussion in which Jean did not join. During it, she tried to edge Dominique into talking about the islands south of New Orleans that were under Laffite control, but Dominique refused to be baited.

Adélaïde Maselari remained silent, covertly watching him, and he in turn observed Léonore Roncival, his mind busy. The parents had eloped, then. Had they married before or after the birth of the child? Perhaps never. And was she in flight from him when she drowned, heading back to Martinique after all? A singular household, a weird upbringing. Yet the daughter preferred San Stefan. Presumably because it held everything she could ever want, including an endless parade of bedfellows. The thought made him obscurely angry.

They were in a lull between courses, and he gestured to another servant to refill his glass. Baudard? The brute sprawled among the split sacks in the cellar . . . God forbid. Yet for her to look lower than him in rank would provoke discontent, jealousies, then mutiny. It was a miracle she had held on so long. He was doing her an immense favor, even if she refused to recognize it.

He caught the black woman's eye at last. She was not drinking wine; he poured her more water from a crystal jug and allowed his own glance to express the full extent of his genuine regard. She was in an odd situation on San Stefan. A possible reason for her having stayed on was fondness for the daughter, but it did not prevent her from returning his look in kind, with her usual hint of irony. With infinite care, he set himself to entertain her.

Léonore felt ill with the strain of trying to cope with what was happening in the room and keep alert to what might be going on outside it. She did not need the sight of Laffite's two sentries walking the terrace to remind her that he had the house absolutely secure. He had not requested that she talk the household staff into giving their cooperation over the supper, but she had done so anyway, with carefully worded reassurances offered under the watchful eyes of the sentries. There were no armed men in the room, and her servants acted as though the ones downstairs did not exist, so the panto-mime of a civilized meal was complete.

As seemed to be his habit, Laffite was quite at ease. While the roast for the main course was being carved behind her, she observed him as he carried on an inge-nious flirtation with Adélaïde. At some point after fetch-ing her from the cellar he had returned to the ship and discarded the bloodstained shirt, the heavy sword belt and trousers. Instead he wore narrow shoes with white hose, and black breeches with satin buttons at the knee. The evening coat was of fine black cloth, exquisitely tai-lored for his tall form. The high collar and open neck framed a shirt as white as the froth on a breaking wave, and the lace that cascaded onto his chest was pinned with a diamond like a drop of pure water.

He had complete control over her, and he wanted her to feel it with the same certainty that ruled in the minds of the hundreds of men under his command. He was rich, and he knew that she knew it. Whatever he snatched from San Stefan would weigh little against the wealth he derived from New Orleans, where the greed for his smuggled goods—fabrics, jewelry, foodstuffs, weapons, wine and slaves—meant that he walked un-scathed through the city streets, on nodding terms with gentlemen and bankers, merchants and lawyers. The Roncival treasure would hardly make or break him—but he wanted it just the same.

It troubled her desperately to have him so near, and she tended to listen rather than meet his eye. His voice suited his good looks—expressive and winning, with a warm, manly timbre. If she went by the mere sound instead of what he said, it had a kind of generosity to it, as though he were just about to convey pleasing se-crets, or make delectable promises.

She shook her head slightly: this man took rather than gave, without a qualm.

He turned as though she had spoken. "Mademoiselle?"

Gathering her courage, she looked deep into his eyes. They were not quite black; rather the very deepest brown. In daylight, when he glanced away from her, they were ironclad, opaque. Tonight, as he gazed fully at her, the candle flames danced in his expanded pupils and picked out russet hues on the surface of the irises that made Léonore think of leaves drifting on a dark pool.

But they told her nothing she wanted to know.

She took a breath. "Before you taste the roast pork, monsieur, I must tell you there will be no dessert tonight."

"Fresh fruit is all we require, I thank you."

"You misunderstand. I mean that after this course you will be indulged no further. I will never sit at my own board with you again, and you will get no information out of me."

He considered this for a moment and then gave a wry smile. "Will you believe me if I say the first idea desolates me more than the second? No. You do not think well enough of me for that."

"I have no opinion of you at all, monsieur." As his smile broadened she concluded. "You are a pirate. What more is there to say?"

The smile vanished, the hand on the table clenched, and to her astonishment his eyes narrowed as though she had been about to strike him across the face.

"Before you decide to trade insults, mademoiselle, have you thought how you would best describe your own father?"

"My father was a privateer, operating with letters of marque against English ships."

"And what of other shipping? Spanish, for instance?"

"Granted, he sometimes raided the Spanish. As you do."

"But he had no authorization to dispose of Spanish prizes. We on the other hand hold letters of marque from Cartagena. Our privateering is legitimate. So whom would you deem pirate now, mademoiselle?"

She rejoiced at having gotten under his guard for

once, even if it was over a word. "And you touch only what comes from the Spanish Main? I am not so ill informed: what of the Atlantic slave traders you intercept off Cuba? What of the English navy—judging by her name, there is one of their sloops here right now!" A quick glance at Dominique You's face confirmed this at once.

Laffite shrugged. "We have our loyalties, you and I, and they are French, in language and in many other ways. Think what the British have stolen: your mother's birthplace, for one. They have seized every French island in our seas except for Guadeloupe. Napoleon rules Europe, but he is powerless in the Caribbean since the British gutted his navy—in that situation, why not maintain a navy of my own? But it's not just a personal crusade, mademoiselle: France has been at war with England for more than a decade."

"But America is not."

He frowned but said nothing.

"You have a house in New Orleans, and warehouses on Lake Barataria, I believe. Louisiana has belonged to the United States for six years and America is at war with no one. If you were concerned about loyalties, Monsieur Laffite, I would say that you are living in a dilemma. But of course you couldn't care less. Piracy takes no account of flags and nations and maritime law. A pirate's only fidelity is to greed."

His response was simply to take up his knife and fork again.

Leaving her plate untouched, she glanced around the table. Dominique You was eating, Maurice the lieutenant was looking at her with fascination, ready to address himself to his plate if Laffite raised his head, and Adélaïde gave her a speculative look over the top of her glass. They had been separated before the meal and had had no chance to confer: Adélaïde had told her all she could in a hasty murmur on the terrace in the afternoon, so whatever happened now was her responsibility alone.

The breeze from the sea had become stronger, dispersing other sounds, but she caught a surge of men's voices from the other end of the beach and took up her fork so suddenly that it knocked against her plate. Laffite looked up.

She put the fork down again with a clatter and, holding his gaze, said in a louder tone, "It is time you told me exactly what you are doing on my island, Monsieur Laffite."

"And I have been waiting all afternoon for you to ask. It will be a pleasure." He put his fingers on the stem of a fresh glass, and her servant poured him the first taste of her Bordeaux. He went on. "We have just been talking about the complexity of our world at present. Who has any hope of predicting what will happen next? The English, God rot them, have their eyes on Guadeloupe. The proud independents of Haiti change their tune by the season—one month my ships are welcome, next they suddenly recall that our relatives once manned French cannon against them. Like you, I am unwelcome in Jamaica and a scourge and an abomination to Cuba." He took a sip of the wine and nodded. "This is excellent."

Léonore turned and said to the only servant at that moment in the room, "Go below and fetch up another bottle of the same. Take Paul with you; he knows where to look." At his hesitant look she said meaningfully, "Go."

Preoccupied by the wine and his subject, Laffite hardly noticed. "In short, for privateers like ourselves, safe havens in these waters are becoming scarce. When we operate far from home, there are fewer harbors to give us concealment, or fresh water, or a place for repairs."

"You find yourself in need of friends, Monsieur Laffite? Then you go quite the wrong way about making them."

He gave her a smile that bared only the upper row of his white, even teeth. "You are about to offer me some lessons in diplomacy?"

There was a crash somewhere downstairs and a burst of voices. "I am about to chastise my servants—they are making a sorry business of bringing that wine. But I shall wait until you spit out why you are here."

The solidly drawn black eyebrows rose a fraction. "But—to form an alliance, mademoiselle."

She gasped. "Like *this*?"

"Why not? In essence, this is how everyone does it, where there is a prospect of mutual gain. My approach to you has been swifter and franker than most, that is all."

She could not suppress a mocking laugh. "What could I possibly gain from *you*?"

He put down his glass and his hand rested on the table between them as he leaned back. His voice was mild and contemplative, but he was not looking at her; instead he gazed through the candle flames towards Dominique You. "In these troubled times, the situation of San Stefan is precarious. The English have the ports of Jamaica, so there would be no profit in their seizing this tiny lagoon, for it holds how many vessels at most: four? But the English dispute these waters with France, and if they suspect you of aiding her, what is to stop them retaliating? It would be very simple for them to declare this a nest of pirates, arrest you and seize the island." She was about to interrupt, but he went on in the same tone. "Haiti is another matter—who knows what that administration may do from one second to the next? But there you do have at least the fragile ties of friendship that we share. And finally there is Cuba. Where they are fully aware of your father's inroads on Spanish trade. They have no pressing interest in this island but, of all nations, Spain would have the strongest case for claiming it definitively as her national territory."

The room was very still, which magnified the sound from the terrace as a sentry's shoe slipped on the tiles. She said quickly, "Spain is ruled by France, and San Stefan has good relations with the French. There is no threat from Spain."

"Until she manages to shake off Napoleon."

She shrugged. "Even so, it would take years of fighting to clear the French out of the Peninsula. Granted, Spain may one day be a useful ally to England, but I do not plan my life around the fate of nations, monsieur. I run this island here and now, and shape my strategy accordingly."

"But what now, mademoiselle? San Stefan needs allies. It needs a master even more. I happened to realize this a little before you, and that is why I am here."

Her voice shook, though she raised it an angry notch. "You filthy liar. You were more honest than this a few hours ago—you are here for the brigantine, the arms and the treasure."

His voice hardened, but in his eyes she saw an odd hint of compassion. "I do not deny that. And it is my *honest* belief that they would be safer in my hands than in those of a woman. Despite your best efforts, you were destined to lose them all. So why not lose them to me?"

She had had enough. With a movement that took everyone by surprise, she pushed back her chair so that it grated on the floor and stood up. He showed no alarm, but his eyes flicked to her hands and then back to her face, as though looking for hidden weapons. She said, "You shall have nothing of mine."

His gaze darkened and sped once more over her body. This time he was not searching for a weapon, and she shivered as though he had touched her. When he raised his eyes to hers, she saw in them a kind of regretful amusement, which lingered in the silky voice. "And who is to prevent me?"

She pointed with outstretched arm. "They are."

All heads swiveled, and a great many things happened at once. The instant Laffite turned, Léonore set her foot against his chair arm and thrust the chair and his tall body to the floor. Adélaïde gave a cry of glee, flung out one powerful arm, took the lieutenant by the throat and with a mighty tug plunged his face into her lap and applied to his neck a knife that had come from the ample bodice of the scarlet dress. She was laughing. Dominique might have given them trouble, if the men outside the dining room door had not moved smartly into the room on Léonore's signal. He managed only one convulsive movement before he was pinned to his seat, while the men who had overpowered the sentries on the terrace vaulted through the open casements and took care of Laffite.

"Ah!" A great sigh escaped from Léonore when she saw her tormenter disappear under the weight of four bodies. "Hold him." She gestured towards Adélaïde and the lieutenant as more men poured through the door. "Lash that man to his chair. Where is Monsieur Santo?"

"Here, Maître."

If the young man who leaped through the casement had been an angel, she could not have looked at him with greater joy. A laugh bubbled up out of her, he looked so untouched by what he had just achieved: the tanned skin without blemish, his thick, sun-blond hair scarcely out of place, a blunderbuss swinging from one hard-muscled arm like a shiny toy.

"You took your time."

The lilt of approval in her voice was unmistakable, and he grinned in reply. "They had the edge in numbers, so we didn't jump them until they went into the mine. I'm glad you signaled for us to wait, Maître, or we'd have tried to hit them on the shore first, and we mightn't have done the deed."

"Curtis, the captain?"

"Still alive and kicking. But he's lost two fingers and nine men."

Nine. She looked at Laffite, who had been dragged to his feet and stood with a pistol jammed into his ribs. Their eyes locked. There was a terrible moment when his mind seemed to blend and quiver with hers, as though a knell had been rung that only he and she could hear. She had destroyed nine men.

She wrenched her gaze away and smiled at Andrea Santo. "Come onto the terrace and show me just what you have done." Whereupon she turned, without waiting for him to follow, and walked out into the night.

Three hours later, she stood on the beach within a circle of flares and studied the last of Laffite's force drawn up to face her. Behind them, rocking gently in the waves, was the tender from the *Raleigh*, with four of her seamen seated between the oars. The rest of them, including the nine dead and seven wounded, had already been ferried across to the brig. She had left the vessel

itself untouched, but she had ordered the removal of
two thirty-two-pounders, which had been winched over
the side, brought ashore with immense care and balanced on their carriages on the sand. Looking along the
beach to where they loomed above the tide mark, she
felt a surge of relief that Laffite's gun crew on the *Raleigh* had been too indecisive to use them against the
fort when they woke up to the attack onshore.

The lesser cannon she had left on the brig, but she
had ordered half their ammunition taken off—another
lengthy task. They might fancy using some of what remained before they sailed out of the lagoon, but she
rather thought not; it was a risk she was prepared to
take.

All the inhabitants of San Stefan, men, women and
the few children, were gathered about her. Adélaïde was
some way off with a small group of women, but Santo
stood at her side, watching the six men who waited before them at the water's edge.

Barrel-chested Dominique You, his gray eyes narrowed, paid no heed to the weapons trained on him. He
was clearly a man without fear, but she had seen his face
when his cannon were heaved ashore and the sight
seemed to bring him physical pain. Curtis, beside him,
was a picture of resentment. One hand was bound up in
clean linen and held in a sling across his chest, his skin
was gray and he was swaying on his feet, but the look
he gave her and Santo was murderous. She recalled her
cautious talk with him in a back room of the Amiral
de Grasse in Haiti and smiled to herself; he had acted
differently then, while he was trying to guess whether
she would offer him the chance to serve her by sup-
planting Baudard.

Baudard stood between Curtis and You, looking down
at the sand where two trunks and a bag of his effects
were waiting to be loaded. People had murmured at this,
now that everyone knew his treachery. But Léonore had
insisted that he be allowed his possessions. He was leaving behind him the achievements of ten years, forced to
join people who held him cheap, and he must witness

Santo standing already in his old place. He was a broken man.

On the other side of Laffite were two slaves, one of whom had been bringing Curtis's message from inland when they intercepted him. Santo had deciphered the message and seen good reason for allowing it to reach Dominique You. When it was explained to the African that there were no slaves on San Stefan, and never would be while a Roncival held it, he became very attentive. Then, when he realized that he was being promised his freedom merely to do what he was already commanded, he could scarcely run fast enough to deliver the message.

Now he stood alongside the other slave, between the water and the San Stefan guns, his questioning eyes on Léonore and one protective hand resting on the shoulder of the other youngster. Neither could be more than sixteen.

"Do they speak French?" she said aside to Santo. When he nodded, she said clearly, "You two: do you want to sail with Laffite or stay here? There are no slaves on San Stefan. But there are no slackers either— if you stay you must work for your keep, and it may be months before you go to sea again."

The young man held on to the other's shoulder hard as though he expected him to run off.

She caught sight of the lined black face of a friend in the crowd and called out, "Mirliton: will you come forward?"

The others parted to let the old man through, and he paused on the edge of the group, observing the slaves from under the peak of a faded forage cap.

"If they want to stay, Mirliton, will you show them what to do and where to sleep tonight?"

Mirliton gave her a wry look, but signaled his assent with a twitch of his thin shoulder. At that the youths rushed up the beach and stood behind him, looking at Laffite with the utmost alarm.

She felt so sorry for them that she said sharply to Mirliton, "Take them to the village. We'll sort this out tomorrow."

She did not watch them go, but addressed the armed men at the shore. "Shove them into the boat. All except Monsieur Laffite."

Baudard's gear was thrown into the tender and the men forced to board. Dominique You was reluctant to leave Laffite on the sand but eventually climbed into the boat under the influence of two bayonets and a quick, low word from his leader.

She said, "You are all free to go. But do it in the next twenty seconds or we open fire."

There was a deep growl at this from the people around her, and she saw even Santo stiffen. No one comprehended what she was doing. If she were to keep their loyalty, the events of the next few moments must be as clear as crystal to their understanding.

"I am counting."

Again at a signal from Laffite, the boat began to leave the shore. It was a strange departure: the group onboard sat at awkward angles, gazing back at the flame-lit beach and out to the *Raleigh*, moored amongst the reflections of its yellow riding lights in the indigo water of the lagoon. And in the foreground was Laffite's tall, nonchalant figure, facing the hostile crowd.

She walked towards him, and the others drew in. "Monsieur Santo, two men. I want his arms behind his back." Santo gestured and the men moved to his bidding. "You have what I asked for?"

Her new lieutenant nodded, and she saw his broad shoulders relax. She was making it evident that she had conferred with him before taking these steps. It was a confirmation of his new status that would ensure respect for him and order on the island—for at least one more night.

Then she faced Laffite. She should be triumphant, but instead she trembled inwardly, with exhaustion and fearful resentment. All her choices, from the second he set foot on the island, had been in response to the situation he had dictated. In one day he had changed forever her vision of the future, and the only relief in this extremity was that no one but he could possibly guess what he had done to her.

"The tide is high again. The *Raleigh* must leave now, to get over the reef. If she strikes it in the dark, it will be your mistake."

He said nothing, and the midnight gaze was unfathomable. The diamond in his spotless shirt winked with the easy regularity of his breathing, and his face showed no hint of the brutal pressure the men behind him exerted on his arms and shoulders.

She took a deep breath, then pitched her voice so all could hear. "Monsieur Laffite, as you confessed to me tonight, you came here for the brigantine, the arms and the Roncival treasure."

There was a rustle of interest behind her. But she was not going to tell him where the brigantine was, beyond the western end of the beach, in a channel cut in the stream where they careened the big ships. When he arrived, most of her men had been working on the vessel, which had been dismasted and hauled up into the trees to keep it concealed.

"The brigantine is a phantom that is not destined to appear to you. But Monsieur Santo and his men were with her when you sailed past the point. That is where my sentries ran with the warning."

He spoke for the first time. "So you had them hide first and attack later. How did you make the signal?"

"With a mirror. From my chamber." She kept her voice quite clear. "I shall leave you to speculate about the magazine. As for the treasure: I am the only person on earth who knows where that is. And you are the last person on earth I would choose to tell."

The crowd was now quite silent around her. A few moments more, and it could be the silence of complete approval. But everything depended on how she handled Laffite. She was facing one of the most feared men in the Caribbean and the Gulf, and something about his very stillness underlined the multitude of means he could use against her if she let him go. Yet on the other hand, in his arrogant and perplexing way, he had talked of an alliance.

She stood even closer to him, and the silence intensified, as though everyone's thoughts were leaping high like the torch flames into the night air, without a soul daring to speak.

She forced out the words. "You were right, Monsieur Laffite. You need some lessons in diplomacy." She managed a slow, taunting smile, into his eyes. "We all know what you came for. And you got none of it." She raised her bare arms and put them on his shoulders, against his neck. He moved involuntarily, as though at the sudden coolness against his hot skin. The people behind her drew a concerted breath.

"You spoke of allies. That's as may be. For the moment, this is farewell."

She had planned it. This was a gesture calculated to sweep into oblivion the imposition of his body on hers in the palm grove. To stage another encounter where the ambushed prey this time was male. To burn away one searing injury with another.

There was a murmur of startled amusement when her arms tightened and her lips approached his; there was a roar of ribald disbelief when she closed the embrace; but she heard neither. She had expected resistance, yet he did not—or could not—summon it. The response, from his lips alone, enveloped her as though his trapped arms encircled her waist, and they stood pressed together in a dark haven, far from the shouts and laughter and fire of their present meeting place. It was as though he spoke through the firm lips that were molded to hers, in words that hummed in her ears, filled her head, seized her by the throat. Her arms tightened and her body swayed against him. The moment swelled, occupied by one loud, single heartbeat. His mouth moved on hers and her senses expanded to take in the scent of his skin, a hint of oak from the sea chest where he kept his clothes, smoke in his hair.

It took memory and will to break the bond. It took a flash of her former outrage to erupt into her mind, and she flung her arms wide and staggered back. The white fire burned behind her eyes again and for a second she could not even focus on his features. Another tremor ran through her, and to stay upright she retreated another step and rested one hand on Santo's shoulder.

"Now take off your clothes."

The air exploded with a raucous shout, and her gaze concentrated in time to see the handsome face before her alter at last. He grimaced in disbelief, then clamped his teeth together so that the bones stood out starkly above his lean cheeks. His eyes, glittering, raked hers briefly, then looked up and beyond her as though searching for help from the sky.

Around them laughter, whistles and catcalls expressed, in delicious compliment to them both, just what everyone expected to see when he was stripped of his breeches.

Then she beckoned forward the man with the grenade.

Laffite saw him at once and froze. She repeated her order, and the two men behind Laffite tugged the black coat from his shoulders and over his arms. Twisting, he ripped it from their hands and flung it on the sand.

"Stand back." They could not have moved more promptly if he had held a pistol.

He did not meet her eye. Instead, as he began to unfasten the shirt, he directed all his mute scorn at Santo. She kept her hand on Santo's shoulder, watching the methodical disrobing as the cries, whistles and hooting around them, by some strange sympathy, began slowly to diminish.

He kicked off his shoes. Then his long fingers finished unraveling the ties of the shirt, slipped the diamond from the lace cravat and let it fall. At that moment the tide, creeping farther up the sand, sent the tip of a wave around his feet and the jewel tumbled forward under a sheen of water. There was a quick murmur from the onlookers, but he did not glance down.

He pulled the shirt from around his waist, twitched it over his head and threw it up the beach. Still he did not look at her, but there was no fear or embarrassment in his eyes, and no hesitation as he bent over and stripped himself of breeches and hose.

He straightened, and there was a hush.

In the light of the torches the tall form was golden. The one mark upon his skin, the bloodied bruise made by her teeth, served only to emphasize the smoothness of the hard, curved contours of his chest. His body seemed shaped not by his rough life of seafaring and enterprise but by some sculptor who had thought only of beauty and pleasure in its fashioning. He stood as he had when he faced her in the palm grove, and the set of his straight shoulders, the easy stance of his lean hips, lent him the same unconscious grace.

She would never know how much she might have thrilled or terrified him in the last few minutes. All she knew was that the sight of the weapon had quelled some of the havoc wrought in him by her embrace. And meanwhile what filled her eyes was the lithe, strong body where ease and strength resided together in generous proportions, perfect balance.

The black, unreadable eyes were fixed on the brute with the grenade. She had not the slightest doubt that he recalled her first angry threat, when she told him what they did to dogs on San Stefan. She presumed he would have noticed there were none on the island. Now she tried, and failed, to read his expression as he examined the grenade she had chosen: the tight cylinder packed with gunpowder, the corded wick, the rough wooden shaft in the grip of the man's broad hand.

She took her fingers from Santo's shoulder, and Laffite instantly looked up. She beckoned to Adélaïde. There was movement in the murmuring crowd as Adélaïde came to her. People's voices sounded overwrought, uncertain. Feet shifted in the sand, and she sensed the subtle beginnings of doubt and withdrawal.

She smiled at Adélaïde and took a money bag from her, and a length of cord. Making sure everyone could see, she plunged her hand into the bag and held up a fistful of coins. "I should regret to see a guest depart with nothing to show for his visit. So here is Spanish silver, offered with our compliments."

She gestured to the man with the grenade, and he came up the sand towards her. "Wrap this around the cap and tie it." She watched him as he fastened the money bag, listening to the sounds of speculation, amusement and guarded approval stirring amongst the bystanders. When the weapon was ready she gave it to

Santo and sent the other man to light a taper at the nearest torch.

Intent on this last maneuver, she watched Santo walk to the water's edge and take up a position facing the lagoon, a yard away from Laffite. She waited until the man with the taper joined him before she could bring herself to look into Laffite's eyes again. Thus she did not witness the moment when he realized that, against all the odds she had lately proposed, he was going to live. So she was not ready for his grin. Alight with savage irony, it held also a spark of his laughter in the cellar, of the flash in his eyes when she first entered the dining room.

Santo kept one shoulder turned from Laffite's motionless figure. Without waiting for her command, he touched the wick of the grenade to the taper and extended it behind him. There was a tense hush, pulsing with the beat of the count; then Santo's brawny arm swept forward and the grenade arced, end over end in a spinning tracery of sparks, out over the sleeping lagoon towards the ship.

A few feet above the surface it exploded with a crack and a red gout of flame opened like a wild rose in the darkness, scattering the coins in a burst of incandescent seeds that flashed over and over across the water until the last one hissed into a wave top and went out.

"There's the treasure, monsieur. Now swim for it."

The torch flames quivered with a boisterous outrush of air as everyone on the beach uttered a final shout of mirth.

He wasted no time. He stepped back into the sea, swept the deepest of bows to the multitude, straightened and gave her a look from which all hint of a smile had disappeared, then turned and dived smoothly into the waves.

CHAPTER FIVE

✑

Madame Ch'ing

The brigantine *Fantôme* was sailing northwest within the Great Bahama Bank, along the northern coast of Cuba en route for the Straits of Florida. Picked out in dark blue from stem to stern, her scrubbed decks drying pale under the morning sun, her brightwork gleaming at her waist, the *Fantôme* for the moment belied her name: this was no specter from the past, but a fresh, supple-timbered vessel primed for action and enterprise.

If Jean Laffite had chanced to see her earlier in the year, when she lay hauled over on her beam-ends in the San Stefan careening yard, he would scarcely recognize her now. Three months had gone into scraping, patching and caulking the hull, and as many more into stepping her raked masts and refitting the decks. Skillful planing along her bow and sides meant that she cut through the water as sleekly as a razor, and with the wind dead aft spun a wake of diagrammatic symmetry.

She was a sea phantom nonetheless, with no figure-head at the bow or mark at the stern, and she flew no nation's flag—only the Roncival pennant at the mast-head. The pennant was new, replacing the stained and shredded remnant of the one Léonore had first created for her father seven years before. He had laughed when she suggested it, for his ships hoisted only the French ensign at the stern, except for rare occasions when different colors were brought into use—including the red flag of piracy. He also doubted that she could fashion a pennant, despite her canny use of a sailmaker's needle. And he had scoffed when she said the symbols on it would depict the family name.

"Ronce and Val? I never yet saw brambles on a flag. And how will you show a valley? You'll end up with a blackberry stuck between anthills."

But the berries she contrived looked more like a triangle of black grenades against the twin, blue-green peaks, and they were ringed by a thicket of thorns that spread to the tip of the pennant and stood out, stark and menacing, on the clear canvas ground.

Instead of laughing, he had flown it at once atop the mainmast of his corvette, the *Espérance*, and she had roped in the regular sailmakers and made one for each of the other three vessels. It was not until recently, when the men demanded that the *Fantôme* fly the colors, that she knew whether she had been indulged or genuinely approved in that long-ago endeavor.

It seemed impossibly distant now, the last period of her childhood between the death of her mother and the arrival of Adélaïde. When her father was a hero and she greeted his every return to harbor with bloodthirsty homage. When her boy's soul, trapped in a girl's body, clamored for recognition, and the bemused sailors of San Stefan shared their sea knowledge with her, first for her father's sake and then for her own. When her heart's home was in the tops and she fell in love forever with the swelling thunder of the canvas and learned in intimate detail how each piece was made and where it worked within the ranks of a ship's living, breathing sails.

Léonore stood in the stern of the *Fantôme* and looked up at the pennant streaming along the wind and wondered whether her fierce desire to learn masculine skills had been in response to her father's unspoken dream: for he must surely have wanted a son. If he was to have only one child, then it was a boy he needed, to be trained in all his ways, to maintain the fleet and defend the island, to lead the forces of San Stefan when the time came. Perhaps this was what made him yield when his men, half in jest to begin with, took her under their tutelage. Perhaps it was muted pride that tempted him to take her on that first voyage, a routine supply trip to Guadeloupe, and on the way to give her the first of his lessons.

It was her mother who had taught Léonore to read, but it was her father who taught her the language of flags. She learned the numbers and single letters they represented and then the combinations. She remembered the magic of it when she spaced them out and mastered the knots and watched as they were hauled up on the lee side of the mizzen topsail, to swing out in an arc beyond the canvas and flutter free against the azure sky.

Forever after, they reminded her of the days when she and her father spoke the same language. When he called her "lion cub" and allowed her into the wilderness of his mind. Before she watched him retreat, baffled and without resources, before the dilemma of her womanhood. Before he sent her far away from her coral sea, to receive an education she had never asked for, in a city where the flags that flew against the rain clouds conveyed not a syllable of meaning to her starved senses.

It was her father's lore that lingered in the memory of the old-timers who were still with the company, and worked a certain covert influence with the younger men. She had had to rely on it blindly when Laffite forced her hand, and it had been just enough to get her through Baudard's treachery. No one knew better than she that Santo, victorious on his descent from the peak, might have chosen that critical moment to displace the Roncivals. But instead they had all been catapulted on into a new era.

This day sailing up the coast of Cuba was a reward after the months of preparation on San Stefan. There was a distinct impression onboard that the refloated *Fantôme* was lucky. She had already had one success in her new guise, when Léonore sent Santo to Port-au-Prince to recruit and gave him leave to act if he saw likely prey. On the way back he had intercepted a Jamaican sloop— two masted like the *Fantôme* but smaller—and slower

as well, for she had been laden with spars intended for
a British flotilla laid up in the Virgin Islands for repairs.
After a short chase, the little *Seraph* struck her colors,
the crew was set adrift in their boats and Santo's first
lieutenant sailed her jubilantly home in the wake of
the *Fantôme*.

So now San Stefan had a flotilla of its own. It was
meager, with insufficient men to make it a fighting force,
and there were not enough arms for the three vessels to
be taken out together; so the *Fantôme* sailed alone and
the signal flags stayed in the locker. But a beginning had
been made, of a kind to stir the men's hopes, for they
had just dived for treasure on a Bahamian reef and there
was a casket of specie in the Maître's cabin below,
counted and divided for distribution when they reached
home.

Many years before, Edouard Roncival had happened
upon the exact location of a famous wreck, that of the
Barbadoes, an English merchant ship that went to the
bottom on the Shoals of Heniagoe, not far from Great
Inagua Island in the Bahamas. The shoals were north of
the waters where Roncival used to lie in wait for ships
leaving the busy lane between Cuba and Haiti, on their
way to the Atlantic. It was this very route that the *Barbadoes* had taken just over a century before, when she
was leaving the Caribbean after a trading trip, bound for
England with her cargo of cash in gold and silver. She
was attacked by a French vessel, and her captors plun-
dered her, but they were not quick enough to remove
all the treasure before she sank and settled on the reef,
just too deep for salvage and visible only when the seas
were abnormally low and calm.

Roncival had made his own chart of the wreck and
returned twice to send divers down, but although the
second trip yielded a bag of coins, it became too dangerous to continue. Léonore, who was with him on that
attempt, was fascinated by the thought of the riches still
below the waves.

Santo navigated for the *Fantôme* and was also finishing the training of Philibert, ex-French navy and coached
by her father, but for the *Barbadoes* search she navi-

gated herself. Once in the area they found the wreck within a day, and the divers they sent down were the two African youths taken from Laffite.

She smiled, thinking back to the morning after the *Raleigh*'s departure, when Santo had come to her with the request that people be allowed to dive in the lagoon for the scattered Spanish silver. She said if they were so keen they could keep what they recovered, and minutes later the pirogues put out at the good news and there was a free-for-all. Some found money easily not far from the shore, but no one could match the two former slaves at staying under in the deep area where most of the red-hot coins had spun into the dark. They returned exhausted to shore with their booty, but enterprising new friends coaxed them to go back later and share the findings. Wisely they agreed, and thus became the most popular people on the island.

There had been the same kind of festive frenzy over the Shoals of Heniagoe when the *Fantôme* anchored in slick, limpid water under a calm sky and the crew lined the waist to watch the youngsters plummet down to the ghostly ship on the rocks below.

Santo, pacing the deck, saw her half smile and drew nearer. "Shall we be scouring the *Barbadoes* again on the way home, Maître?"

"I'm hoping we'll have more on our hands by then. We could do with a big prize, don't you think?"

He narrowed his blue eyes before asking the next question, half expecting a rebuff. "We held on just two days after the weather turned rough. You couldn't have stayed in wait a bit longer?"

"Finding the gold has put heart in the crew, Monsieur Santo. They want action and I don't blame them. Best to keep on the move."

"So you think we'll have luck in the Straits?"

She shrugged. "If we do sight anything likely, it all depends on how many ships we spy and what size they are. I don't want to put the *Fantôme* at risk too soon. But I should like to snatch us a larger vessel."

He nodded. "We could do with another *Espérance*." After a pause he said, "One thing I can't figure out—

why Laffite came after us with a two-masted ship, and only sixty men. Even that *Raleigh,* they could have crammed her with more than a hundred."

She put both hands on the rail. "They were a long way from home and we don't know what happened on the voyage down. They might have taken a prize before they got to us, and sent some of the crew to sail it back to base. But they didn't hesitate to take us on, for they were told how unready we were, down to the last man. They expected it to be easy—and up to a point, it was."

There was a pause, as both remembered that precise point, and what had happened after it. It was this kind of situation—when, despite his abilities, Santo depended on her for strategy—that defined their relationship. And left the initiative in her hands.

"Maître, you'll forgive me for mentioning it, but it troubles my mind that you—we—let them go."

Her fingers clenched on the rail, but she deliberately relaxed before she looked up. "What would you have done, Monsieur Santo? Not at once—I mean, if you'd had a chance to think it over?"

Silence. Even though there was no one in earshot, she could not prolong it, for fear of making him look and feel slow, inadequate.

She waited only until he glanced away, then said, "They didn't get off lightly, after all. You cost them nine men and two of their precious cannon. And no one can ever have turned the tables on Laffite in such a way before. If we had seized the brig and set them all adrift, or worse . . . They say Laffite can rally five hundred men. I don't know if that's true, but I'd certainly hate to find out."

"You think the rest of them would have upped and done anything, from so far away, once he was gone?"

"Those brothers are legend. Pierre and Jean are as close as twins: harm one and the other will hound you to your dying day. That's the word on the Laffites, and we'd be safest to believe it."

"But he could come back now himself! With a whole fleet if he wanted."

"And has he?"

He shook his head slowly. "I guess he knows we're ready for him this time."

"He satisfied his curiosity—maybe he's content with that for now." When Santo looked puzzled, she went on. "He heard about us from Curtis, and he decided to wander down and take a look himself. He fancied knowing how strong we were, what kind of rivals we would make if we got San Stefan running again. And he was thinking of the future, looking for a handy port. But a man like that doesn't come visiting, he strikes. Hard, so we know who's boss."

Santo digested this and then grinned. "Well, I reckon we taught him a lesson!"

She returned the grin, wrapping her arms around her ribs to reduce the hollow ache inside. "Let's say it was mutual."

Next morning in her cabin she woke to fear. For a moment she believed something had roused her: a disturbance on deck, a voice outside her door. She listened with her whole body to the sounds and feel of the ship, then let her head sink back into the feather pillow. From the friendly creaking of the timbers that enclosed her she gleaned a reassuring message: the southeasterly had continued steady through the night and the *Fantôme* was sailing easily in a moderate swell.

No, the fear lurked within. She lay and looked at the narrow cabin as dawn rose behind the stern window, and fought down panic by observing each article in turn. The chart table, which doubled as a dining board when she invited the first officers to a meal. The six chairs around it. The mahogany chests containing the nautical instruments. A shallow armoire for her gowns, and two trunks against the opposite bulwark for shoes and other garments. A fold-out table against the wall, at present stowed away, with a stool beneath it. A tall bookcase, the shelves all crammed with books except for the bottom one, on which there was a box containing a brace of pistols.

She was afraid of what she might do in the conflict to come, if she lost her head, abandoned all control in the midst of mayhem. And she was terrified of the reverse: that when action threatened she might come to a dead halt, that she would not be able to command the men to do what they were trained for—take another ship by force. Fight and kill.

Yet there was no going back; Laffite had seen to that. By invading San Stefan, by revealing the fragile foothold she held on the Roncival heritage, he would have awakened the interest of many others in the Caribbean and the Gulf who shared his marauding appetites, if not his talent for the lightning strike. She could not afford to let the months pass in idleness, as she had done in the disarray that followed the loss of her father. She no longer had the luxury of dreaming up plans for the future, seeking the right people to carry them out. Laffite had defined her future for her: she must defend what she held, or be annihilated. All she had in the world was San Stefan, and from now on she had but one goal—to hold on to it, for the people's sake and her own.

So she had to plan. If Laffite still wanted the island, he would come back with a greater force and subdue her once and for all. The only security she had against this prospect—and it was so slender she could never confide it to anyone else—was the look in his eyes as he left. She had tried him, but not too far. She had challenged him, but he had laughed when she did so, with a wild flash in his eyes that gained the respect of his audience on San Stefan and at the same time sent a secret message to her. She could not predict what he would do, but whatever his choices, they now had as much to do with herself as they did with territory.

She turned over on the bunk and pressed her face into the pillow. Perhaps she should be grateful to Laffite for compelling her to make up her mind. But what of her dreams, her deepest impulses, that she had been striving to understand since her father died? If she had had time to take them into account, would she now be throwing herself into the ancient arena of violence and greed where her family had seized its livelihood for the last two hundred years? She had no idea. Thanks to Laffite, she would probably never know.

Images of his midnight departure surged back, and she relived her relief when the *Raleigh* weighed anchor seconds after his men hoisted their bos from the black water of the lagoon. She had known they would not dare use the ship's cannon while he was hostage on the beach, but as soon as his naked body hit the waves she sent her gun crews speeding to the cannon on the roof of the mansion, in readiness for retaliation. There was no need: the brig, showing them her stern at once, raised just enough canvas to tack against the landward breeze and wriggle out over the reef, with such skill that she might have been a home ship leaving harbor. There was no parting shot, no threat of a vengeful return— they just melted away into the darkness.

She had doubled the sentries and the night watch, spent an hour at the village hearing reports and making sure all those in need received attention, and then returned to the house. Adélaïde had somehow brought it to order, so after telling Santo they would talk in the morning, she had gone to her room and collapsed on the bed fully clothed. It was only then that her eyelids clenched, she curled herself into a ball under the muffling sheets, and at last allowed herself to weep.

For the first time since her tomboy days, she wore male clothing to the deck. Reason number one was pragmatic: if they grappled and boarded another vessel, she could not possibly manage it in skirts. It was true that from long practice the decks and companionways of the *Fantôme* presented no difficulty to her in a dress; she had after all brought other San Stefan women onboard, and it was years since she had felt it necessary to go scrambling up the ratlines—but she still could not see herself taking another vessel in a gown, nor looking entirely convincing to their captives when it was done. Reason number two was tactical: she, Santo and the first lieutenant on deck would be visible to the opposing crew throughout the engagement, and snipers would be trying to pick off the commander as they approached. Startled at the sight of a woman, they would aim to spare her, so the two men would be the prime targets. She refused to see her men fall at her side because she wore a dress.

Santo could not help a slow grin when she came up on deck, for she had chosen the same uniform as he: a long, blue cutaway coat with a white shirt and cream breeches, in the style of an officer of the English Royal Navy. Santo's most prized possession was an English captain's coat that dated from the time when the young Horatio Nelson served in the navy of the West Indies; Santo even liked to claim that it had once been worn by the hero himself. Everyone knew that this was out of the question, the late admiral having been a much smaller man than Santo, but this did not stop him from wearing the captured coat in action.

Léonore had had her coat made on San Stefan, but unlike Santo's it bore no epaulets, and she wore it buttoned for modesty. It was a glaring signal to the crew, nonetheless, confirming the line of command between herself and her captain and hinting at other, more intimate links that they were at liberty to speculate about.

She stood beside him while he gave instructions to the first lieutenant, and then orders were bellowed out across the deck for a man from the starboard watch to go up and relieve the lookout.

Santo glanced sideways at her. "Are you satisfied with Clothilde, Maître?"

"Yes. She and the others all know to keep belowdecks if we go into action?"

"Yes, Maître."

Many of the San Stefan women besides Clothilde had been eager to sail with them, but Léonore had brought only those who were most useful and whose relations with the crew would prove no distraction during the weeks away. Léonore believed in the value of women's skills at sea. The seamen clung to the old superstition that women onboard ship brought disaster, but if she were to command them, she had to prise that idea out of their heads. Now if they dared to doubt her luck, she need only point to the treasure from the *Barbadoes*.

Two of the six women in the crew served as assistants

to the surgeon and the cook, one was training to be an expert sailmaker like herself and the others had mixed duties alongside the stewards and storekeepers. Clothilde helped Léonore as a combination of tiring woman and laundry maid, replacing her personal maid, Christina, who had been left behind on San Stefan.

"You know that Christina asked if she could come with us?"

He nodded.

"And you realize why I refused?"

"I think so, Maître."

"I applaud your discretion. You understand, Monsieur Santo, whatever happens within the walls of my house is private business. My affairs, and yours, are spoken of to no one—not the landsmen, nor this crew, nor anyone else."

"Rely on me." A slight reddening along the lines of his prominent cheekbones somehow lent his eyes a more intense blue.

"Above all, if anyone tries to press the subject, even with insults to my name, you must not be drawn in."

"I'll not open my mouth, Maître, but you give me leave to put an end to such in my own way?"

"Provided there is no bandying of words. I know I am called Madame Ch'ing, and I have no special dislike to that. As for the rest . . . I did overhear worse, spoken in Port-au-Prince months ago, but—"

"But not by your own people. And never to me, anywhere. I swear it, on this." He put his broad hand at once on the hilt of his sword.

Touched, she murmured, "Thank you." Then, after a deep breath, "But I care nothing about words: I intend my deeds to speak from now on. The world will very soon know me better—and probably come to like me even less!" Which drew a hesitant smile.

It was not until the afternoon that they heard the sound they longed for: "Sail ahoy on the port bow!"

The brigantine came alive and in ten minutes the *Fantôme* had on as much canvas as she could carry. The nets were stretched and packed tight with rolled hammocks to repel boarders, the gun crews ran to the shouts of the gunners' mates, and even while the approaching vessel was still invisible the sails were trimmed to bring the *Fantôme* onto an interception course. Rigaud, the quartermaster, carried out Santo's orders with a smoothness that gladdened her to see. A stocky Haitian of French ancestry, Rigaud was somewhat taciturn, but she had known him and his capabilities for five years. Occasionally, after receiving a directive from Santo, he would favor her with a grin that seemed to tell her that she could rely on him. It felt good to smile in return.

While the bustle went on in the waist, Léonore and Santo armed themselves with spyglasses and stood side by side in tense silence until they gave a simultaneous exclamation: far-off sails had floated into view.

Santo gazed intently. "Three masts. Does she look high in the water to you?"

"Yes," she said, "larger than us altogether. Can you make out the colors?"

He shook his head, lowered the lens, and spun out more orders to the lieutenant. Everything was to be lashed in place on deck and the yards secured. Then all hands were to be fully armed and piped to quarters.

He said to her aside, "When do you want snipers aloft, Maître?"

"I leave that to you, Monsieur Santo." She looked up at their mainsail, rigged fore-and-aft between the masts, and noted how the wind bulged within the vast new piece of canvas. "We've a lot of sailing to do yet. I'd say wait until we're close in, ready to maneuver. That's our great advantage with this rig—we're agile."

They fell silent again as they observed the ship's approach. Earlier, Léonore had enjoyed the playfulness of the wind that tossed her plait of hair over her shoulder, but now its strength had become vital. She jammed her hat down on her head and prayed for the wind to stay steady.

"She's a merchant ship, surely?"

"Indeed, Maître. If only I could make out—yes! English, by God."

Léonore turned to the lieutenant for the first time. "The French ensign, please, Monsieur Martineau." Then she stared anxiously at the approaching hull. "How well armed?"

"I see no gunports. But she has at least two big pieces on the forecastle."

"So large, and no escort!" She added quickly, "What says the lookout?"

At that very moment there was another cry from aloft: just over the horizon were other vessels bearing from the same direction.

Santo frowned. "If they're escorts, why lag so far behind?"

Within the next few minutes, their answer surged into sight. From a distant melee, wrapped in a pall of gun smoke, they figured out that there had been a frigate escorting the merchant ship, but she had been drawn off by a pursuer. The frigate seemed to be getting the worst of the encounter, leaving the larger and slower merchant ship to make a run for it.

Santo said eagerly, "What might she be carrying, Maître? Is she worth it?"

"Whatever the cargo, we want her."

He had the glass to his eye again. "That English escort: it's a navy frigate."

"Engaged by what?"

"The masts are raked. It may be French built—a corvette."

"Faster than us, no doubt. The devil grant the English keep her occupied."

Santo grinned: the expression was Roncival's.

They kept up the *Fantôme*'s speed. The prospect from onboard the English vessel must have been terrifying, with their escort tangled in a losing battle miles behind them and the enemy brigantine in full sail, flying towards them. Expecting no help from the frigate, the merchant ship held to her course, tacking widely to beat against the wind.

The impact of their meeting depended on the merchant ship's direction: if she were tacking away, she could deliver a broadside as the brigantine came within range. There was no way of knowing whether the vessel had the wherewithal, however, and the *Fantôme* would

present only a slim target. If the English ship managed
to get across the *Fantôme*'s bows and then at once
change tack, however, she could steal the wind from her
and deliver a broadside from the other direction before
slipping quickly out of reach. Léonore and Santo found
it impossible to calculate what the English captain might
decide to do within the next hour.

It was a considerable time before they sent the snipers
at last to the tops, armed with the long-barreled American rifles that Roncival had always favored over muskets. Santo made out the name of the vessel: the
Jubilation. He shook his head as he scanned her. "She's
not pretty. A dirty ship and poorly armed—a three
decker but I see no sign of cannon."

"Concealed gunports?"

"I don't reckon so. I wonder if she's a slaver, crammed
to the gills? That would explain it—no room for the
big guns."

"Confound them. And confound that corvette if she
breaks off: I've no mind to get into a contest for slaves."

Santo looked at her in consternation. "But we hold
course, Maître?"

"We do. There's no choice now. Be careful with the
timing: whatever she's doing we mustn't get too close on
our first sweep. Not until we know her artillery. If she
tacks towards us, veer to starboard at once and get well
forward of her. If she stays on this tack, we rake her
astern."

If they had not been wary of what the enemy frigate
might do, if they had not feared interference from the
mysterious corvette, their strike at the *Jubilation* need
not have been so hasty. As it was, as soon as they came
within range the forward guns fired at will. There was
no response from the *Jubilation*: at that angle it seemed
she could not bring her own to bear. Mindful of Léonore's warning, Santo sent the *Fantôme* veering to port
so that the heavy guns amidships could fire as they
passed her stern—and then the English captain did precisely what they had feared.

For a slow and ponderous vessel the maneuver was
completed with amazing dexterity. The *Fantôme* was a

mere thirty yards away when the *Jubilation*'s quarterdeck cannon spat fire; then she swung onto the opposite
tack, bringing her forecastle guns briefly to bear before
she caught the wind again with snapping sails. It all
happened with such swiftness that the *Fantôme*'s impromptu broadside was seconds late, and ragged. She
had no choice but to tear past the *Jubilation* and out
of the wind, then sweep on under her own impetus
while the English ship took a gulp of air and sprang
for freedom.

When the *Fantôme*'s forward guns thundered, Léonore shuddered and her mind went blank, as though
they were firing at her rather than the *Jubilation*. She
felt the crash of arms in the center of her body. She
heard the crack of timbers from across the waves and
saw a splintered gap in the gunwale. At that point the
Jubilation achieved her stupefying about-turn and
opened fire on the *Fantôme* from the bow. This time,
paralyzed, Léonore watched the swing of the *Jubilation*,
saw the bloom of flames from her forecastle, heard the
roar, without moving a muscle to duck for cover.

Their own shots, tilted high, had been intended to dis-
able. The *Jubilation*'s on the other hand were aimed for
their hull, but the shock of the wind as she swung about
brought her head high and instead her shot tore through
the *Fantôme*'s mizzen.

When the top of the mast and the yard fell, Léonore's
instant thought was for her snipers—but she had placed
none on the mizzen. Her next was for the sails—and she
realized she was well equipped to replace them, now
that they had the new spars from the captured *Seraph*.
She hardly took in the fact that the falling timbers had
barely missed her—but, as Santo leaped to the rail and
yelled above the din at the quartermaster, she looked at
the yard and fragment of mast that had smashed their
way to rest in a tangle of sheets and pulleys and torn
canvas, and saw what a weight had plummeted to the
deck. It was then that she realized Martineau was beneath it. And that he was dead.

Santo yelled himself hoarse getting the *Fantôme*

hauled around for the pursuit. Léonore watched as the mainsail, untouched, gathered in the breeze and bent eagerly to its task. Damage reports came in: the only casualty was Martineau. She approached him then, but the gunners about to take him below looked up from their task, and the mate gave her a sympathetic shake of the head. She could see only Martineau's legs. She realized she did not really want to see more.

With Santo, she closely observed the *Jubilation* and saw that her foremast, damaged by the *Fantôme*'s broadside, had now toppled and sent timber and canvas crashing down to hang over the starboard side; the drag was already slowing her. Then they spared a glance astern, to discover that the other ships were no longer so far off. They had disengaged, and the sleek corvette was slicing towards them—now that she was closer they could see that she flew the colors of Cartagena. The other vessel had struck the English navy ensign once she was seized, but the crew who had taken her over were slow in following the corvette.

"They must have been boarding the frigate when we saw them!" she shouted to Santo. "She's barely moving—perhaps they've got repairs to make. But I don't like the look of that corvette."

"Nor do I. She's not content with the frigate; she wants our prize as well."

Meanwhile they were gaining on the *Jubilation,* but not very fast despite the damage she had sustained. Léonore looked up at the *Fantôme*'s sails: they had been shortened and trimmed within an inch of safety. There was nothing to be done but hope that they would come in range of the *Jubilation* in time to finish their business before the others caught up.

"Monsieur Santo. When we come close to the *Jubilation*, keep us between her and the corvette at all times."

He looked at her inquiringly.

"If the corvette tries to blast us, they risk holing the *Jubilation* too. We must board her before they make up their minds to try it."

They could see they had one further advantage over

the merchant ship: she had only swivel guns mounted in the stern, which would present a problem at close quarters but could do nothing to discourage pursuit.

Santo reviewed the gun crews, who were armed with swords, cutlasses and small arms. Somehow, for Léonore, all the doubts that had plagued her in the morning flew from her mind into the blue air above: all that mattered was seizing the *Jubilation* while they had the chance.

It seemed an age before they came within range. The instant they did, the forward guns spewed grapeshot to clear the decks and moments later the snipers opened up, keeping up a hail of fire over the length of the struggling ship. They could spy not a man standing on her main deck as they drew abreast of her, and when the grappling hooks snaked out over the gap no one tried to prevent them from taking hold. As the barbs bit into the timbers, well above the *Fantôme*'s deck, Santo sprang up into the ratlines to maintain his line of sight.

Neither ship was taking in canvas—the *Jubilation* because only the helmsman was still on his feet on the main deck, and the *Fantôme* because for the moment she must keep level but avoid grinding against the other hull. The speed was dangerous, and at the *Fantôme*'s bow, sailors stood ready with long staves of timber to hold off the tangled debris draped over the starboard bow of the *Jubilation*, in case of damage to the brigantine's timbers. Sick with suspense, Léonore looked up at Santo perched amidst the rifle fire above.

Suddenly he raised his arm and gave a great roar: "Hold! Hold your fire!"

The riflemen obeyed, and the men who were hauling on the grappling cables froze too, staring at him. For a heart-stopping moment there was dead silence as the two vessels bounced onward beside each other with only a narrow channel of choppy water between them.

Santo shouted, "*Jubilation*! Do you yield?"

From his angle he had seen someone invisible to those who waited breathless below: an officer emerging onto the quarterdeck, holding a white handkerchief.

At Santo's signal, he walked to the starboard side and showed the sign of surrender at the rail. A mighty shout rose from the *Fantôme,* which filled Léonore's chest and head and made her ears ring. The officer at the rail transferred his gaze from Santo to the deck, seeking the commander. When he fixed on her, Léonore swept off her hat in acceptance of his gesture, and the men cheered again.

They had had over an hour to decide what to do and who would do it if the merchant ship gave herself up, so Léonore merely had to stand and watch as the crew of the *Fantôme* took over the division of labor, in obedience to Santo's commands and with the skill of long training.

He had guessed aright: the *Jubilation* was a slave ship—bound for Charleston with two hundred Africans, thirty marines and a crew of fifty. Their last landfall had been on the British island of Antigua, where they had sold some of their cargo, taken on supplies and been joined by their escort, the frigate *Hero.* On leaving the Leewards they had aimed for a clear Atlantic run to Charleston, but instead they fell afoul of a violent storm that forced them towards the Bahamas. Finally they had changed plans, chosen the line of least resistance and sailed across the Great Bahama Bank towards the Straits of Florida, their best escape route to the north.

If the *Fantôme* had set her ambush half a week earlier, she might have surprised the *Jubilation* and the *Hero* south of Great Inagua, over the treasure shoal. As it was, she had been chasing them for several days without knowing it.

Léonore kept an eye astern for the approaching corvette while the bosun supervised the clearing of the *Fantôme*'s decks. The quartermaster, Rigaud, had gone across to the *Jubilation* with Santo and the boarding party, who were busy accounting for the men and arms they had secured on the prize, righting her course and slowing her rate of knots. Very soon after they swarmed over to the other ship they cast themselves loose, leaving the *Fantôme* free to maneuver when the corvette mounted her challenge.

Sailors had joined the gun crews on the brigantine to get rid of the timber and canvas draped across the carronades in the stern, and Léonore was side by side with members of the crew for the first time on the voyage. Knowing them all as individuals was a distraction when it came to command, and she had tried very hard to see and treat them as a team. They played the same game, shouldering their tasks at once without seeming to notice whether an order sprang first from the bosun or was conveyed to him by her. It was she, however, who decided at once to jettison the mizzen yard—it was badly smashed and there were spares enough below. While they were disposing of it overboard, she moved to inspect the mizzen topsail.

The bosun, the man who had in his keeping all the sails, sheets and ropes on the ship, was at her side as the sailors fought through the heavy folds to see whether there was any damage.

"Look at that, it's almost intact. Excellent: have it cut loose, Monsieur Robert, and stowed below, the pulleys as well."

She moved to the rail while he gave the order, to see what was happening in the waist of the ship. They had reduced speed to match that of the *Jubilation,* which traveled only yards away, well within hailing distance. The wind meanwhile was swinging round to a new quarter—it was more favorable for their return home, but it was also lending wings to the corvette.

They could not avoid her—they could only ensure that they were primed for action when she burst upon them. The gun crews had set all to rights in the waist and the stern was almost clear. As a small group struggled below carrying the folded topsail Léonore realized, with trepidation, that she was being commented upon.

What she overheard was a long, ingeniously decorated sentence, the gist of which was, "She couldn't give a curse for us; she only cares about the sails." The oaths uttered in reply were unequivocally admiring.

With the corvette a few hundred yards away, she had Santo fetched to the *Jubilation*'s rail and ordered back onboard. His stance altered when he heard the bosun roar the words through the loud hailer, and he did not reply at once. He clearly wanted to stay and command the slave ship if she had to make a stand against the corvette—with his hands on the prize, he could not bear to let it go so soon.

Léonore stayed stone-faced. She was not going to show weakness by repeating the order. *Damn you, Andrea Santo. I need you,* she thought. *Don't make me fight you now!*

Then he shouted back, "Who will command the *Jubilation*?"

"Monsieur Rigaud," Léonore said at once to the bosun. "He's to hold course and we'll approach with a line."

She moved away to observe the corvette. No one could object to that arrangement, at least: it was tradition for a quartermaster to take over a prize.

A man went up to the main topsail yard and fixed on the long rope that would be tossed to the *Jubilation* so that Santo could swing onboard, and the brigantine closed in with the other vessel. None too soon for Léonore: the corvette was gaining. The single, flush deck was crowded with armed men who preserved an eerie silence, and Léonore could hear no orders being called from it to the skeleton crew that sailed her. The defense nets were impeccably placed and she counted enough snipers in the tops to pick off one man apiece on the *Fantôme* in the first volley.

There was movement on the main deck behind her, but she did not turn, she was too intent on the corvette. For now it was veering, in a smooth curve that would take it across the wake of the brigantine and out to the other side of the *Jubilation*.

Santo appeared at her elbow and she said, "Look. They're going to make a survey of the prize first. To assess any damage. But the hull's sound?"

"Yes, Maître. *Gesù, Maria e tutti i santi,* if they open fire . . . we've got no answer to that."

"Why should they? They want her intact."

"Then they'll try to board."

"What, engage our men when we're right alongside? They'd be crazy."

At that moment the sinister hull of the corvette, still out of range of the biggest of their guns, vanished from view as it began a wide sweep around the opposite side of the *Jubilation*.

Santo was in agony. "There's nothing we can do!"

Distracted by the calls of the lookout aloft, Léonore did not answer for a while. Then she said, "Yes there is. Put the forecastle gun crews on the alert and clear the decks and tops of everyone else. They're going to charge in across the *Jubilation*'s bow and open on us at once: it's their only chance of hitting us without damaging her."

"We're wallowing here like sitting ducks! We should pull out and take her on, for God's sake."

"And leave her to batten on to the prize? Get the men below, and I want a blind put up around the helm." He stood looking at her, his mouth compressed into a hard line, his blue eyes brittle as eggshells. She chose her words carefully. "We made our agreement about this voyage, Monsieur Santo. If you have anything to say, you may speak, of course—when it's over."

With a muttered oath, he turned away. Ignoring him, she looked up towards the lookout again and strained to catch his words. Then she realized what she must do. It was time, after all, to see what could be achieved by trading on her sex.

There was no chance for Santo or anyone else to prevent her, for it was plain that the corvette was just about to shave across the bows of the *Jubilation*, as close as she dared without the risk of being rammed. At that very moment, the tips of three masts could be seen slipping past those of the merchant ship.

Léonore sprinted the length of the brigantine, tossing away her hat and ripping the ribbon from her queue of hair as she ran. When she tore up into the bow, some of the gunners crouched around the cannon leaped to their feet.

She flung her coat onto the deck and raked her fingers

savagely through her hair. "Stay down! Don't fire unless they do."

Then she turned, moved swiftly over the bow, scrambled out along the bowsprit, and found a foothold where she could stand upright, hanging on to the shrouds and facing the expanse of sea ahead.

The wind streamed over her shoulders, shaking out her tresses and tossing them around her head, and in her light clothing she blazed like a beacon in the sunshine. Once the enemy swept into view, they could not fail to make out her figure at the prow, fixed among the shrouds—unmistakably, shockingly female. If the quartermaster hesitated even a second before giving the gunners the order to fire, they might throw their choicest opportunity to the wind. And, if they were not skillful, the next minute might expose them to the *Fantôme*'s starboard cannon—to which they could not reply without risking the prize as well.

The corvette exploded into sight. In the blink of an eye, there was a massive silhouette etched onto the sparkling waves, so close it seemed she could have reached out and touched it.

She gasped, and her lungs kept on expanding, as though a pitiful gulp of air could turn aside the metal that was about to be hurled at her from a dozen cannon mouths.

Desperate to keep her back straight and her face to the foe, she gripped the shrouds on each side of her and fought to steady her gaze. The corvette's gun crews were sheltered like hers below the gunwales and there was a flock of snipers in the tops. They did not fire. Another fraction of a second flashed by. Half the corvette's deck was visible, but not a single officer or man.

She took another shuddering breath and looked again, all her senses straining: and then she saw him. If she had not been dazzled in the first moment she could have picked him out easily, for he stood in the bow, erect and dire as a totem. One arm was raised to give the signal to fire, but it did not fall. His eyes riveted on her, the commander shot by in his dark-painted ship without a sound or gesture.

It was as though a lacquered screen were unfolding before her, painted with a silver sea, the shadowy mass of the corvette and the stark shape of its lone navigator—and rendered in the boldest strokes upon it was his honey-colored face with its black, iconic eyes. The face of Jean Laffite.

CHAPTER SIX

Hero

The cry came to them staccato from the speaking trumpet on the corvette, fragmented by the breeze, but there was no mistaking the words "parley" and "reduce speed."

Santo said, "They're bluffing. It's to give the frigate time to catch up."

"I'm aware of that."

"Then we'll have two men-of-war against us. Damn their parley—we must take them on now."

"Monsieur Santo, while they're conveniently out of range, how do you estimate their firepower?"

"Thirty guns."

"To our twelve. And men aboard?"

"Upwards of two hundred."

"Even though she's had to put a crew on the frigate."

She left him to think about that while she paced along the starboard rail. Laffite's corvette was sailing parallel to the *Fantôme*, with a host of sailors swarming up her rigging to take in sail. The snipers had been withdrawn from the tops, and the long, level deck remained as clear of armed men as it had been when it swept across the brigantine's bow ten minutes before. After that heart-stopping maneuver the corvette had lunged out in a broad arc and onto her present course, without further challenge and without a shot being fired.

At this polite distance the corvette was still close

enough for Léonore to see Laffite's tall figure, standing now in the stern. He had put on a broad-brimmed hat and his face was in shadow. There was no way of reading his thoughts and they should not matter to her anyway, for the situation was perfectly decipherable to a cool mind. But hers, jarred and confused by this nightmare meeting, was anything but cool.

She clamped her teeth together and looked in the opposite direction. The *Jubilation* rose like a wall beside them, the old, worn timbers russet in the afternoon light, the setting sun glinting on the swivel guns at her waist and pointing up the men of San Stefan posted behind them.

Suddenly Léonore wheeled. "Take in sail, Monsieur Santo, and when we've less way on, grapple us to the *Jubilation* again. Winch the sixteen-pounders from the port of our main deck to the other. Make us a floating fortress."

He let only a moment go by before he relayed the orders. She watched him as he surveyed the crew, who leaped to their tasks without demur. Santo liked above all to be doing, and so did they. Heaven help her if all that massed energy and will should ever take a course against her.

Five minutes went by without her composing any reply to the corvette, but the activity onboard the *Fantôme* was signal enough. The three ships trimmed sail, gradually slackening speed, the corvette keeping her distance as before. Then, when the brigantine was made fast to the *Jubilation* and the men were occupied reinforcing the merchant ship's artillery, they were hailed again.

Santo came at once to Léonore's side. His voice was explosive. "Permission to send over a boat? I know what I'd give them!"

All at once she lost her temper. "You realize what they could give *us*? What they could have poured into us when they came across the bow? We've had ample chance to go to the bottom. Instead we've lost one officer, we've kept this vessel intact and we hold our prize. Do you have any complaints so far?"

"If you put it that way, no. But—"

"But you don't think it necessary to know what terms our opponent has to offer. Permission to state your views, Monsieur Santo, but be brief: I am about to send the reply."

Suddenly the formality was beyond him. "*Jésu,* I just couldn't stand to yield to that bastard. You wouldn't dream of it, for God's sake! Tell me that's not what you have in mind." He looked around the ship in anguish. "We'd as soon go to perdition as lose what we got today. Wake up, and you can see what these men will fight for."

"I'll remind you, what they fight for is your responsibility. They elected you captain for this voyage and there was not one dissenter in the vote. Are you suggesting they won't jump to your next command?"

"No!" There was such confusion in his eyes she almost felt sorry for him.

The crew, always alert to what passed between them, were slackening in their work and turning to catch what was being said. And also, no doubt, wondering how far Laffite's patience was to be tried before he received an answer.

She moved nearer and kept her voice low and steady. "Listen. I have one desire, one strategy—not to go home without a prize. I pledge to you, whatever happens from now on, that aim never leaves my mind. Do I have your pledge in return?"

"To do what?"

"To back me up, in whatever I must do to deal with Laffite."

She could see the struggle, knew that he was piqued by her remarks about his leadership, yet flattered by her plea for support—and she prayed that his male pride, of which she took such tender and constant care, would win out.

"You have my complete confidence, Monsieur Santo. If you will only shake hands on it."

They were standing so close together that from the point of view of the bystanders, when his head bent towards her and his broad hand took hers, the firm handclasp might just as easily have been a caress.

*   *   *

As he was rowed over in the longboat, Jean Laffite reflected that the issue was crystal clear, yet somehow there was everything to distract him, and in search of calm he scanned the brigantine. She was lovely: sleek, irreproachably fitted out, her canvas fresh and supple enough to wrap a newborn babe. At once he longed to take her, and he had to remind himself of his plans.

The moment he had seen San Stefan, he had wanted that too. But there were other ways to possess than by force. The island was not vital—he had Barataria under his hand, which more than sufficed in strategic terms. Roncival's little ship was not necessary to him either. He had other prey in his sights, which would not slip through his fingers a second time.

He climbed a rope ladder up the brigantine's side and the longboat pushed off before he reached the rail. Two seamen were posted above to help him onboard and another with a tin whistle piped him on as though he were a visitor to a naval vessel. This might have tickled him in less trying circumstances, but it had been a long day.

He found himself standing between two widely spaced sixteen-pounders and noted that the corresponding positions on the other side of the waist were empty. It was clear what had been done with the missing pieces. He tried to be angry about that, but all coherence of thought and emotion dissolved as he looked towards her.

She was in the stern, facing his way. He wondered whether she really imagined that the English officer's rig, now tidy and complete, made her look anything like a male—and his senses instantly blazed a negative. He began walking aft, grasping for cogent details.

The blond six-footer with the scowl was standing at her side, almost as close as during the intimate exchange that he had just observed from his own deck. Andrea Santo: born in Genoa, went to sea on Portuguese traders as a boy, fetched up in the Caribbean in his twenties. With Roncival for at least three years, the last as lieutenant to Baudard. In a bitter tirade to Curtis lately, Baudard had said Santo would have lost no time in claiming all the usual rights of San Stefan's man in command.

When pressed, he boasted that his own privileges had
dated from a week after the demise of Roncival. He was
lying, almost without a doubt. Which made it at least
possible that he was also lying about Santo.

As he drew nearer to her, the low sun darted a ray
into his eyes, so she appeared to him in that second as
a silhouette, limned by a sickle of gold where the light
caught one side of her gathered hair, below the hat. He
swept off his own to make a bow and, rising, closed one
eye against the glare. Her face and body swam into focus
and it was impossible to suppress the dazzled smile with
which he greeted her, nor to miss savoring what it might
do to the vitals of the man at her side.

"Mademoiselle, life never seems more extraordinary
than when I cross your path. I cannot help wondering
whether I shall ever meet you in a gown."

"And I wonder whether I shall ever farewell you
clothed, monsieur."

His burst of laughter did not prevent him from seeing
the discomposure in Santo, who looked at them both
without amusement.

Despite the breeze eddying over her right shoulder, her
voice reached him with the melodious timbre that he remembered. "You suffered no ill effects from your swim?"

"I confess there were some, mademoiselle. Once I got
to the *Ruleigh*, my invention was a little taxed when it
came to explanations—my men were perplexed by your
fireworks. And ever since, I have regretted the interruption to that meal at which I had the delight of your
company."

Santo answered for her. "Well, it was none too soon."

He went smoothly on. "So by delicious paradox, your
intrusion today brings me the greatest pleasure."

"What?" Santo said more loudly.

He looked at her with irony. "You know, mademoiselle, that having engaged these ships before you came
in sight, I have the prior claim to both."

"I've seen no evidence that you engaged the
Jubilation."

"But your captain has. How many dead and wounded
lie below—twenty?"

She looked sharply at Andrea Santo, whose expression became surly; he had obviously had neither the time nor the sense to give her a full assessment of the capture. But why else did she imagine the slaver would yield with such ease? The English marines, picked out of the shrouds or from the deck as the corvette sprang rapidly within range, had paid dearly.

"However, I have no doubt that we can find a solution to your mistake, mademoiselle. Are you prepared to debate this now?"

She glanced over her shoulder to check on the distant *Hero*. Jean could see the frigate was still having trouble holding her course; the jury rudder was scarcely doing its job. When the turquoise eyes came back to his there was a sheen of tears on them, caused by the wind. "Mistake?"

"For which you might have paid with your life! But I could not fire on you."

His tone for the moment was uncontrolled, but she ignored whatever feeling it might have expressed, saying at once, "And why not? Because you have no legitimate grievance. Also, you don't care to waste ammunition. I wonder if the frigate is carrying any more than you, after such a costly encounter?"

With difficulty he concealed the absurd rush of admiration that so often came over him when they confronted each other. "Such details, mademoiselle, are precisely what I am here to discuss. Would you prefer to receive me below, or hold our parley aboard the *Mélusine*?"

She glanced across at the corvette. "So that is her name. I must say I was not thinking of sea sprites when you chose to *intrude* on us." He half smiled at the emphasis as she turned to the captain. "Escort Monsieur Laffite to the chart room, if you please."

Below, he had a keen look at what he could see of the brigantine's appointments and spoke to Santo in Italian, eliciting a few tight-lipped answers. At one point he caught sight of a skirt disappearing round a corner—she had women onboard! It surprised him more than anything so far; then he wondered whether the air of com-

fort and order on the vessel derived from that very
presence. He had a mischievous impulse to ask the captain, and also to inquire of Adélaïde Maselari, but next
moment he was ushered with bad grace into the chart
room and left alone.

For a ship the size of the brigantine, it was handsome,
with its smooth, polished wood gleaming in the last rays
of the sun that crept through the stern window. The
strange sixth sense that he had about her told him that
this was her cabin. There was no sign, for all the doors
and brassbound drawers were shut fast, and her bed was
folded against the wall. None of her clothes or trifles
were about, but he felt her touch in the place, as though
she had just put down the parallel ruler that lay by his
hand on the table. He half closed his eyes and breathed
in a trace of her perfume that lingered in the still air.

She had stayed on deck to give orders, for by the time
she joined him the brigantine had lost way and, still
yoked to the slaver, continued peacefully on a calmer
swell. Astern, the vast, shimmering fireball of the sun
was up to its middle in the sea, and the hot light caught
her as she paused in the doorway, coloring her midship-
man's shirt, breeches and hose a blushing pink and lending a rosy tint to her cheeks that made her look
embarrassed, disturbed. He hid his own disturbance by
getting to his feet and drawing out a chair for her.

A steward, entering immediately after her, lit two lanterns slung on the crossbeam in the center of the cabin:
when the sun disappeared, their light would illuminate
his own face more clearly than hers, which was directed
towards the window. She did not speak while the man
was in the cabin and Jean simply looked at her, waiting
while the last sparks of day flickered out and watching,
fascinated, as the sun drowned and the tropic night
flooded in across the sea-blue of her eyes.

Once the door closed behind the steward, she began
by asking him about the *Hero*. He gave her the information concisely, including the damage the frigate had sustained and the subsequent repairs.

"I see. Just by the look of her, she needs a lot more

attention before you can sail her home. And as for being of any use to you when she catches up tonight—she maneuvers like an upturned punt!"

"But she fires like a floating blockhouse. I'm afraid it was unwise, mademoiselle, to venture between us."

"I am not between you. And if I were, that would scarcely guarantee you this cargo. I presume you have no inclination to send it to the bottom?"

"It?" His eyes probed hers unsuccessfully. "You are aware the *Jubilation* carries slaves?"

"Indeed." Her voice was cold. "In excellent condition, I am told. The quartermaster has instructions to bring them up on deck for air this evening, in batches, and their meal is being prepared as we speak. Everything will be done to preserve their negotiable value."

Baffled, he persevered. "You have not inspected them yourself?"

"I have not been onboard the *Jubilation*, nor do I intend to. I am sure this is quite impossible for you to conceive, but my mercantile ambitions will never match the vileness of yours."

He expelled a sudden breath. The chill in her eyes and voice was contempt. "You do not deal in slaves."

"I abominate the trade and all who engage in it."

"Yet in your fond imagination you hold a slave ship at present. To what end?"

For the first time, she summoned a smile. "We are here to strike a bargain, Monsieur Laffite. It would be pointless for me to sit down at this table if I had nothing to bargain with."

"Then the moral distinction escapes me. You do deal in slaves."

"I am sure all such distinctions are beyond a mind like yours, so I shall not waste time debating them with you. Instead, perhaps you would like to hazard an estimate of what this cargo would fetch on the American market."

Her lingering scorn lent an odd tone to her fluid, mellow voice, but he ignored it, saying calmly, "That would depend on where the merchandise was landed. Importation of slaves to the Territory of Orleans being illegal, they must be smuggled in. Otherwise they may be auctioned at ports on the eastern seaboard. None of these operations is easy, or, I would have thought, quite within your scope."

"The *Jubilation* is sound and seaworthy and I can simply trade the merchandise in Guadeloupe, though perhaps with less profit. So there is nothing to stop me setting course for Pointe-à-Pitre at once if I choose."

"With respect, mademoiselle, I should have an objection to that."

"And it would be even simpler for me to sink her."

She held his gaze defiantly as he flashed at her, "You're not serious. You'd not send two hundred souls to perdition."

"Ah, they have souls now?"

Exasperated, he shook his head. Into his mind, amongst the indelible images from the night on San Stefan came that of her face, when Andrea Santo told her how many of his raiders were dead. There was no mistaking the spasm that had crossed it, marring the perfect features, turning the skin so sickly pale that he had thought her about to faint. At her first kill, she had weakened to the core.

Before he could reply, she continued. "Or supposing I scuttled the *Jubilation* but left the Africans floating for you to pick up—that would be troublesome for you, would it not? No, I think the prize is most valuable to you in one piece." When he still did not speak, she said softly, "You do want it?"

He raised his head, about to give vent to a justifiable stream of sarcasm. Then his eyes met hers and all at once he understood. "First tell me what you desire."

"I want the *Hero*."

He breathed out slowly, his mind racing. "There is a disparity. She is magnificently armed, as I told you."

"She is also unnavigable. I must inspect her when she arrives, before I can even consider her as an exchange."

"An exchange? For a ship and cargo you hold through my indulgence and which you have no way to dispose of?"

"But I have. One shot from the big cannon amidships

will do the trick. The muzzle is kissing her hull this instant. Come now: surely from your point of view the *Hero* is a mere trifle beside the *Jubilation*. Rumor gives you forty ships, Monsieur Laffite, and even if you possess only a quarter of those you are well supplied with gunpower. Why not strike this bargain now, and leave me to worry about the *Hero*? My carpenters will have to work all night to get her in a fit state to sail tomorrow. But you can be homeward bound within the hour."

He transferred his gaze to the table again and began an unhurried deliberation. He found himself staring at her hat, which she had folded flat and laid next to the parallel ruler on the shiny tabletop between them. Neatly fashioned, it had once belonged to an English flag officer's dress uniform—it was bound with gold lace and the cockade was of fine black silk. All at once the bizarre nature of the whole encounter surged into his consciousness on a wave of mild hilarity.

He smiled at her. "We have covered all the major points. In fact, I believe we are very near agreement." He rose. "I suggest we adjourn until nine o'clock, at which hour I shall be honored to receive you to supper onboard the *Mélusine*."

It was ridiculously gratifying to see that she had not predicted this, and it was also some salve for past injuries to read the realization in her eyes that her own lessons in diplomacy had only just begun.

She collected herself, however, and rose gracefully. "I have your assurance that we preserve the status quo until then?"

"Yes. When the *Hero* approaches she'll be told to keep her distance."

"My inspection party will be allowed onboard?"

"Just tell them to indicate when they are ready."

"Thank you, monsieur."

He governed his voice to solemnity and his body to patience. "Until nine, mademoiselle."

CHAPTER SEVEN

~<del></del>~

Sida Al Hurra

The wide stern gallery of the *Mélusine* was furnished in a style more sumptuous than Léonore had seen, even in the wealthiest houses of New Orleans. It was paneled in costly oak, but the gleaming timber was scarcely visible, except where lamps of venetian glass were bracketed to the walls. Elsewhere it was draped in richly patterned North African rugs and hangings, which she recognized because her father had shared the same tastes. Some of the Roncival treasures had been obtained through French corsairs who operated from the northwest seaboard of Africa—Laffite's came perhaps from the Mediterranean, along the Barbary Coast or farther east, for set in a socket of ebony near the door she saw the gold statue of a young woman whose snakehead diadem, high breasts and immense, catlike eyes pronounced her from Egypt and the Nile.

Léonore had resented what amounted to a summons from him, but she had nonetheless prepared for the visit with great care. Her Parisian gown was of finely figured Chinese silk caught under her breasts by a narrow gold ribbon, and her wrap was cloth of gold, with a long fringe that brushed the floor. There were no servants in the room when he ushered her in, so he took the wrap from her himself, laid it over a high-backed chair and paused for a moment before turning to look at her.

The still silence seemed very long to Léonore as she

stood in the middle of the room. She had not felt the touch of his fingers as he removed the wrap, his eyes were unreadable and his voice was remote when he eventually said, "Pray be seated, mademoiselle."

She moved to a sofa under one of the lamps. When she sat down, there was a sensation of coolness as her gown came into slippery contact with the satin surface. She put one hand on the armrest and with the other smoothed the narrow panels of silk that shone like nacre against the coral-colored cushions.

This meal, she promised herself, would be different from the one on San Stefan. This time there was nothing to threaten her personally, not while her men held the *Jubilation*. And Laffite was too intelligent to try holding her to ransom, for how could he know whether Santo was loyal? In the event, her young lieutenant might simply try to escape and sail off with the prize.

There were a few seconds of strange suspense; then he seemed to rouse himself. "You're comfortable there? It's a warm evening."

"Perfectly, thank you."

Nonetheless he strode across to the windows and pushed two tall panels of lead lights fully open, latching them to hooks outside. She did not feel the light breeze, but at once she heard the music that drifted in upon it, played on a guitar, a honey-toned wooden pipe and a violin.

"Who are your musicians?" she said in surprise.

"Two gunner's mates and a foretopman. The sailor favors us with the violin only at sea—the rum always does for him on land." He leaned one shoulder against the casement and contemplated her with a faint smile, as though amused by her interest.

"They play every evening?"

"Below on the gun deck, usually. Tonight they're perched in the stern."

"As far away from the rum cask as possible?"

The smile became a grin, and he pushed himself upright. "Speaking of which, I must offer you some refreshment." He walked to the wall opposite her, where a long polished sideboard occupied the space below a gilded mirror. "Let me see." He laid a finger on the top of one of the decanters. "We have cordials: grenadine, barley water, and the bilious one is lime. And there is another concoction, described to me by the cook, who hails from Savannah. I've forgotten what's in it now, but never mind—all one ever tastes, I must warn you, is mint." He raised an eyebrow. "No? Very wise. Though I vouch for the freshness of the water. There are the usual others, canary, Madeira wine. And I think, in our rare stab at refinement, someone has dug out some ratafia." He looked doubtfully at a dusty bottle. "Which on second thoughts I cannot vouch for."

She asked for a finger of canary wine and watched him in the mirror as he half turned to pour it. The smile vanished from his lips as though he had stepped alone into another room. The intricately patterned fabrics on the cabin walls appeared darker in reflection, like somber tapestries in a twilit chamber, against which his face stood out with grave clarity, like that of a Spanish prince in an old palace portrait. The lamps set at each side of the mirror touched him with warm light, defining the strong lines of his smooth, bronzed cheeks and determined jaw, casting shadows from the thick eyelashes against his straight nose, finding ruddier tones in the long, full lips and beneath the fine skin at the corners of the downcast eyes.

Then he looked up, caught her studying him, and his expression changed. It seemed to her that a question sprang into his eyes, but the mirror was too elevated for her to see her own reflection, so she could not imagine what it was about her that puzzled or perturbed. For the first time she felt the hint of something vulnerable in him and, oddly enough, in that instant he appeared younger. No one had ever known Laffite's precise age, but he was clearly some years older than she. Yet at this moment it seemed as if her covert glance had stripped him of the advantage of his extra age and experience and broken through to him in a new way.

He turned, holding the glass of wine. The mysterious question lingered in his eyes, but he merely said, "You did not bring Monsieur Santo."

"You did not invite him."

He shrugged, crossed the room to give her the glass, then sat down opposite her.

"Thank you. Am I to have the pleasure of seeing Messieurs You and Curtis this evening?"

"No. They are not on this voyage."

She took a sip of the canary and glanced around the gallery. "You could entertain a vast company in here."

"Indeed. But never ladies, until tonight." He paused, then said in the same even tone, "And this room will never again hold such beauty."

She snatched her lips from the glass and lowered it to her lap, and a rush of confused feeling betrayed itself by a blush that threatened to rise from her neck to her cheeks. She put a hand to her throat, took it away, then avoided his eye while she struggled for an answer. If she said nothing he would suspect the compliment had moved her, but it would be absurd to murmur "Thank you" as if he had just handed her another glass of wine.

She had come onboard to seal the bargain with him—the *Jubilation* for the *Hero*—then leave and eject him from her life. As an enemy he was formidable, for the defeat on San Stefan must rankle in a man so used to conquest. And as an ally, he was the most dangerous she could possibly contemplate. Yet the way he spoke to her was so calculated to disarm that at times he almost succeeded. She should be wary of him for this alone!

He spoke again, either to rescue her or to conceal his amusement at her disarray. "I have been meaning to ask after Mademoiselle Maselari. She is well?"

"She was when last I saw her." Léonore managed to raise her eyes. "She has left San Stefan and gone to live in New Orleans."

"She must have left a considerable gap in your household."

"That's true. I miss her." She recalled the day Adélaïde left, and the sense of betrayal she had felt then caught up with her again. To banish it, she went on. "But I understand her choice. She . . . there is a son. She left him behind, with a relative, when she came to

San Stefan with my father. He never knew about the child. No one did. He is eight years old, and now she has rejoined him."

He said with a slight sneer, "None too soon. Or rather, far too late."

She glanced at him in surprise, but at that moment there was a tap on the door, a steward announced that supper was ready, and he rose to usher her to the table.

The food was fresh, flavorsome, beautifully prepared, and presented on gold plate. In another setting, Léonore might have found the meal and service wildly ostentatious, but with Laffite on the *Mélusine* it all seemed natural and effortless. The awkward checks that had crept into their opening conversation did not recur, and to her astonishment she and her host managed to talk for an hour without referring once to the bizarre events that had first thrown them together, nor to the heavy blows they had struck against each other since. She put off talking of their bargain and allowed herself to maintain this conversation between equals. The cabin became briefly an enchanted space, where they could talk of ships and sailing, of coral gardens and dangerous reefs, of celebrated commanders and unreliable crews, of New Orleans and its notables, just as though the candlelit table were their first place of meeting, and they were surrounded by a social crowd instead of the dark vastness of the sea.

It was he who at last mentioned their purpose. The musicians above had summoned another plaintive Irish ballad from their repertoire and the sweet voice of the violin was flowing down to them on the warm night air; Laffite was holding a glass of burgundy up to the candlelight and contemplating its ruby glow with a smile. She had seen him drink a quantity of wine with no noticeable effect, for the firm timbre of his voice had not altered while he subtly guided their talk throughout the meal— always onto impersonal subjects that could give her no cause for defensiveness.

He transferred his approving gaze from the wine to her. "Your party is confident of fixing the *Hero,* I gather."

"Yes. They are ready to start work. I should be glad to give the order when I return to the *Fantôme*."

"And what did Andrea Santo have to say about letting the *Jubilation* out of his clutches?"

"He didn't agree at first. But that's of no consequence. He captains the ship, but he does not command me."

"Really?" Again the hidden question betrayed itself in his gaze, and she felt a tingle at the back of her neck. Was he toying with the idea of holding her on the *Mélusine* after all? She had imagined he had guessed the risks of this—but perhaps not. The time had come, then, to show him that the links between her and Santo were strategic, not sexual.

If she had not just enjoyed rational conversation for the first time in months, if she were not surrounded by pleasures that aroused her senses as well as her mind, she would have taken longer to consider all the implications of what she was about to say. But the impulse to explain herself on this one subject was too strong.

"The people who choose to stay on San Stefan are sustained by the Roncivals. That is a given. The island, the ships, the enterprise, are ours."

"And in return they pay you allegiance? That is positively feudal, mademoiselle. Even your legendary treasure could not exert such power."

"No, of course not. San Stefan is democratic. The Roncivals may fit out the ships, but we don't elect the captains for the expeditions. That's up to the people who sail in them."

"Which still smacks of the feudal. You are not required to gratify the crowd to remain secure—you need only please the barons."

She nodded. "I knew you would understand, monsieur, being in very much that situation yourself."

He said softly, "With one compelling difference: I am not a young, beautiful, unmarried woman."

She could feel a blush building again across the base of her throat. "You mean I require either a father or husband at my side. Or a lover. Or at least the appearance of one." At that point she saw him take the mean-

ing at once, as though a flame had darted towards his
eyes.

"Baudard . . . Santo . . ."

"I gave Baudard quarters in my house when I confirmed his command on San Stefan. When Monsieur
Santo succeeded him, I did the same, and it suited him
well—much better than anyone on the island suspected.
For more than a year, he had been carrying on an intimate affair with my maid, Christina. It was not encouraged, for there is a tradition on San Stefan that keeps
the crews and the household staff apart. When he moved
into his new quarters, it was natural for the others to
believe that he would overlook her once he had . . .
other favors in prospect. But he and Christina are devoted to each other. Monsieur Santo is very happily provided for. And so am I."

The look in the dark eyes became more intense and
demanding and too late she felt the consequences of
letting down her guard. He was riveted on every word
she said and on every inward tremor that accompanied
the words, for he seemed to understand what they cost
her—and yet he was poised for more, ready to stride
over all her barriers and engage her on the home ground
that she needed so much to defend.

She tried for a lighter, ironic tone. "There are prece-
dents, even more or less feudal ones. If I dared compare
myself with English royalty, I might name Elizabeth
the First."

"And what a life she had! The only way she could
manage her men was to slice their heads off. Can you
envy the Virgin Queen?"

The last two regrettable words hung between them
like a challenge, a threat, or a veiled insult.

She succeeded in keeping the smile on her lips. "I am
not so ruthless, I hope. Monsieur Santo has no cause for
complaint. And as for Baudard—his head is no doubt
still on his shoulders."

He laughed at that and put down his glass. "I shall
never forget! He looked as though someone had thrown
him off a balcony onto a vegetable stall. These days I

can't walk past a bag of onions in the market and keep a straight face."

"It was potatoes, actually."

"It was the whole cornucopia!" Suddenly he rose to his feet. "Mademoiselle, before they serve the last course, would you care to join me for a turn on deck? I can offer you fresh air and a story that may entertain you."

"A story?'

"About a remarkable woman. She was known as Sida Al Hurra."

Léonore put her hand on his outstretched wrist and stood up, then swayed on her feet. At once he put the other hand under her elbow, but a second later she disengaged herself. "Thank you. I don't know what came over me."

He was standing very close. "It was certainly not the wine—you have scarcely taken food or drink tonight. You are worn out. I should not have suggested—"

"No, let us go on deck. I shall welcome the breeze."

At the door, he arranged the wrap across her shoulders, and this time she did feel the touch of his fingers, featherlight on her bare skin.

As she went up the companionway before him, holding the hem of the gown just above her ankles to negotiate the steps, she remembered the hot day when she had walked before him with only an Indian shawl around her—and she recalled her fear of his maleness, of his power. Things had changed since, but not the reality of what he was.

On deck, however, the scene was totally different from that brutal afternoon. The corvette was gliding through a gentle swell, the deck was deserted except for the helmsman and the watch looking out to sea, and there seemed to be no sound but the music. The playing ceased when she and Laffite approached the musicians, and he dismissed them with a gesture. As they trailed off to go below, Léonore murmured her appreciation; the foretopman, tucking his violin under his arm, gave her a grin and a duck of the head that proved him surprisingly grateful for the attention, considering how long he had been kept from his rum and his hammock to entertain her.

They stood at the stern looking at the three ships, silent as ghosts, sailing behind them. On the night air she could hear muffled voices from the deck below, where the men who had rowed her to the *Mélusine* awaited her departure, the rustle of water under the stern, the ever-present whisper of the sails.

Laffite leaned with both hands on the stern rail, close beside her. "A wonderful sight. Who needs sleep when the night affords such splendor? Sometimes I stay on deck until dawn just watching."

"Admiring your prizes, Monsieur Laffite?"

"Yes. Think what a marvel it is—that these fragile shells are still on the surface after wind, waves, shot and hellfire have battered them today. Think of what lies ahead, the leagues to cross before we get them home, the thousand and one chances they'll have to sink out of sight forever. Think of the devils who are roving the ocean out there, avid to pound us to pieces and get their hooks into these beauties in their turn." He swung towards her. "I still can't believe you've chosen this."

"What?"

"That you want this . . . struggling in the dark, taking scores of men with you into the teeth of God knows what, snatching a living out of the whirlwind, and always solitary, always in danger."

She smiled ironically. "If you can put up with it, why shouldn't I?"

The black eyes widened. "Mademoiselle, *I like it.*" After a pause during which his keen gaze did not waver, he said, "And you do not. So why continue?"

"That is my business."

The heels of his hands struck the rail in a soft movement of impatience. "Your business should be better safeguarded."

Just avoiding bitterness, she said, "How?"

He faced her, leaning one arm along the rail and crossing one long leg over the other. He was dressed as he had been at her supper table on San Stefan, except that the ribbed cloth of his coat had a subtle gleam even in the semidarkness, and his shirt and cravat were ivory instead of white.

"Let me tell you the story of Sida Al Hurra. It was a sailor from Morocco who told me about her, and he was by no means sure of the century when she lived—but it was after the Spaniards threw the Moors out of Spain. She went with her family to a port called Tetuan. She must have been very seductive, extraordinarily clever, for she rose from obscurity to marry a rich merchant and became even richer herself, operating pirate ships along the North African Coast and across the Straits of Gibraltar. 'Al Hurra' is a title, in fact—it means 'woman of power.' "

"Lucky her."

He shook his head in melancholy reproach. "There was no luck involved. She secured her enormous enterprise by making a strategic marriage and by keeping the reins in her hands when her first husband died. Can you imagine whom she married next? The ruler of Morocco. And for the wedding, an unheard of event occurred: her prestige was such that her bridegroom traveled to her, instead of her going to Fez, his capital."

"I see: this is your old theme—the only safe foundation for a woman's life is marriage. So you are advising me to attract a husband, Monsieur Laffite." She paused, her heart thumping in her throat. "Or are you proposing to me yourself?"

The reaction was instantaneous—he was as startled as she had meant him to be. But her angry mockery, instead of injuring him, seemed only to strip away another of the shields she put up between them. For he replied at once, with an intensity that seemed driven by the force of his own surprise. "I would marry you tomorrow! If it could do good to you. If you would have me." He took a breath, then remained in suspense, one hand on the rail and the other advanced towards her, as though he were about to touch her. But he did not.

She stood staring at him, astonished and unable to move, until he spoke again, less rapidly. "As for the first, there is no good I could do you or any woman. I work beyond the law; I have legal title to scarcely a single article of property and no fixed abode. As for the second—spare me your comments on that. I know your opinion of me."

For a wild moment her sympathy went out to him, as though she really could wound him by a harsh word, but she said, "Monsieur—I act as I find. We were ill met in the beginning, and you have given me every reason to resent you since! Good heavens, do you think I want your advice now?"

He shook his head. He had gotten over his own surprise and his tone was dry as he said, "Of course not. My ideas ran away with me. I was thinking aloud, of your interests—but naturally that is impossible for you to believe. From my selfish point of view, the idea of your marrying is anathema. It would strengthen you as a rival, and I do not enjoy having rivals of any kind. Nonetheless, since I left San Stefan, I have often meditated on how precarious your life is, and will continue to be, without protection."

There seemed no end to the twists and turns of his extraordinary conversation, in which arrogance and more generous emotions were so confusingly mingled. She was not going to tell him why she could never marry; she would not trust him with any more truths about herself. But she did not turn away from this strange onslaught, or flinch from his nearness. Instead she remembered her own dramatic cruelty on the night she had banished him from her island and, looking into the dark eyes so close to hers, she realized he was thinking of it too.

"Thank you. I am sorry. For both our sakes, I think it best if we change the subject." She took a breath. "I brought something here tonight that belongs to you, and I should like to return it." He said nothing, so she went on. "You do not recognize the pin I am wearing? It is yours."

She raised her hand to remove the diamond from the headdress of ostrich feathers fixed in her hair, but he took her wrist and arrested it.

"Please, don't. I never want it back. To my memory, it is full of ill luck." He brought her wrist down between them within the firm band of his fingers. "If you don't want the thing either, you may throw it into the sea."

"I don't think that's necessary." Her voice sounded odd. "You really did not notice it?"

"No. I was too aware of the feathers. With the slightest movement of air, the tip of one floats down and just brushes your face. Here." His fingers let go of her wrist and followed his glance, to touch her temple with the lightest caress.

An incredible impulse overcame her to turn her lips into his palm and lean her whole body into the warmth of his. All the resistance she could summon was to close her eyes for an instant, and he withdrew his fingers, but only to place both hands over her shoulders. She felt his breath soft on her face. "Look at me. Ever since that night I have wanted to obliterate the piece of madness and misfortune we forged between us."

She opened her eyes and felt as though she were spinning into the blackness of his. "But how?"

She knew the answer. She wanted the answer.

Once again his lips spoke to her alone, but this time he was not at bay before a hostile crowd and she offered no opposition. The instant his mouth closed on hers she was engulfed by a wave of sensations that swept her against him, so that in one smooth movement she found herself within the strong circle of his arms, and her hands slid in beneath his coat.

Drowning, she locked her fingers over the hard muscles of his waist, into the fine shirt that was soft and fresh despite the hot humidity of the night; perhaps he was impervious to heat. But he was not impervious to her. His arms tightened, his mouth urged irresistibly and her lips parted. She clung to him for a kiss that went longer, deeper than anything she had known.

When they disengaged a fraction to breathe, he did not speak and she could not. He repeated the kisses, until it seemed to her that somehow, while standing molded to him in the same spot on the ship's deck, she was at the same time exploring undreamed of territories, crossing oceans of knowledge and desire. He was insistent and gentle by turns: the gold wrap slithered unheeded to the deck and settled around their feet, but he took no liberties with the body thus revealed to him by the binnacle light and the faint luster of the stars. Eyes closed, with her head tipped back, she sensed protectiveness in the hands that caressed her bared shoulders; then he wound his arms around her waist and pressed his lips to the base of her throat with a suddenness that made her gasp, as though his lips scorched her.

Was this how he bargained, then? No, they both knew the bargain was already concluded. Was this the seal? It felt like more than that. It felt indescribably dangerous.

She raised her arms and slid them across his shoulders, feeling his warm neck above the cravat, the faint rasp of the jaw he must have shaved that afternoon, the smooth hair of his sideburns slowly brushing against the tender skin of her forearms. She opened her eyes, remembering the way he had shivered when she taunted him with the same gesture on the beach at San Stefan, wanting to see and feel him to do it again, knowing now what it was like to be a body in thrall to another, subjugated by a single, potent impulse.

She was not in time to read his eyes: the black lashes dropped across them and he interrupted her languid, sensuous movement by angling his face to plunge his mouth onto hers. His hands gripped each side of her waist, and she was drawn to him with a strength that matched her own longing, so that she fastened her arms around his head and felt in her own a silver flash of fire, like moonlight in the eyes, the announcement of something new, unpredictable, fateful.

But almost in the same instant there came a quiver that set up a counter movement. Perhaps it was merely a subtle change in the *Mélusine*'s contact with the sea under her keel. Perhaps there was a pulse in Léonore's veins that had vibrated to the same rhythm during her first bitter parody of an embrace on San Stefan. In the midst of her ardent response there was a stifling sense of seeing herself from without—as though she were a witness to her own actions, as though there were others also gathered around, like shocked sentinels.

Her arms loosened. She released his lips, lowered her head and took one step away. He made no attempt to stop her: in a moment they were no longer touching. She held on to the rail with one hand.

His voice reached her through a kind of mist in her brain. "What?"

She shook her head. "This is not—"

"No. Don't say it yet." He swept up the cloth of gold from the deck and spread it open, and like a New Orleans demoiselle about to go home from a ball she allowed him to put it around her, to adjust it across her shoulders. His hands closed over hers as she drew the folds across her chest, and she could not help imagining what it would be like if he cupped her breasts and drew her back against him.

"I want you to do something. Trust me, it's quite innocuous. Just close your eyes and let me take your hand. For a few moments." She did so because it was beyond her to do anything else. His fingers laced themselves into hers and led her a few steps inboard. "Keep your eyes closed and let me turn your head where I want you to look. When I say 'Now,' open them and tell me what you see. At once, without a second thought. Exactly what you see."

"What kind of parlor game is this!" She was about to open her eyes, but his fingers slid from hers.

"That remains to be seen. Patience." The voice came from behind her. Next moment she felt his hands on each side of her head, gently tilting it upwards. "Keep your eyes closed. You open them only when I say. Remember, the first thing that springs to your mind. Now."

The view was vertiginous, but in the foreground something pale moved against darkness. "Mizzen topsail."

Soft laughter. "The one woman on earth who . . . And above?"

"The stars," she said in the distinct voice of an obedient child.

"Close your eyes again." His fingers on the tips of her shoulders, turning her. Around her wrist, leading her back to the stern, but directing her another way. Facing straight into the breeze, therefore southwest. "Now."

A black expanse scooped with pewter, bounded by a backdrop of indigo. "The sea."

"Ah." Contented approval. "Close again."

His hands on her waist, turning her. A full circle, then another, and she was about to protest when he halted her. She was too dizzy to recognize windward.

The voice behind her said, "Ready?" She nodded, and he took his hands away. A second passed. "Now."

You. It rang in her head, but the surprise held her mute. She was most aware of his eyes, dark-ringed and intent, willing her to answer.

She shivered and pulled the wrap closer. "It's not that simple."

"But it is." He took two steps. "It is." He lifted the wrap aside and took one hand, clutching it to him so that her fingers spread out upon the pale shirt and her palm was flattened to his chest. "What you see—" The voice had a tremor in it, almost like anger. He waited, then said more steadily, "What you see is a man. Who will never be free of your image."

"I can't help that." It was a whisper.

"Nor can I."

She tugged the hand free, broke away and stood at the rail looking astern, towards the *Fantôme*. She could not speak. After a minute or two he came up behind her and placed both hands on the barrier before her so that she was trapped in the cage of his arms. He put his forehead against the nape of her neck and she rocked slightly with the pressure, caught again within the warmth of his body, though he was scarcely touching her.

"You're going." His voice was muted. "Aren't you? You're going." He let the silence continue another half minute, then abruptly took himself away. She heard him stride across the deck and soon his voice reached her from some way off, giving curt orders to the watch. They would be at work in a second, lowering the *Fantôme*'s boat that had been hauled inboard, summoning her oarsmen from below.

When he came swiftly back she did not turn at once. He placed his hands in front of her again and then snatched his arms up and gripped her hard, riveting the length of his body to hers, bending her forward with his weight so that the edge of the rail against her midriff was painful. They did not speak. There was nothing to say. His lips burned on the side of her neck, and her shoulder; then he stepped back.

When she turned he was standing at a polite distance, there were men everywhere and the bustle of leaving had begun. Her crew of four appeared from the companionway in the waist, accompanied by two of Laffite's men to bid them farewell. They looked much the worse for wear and the atmosphere was convivial. At her bleak stare, however, they achieved a more sober demeanor.

On Laffite's orders her reticule and fan were brought to her from below. When all was ready she moved to the gap in the side where her first oarsman was dutifully poised, only his head and shoulders visible as he waited on the wooden ladder to help her down. The corvette was well fitted out, in comparison to the *Fantôme*. No doubt the English frigate would be similarly appointed.

She tried to keep such thoughts concentrated in her mind as she met her host's eye again. She did not dare try to read what was in his.

He made her a low bow. "Thank you for the honor of your company, mademoiselle. You have my word on our agreement. I suggest the transfers be made at dawn."

"Granted. Thank you very much for your hospitality." It was impossible to go without touching him for the last time; she extended her hand. "Adieu, monsieur."

He bowed again, his lips just brushing her knuckles, and released her.

When she turned to the rail her own man indicated where she could place foot and hand. He stayed close behind her as she descended—not far enough below her to make managing her skirts an embarrassment, and near enough to support her if she slipped.

She looked up when she got to the boat, but Laffite was not in view. She sat in her usual place in the stern, facing forward, and the rowers struck out, at a good pace considering their jovial visit belowdecks. She had hand-picked them for what they could relay to her afterwards about the *Mélusine* and the rest of the fleet, but she said not a word to them on the way back to the *Fantôme*. Nothing mattered except the man who stood on the deck behind her, whom she did not turn to observe.

He had said not a word in farewell, but he had let her go. He had as good as said that he would not be disputing with her for the island of San Stefan. But could she believe him? She had no way of knowing—not while his touch enveloped her body and possessed her being.

Jean ordered the gallery cleared and a box of cigars brought up to him. He smoked while he paced the full length of the *Mélusine*'s level deck. From time-honored practice, the men pretended he did not exist unless he spoke to them. Also from long habit, he was silent.

Reliving her kisses was like choosing to walk through flame. Yet from the first moment he touched her, right up until the very last, when suddenly she abandoned herself against him for one searing moment, he could have sworn . .

When she sat down in the gallery at the beginning she had blushed under his scrutiny. Not from the heat, for she had been as cool as glass.

He flicked a spent cigar out over the stern and watched the little red eye wink out in the silver wake. If she had looked over from the *Fantôme* in the last half hour she would have been able to tell exactly where he was and what he was doing. Deliberately, but without his usual relish, he lit another and began strolling again.

He had no such clues about her. He clamped the cigar between his teeth and his lips drew back in a savage grin as her words flashed across his mind. "I am sorry. For both our sakes, I think it best if we change the subject." A singular reply to any proposal of marriage, be the circumstances ever so bizarre. But then he had not, of course, proposed.

There would be no occasion for contact on the morrow, and once the crews were exchanged the two flotillas would part, sailing in exactly opposite directions. With the frigate patched up, she could head back to her island with Santo.

Her words echoed again. "Monsieur Santo is very happily provided for. So am I."

He stopped at the capstan, tipped his head back and blew a smoke ring towards the languid sails above, watching it spin and wobble in the eddies of warm air. She had not denied that she had a man on San Stefan. She had only said that he was not Santo.

CHAPTER EIGHT

Indigo

Léonore badly wanted to keep the *Hero*, and had meant to put the proposal up to the full council for a vote when they returned to San Stefan, but instead she called the crew together in the morning.

Once again, Laffite forced her into a defensive move. The moment she could make herself think, she saw that by not inviting Santo to their discussion, he called into question Santo's powers to act in the best interests of the crew and made it look as though she might be by-passing him. Next, their parley had taken place below-decks and without a single witness. Following which, above board, he and she had probably had all too many witnesses to a scene that gave the strongest impression of self-interest on the part of both. If Laffite had been deliberately planning to drive a wedge between herself and her company that night, he could not have acted with a better chance of success.

Then again, despite the fact that the whole encounter would have received a salacious review belowdecks on both ships, so too would its conclusion. Laffite might have been seen in temporary possession of her, but her disengagement had also been witnessed, followed by her cool departure. Her crew would probably laugh to think of her making a deal with a kiss—they would frown only if they thought they had come off worse because of it.

At first light they performed a burial, consigning the

body of Martineau to the deep, and then the council was held, with the quartermaster presiding as usual. Léonore spoke first.

"Monsieur Santo and I have a proposal to put before you: that we hand over the *Jubilation* to Jean Laffite and take home the *Hero*." Over the murmur that arose, she went on, "We judge that San Stefan needs another well-armed ship. We would like to make the *Hero* part of the fleet, but that would leave us without a prize from this voyage, which would be a poor reward for your endeavors. There is a solution, and I meant to present it to council in due course when we reached home. But here we are with the *Jubilation* in our hands, and if it is to be relinquished for the *Hero,* you should have your say now."

A voice was raised at this point—only one, where she had expected more, but it was nonetheless powerful: "Looks to us like the deed's done!"

She shook her head. "You can send another delegation to Laffite and reopen the discussion if you choose. But hear me out first. I consulted with Monsieur Santo yesterday, and then I met with Laffite. Alone. I make no bones about this: I had a private matter to resolve with Jean Laffite. You were all there when he paid us the indignity of a visit to San Stefan. You were all there when, as Monsieur Santo says, we taught him a lesson he will never forget." There was a growl here, which was not discouraging.

"I freely confess to you, I harbored a grudge against Laffite, which has nothing to do with his prizes or ours." Again she paused. The hush was deeply expectant. "When he moved against us on San Stefan he breached one of the age-old privateering principles we all recognize. He broke the rule of the seas that makes brothers of crews like his and ours. I was not happy about that. I have not been happy for six months." There was a ripple of harsh amusement. "But when we took the *Jubilation* yesterday, even though he had opened on her first and so had prior claim, he did not fire on us. That showed respect. To my mind, that earned him a hearing."

She still had them. She looked around the hard, attentive faces and read the wish, as plainly as if it stood on
their foreheads—to go forward with the knowledge of
gain and with their own kind of honor intact.

So she gave them succinctly her argument with Laffite
over the slave ship and the reasons for exchanging it for
the *Hero*. She managed in the process to ram home what
they all knew—that they had never stood a chance of
sailing away with both vessels.

"I think we should add the *Hero* to our fleet. But you
elected Monsieur Santo for this voyage, and you trusted
him and me to bring back a prize. Consider this: we
already have one. When we get home, I propose that
we take your last capture, the *Seraph*, to Guadeloupe
and claim her as a prize. We will leave on San Stefan
the spars and anything else we want to keep—but we
will demand our share from the governor for the vessel
herself. Which will give us a just reward for the last few
weeks' adventuring. While we are in Pointe-à-Pitre, I
will have the letter of marque renewed, so that we operate officially as privateers, under the French flag. I have
discussed every aspect of this with Monsieur Santo. That
is the proposal. Before you make up your minds, let us
hear from the inspection party about the condition of
the *Hero*."

She carried the day. There was a lot of talk, in which
Santo did not take part, for it was not his forte. They
all knew his strengths, which were his swiftness in action
and his iron courage. They also knew precisely whose
boldness had hurled them into the encounter and whose
mind had conceived how best they could profit from it.
They too had been piqued by the first bloody conflict
with Laffite. Now that they were squared with him there
was a sense of new horizons opening up. The four men
who had been so royally treated on the *Mélusine* were
enviously questioned, and the rest began to look forward
to rubbing shoulders with the other crews during the
exchange of vessels, as though the deal was a brother-
hood pact, perhaps the first of many.

So the exchange took place and the ships parted.
While the hard work went on, Léonore could see Laf-

fite's influence in the speed and smoothness his crews displayed. But of the man himself she saw not a sign.

She asked Santo to accompany her to the official meeting when the *Fantôme* escorted the *Seraph* to Point-à-Pitre a few weeks later. There were two good reasons: she was hoping he would be capable of handling future matters of this kind alone, and she needed someone by her side.

In the past, her father had twice taken her along when he paid his regular visit to the governor of Guadeloupe. She doubted whether that was intended for her benefit: it was much more likely that it had been her father's way of subtly shifting each encounter to his own advantage. The governor, forced into greater politeness because a woman was present, was disinclined to look grasping when it came to valuing the prizes and paying out to the privateers. Having smiled and chatted her way through the meetings in her father's day, she at least knew now how to behave. It helped that he was the very gentleman to whom she had first been presented.

The governor might have looked bemused at various points during the discussion, but she obtained a just return for the *Seraph* and her cargo, and was granted the letter of marque for San Stefan. He also invited her to a reception that evening at the residence, and she did not miss the odd mixture of relief and chagrin that crossed his face when she declined in time-honored form. Her father used to receive similar invitations and make the same welcome refusals—but the governor regretted that he was unlikely to see her again for months and tried to detain her for a while when the business was over.

"Mademoiselle, it is clear to me that your father's enterprise has been left in capable hands. My duty is just as clear—France needs privateers in these waters as never before. Otherwise, you will forgive me for saying that I should have hesitated before granting your request for the letter of marque."

She smiled. "I would not like the authorities in France to make difficulties for you. That is why Monsieur Santo is with me. His signature sits alongside mine. If you need any further guarantees, may I suggest you await his next visit? We hope to provide you with even stronger evidence of our success than the *Seraph*."

The governor's thin face relaxed in a sly smile. "The evidence is not wanting, I assure you. In the last few weeks, some remarkable tales have reached us of your . . . exploits . . . on the high seas."

She caught the knowing look in his small gray eyes and said more sharply than she intended, "From whom?"

A dismissive movement of the hand. "You know Pointe-à-Pitre—rumors fly to us like homing pigeons. But perhaps the plumpest of the breed would be those of the redoubtable Jean Laffite. One of his ships put in about fifteen days ago. The stories may have sprung from that visit." Catching Santo's eye, the governor took a more prudent tack. "Needless to state, however, I do not deal in hearsay, but in much more substantial matters. And nothing could give me greater pleasure than to ratify what we have agreed upon today."

She rose, she hoped not too abruptly, and Santo rose with her. Just concealing his disappointment, the governor bowed low over her hand and promised that one of his secretaries from the bureau would attend on her with papers the next day.

The papers came, along with an official letter. When she unsealed and read it, she found that there was a plain sheet of paper folded inside it. She was finishing a solitary meal in her dining room on the first floor of her dockside inn, so she took a few more sips of wine, looking out the window at the sunlit, bustling scene beneath, before picking up the private letter. It was unsigned.

Mademoiselle,
Words fail to express the delight you afforded by honoring me with your presence yesterday. I trust that the enclosed documents address every matter we discussed, in accordance with your desires.
What I am about to relate here is confidential, and I should not perhaps broach it at all, but my

regard and concern for you has been increased ten-fold by yesterday's meeting—which seemed to me, dare I say it, far too brief.

You may recall my mentioning that your actions over the past few weeks have become known in certain quarters. You will judge of my concern when our bureau received a communication this morning from the English incumbent in Martinique. I may not give you the exact wording of this official dispatch, but I should warn you it was couched in terms of complaint, not to say outright threat. It mentioned the capture of the Jamaican sloop Seraph *and of an English navy frigate* Hero, *attesting that both seizures were in contravention of maritime law, since you were not at the time operating under letters of marque. How our correspondent learned about the* Hero *I cannot say, since I myself did not even know the vessel's name until I read the letter. He continued in ominous tones, referring more than once to "piracy," and in the last paragraph proceeded to a very serious matter.*

Mademoiselle, English indignation seems to have been touched to such an extent that a representation is to be made to France, claiming the island of San Stefan as English territory. Whether a naval expedition is planned against you I have not been able to ascertain, but in the present state of hostilities I should imagine the ships of His Britannic Majesty are employed on graver enterprises. However, even if the island is merely a catspaw in the larger struggle between nations, this does not lessen the danger to you.

I have not yet penned a reply to this morning's letter. You will note that I have done what I could at once, by antedating your letter of marque so that it covers the capture of the Seraph. *It would afford me great personal pleasure to be of further service to you in this troubling affair. Given its delicacy I would suggest that we arrange a discreet reunion at your hotel, where I shall visit you unannounced and unattended.*

*If you wish my advice and assistance, send me a
line today.*

*Meanwhile, be assured, mademoiselle, of the ut-
most zeal on your behalf and the eternal admiration
and respect of*

Your most humble and obedient servant.

She sat staring at the letter for so long her eyes began
to smart. Then she rang the bell, and when a servant
came to clear away the meal she sent him out after
Santo, with a message to return from the docks at once.

Alone again, she put her head in her hands and felt
the blow, like a kick in the stomach. They could take her
island. She did not cry—she was too breathless for that.

Then she took her hands away from her face and
looked again at the piece of close-written paper that the
governor had penned that morning. So far, it was all
words. Nothing had happened yet. No real blow had
fallen—there was room to act.

She got up from the chair and stood looking out at
the harbor. Santo was not in sight, but as soon as he
reported to her she would order the *Fantôme* to sea and
head back to San Stefan. They had what they had come
for and their business was done. She would send no
reply to the governor, which would thwart whatever private expectations he might have but give no cause for
official disapproval. He must handle the correspondence
with the British on instructions from France; there was
no point in his discussing it with her alone, as well he
knew. She must get away before he learned that he was
to be disappointed and took it into his head to delay her.

What was happening that the British should suddenly
care about her island? Of all the privateers that operated
in the Caribbean in this time of war, why inquire so
closely into the status of a company that so far had taken
only two vessels? And how could the men of the *Jubilation* or the *Hero* have given such exact details, so
quickly, to the British authorities, when in fact they had
both been fired on first by Laffite, and the *Hero*'s crew
had actually been set adrift miles away from the *Fantôme*, while she herself was still approaching the scene?

Then with a jolt she realized: there had been no inquiry, no British interest. It was even possible that the captains of the *Jubilation* and the *Hero* had yet to present their reports, wherever they had made land, separately or together. Someone else, with different motives entirely, had stirred British curiosity and ire by pointing out all they knew about her obscure island and her fledgling activities.

She closed her eyes and swallowed, feeling sick. She remembered the night when Laffite, at his most dry and ironic, counted off the nations that might at some point decide that San Stefan was strategically useful. The English, he had remarked, could well declare the island a nest of pirates and annex it. And she remembered a much more recent remark, and detected veiled menace in his voice as it echoed in her brain. "I do not enjoy having rivals, of any kind."

He had tried to deal with her first himself. On their second encounter he had willingly relinquished the *Hero*, because he knew its loss could serve him. By the time he received her on the *Mélusine*, she had already been outmaneuvered. She had been permitted her single chance of capturing a knight on the vast blue chessboard that had been his field of play for so long. Since then, he had opened the center and was now standing back to watch—waiting until she was sidelined forever, like a pawn exposed by a rash player in the very first moves of the game.

It was no matter for surprise. From the stark moment when he appeared in her life, the man had taken no trouble to conceal that he was her enemy. On the contrary, he had made her privy to his relentless purpose, which must have begun when he first heard that she was recruiting men to repair the brigantine. He expected her to fail; he warned her she would fail; he was making sure that she did. Behold the truth of Jean Laffite.

Léonore and Santo left the *Seraph* in Pointe-à-Pitre in January 1810: in February, Guadeloupe fell to the English. Whatever its governor might have tried to do for or against her must now be pursued by the Foreign

Office in France. However many prizes San Stefan captured under its letters of marque in the future, there was
not a free French port in the Caribbean at which they
could be declared.

Léonore devoted herself to the island's defenses and
left the forays to Santo. She kept the *Hero* in harbor,
overseeing the last of the repairs and knowing that the
frigate's massive battery, which now included Dominique
You's thirty-two-pounders, provided the extra security
that the island needed, whether she prowled the perime-
ter or occupied the lagoon. The *Fantôme,* easier to take
out over the reef and more agile in attack, was their
mainstay at sea.

She did not tell Santo about the letter from the erst-
while governor of Guadeloupe, and confided in no one
about Laffite. Since Adélaïde had deserted her, she had
no listener. Adélaïde seldom offered advice, but the satirical look in her dark, almond-shaped eyes had sometimes arrested Léonore when she was about to attempt
a foolish move, and she valued the older woman's rare
moments of affection.

Léonore had already made her next plan and only
awaited Santo's return from the latest voyage to put it
into action. She was thinking about it one day as she
strolled along the slopes of the peak with her old friend
Mirliton, watching the rope makers at work. For a genera-
tion, the islanders had made all their own cordage, using
henequen that grew in the swamp near the mouth of the
stream. The preparation of the spiny, succulent leaves that
provided the fibers was done by women, but twisting the
ropes, from fine halyards to the thick, plaited cables that
supported anchors or guided tillers, was the work of men.
The islanders were as good at cording ropes as they were
at privateering. So why not see if there was a market for
their produce in New Orleans?

Léonore looked at the vast fan of yellowy ropes that
stretched up towards the peak, from the waists of the
spinners to their partners who worked the capstans
below. "We'll have even more cordage than last year,
Mirliton. And the quality is good?"

"No question, Mademoiselle Léonore."

He was the only person on the island still permitted to call her so. She looked at the fine, papery profile below the ever-present forage cap and smiled. "Those two youngsters we took from Laffite are working well. You've done wonders with them."

"Dani and Amirou? They're good with their hands. I'll teach them to plait cables soon."

"Good. I can't make sailors of them. They're too old. It would be murder to take them to sea."

"Unless you want them to dive again."

She shook her head. "I regretted it last time—Laffite would have snatched them back if he'd guessed they were with us. When I made them hide belowdecks they were only too willing—I never saw lads more terrified."

Mirliton said in his soft voice, "They were treated well under Jean Laffite. What they feared was being sold."

She turned to go downhill, following the well-worn path, her gaze drifting beyond the fringe of palms below, to the ring of turquoise water within the reef, then out to the ultramarine and cobalt of ocean and sky. "How does he do it—smuggle so many slaves into Louisiana? He doesn't just supply New Orleans; they say he has buyers all the way up the Mississippi to St. Louis."

"Most times he holds auctions, just for slaves, at a special place in the bayous. Dani told me; it's a regular thing. Advertisements go out—bills are posted even, in broad daylight, cocky as you please. Hundreds go to Barataria, the market lasts until they're all sold, and there's eating and drinking and all get-out, like a festival. And any minute, anywhere you look, there's Jean Laffite walking about amongst it like a prince and potentate, with his eyes ashine and all his teeth on show."

"Bastard."

She felt him falter beside her, less shocked by the curse than by her vehemence. She stopped and looked into the lined, compassionate face.

The old man said quietly, "You hate him that much?"

"I hate what he does. I am sick at heart for all those people. If I could end slavery by cutting out Jean Laffite's liver, I would do it."

He shook his head at her savagery. "Not that simple, though, is it?"

"If you don't understand, Mirliton, then no one ever will."

He smiled. "I make no claims to that. But as to understanding you, Mademoiselle Léonore . . . there's a few things I see clear enough."

She smiled back. "Tell me, then, for I'd rather hear them from you than anyone I know."

They resumed their walk downhill, towards the big shaded compound near the stream where the sailmakers on good days worked in the open air.

"I know you're set against all slavers." He paused. "I understand why you feel that way. Because of your mother. She taught you to hate the black trade, and there's no way I'd be telling you to think otherwise."

She looked at him, waiting for him to resume, and when he did not a familiar feeling stole over her, one that belonged to her girlhood, to the age of confusion. She spoke quietly.

"Did she talk to you about this?"

He nodded.

"If she shared her notions with you, Mirliton, tell me. I stand in her place now."

"True."

After a few more slow paces, when he would not speak, she knew it was up to her. "She confided in you, didn't she? So you know. She had African blood. Through her mother, and her mother's mother."

He drew in a slow breath, and nodded. "Who would have believed? With that hair and those blue eyes? She said her mother was born a slave."

"When did she tell you? And how—what were you speaking of? She made me swear not to say, not to let a living soul find out."

They reached the edge of the compound where half a dozen men and women were sitting cross-legged on the beaten earth in the shade of the flame trees, stitching canvas. She indicated a bench to one side, just out of earshot of the others, and they sat down. Mirliton leaned his back against a tree trunk and gave her a melancholy glance.

"It was once only. We'd just came back from a voyage. Your father was pleased, for we'd captured and declared two ships, and one was a merchant vessel with a cargo so rich you would scarcely believe. We collected on the prizes and celebrated for a week at Port Saint-Pierre and then rolled home like kings. But before we put into the lagoon, your father ordered us not to talk of where we fetched up or to let on there'd been three slaves aboard the merchant ship, that we traded with the rest."

"Ah. I see. And such is the way on San Stefan, that my mother found out within hours." Sorrow seized her. "My father promised never to set foot on Martinique, and never to sell slaves. How often did he lie to her, Mirliton?"

"That's not for me to say. She talked to me only that once. She thought we had taken more slaves than that; when I said there were three, she calmed herself a little. And I told her the truth about Port Saint-Pierre: your father had no contact with anyone outside the harbor and there was no talk of her relatives, let alone sight of them. Don't they have a plantation well inland? When she first asked me, I thought it might be news of them she wanted, and I was sorry I had nothing to tell her. But no."

"No." The old feeling of despair came over her, as though she were still a child, helpless before her mother's pain. "She chose never to see them again. She cut herself off. The only times she ever talked to me about her life, all the stories were about her father. But she'd never answer a single question about her mother."

He nodded, then said in a neutral voice, "She was ashamed. That's why the word 'slave' could never be said in front of her. Even 'black' was a dirty word to her. I always thought that made her life extra hard, and I was sorry. She could care for people, no doubt about that. And she was always decent to me. But when she took a set against something . . ." He shook his head. Then he looked up, afraid that he had gone too far.

She gazed into the kind, careful eyes. "She was ashamed. I was old enough to know that. It could not divide me from her. I adored her too much. But I've never been able to understand her. It makes no sense to me, Mirliton. It does not shame me that part of me springs from Africa. One day, if Martinique is ever free again, if my grandmother is still alive, I'd like to go there and find her."

He shook his head again, but did not reply. After a little while she said, "Do you remember the humming-bird?"

He twitched one thin shoulder. "Not likely I'd forget."

"I never told you I was sorry. For lying to you. I should never have made you believe my parents had given permission."

He sighed, then said, "Finest tattoo I ever did. And I had to do it where no one can see it!"

Except Laffite. But no, all the time he was stalking behind her from the cove, she had held the shawl up high under her arms, so the tiny, iridescent bird between her shoulder blades remained hidden.

"It still looks perfect in the mirror. You made it so beautiful, so accurate."

"I wish I hadn't done it, though. I had no call to go tattooing an eight-year-old, however convincing you were. With that message you reckoned came from your father, every word to the life. Oh, were you determined!"

She closed her eyes. The terrible day came back. She had been so proud—for not having cried under the pinpricks of pain, for wearing at last a special badge, like the seamen she worshipped. She had run from the village to the house with the new decoration smarting on her back, avid to show her mother the magical image that was so like the picture on the pretty miniature she always wore around her neck.

Now, thinking of how all that childish joy turned to horror, her breath stopped an instant in sympathy, as though it were another little girl who had heard her mother's piercing cry, whose arm had been seized in a cruel grasp, who had been hauled into her father's room and flung down before him. As though the child who crouched sobbing on the floor with the dress ripped from her shoulders belonged to someone else, not to the two people who shouted and cursed over her head.

She heard again the violence and despair in her mother's voice. "This is your doing. No matter how I try, she's your daughter. Look at her. Look at this barbaric life we lead. You've ruined me and you'll destroy her. There's nothing I can do. It's already too late."

Terrified, she had flung herself at her mother and clasped her around the knees, crying so frantically she heard not another word of their quarrel, the fiercest and most bitter they ever had. In the end it was her father who pulled her away, made her stand, rearranged her dress, put his arms around her in a quick, possessive embrace. And as she clung to him, shuddering and incoherent, desperate for comfort, she saw through her tears her mother's distorted face; and the guilt of the crime she had just unthinkingly committed took on the doom-laden cast of treachery and betrayal.

Mirliton's voice reached her, like the dry breeze through the broad leaves above their heads. "No call to fret over that. It's all past. If they could see you now, father and mother, they'd be proud of you."

She opened her eyes. "Did they make you suffer for doing the tattoo, Mirliton?"

"No. Had too much else on their minds, I reckon."

It was time she changed the subject. She gestured towards the sails laid in front of them, which she had had laboriously dyed in a vat sunk alongside the stream. Expensive indigo, purchased on the last trip to Point-à-Pitre, had washed like fresh ink into the weave, then dried by slow degrees in the sun, and the new-fashioned sails held all the magic of its deep, penetrating blue. "These are perfect. The *Fantôme* will look like a carnival ship when we sail her up to New Orleans."

"So that's where you're going! The Mississippi."

"Never fear. We'll get home safe. We're going as good honest traders, not as privateers."

He nodded. "Of course you'll be back safe. I made sure every one of those sails is fit to bring you home."

She felt a sudden thrill. "What have you done? Did you say a spell over them? Can you tell me, or does that weaken it?"

He looked at her severely. "There are things you've no call to know, Mademoiselle Léonore. All I can tell you, there's a piece of coral from San Stefan sewn into a corner of every piece of canvas." He gave a subtle smile. "Not heavy enough to sink the ship. But solid enough to bring it home."

Her eyes locked with his and the smile faded. "Do you sing everything you make?"

"Most times."

"Did you sing my hummingbird?" He said nothing, but she persevered. "And what was the song?"

He shook his head. "If you don't know yet, it's not time. When it's time, you'll have the strength to know."

CHAPTER NINE

~~~

Creole

On a gray, damp day in carnival season, a brigantine from the Windward Isles sailed into the mouth of the Mississippi, announced herself at Fort St. Philip as a French ship, the *Spectre,* with a cargo of timber and cordage, and was allowed to continue upriver to New Orleans. On her way she passed swamps tangled with cottonwood and tupelo, narrow bayous that snaked out into the river amongst reeds and mangroves, the cracked and polished sides of the mudbanks where alligators turned a basilisk eye to the stream. Plantation workers along the great curve of the Mississippi below New Orleans stood still in the fields to watch as a flock of blue sails glided past above the top of the levee, and they wondered who guided the invisible vessel beneath, and what mission its sky-colored canvas might denote.

On her arrival at the city, the *Spectre* paid her customs dues and tied up at the docks, amongst a crowd of river barges, fishing craft and a few ocean-going ships. All her goods stayed onboard until such time as the supercargo found buyers and could order the unloading and delivery. Meanwhile her towheaded young captain put up at one of the best hostelries near the dockside, and the crew, with full pockets and a great frenzy to empty them, blew like spindrift into the streets of the city.

The owner of the vessel, Mademoiselle Eléonore de Rochambeau, did not stay on the *Spectre* or seek rooms at an inn. Having dispatched a message several weeks before from Guadeloupe—not long before its capture by the English—she went almost immediately to the house of the friend to whom the letter had been addressed, and received a warm welcome.

The fact that there was a supper party at her friend's house on the very evening Léonore arrived was accidental, but it seemed somehow typical of Sophronie that there was scarcely a moment for them to exchange the news of four years before they were inundated with company. Perhaps it was for the best, since Léonore's news was for the greater part fictional.

She and Sophronie had first met when Edouard Roncival decided his twelve-year-old daughter should go to New Orleans for a ladylike education. He had sent her there partly out of respect for the memory of his wife, who had always longed for Léonore to have an upbringing that would allow her to move in the highest circles. He also did it in the hope of countering Léonore's own willful tendencies and her scorn for polite society—such of it as she had glimpsed during her strange childhood. She was clever, robust, expressed herself only too fluently and had a great love of reading and a wide knowledge of the sea and ships, but not one of these accomplishments was considered essential in a lady of quality. Edouard Roncival had begun to think that Léonore's mother had been right, and she was growing up as a savage.

He did not want her to waste her life on San Stefan, and to his dying day he never admitted the notion of her taking over his enterprises. He imagined her in a fine establishment in one of the ports of the Caribbean, married to a merchant or a planter, holding court to a select society that would appreciate her brilliance, her beauty and her endowments and be pleased to overlook her singular origins, if they ever guessed them. His nobly born wife had dreamed of Léonore traveling to Paris and somehow making a splendid match in France. After all, the noble daughters of Creoles—that is, children of French or Spanish families born in the colonies—could find illustrious marriages in the home country, the most spectacular examples being those of Joséphine de la Pagerie, with a French general and then with Napoleon Bonaparte. This idea irritated and disturbed Roncival; he knew it could never happen for Léonore and he did not want it to, for he could not countenance her being so far from home—New Orleans was distant enough. But if she were to find a place in the French high society of the West Indies, he must make the sacrifice and send her away, to mend her manners and her mind.

To Léonore, the sacrifice had been all on her side. She arrived at the convent of the Ursulines miserable and mutinous, and everything that happened at first made her feel more so. Whatever she took it into her head to do—climbing the biggest tree in the cloister garden, exploring the attics, hanging over the gallery to watch the passersby in Chartres Street—drove the nuns to near panic. If the truth about her origins could have made them expel her on the spot, she would have revealed it, but her father had sailed back down the Mississippi within the hour. She could not go home, so there was no point in betraying the shocking facts that her fees, her impeccable accoutrements and considerable allowance all derived from plunder on the high seas, and that her family property was not a sugar plantation on an island west of Martinique, but a remote fortress defended by a coral reef and a band of cutthroats.

The nuns, more impressed than they should have been by the fine appearance of the gentleman who commended his daughter to their care, clung in that first discouraging day to the account he had given of her background. Not only did he hold a title, but both the mother's parents had been from the nobility and the mother herself, born into a prosperous family on Martinique, had been a childhood friend of no less a person than Joséphine de la Pagerie, first wife of Napoleon Bonaparte and Empress of France. The father claimed to be descended, along a lesser branch, from the famous Comte de Rochambeau, whose French armies joined those of America during the War of Independence. The nuns also tried to make allowances for the girl's having lost her mother young, and possessing no other near female relatives to refine her tastes or her language.

Locked in the dormitory while the nuns searched for a solution, Léonore reached the depths of loneliness; and it was then that she met Sophronie Bosque. This dark-haired, willowy schoolgirl already had the captivating looks that were to make her one of the beauties of New Orleans, and the poise and confidence of a child born to one of the great families of Louisiana, who had ruled it from the time it was ceded to Spain by the French in the 1760s. With a lineage that was aristocratic through several generations, Sophronie had pure Castilian features along with the flashing eyes and effortless charm that seemed as much a heritage of the high-born Spanish Creoles as their sumptuous haciendas.

Sent to welcome Mademoiselle de Rochambeau to the convent and to explain the expectations of her teachers—or, as Sophronie roundly put it, "told to spy on her and make her look a fool," she had no intention of furnishing an example of rectitude to this fascinating girl. Once the matron had turned the key in the lock behind her, Sophronie sat down gracefully on the bed opposite Léonore and looked at her with open curiosity. "Have you read *Paul et Virginie?*"

Startled, Léonore answered at once, "Yes."

"Did you like it?"

"No!"

"Oh, marvelous." Sophronie sat back, her eyes brilliant. "I've spent a year telling Soeur Marthe that it's drivel from beginning to end, but no one else will support me. They say you're from a tropical island, so you know just what it's really like to live in the pristine splendor of nature and all the rest of it, and if you think it takes shameless liberties with the truth, they'll have to listen to you. What did you specially hate about it?"

"Virginie. Life on an island is nothing like that book, but still, who on earth could be satisfied with going off to molder away in France? Nothing but cold streets and boring people. And Paul made me furious. All he could do was sit around and wait for her—why didn't he *do* something if he loved her that much? It served them both right when she drowned."

Sophronie laughed. "Promise to back me up when we tackle Soeur Marthe. She's actually quite bright. You'll find her interesting on almost every other subject. Some of the other nuns are deeply obtuse, but you've found that out already."

Léonore was never quite sure whether Sophronie would have been so ready for friendship if she knew who she really was, therefore she shared no confidences with her. As time went on and so did her intimacy with this sparkling, sophisticated girl, her own version of life on the plantation with her irreproachable parents became second nature. She based what she said mainly on her mother's stories of growing up on Martinique, which were all about idyllic times when her father the marquis was home—riding through the cane fields and up to Mount Pelée, attending balls at Port Saint-Pierre, visiting other planters and their families, including Joséphine de la Pagerie (there, Edouard Roncival had not lied), reading the latest books in the marquis's library and learning about the courtiers, commanders, philosophers and artists who were his friends in France.

Léonore not only grew very fond of Sophronie, but eventually resigned herself to the school and even learned to like New Orleans society, with its pride in the French freedoms laid down since the seventeenth century, tolerance of the recent Spanish rule and sturdy mistrust of its new master, the United States of America. In the months when studies ceased, her father faithfully arrived to carry her away to her exotic island home. In between, invited to other pupils' houses, she enjoyed bright snatches of Louisianian life. She went with them to supper dances, implacably chaperoned and dressed in the white, flowerlike dresses worn by the young maidens of New Orleans. She ventured out of town in elegant carriages to stay with them in plantations along the Mississippi, and picked up the graces and courtesies of the Deep South along with a knowledge of its more complex evils—floods, the Indian question, yellow fever, the doubtful value of the paper dollar. She found that the

greatest differences between her existence and that of
her fellow pupils lay not in richer comforts or in any
mysteries of style and behavior but in their being surrounded by family, for which she sometimes envied
them. On the other hand, when she observed the young
men amongst them, she realized that there was not one
with whom she could be persuaded to share such a life.

Tonight the mansion on Toulouse Street provided
pleasures that belonged to the time of might-have-been.
Seated alone on an ottoman, near French windows that
led onto a gallery, Léonore could observe the scene
while sharing in its warmth. Supper was long over and
the gentlemen had just walked into the salon to join the
ladies and take coffee, which Sophronie was dispensing
from a low table at the other side of the room. Two
matrons sat under the central chandelier. The candlelight
rippled over their silk dresses, catching in the rings on
their plump fingers and kindling sparks as they spoke to
each other and plied their fans. In a corner sat five much
younger women, balancing fine cups over their laps as
they bent towards one another to chat.

The males were just as eye-catching as the women.
The clothes of Sophronie's American husband, William
Claiborne, governor of the Territory, were dark and
sober apart from his dazzling white holland shirt, but
three younger guests, all countrymen of his, wore evening dress with colorful waistcoats and elaborate cravats.
The Territory had not been part of the United States
for long—a mere eight years—and somehow it had attracted a certain kind of American into this unique
Franco-Spanish society—keen on business and easygoing
about the law, ready for adventure and enterprise, and
fonder of luxury and ease than of principles. Beside
them, the upright governor seemed slightly out of place,
even in his own home.

The French Creole gentleman, Monsieur de Marigny,
had chosen silver-gray breeches with a brocade waistcoat
and an evening coat in different shades of blue, decorated with twists of glittering braid. But the most splendid
figure was the only foreigner in the room, the hidalgo
Don Julio de Oleron y Siqueiros, who wore a cutaway

coat in figured velvet lined with scarlet, with waistcoat
and breeches striped in charcoal and gold. As soon as
he caught Léonore's gaze he came over to stand before
her, and she noticed without surprise that his stockings,
molded to his thin calves, also had a subtle gold sheen.

He said in his suave, meticulous French, "Mademoiselle, how kind of you to await us so long. While my
young companions were savoring the governor's excellent port, all I could think of was that you would retire
and leave us bereft. How little you ate at supper! You
hide it, but I am concerned that you are exhausted."

"Not at all, monsieur. However tedious the voyage,
simply to be in this house at the end of it is refreshing."

"How true!" Then murmuring, "May I?" he sat down.
"Madame de Oleron y Siqueiros and I have just returned from a trip to Pensacola, and this is the first time
I have felt restored since we landed. I consider myself
fortunate in my friends; I would not have missed this
evening for the world."

She smiled. "I am sorry not to be meeting your wife.
It is not indisposition that keeps her away, I hope?"

"A little fatigue. She does not enjoy traveling by
water."

"Your voyage from Spain cannot have been very
pleasant for her, then."

"We sailed from Le Havre—my wife is French and
has not yet seen Spain. No, I am glad to say the Atlantic
crossing was without incident and she bore it magnificently. It was only when we approached the Floridas
that she became prey to nervousness. The terrors of the
deep she can face with fortitude, but the risk of attack
by pirates make her pitifully anxious. I was obliged to
be at her side day and night."

Léonore looked up into his narrow face, with its cav-
ernous cheeks and the perfect black arches of his
haughty eyebrows, and wondered how much comfort his
measured courtesy would afford a frightened new wife.
The lady, Sophronie had told her, was a Parisian beauty
of noble birth and spectacular means, who had married
him very shortly before they set out for America. No-

body knew quite why they were in the region, but the hidalgo's interests were thought to be in tobacco.

"I'm sure you convinced her that her fears are exaggerated. There are so few pirates these days. Privateers, perhaps, but they—"

"Privateers, freebooters"—he waved a slender hand—"call them what you will. The prospect of a shipful looming over the horizon strikes just the same chill into the heart, when all you hold dear is riding the waves with you." There was keen curiosity in the dark eyes that locked with hers. "You of all people must understand. You are surely uneasy whenever you venture from your island?"

"I take precautions, yes. There are one or two cannon aboard the *Spectre*—beyond that, I must trust to fate to bring my cargo through."

He shook his head in admiration, then asked, "What do you carry?"

"This time, mainly cordage. And what goods did you bring here, monsieur, with so much care and anxiety?"

His lids fell lazily over his eyes. Then he looked away. "All my anxiety, I assure you, was for Madame de Oleron y Siquelros."

Late the next morning she and Sophronie were together in the same salon as Sophronie prepared to pay some calls. She wanted Léonore to go with her, but Léonore declined, saying she had business to attend to.

"Then I should leave you the carriage and take a cab myself; it still rains." Sophronie nodded towards the tall windows: a fine drizzle was putting a gloss on the iron-work of the gallery outside.

"Nonsense. I shall not deprive you of your carriage! I hope I know how to cope with a little moisture."

Sophronie was pulling on her gloves. "Before I stir," she said, still looking down, "you must tell me why you are here."

"But, to visit you," Léonore said lightly.

Sophronie smiled. "Having avoided the pleasure for the last four years? You know I should have welcomed you anytime you came to New Orleans." She raised her eyes, allowing Léonore to see the challenge in them.

"If I had been here, you would have been the first to know."

"But you have not?"

"No! I told you last night, my affairs are much nearer home."

Sophronie rose gracefully. "You told me a great deal, except the thing that signifies most." Unexpectedly, she laughed. "Do not look so wary. This is not the Inquisition. It is just that if you do not tell me what you seek in New Orleans, I cannot help you find it."

"I have no right to ask your help."

"I watched you last night, subjecting each guest to your subtle scrutiny."

"And what did you conclude?"

"That you judge none to be of the slightest use to you. Except, perhaps, my husband."

At Léonore's start she laughed again. "Come: I am married not only to a politician, but to politics. Make use of me."

Léonore sighed, then began. "I'm in New Orleans for advice, but I've no idea whom to apply to. The issue is a diplomatic one."

Sophronie brightened. "To do with what—customs, trading rights?"

Léonore shook her head, wondering how much to confess. It would scarcely solve her problem to have it broadcast to all of New Orleans, and she knew that part of Sophronie's love of secrets came from the pleasure of revealing them at a judicious moment later on. But her friend was the key to Governor Claiborne.

"I am concerned about the security of my island."

"Are the English making things difficult for you?"

"Not as yet. But I have no guarantees against interference. It would be wise for me to seek support."

"From where?" Sophronie finished doing up the buttons of her pelisse, then began counting on her fingers. "France is ousted from the Caribbean and the Gulf. Spain—"

"Has its hands tied by France," Léonore said dryly.

Sophronie contemplated her third finger, upon which a large cornelian glowed against the pale satin of her glove. "The United States of America." She gave Léonore a serious, sidelong glance. "You would like to make an approach to an American diplomat. To discuss what, exactly?"

"Tell me whom I can speak to, and if the outcome is favorable I promise to tell you what was said."

Sophronie gave a quick laugh, then considered. "Can you wait a month or two?"

"I could return sometime, yes, if you think it worthwhile."

"It may be. A gentleman named Albert Gallatin from Washington pays us an unofficial visit, I think in May. You should consult my husband tonight, and if he thinks Gallatin can shed any light on your affairs, we'll send you an invitation so you can meet him."

"You mean the Secretary of the Treasury?"

"Indeed. Why go lower when you have the chance of speaking with someone in power—and an intelligent man into the bargain? Just tell me where I am to write to you."

Léonore rose. "I'll give you an address on Haiti. You are very good."

Sophronie laughed again. "I am very intrigued. And I mean to have at least some of my curiosity satisfied before I let you sail back into the blue yonder."

Sophronie left the house before Léonore, so did not see her set off on foot instead of by cab, sending back the Claibornes' servant from the first corner. Léonore needed to be on her own, to explore the once familiar streets. The rain did not ease and the gutters in the middle of the thoroughfares were beginning to fill and spread their filth over the unpaved surfaces, but for most of the way she could keep to the banquettes, the raised wooden sidewalks made from the remains of flatboats that had passed their days on the Mississippi. They were rotting in places, and it amused her that the planks designed to keep her out of the mud should feel more unsteady than the deck of the *Fantôme* in full sail.

She was allowing herself a ramble. There was no need

to check on the brigantine or contact Santo, for she had given him two days to locate buyers for the timber and cordage and to plunge meanwhile into the pleasures of the great port that he and the crew had for so long been denied. She had given herself slightly longer to locate the best rate of exchange for the Spanish and other specie that had lain in bags, deftly concealed from the customs officers, inside each coil of henequen rope in the *Fantôme*'s hold. Kept in lots since its allocation after the *Barbadoes* salvage, it was entrusted to her to be disposed of in a commercial center that still put a considerable value on currency other than that of the United States. Given the crewmen's spendthrift tendencies, she would hand out their personal shares as close as possible to departure, to save them regrets on the voyage back to San Stefan. She did not intend telling the banker or dealer where the coins came from, and the crew had good reason to keep silent about the *Barbadoes* too: therefore, if they spoke in their cups about their successes and hers, their boasting and crude air of mystery would enhance the only rumor she wanted to circulate in the low dives of New Orleans—the story of Roncival's treasure.

The wet weather kept the balconies and galleries of the houses empty and the jalousies closed, but life at street level was as she remembered it: busy and varied. At the crossroads, whips cracked above the shouts of drivers as vehicles vied for right of way and splashed through the mire. In the lanes there were people on foot, and the sounds of laughter and music escaped now and then from ale shops and taverns, enlivening the grayness like sparks of sunlight. Carnival in New Orleans meant balls, soirees, parties and dancing all night; by day the gatherings were more scattered—apprentices taking a decorated wagon on an impromptu parade; a trio of young blades conferring outside a coffeehouse, still dressed in the gaudy clothes of the night before; groups gloriously cloaked and masked, passing by with caked shoes and jaunty voices.

Whether it was carnival time or not, Sophronie and women of her station would find it unthinkable for

Léonore to walk the town alone, but she had never been
able to take the edicts of New Orleans high society seriously. If she had gone on the hunt for a husband once
her schooldays were over, this attitude might have been
a disadvantage, but she had cared nothing about scan-
dalizing eligible bachelors. She could never wed any of
them anyway—marriage between a citizen of New Orleans and a woman of mixed blood was illegal. If such
a union did take place, and the wife's black ancestry
were later revealed, the marriage became void and the
husband could repudiate her and her children. Jean Laffite's high-handed advice that she take a husband was
doubly impertinent, if he did but know it, for she could
find no partner in the United States.

Not far up Toulouse Street, just as the rain began to
fall a little more vigorously, a carriage came to a halt
beside her.

"I declare, Mademoiselle de Rochambeau!"

She looked up into the keen brown eyes of Don Julio
de Oleron y Siqueiros, who put one arm along the half
door of his vehicle but was careful not to lean out into
the shower. On his other side was the figure of a woman.

"Good morning, monsieur."

"But it is far from good: it is a detestable morning!
How is it that you are caught in the rain? And alone—
there has been some accident?"

"By no means. I was taking a stroll."

"May I ask where you are going?"

She said at random, "I thought of the shops on Bourbon Street."

"Then we shall convey you." As the groom jumped
down on his order from the back of the carriage and
opened the carriage door to let down the steps, the hidalgo
continued. "You will not refuse, I hope, nor deny my wife
the pleasure of meeting you in this fortuitous way?"

It was more of a command than a question, but Léonore obeyed, folding her umbrella and giving it to the
groom as he handed her into the carriage. She would
have hesitated to muddy the floor of the hidalgo's elegant equipage, if she were not so curious about his wife.

Don Julio greeted her apologies about her damp hems

and boots with forgiving courtesy and at once began the introductions. The carriage moved off. Léonore raised her eyes to take her first good look at the lady opposite and felt a small shock. The face was masked. With this jolt to the senses, Léonore failed to distinguish the words the lady pronounced in a low, muffled voice, as they bowed and acknowledged each other. Léonore observed her while the hidalgo carried on the conversation in his unhurried way. The mask was covered with dark blue velvet, molded to conceal the forehead, temples and upper cheeks, and the eyeholes were edged with tiny diamonds. A black cloak of shorn velvet swathed a walking dress of blue merino, in the same shade as the mask. The hair was caught up and bound with fine plaits that shone like gold wires against the bright locks, and the diamond-framed eyes that met Léonore's were the color of the palest sapphires.

The aspect was deliberately Venetian. Yet beneath the cool, contrived air of mystery Léonore sensed something else—something like animosity, not quite concealed by the half smile on the lady's full lips. The hidalgo had perhaps been too generous in his praise of the women he had met the night before. Or his wife did not relish sharing her carriage with a new acquaintance.

Léonore tried an overture. "The señor tells me you have been in New Orleans some months now: are you intending to settle?"

All the lady did, however, was incline her head, without improving the smile, and let her husband reply.

"Alas, mademoiselle, we are homeless, as you point out. The decision has been taken from our hands—we must perch where we can."

"Are things so grave that you cannot return to Spain? Napoleon seems to have achieved some stability there."

He gave a thin smile. "With respect, true stability for us can only derive from Spanish rule, not French. And despite her love of France, Señora de Oleron y Siqueiros is of the same mind."

Again his wife inclined her head and Léonore, annoyed by this outlandish silence, addressed her again. "You must be disappointed, then, that the English have been beaten back into Portugal. A successful invasion may be Spain's only hope."

"There is some support within the country," Don Julio replied. "The peasants of the north are mounting skirmishes, which we call guerillas. But I agree with you—they can achieve nothing alone. If Wellington takes his army back into Spain, I shall view their progress with interest."

"And cheer them on?" Léonore said lightly.

He did not reply, and not long after that he ordered the carriage stopped. "Mademoiselle, I believe this is the corner you were seeking. I have accompanied my dear wife too often not to recognize that here is the most expensive haberdasher in town."

"Indeed, señor," Léonore said cheerfully. "And the rain has ceased. Thank you for the rescue and your voluble company."

It occurred to her as she descended the steps that the last remark was not quite polite; nonetheless it was still several degrees removed from the bizarre rudeness of the wife, who conveyed her farewell in dumb show, to the accompaniment of the señor's elaborate good byes.

The whole encounter had been so perplexing that instead of entering the shop Léonore stood on the banquette outside, absently pleating the folds of the umbrella, and stared after the carriage as it moved slowly away down the crowded street. Was this a new carnival game? If so, she must learn the rules at once or be unable to communicate with fifty percent of the population of New Orleans. She wished she could talk to someone informative.

Then all at once she saw a tall figure walking down the street from the direction in which the carriage had just departed. In the same instant that she caught his eye, he touched one finger to the wide brim of his black hat, then swept it from his head and grinned, his teeth flashing white in his smooth face. The easy but purposeful stride, the glint of amusement in his black eyes, visible even from this distance, told her he had seen her long before she glimpsed him. Her wish was about to come true—but the last person on earth she wanted to talk to was Jean Laffite.

CHAPTER TEN

Crescent City

God knew what the encounter would bring, so Jean savored every second of his approach. She remained stock-still, on guard. As he drew nearer he saw how the eyes, shaded by a wide bonnet brim but catching reflected light from the rain-washed street, fixed him with a pale, leonine stare.

"Mademoiselle Roncival, by all that's wonderful."

The gaze flicked away, checking for bystanders, before coldly returning. She was shy of people hearing her name—but she pronounced his with scornful clarity. "Monsieur Laffite, by all that's lamentable. And what mischief might you be doing here?"

His smile did not waver. "I should more properly ask you the question, since I live in New Orleans. My business in this street is usually nothing more nefarious than buying a pair of gloves. You were about to enter Feversham's. May I escort you inside?"

She half turned her back on the haberdasher's, which brought her closer under his scrutiny. Her face was full of enmity, but obviously she would rather put up with him for the moment than hear her name pronounced before others. She said at random, "I thought you lived at Barataria."

"I am touched that you think of me, mademoiselle. As a matter of fact, we have a family business a stone's throw from here."

"Don't let me keep you from it."

"I cannot leave you in the street alone. I am not so cavalier as the friends who abandoned you just now."

She said in a venomous undertone. "I have no friends."

"I am glad you do not number those two amongst them, at least."

"You know Señor de Oleron y Siqueiros?" It was a challenge.

"Only by reputation." He pondered telling her that Don Julio was supposed to have been trading arms in West Florida on the way to New Orleans. But only for a second. "And his wife not at all." He could also have told her that when the carriage passed him the lady's face, half-hidden by a golden fall of unpinned hair, was bathed in tears. "If you are friendless, with whom are you staying? Not at an inn, surely."

"I thank you for your concern, monsieur." The tone was acrid. "I am comfortably housed and ask only to be able to conduct my affairs in peace."

"Here? The banks are a considerable step from this end of town."

It had been a shot in the dark, but the haughty lips were suddenly compressed. So this visit involved exchanges of currency, as well as the sale of her goods.

She retorted ironically, "My affairs just here, monsieur, run to nothing more exciting than the purchase of gloves."

He allowed his gaze to glide over her. She was all in russet, and the high-necked pelisse, trimmed with dark swansdown, made her like a lithe bird of prey. "But you are exquisitely provided for already." Her right hand in its fine kid glove tightened on the umbrella. Then she slipped her wrist through the loop on its ivory hilt and the hand disappeared inside a feather muff, held against her midriff. He had a sudden, blazing consciousness of the smooth body within the warm envelope of cambric and plumes. His voice sounded thin as he said, "And you look remarkably at home."

"I have already told you, I was educated in New Orleans."

"But you have not told me when. Nor what name you bore at the time."

All at once she was furious. "You commandeered chapter and book about me when you thrust yourself in my way. Twice. If you want another syllable, you must use your talents as a spy."

She almost spat the last word at him, but he was more surprised than provoked, and said at once, "Who needs spies in a town like this? You could scarcely expect me not to notice the *Fantôme* when she paraded by in her gorgeous new guise. And I heard a description of the captain that could only fit Andrea Santo. Where he appeared, there I guessed you would be." She looked even more angry at this, and he said quickly, "Since you have to keep an eye on him. You must know the man is not to be trusted." When she did not reply, or soften her expression, he went on. "So when I saw you today I was not astonished. Charmed, overwhelmed, transported, but not astonished."

"I feel exactly the opposite, monsieur."

"On all counts? Yet you seem amazed I am not at Barataria." He stepped beside her and offered her his arm. "It looks like rain again. Let me take you to a sheltered spot and find you a cab." She hesitated, but noticing he was not about to lead her into the haberdashery, she took the best of the poor bargain and disengaged a hand from the muff to lay it on his sleeve, sending a warm tingle into his arm that was quite out of proportion to her light touch.

As they walked down the street they were constantly looked at, but she seemed not to notice, for which he was thankful. She was preoccupied, looking down in a pretense of negotiating the damp boards under their feet.

He tried for a more detached, conversational tone. "You are perhaps not aware how long I have been a citizen of the Crescent City. I first came here five years ago when I sailed up the river with a cargo of cash. In quite an assortment of currencies." He had her attention now, though she still did not look at him. "It proved pretty welcome on the exchange market. My brother

Pierre was already established here, and I decided to join him, so we opened up a shop together in Royal Street. We closed it recently, but there is another, which he still runs. I am in town only occasionally these days, but I walk on the same footing as the rest of New Orleans. As you see. Though never before in such dazzling company."

"With your other activities so well-known, how is it you don't face arrest?"

"Here be mysteries. Ask Governor Claiborne. Or even ask President Madison. My assumption is: because I am not known to molest United States vessels." There was a tremor when he mentioned Claiborne but no reply. After a moment he said, "And what did you bring up the river, mademoiselle, along with your spars and cordage? Anything I can assist you to dispose of?"

The hand was snatched from his arm, she stopped dead, and the eyes she lifted to his were hard as gemstones. "Stay out of my affairs, I warn you, or your arrest may be sooner than you think."

"You could denounce my dealings without uncovering your own? Think again. The same applies to me with regard to you. Fate has made us equals. Accept it: I am your ally."

"You traitor. How dare you utter these lies! When you have harmed me to the ultimate degree."

"Never." She tried to reply, but a quiver of anguish crossed her face and she could not speak. He took her hand. "For any crime against you, I swear to make reparation. Just tell me what I must do."

She tugged her fingers away. "An empty promise. Can you call back the cannonball when the piece has fired?"

"I have never fired on you. On San Stefan, yes, but that you still hold."

She drew her lips back from her teeth. "For how long, thanks to you?"

He was seized by a cold anger that overmatched hers. "You fear another invasion? San Stefan may drop off the edge of the universe for all I care. You misunderstand me radically if you think I shall ever set foot in that accursed place again."

She took a step back, discountenanced despite herself. Her nether lip quivered, but she spoke with almost the same vehemence as before. "I do not care to understand you. And I would be fool to expect any straight answers. Nonetheless"—she lifted her chin—"I should like to hear you deny that you have tried to ruin me since we last met."

"I do deny it."

The answer seemed to take her in the chest. After a second she dragged in another gasp of air. "And you can invite me to trust you!"

"I don't know what you mean. Of what do you accuse me?"

She shook her head, and he was astonished to see that she looked close to tears. "There's no point in discussing this. You are a liar by trade, Monsieur Laffite, and will make no exception for me."

He took her hand again. "Are you such a friend to truth?" She looked up through a sheen of moisture that put a polish on the turquoise eyes. "Admit, you protect yourself as I do: by silence, or by careful management of what others say. Cold facts can strike cruelly if they are let fall at the wrong time. Nonetheless, ask me a frank question and I shall answer it."

Uncertain, she left her hand in his. Then she shook her head and said, "Thank you, I decline the favor."

If she had not looked so bewitching as she spoke, he would have removed himself at once from further insult. Instead he transferred her hand to his wrist and took her a few steps to the next corner. "Let us change the subject. Do you still have the diamond I once inadvertently bestowed upon you?" Her profile showed she remained unsure, so he put a sly smile in his voice. "Or perhaps you came to New Orleans to pawn it?"

"I do have it somewhere. But I have other things to do here than haunt pawn shops. I am happy to say my legendary wealth continues to keep me out of them."

He laughed. A few yards down the lane he came to a stop, startling her again. "By the way, I have something for you. If I can find . . ." He dug in his pocket, and she gazed at him, perplexed.

He withdrew a snuffbox and opened it. Solid gold, lined with gauze, it held a pair of sapphire earrings, spectacular because the solitaire stones were large, and because they were an unusual shade, like waves over sunbaked coral sand.

"You're joking."

He shook his head. "As soon as I saw them I marked them for you."

The response was dry. "And you have been carrying them around in your pocket ever since."

"Yes."

She drowned out his frank answer by saying in a rush, "You cannot seriously expect me to take these!"

"But they would suit no one else. I can assure you, they have no history of violence. They are as innocent as water."

"For a start, I do not wear earrings, monsieur."

"I noticed."

"My ears are not pierced."

This he had not been aware of—and he had believed he knew every inch of her. It was the greatest temptation to say so. Instead, with one fingertip he put aside her bonnet ribbon to see her earlobe. "Indeed. That is easily remedied."

"No. Since— From a very early age— The idea makes me shrink."

He was surprised. "You, the Lionheart? You will not be nervous when it comes to the point. I shall make sure you take no hurt whatsoever. Come now."

In her disarray, she actually allowed him to lead her farther down the street. "This is unheard of. It's utterly ridiculous. Where are we going?"

"To consult an expert, mademoiselle. His name is Marius Thiac, and he happens to be at his post at this very moment. You will allow me, I hope, to introduce you first to my brother Pierre. Our shop is just around the corner, in Saint Philip Street."

She walked as slowly as she could and tried to examine him, but his glance stopped her breath each time and she had to look away. His denial had had the ring of truth—for a moment she believed he had never told the English about San Stefan. Then doubt swamped her again and she felt that she should be walking away from him.

But his hand under her elbow, his body at her side worked a powerful attraction. It was like the encounter on the deck of the *Mélusine*, when he persuaded her for a few blazing minutes that they were simply a man and a woman, not enemies. She had been able to abandon their strange meeting, as though it would never have a sequel. Surely she could withstand him now. Indeed, marching off at once might only make him suspect how she feared his physical influence.

She forced herself to think. What about the very rivalry he had unwisely referred to just now? The fact was that he knew a great deal more about her enterprises than she did about his. If he was fool enough to invite her into one of his headquarters, she would be an even greater fool to decline. There were surely things to be learned from a quick glimpse at the shop he ran with his brother. And to read any significant threat into such an urbane encounter would be the height of absurdity.

They reached the end of the lane and she saw the shop. On the opposite corner was a single-storied, whitewashed building of brick and timber with wide-open double doors on the street and windows that gave glimpses of the spacious interior. Neat lettering on a board above the doors, a massive chimney and the active ring of a hammer on metal from a yard at the rear announced it as a blacksmith's. She would have expected any lair of Laffite's in New Orleans to be a shuttered hideaway in a back street, but this was on a busy thoroughfare.

Then all at once her apprehension returned. She halted him with a firmer grip on his wrist. "I have come to New Orleans on legitimate business. Accompanying you along the lanes with my face hidden in my bonnet is one thing: parading openly into your establishment is quite another. I can't afford to so jeopardize my affairs."

A crossing sweeper approached at that moment and Laffite handed him a coin and waved him ahead. As the tall, skinny black man proceeded over the crossroads with great flourishes of his birch broom, a couple of carters reluctantly paused in their tracks.

"Nonsense. We'll be much less conspicuous inside than here. Afterwards, you can leave by cab from the back door. And I vouch for the discretion of everyone on the premises." He took her elbow.

She stepped off the curb, wondering at him and herself, wondering at this bizarre meeting that he treated like the happiest of everyday occurrences. She was seized with an impulse to pretend the same, to follow the moment and see what happened. "What about your customers?"

He was guiding her across the street. "The tedious ones haunt the front room—we'll go by them in full sail. Within, there's not a soul expected today. You'll be received *en famille*." He said this so reassuringly that she could not help a spurt of incredulous laughter, which put a spring in his step as they got to the great doorway.

There were two men in the front room of the shop, leaning on the counter talking to a beefy youth behind it. Laffite removed his hat, stepped around her to put himself between her and the company. Then, with a hand under her elbow, propelled her towards a closed door in the murky depths beyond. Neither he nor the youth on duty said a word, but both the customers turned.

"The ironware is this way, madame," Laffite said, hilarity audible in his carrying voice.

"Curse your ironware," she said very low, reflecting on how many other women might have swept in here on his arm.

"But that is exactly what we are in search of."

They entered a narrow corridor that had a door at the other end with no latch. He shut the one behind them, and they were engulfed by shadows, the only illumination being one candle in a sconce on his side. He paused, facing her. One half of his still face, catching the soft candlelight, stood out like molded bronze within the surrounding gloom. He was not touching her, but she could feel him breathing. His nearness took her by the throat, and in outrage and quivering expectation she found herself preparing for the touch of his hands.

Her gaze plunged into his black eyes and she suddenly realized that his tension betrayed something else: he was waiting. There had been the faint clang of a bell somewhere when he closed the door. Precautions were being taken while he trapped her momentarily in the dark—the corridor was an observation chamber, well enough lit for those within to be examined through a spyhole in the far end.

As the door began to open she said, "Have I passed inspection?"

"Always. Forgive our measures: you see they apply equally to me. You'll pardon me when you see to whom I have brought you."

She turned her head. The woman standing at the door had most of the light behind her, but Léonore knew her at once. Adélaïde Maselari.

The shock was so great she gasped. Then she swept forward and past her, spinning around at once to take her in: the voluptuous body in statuesque repose, the beautiful face with the knowing eyes, the full lips drawing back from white teeth in a smile. On an impulse that could not be denied, Léonore said her name and stepped into her arms.

"Lionceau!" Plump hands at her back pressed her into cushioned warmth.

When she stepped back, Laffite beside them was grinning. "True surprises are precious. I'll leave you two alone for a while." Adélaïde gave him a glance at this, but he said with easy familiarity, "Please. You do the honors and I'll fetch Pierre."

"He's in the smithy." When Laffite had gone, Adélaïde ushered Léonore into the next room and made her sit near the fireplace and take off her bonnet. It was a simple room, comfortably furnished, with tall French doors leading onto an inner courtyard in the middle of which, hanging between two large oleanders, was a red hammock fringed with tassels that had gone sodden in the rain.

Adélaïde was studying her. "You look different."

"Half an hour with that man," Léonore said, "has aged me years."

A chuckle. "Different, but you haven't changed."

She took a breath. "You live here?"

A satisfied nod. "For the last few months."

"When you came back, how did you— Where did you— What about your son?"

Adélaïde looked up as a slender young woman came in with a tray. She pointed to the low table between her and Léonore, then waved the servant away and poured the lime juice herself, the gathered cuffs of her orange sleeves, oversewn with broad black and gold ribbons, falling gracefully over her rounded wrists. "I found my boy safe and thriving where I left him, with my sister. When I moved in here, I brought him with me." She handed Léonore a tall glass. "Unless you'd like tea?"

Léonore shook her head and took a sip, looking at her over the rim. Adélaïde had never looked so regal, so secure. Her heart gave a thump as she told herself, *Of course.* Everything was *of course* with Laffite. "May I see your son? Where is he?"

"Another day, maybe. He's at school just now. There's an old lady down the street that runs classes. He's learned to read already." There was a soft, musing look in her eyes Léonore had never seen there before. "Pierre pays the fees. He even lets folk believe Joël is his."

"Pierre?"

Adélaïde's eyes widened. "What did you think?" Then she rocked back in her chair and laughed. "Hoo!" she said finally, wiping her eyes with a scrap of lace drawn from one gaudy sleeve. "If you knew what I know, that's one conclusion you'd never come to."

Léonore eyed her mistrustfully, her heart still jumping. Adélaïde never laughed aloud. "Pierre Laffite. You knew him before?"

"Before your father? No." The moment of mirth was over. "There was only one man like Roncival. This is a whole lot different. But I hadn't known Pierre long before I figured I'd be well suited. And I am."

"What have you told the Laffites about me?"

"Some. But not a particle that could do you harm."
She shook her head pityingly at Léonore's sharp look.
"If I had, do you think I'd have opened that door just
now, once I saw who was there?"

"You would have been obliged to," Léonore said in
despair. "This is his house."

"But I'm not his woman. There's plenty of others
around this place."

"Are there?"

Adélaïde laughed again, but softly. "Servants, I mean.
Jean would never have a woman here. I made Pierre
promise me that before I stepped over the threshold."

Footsteps approached the room and Adélaïde fell silent, though she did not rise. Léonore instinctively stood
up, just before the brothers walked into the room. She
looked at Jean first, and it surprised her to see that he
cared what she thought of the man at his side.

"May I present my older brother, Pierre?"

He was shorter, and broad, with softer contours. She
had heard that he had suffered an illness once, some
kind of apoplexy, that had affected the muscles of his
face. It left one greenish eye half-closed, but the other
conveyed a welcome that was echoed in his voice. "Mademoiselle, you do us great honor." He brought his heels
together and a lock of his brown hair fell over his forehead as he executed a quick bow.

"Good day. I hope I am not disturbing you. I do not
usually make impromptu calls. This will be a lightning
visit."

Jean Laffite said, "Time enough for us to render you
a small service. Pray sit down, mademoiselle." As she
did so, he said to his brother, "I have asked Marius to
turn himself into less of a Vulcan and attend on our
guest in here once he's polished up. We won't detain
either of you at that point—mademoiselle is shy of
witnesses."

Before anyone could reply, Léonore said, "Who, may
I ask, is Marius?"

"Our blacksmith." The older man, after a quick glance
at the other's bland expression, chose another subject.
"How long do you stay in New Orleans?"

"As long as my transactions take."

"And where are you staying?"

"With friends." She looked at Adélaïde, but once a conversation was begun by others, even one as stilted and empty as this, Adélaïde withdrew into queenly silence. Nonetheless, after another pause Léonore caught her eye. "If you are wondering about anyone you left behind, they are all well. Nelly had her child—a girl. Christina expects a baby in September."

"Your maid?" Laffite's black eyes caught hers. "You brought her with you?"

"Yes." All at once she remembered the first time she had said Christina's name to him, while she was speaking of the arrangements on San Stefan. At his table on the *Mélusine*, before they went on deck. Before he kissed her. She avoided his piercing gaze and turned cold attention to Pierre Laffite.

"Your brigantine, mademoiselle, is the admiration of all New Orleans. There is not a chandler with enough cheek to claim those sails as his own. Where on earth did you get them?"

"Much nearer home, monsieur."

"They're for camouflage at sea?"

She shook her head. "They're intended to be linked firmly in people's minds with the *Spectre*."

At that moment a tall, black-haired, bulky man stepped into the courtyard from a far door and paused by the hammock, looking through the French doors towards them. He was dressed in a rumpled shirt and worn leather trousers, and held a small canvas bag in one of his enormous hands.

Jean Laffite said as he went to the window, "The ablutions appear to have been pretty scanty, but his hands are clean." He opened the window, jerked his head at the blacksmith and then said pleasantly to the others as the man walked through, "You'll excuse us, I hope?"

Adélaïde rose and advanced on Léonore before she could move, leaning over her to place a feathery kiss on each cheek. "Come back, whenever you like. If you send me word, I'll keep Joël home to meet you."

Léonore contemplated her as she withdrew, smiling,

towards the far door. She might have been schooled in this by one of the brothers. Or both. Or this whole crazy episode was some sort of dream.

Pierre also took a polite farewell, giving his brother a nod as he did so. She sensed between them the special link that rumor had told her of: a profound communication beyond words.

She would have risen, but suddenly Jean was kneeling before her chair, a hand on each armrest. "It will be over in an instant. Marius moves like a firefly—first the needle, then the stud, so fast it's a single sensation."

Trapped, appalled, she saw out of the corner of her eye that the giant had extracted a needle from the bag and was holding it in the fire with a thin pair of pliers.

Her voice shook. "How do you know? I notice you've never submitted to this yourself."

"But I have! Too long ago, perhaps. You may be right, perhaps I should adopt an earring again. I wonder what—a diamond, a gold ring?"

"A skull and crossbones."

His gaze dropped. "Let me relieve you of your muff."

"No, thank you." She laid both hands on the soft mound of feathers.

The black gaze returned, glittering with speculation. "Why not? What do you have in it?"

"My reticule." There was room also for a small pistol, but she had not brought it. However, if he chose to believe she walked the streets armed, he was welcome.

The needle glowed red. "Don't look there. Look at me." Holding her eye, he took out the snuffbox, opened it and held the sapphires out to the dark, silent bulk at her side.

The fire singed her face, and she looked into eyes that glinted like coals. "I don't want this. I don't want to be here. I hate everything that has happened since I met you."

"It will be over before you know it. Tell me about the sails. How did you do it—indigo? What royal tastes!"

"I had pits dug by the stream and flooded them. Then we—" She bit her lip, and he took both her hands, crushing them.

"That's one. Look at me. You'll be free in a second. The cab's already waiting. So, the sailcloth. Fit for the Queen of the Nile in procession."

"It was Adélaïde who gave me the idea of blue sails on a ship, ages ago, though she won't remember. Oh! They sting!"

"And sparkle, like summer rain." He took away his hands and sat back on his heels. "Thank you, Marius."

What did he think he had done? Branded her as his? But she knew better than that and so did he. Instead, what struck her about this moment was the peculiar innocence of it. He had given her the sapphires because they belonged to her. She had raised a practical objection, so he had removed it.

The blacksmith fiddled about with his equipment, then let himself out the courtyard door. She had scarcely felt his fingers on her skin each time, only the searing dart of the needle point. A spark in each earlobe seemed to ignite each side of her neck and spread a harsh glow along her cheekbones, and she felt tears of pain trembling at the corners of her eyelids. She had been savaged, but Laffite was looking at her with a rapt expression, as though she sat before him radiant and untouched.

"I hope you do not expect any thanks for this."

"I have it already." He dropped his gaze and rose to help her to her feet.

Ignoring his hand, she quickly tied on her bonnet. She winced at the touch of the ribbons, however, and had to loosen them. Then she gathered up muff and umbrella and rose to her feet. He had retreated a pace or two and was contemplating her with the same light in his eyes. Unable to think of a word more to say, she willed him to speak, but he remained silent as he indicated the far door and then moved to open it for her.

Walking behind him in a haze of discomfort, seeing very little of what she passed, she went through a smaller room, across the smith's yard beyond and paused before a heavy door set in the stone wall at the back. From inside the forge nearby came the roar of the bellows and the renewed clang of hammer on iron. Laffite's words reached her like burning fragments thrown out into the cool air between each deafening percussion.

"They're set in gold. Don't remove them. Just give them a twist now and then. You'll heal around them."

"I bid you good day, monsieur."

He bowed, opened the door and stepped with her into the lane where the cab was indeed waiting. Laffite helped her in and left a hand on the half door. The hammering was not so loud here, so she could hear him easily when he said, "Until this evening, then."

"I hardly think so."

"You do not expect me to find you—because I do not know where you are staying, or even the identity you go under? True. If it is your schoolgirl name, I am mortified to admit Adélaïde has not yet revealed that. I could of course inquire at the docks." He caught her expression. "Or possibly that's a waste of time." He smiled serenely. "Then you must tell me yourself."

"Drive on!" she called to the cabman. As the vehicle shot forward with a jerk, she said with a last glance into the black eyes, "Try Cleopatra."

His laughter rang down the street in her wake.

CHAPTER ELEVEN

Carnival

Jean arrived at the ballroom of the French Exchange on the stroke of midnight, entering unannounced through Cinderella territory, the kitchen. There was a vast crush of dancers in the grand room on the upper story, at least half of them masked, amongst whom he could move freely. He made the quick discovery that the Claibornes had not yet arrived, and allowed himself a glass of champagne. One, to whet the palate.

A polonaise began, and he watched while the night to come opened in his mind's eye like a flower.

As he was leaving the shop, Pierre had said, "Where will you be?"

He had produced his worst grin. "Where do you think?"

Pierre had said slowly, "Dominique told me about that one."

"And what did he say?" He had waited tolerantly. None of his brothers was known for eloquence.

"Trouble."

"Indeed. In abundance. So I sincerely trust."

The wait for the Claibornes was piquant. He had had many years to observe and delicately try the patience of the governor, but he had never chosen to get so close, despite the pleasure to be derived from glimpsing his splendid third wife. Of course, he did not receive invitations to balls such as this at the Exchange—nor could he expect to, however close his personal wealth might come to rival that of certain pillars of society. Consumed by a vision of the moment when they would walk into the room with their guest, he took a position halfway down one side of the room and talked to no one. A couple of gentlemen came up in the mistaken belief that they knew him, but were swiftly discouraged. No one approached after that.

He was being watched, nonetheless. Two observers seemed especially intent. They were both masked, like himself, but the gentleman was otherwise as usual: a trifle overdressed, with a very formal bearing. The wife had caught more nearly the air of fashion, the mask alone being a concession to carnival mode, for she looked across at him through a perfect hailstorm of brilliants.

The couple became lost in the whirl; he resumed his vigil, then suddenly the Señora de Oleron y Siqueiros was walking towards him from amongst the throng. Her graceful approach brought her within a yard of him and he saw that the black veil onto which the brilliants were sewn, which had hidden the upper part of her face while she was on the other side of the room, proved up close to be made of fine gauze, through which he could now make out every exquisite feature.

"You will excuse me, monsieur, but I cannot locate my husband. Do you see him from where you stand?"

He bowed. "Your servant, madame. May I ask his name, his appearance?"

"But you know him. Forgive me: you nodded to each other in the street today. I believed you to be acquainted."

He perfectly remembered the moment in question, during which the hidalgo's attention had all been reserved for his wife. He saved his reply until he had looked over her head and searched the room. The husband, interestingly, had in fact disappeared.

"I regret he is not visible. But it shouldn't be long before we catch sight of him. In the meantime, how may I serve you? A glass of punch?"

"Thank you, no."

The voice had a low, caressing quality that provoked a desire to hear it again. After a fruitless half minute he said, "Your recognizing me with so little trouble is rather pitiful, I'm afraid. Next time I must choose a better mask."

"Oh no." Blue eyes threw an appraising glance at him through the veil. "It is quite adequate as a disguise—the gold glares, so one cannot guess the face beneath. No, it just happens that you are wearing the same pin in your cravat that you had on today. My husband happened to notice—he is a connoisseur of rubies."

His admiration skipped up a couple more notches. "Beyond rubies, madame."

A woman of her beauty usually accepted this kind of thing as her due, but she chose to look arch, which did not suit her.

He cast another quick glance around the room again, then asked, "Is this the first carnival you have passed in New Orleans?"

"Yes. I keep wondering whether it will ever end."

The note of complaint seemed genuine. "What is it about us that most perturbs you: the crowds, the dancing, the mad license, the endless music, or the fact that everything of importance suddenly seems to happen under the cloak of night?"

The glance was satirical. "The endless music."

"You will not care to accept my hand during this, then. With double infamy, it's a waltz."

"I might, if suitably asked."

He bowed. "If there is anything at all suitable about me, I am afraid it is yet to be discovered."

She took his arm and they walked to the edge of the floor. "It is kind of you to issue the warning, but I am already a little prepared by what my husband tells me of you."

They took their position, and he put out his arm to just touch her firm waist. "I have no need to guess his views on me," he said evenly as he guided her into the crowd. She danced with a suppleness that matched her gliding voice. "The señor and I can possess nothing in common. However much I may begin to wish otherwise."

She stiffened as though he had come too near the mark too soon, then recovered. "Your enmity towards Spain is disagreeable to him, certainly; but here, in a neutral territory, I hope we can find the liberality to understand other points of view."

His voice hardened. "I can promise you never to become so liberal as to like the Spanish."

She chose to be surprised rather than affronted. "Will you do me the favor of explaining why?"

A long pause. "The reasons are personal."

"So you think I shall be less keen to hear them? On the contrary."

They spun in silence for a while; then he said with deliberate detachment, "I was born in a seaside town on the Atlantic coast of France, near the Spanish border. My brothers and I were witness to the effects of the Revolution in our little corner of the world, but it would have taken greater changes than those to alter our childhood. It was a happy one—perhaps more blissful than most people can boast, for our parents both worked to make it so." He withdrew his gaze from hers again to take in the room. "But it was not to last. With France at bay before the monarchies of Europe, it was foolish to think our little town was immune from invasion. Spanish troops poured over the border and the first thing we knew our street was in the hands of pillagers and its unarmed citizens were being put to the sword. My parents paid the price of the Republic before the eyes of their children. You will excuse me from describing the manner in which they died."

"I am sorry." The muted tone brought his eyes back to her downcast face. "I should prefer not to finish this waltz."

"How thoughtless of me. I shall find you a chair. Ah, there is an alcove free—a minor miracle."

It provided seating that was partly screened from the room by a line of potted palms. He installed her on the sofa and was about to look for some refreshment, but she took his sleeve between her fingers. "Please don't go; there is no need." When he was beside her she said softly, "I am sure, if I confided to my husband what you have just told me, his sympathy for your attitude would be as ready as mine."

"And will you?"

A subtle smile. "I discuss most things with my husband. But I prefer to avoid any that might give him pain."

She felt very close. "Your tenderness does you credit, madame." Her perfume held a drifting hint of musk.

The sigh was a whisper of breath on his face. "It makes me vulnerable. For he cannot always extend the same tenderness to me. His business affairs create a distance."

Such as selling arms to the Spanish in West Florida. He introduced a note of awe. "It is beyond me to believe any man would not respond to you with the utmost of true feeling."

"To the exclusion of all else? Of all others?"

"Are you referring now to him, or to me? I would tell you my preference, if you wished to know it."

The gaze was withdrawn, and she looked down at the gloved hands clasped in her lap. "I might wish you to tell me that there is no other person of importance to you at the moment. But I would also wish to believe you. And your . . . companion . . . of today would make that impossible."

He allowed himself a mere second to marvel at her information, then said, "But the simple truth is that I have seen no one today, or ever, who compares with you, madame. No one whose company I would not sacrifice for the honor of paying you homage. I sue for no higher reward."

She raised her face again. "That is wise, monsieur, since I make no promises." Her eyes, however, as iridescent as the floating brilliants, spoke far more than her lips.

He shot a glance at the room. "I cannot see your husband, but I fear it is time I returned you to him. Before I do, will you permit me?" With delicate care he raised the veil from her face, positioning his head and shoulders so that she was not visible from the room.

He murmured, "It was a crime to hide such perfection. Yet having revealed it, dare I confess that what I covet most is the only ravishing feature this veil did *not* conceal?"

The beautiful lips curved in response, and he moved to close the gap between them. She turned her head at the last second, however, so that he merely brushed her cheek. He gave a soft, involuntary laugh. It pleased her to deny him her mouth, but he had felt a shiver. Looking at her averted face, he reflected that her husband, for all his land and titles, was no more than a dull man of affairs. And she had sharper tastes.

Without another word he replaced her veil and they rose to their feet. He guided her back onto the floor, struck by the rather breathless sensation that he had never before found such instant complicity with a woman.

They danced in silence, her expression withdrawn and calm. But the clasp of his hand on her waist now spelled out promise and demand as though they had sealed a binding pact. He was intrigued by the particularity of the condition she laid down, but time would perhaps reveal the cause. The motive, meanwhile, was of a consuming and delightful clarity.

He did not speak until he caught sight of her husband. As she turned her head to look in the same direction, and gave a wifely smile, he murmured, "Your desire, madame, is henceforth my command. On that you have my solemn assurance."

Léonore entered the ballroom on the arm of Governor Claiborne, resigned to the fact that he was useful to her only as a host. When she spoke to him of San Stefan earlier in the day, she could not give its real name or its exact location—she did not want the Americans to descend on her territory as the English threatened to do—so her talk was guarded. She really needed to know whether the United States would be at all interested in laying claim to San Stefan, what concessions it might demand from her, whether it would have sufficient might

to override the claims of other nations, and whether in
the aftermath it would be content to leave her in peace.
But she soon saw that these questions should be put to
a diplomat of wider powers than Governor Claiborne—
and a man less beset by local troubles. She would have
to follow Sophronie's advice, wait a few months, and
arrange a meeting with Albert Gallatin.

The governor's party of twelve had been to supper on
the other side of town and reached the ball in the mood
for merriment, so Léonore came ready to enjoy herself.
She had almost forgotten how splendid the great ball-
rooms of New Orleans could look, and stood for a moment admiring the chandeliers, the lavish hangings
looped around the mirrors on every wall, and the colorful crowd that made the room hum.

The dance in progress was a polonaise, and the parade
of couples showed off the variety of evening dress,
masks and costumes. There was the usual scattering of
Grecian and Roman beauties, warriors clad in armor,
numerous jesters, and a group of feathered friends,
amongst whom was a lanky white chicken that drew constant giggles from its fluffy yellow partner.

Sylvain Audubert, a good-humored young man who
had been one of her supper companions, was examining
the crowd with open amusement. "Don't you wish, mademoiselle, that you had come in fancy dress?"

"Absolutely. But when I inquired yesterday, I discovered all the plumage in New Orleans had long been
plucked."

"If this dance is followed by something less of a me-
nagerie, may I beg your hand for the next?"

It was a Virginia reel—she danced it and a second
with him, then the Boulangeries with another of their
party. By now she had noticed the only other people in
the room whom she knew, Don Julio de Oleron y Siqueiros and his wife. She nodded to them and was acknowledged, and every moment she expected that they
would make their way down the room and join the
Claibornes. For some reason, however, this did not happen, though they were not dancing.

She also became aware of a tall, black-haired gentleman, halfway down the ballroom, who was not dancing either. He wore beautifully tailored black evening clothes, which made his gold mask look all the more dramatic: it was cut like a face from Greek tragedy, with narrow eyeholes that looked unnerving when turned her way. Which it frequently was.

During the first dance she was jolted by the sudden thought that he might be Jean Laffite. And it also struck her, annoyingly, that she had been waiting all afternoon and evening for his reappearance, despite doing everything to ensure he could not find her. She ignored whole passages of Audubert's pleasant conversation while she stole glances in the observer's direction and struggled to make up her mind. He was of the right height, build and elegant attire. There was even a Laffitean touch in the cravat, which was secured by a ruby pin of the same style as the diamond one, which she was not wearing tonight. But on the other hand, she told herself with a shudder, if it was Laffite's face behind that mask, she would have known it the instant she walked into the room.

In the third dance, her partner happened to steer her towards the still, intent figure, but the group of fowl-yard creatures somehow got in their way and she was deflected from getting a closer look. Which was just as well, perhaps, since if it was Laffite, and she met his eye, there was the nightmare risk that he would quit his post and come up to her.

Back with Sophronie and the governor once more, she looked down the room in time to see the señor and his wife departing. He placed a long swansdown tippet around his wife's shoulders, and with a glance around the ballroom they turned to go. If they had seen her polite, farewell nod in their direction, they gave no sign of it.

Not long afterwards the man in the gold mask moved at last, striding abruptly out amongst the dancers. He went straight up to the white chicken and his partner, whereupon a short discussion took place. The chicken seemed to listen attentively. Then he turned and walked away with his shoulders and wings drooping in mock dejection—a sight made funnier by the high-stepping gait he was forced into by his long footwear. Oddly enough the yellow bird looked eager to rejoin this sorry apparition, but the man in the mask prevailed and the chicken retired defeated.

Léonore turned her back on the crowd to speak to Sophronie, who for once was unoccupied. "What an entertaining evening."

"I'm glad you think so. The music is superb. But Audubert tells me you will not waltz. Why not?"

"I have never learned."

"But he is aching to teach you! You simply leave your partner to commence the one two three—nothing could be easier."

"I don't feel dressed for the waltz, somehow. A plain round gown without a train looks unsuitable."

"Plain! With silver filigree like yours? Spare me. And those sapphires are the finest in the room. My word, when you shop, you shop. Where did you find them?"

Léonore had been adjusting her long gloves, and for some reason took a step back—a mistake, for she trod immediately on someone's toe. There was a faint squawk, she looked down just in time to see a scraggy, three-toed foot disappearing, and next second she heard a voice that sent a shiver of horror straight up her spine.

"That hurt abominably. Please do it again."

She whirled around to find herself gazing at the absurd black beak of the ridiculous chicken. "Pray excuse me." It was pitiful, but these were all the words she could summon up. Sophronie was of no help. She just laughed.

He said promptly, "With pleasure, mademoiselle, if you will permit me the next dance."

There was no doubt about the voice, nor about the eyes deep in the mask that glinted with pinpoints of light caught from the chandeliers.

The music struck up again. "I do not waltz."

"Nor do I, in these infernal—" To her dismay, he bent and ripped the footwear off, so that next second he stood before her in his hose.

Sophronie was still laughing. "You are not serious, monsieur. You cannot possibly believe my friend will take the floor with a barefoot cockerel!"

He drew himself up. "Madame, you are addressing *Egretta thula*, the black-billed snowy egret. Well known for its stately bearing. And its terpsichorean skill." He bowed, the movement producing eddies amongst his wing feathers that set off Sophronie's giggles again. "Your devoted servant. Perhaps if mademoiselle does not care to join me, you on the other hand may—"

This had to stop. Léonore threw all the warning she could into her interruption. "Madame Claiborne is about to dance with her husband, the governor."

The eyes within the mask brightened. "Then I take it you are about to do me the honor after all, mademoiselle?"

It was hard to keep the fury out of her voice. "One turn of the room." She could feel Sophronie's surprise beside her.

"I am overwhelmed."

He had the sense not to offer her a wing as they walked onto the floor together. She hissed at him, "I don't believe this."

"Nor do I. Everything I planned tonight has gone damnably wrong."

They stood facing each other, an arm's length apart. "So you decided to include me in your disasters?"

"I vowed to achieve the one goal I aimed for. To dance with you. Have you really never waltzed?"

"I have not. You've drawn the short straw again, monsieur."

"You take the tip of one panel of the gown in the fingers of your right hand and place the left just behind your waist."

"I am obliged, but I know how to stand. Moving will be quite another matter."

"No it won't. I've been watching you."

He increased the pressure on her waist just before a beat in the music, swayed her into the rhythm and took her with him into the midst of the dancers. There was no talk for a while as she tried to accustom herself to the heady pulse of the dance and the sensation of his hand through the superfine silk of her gown.

At last she summoned up the breath to say, "If you wanted to recommend yourself, I'm astonished you dressed in that feather duster."

He replied bitterly, "If you knew how much it cost me, you would not say so."

She said in a rush, "Who is the statue in the gold mask?"

"The man from whom I obtained this unique apparel. I didn't catch his name. There wasn't time."

"Can you tell me why he was staring at me?"

"Yes. I instructed him not to go anywhere near you. When he saw the lady he was not on any account to approach, he was naturally agog. He became ever more fascinated and tormented as the night wore on. As you no doubt noticed."

At the risk of another useless answer, but unable to stop herself, she said, "And who, may I ask, is the canary?"

"I have absolutely no idea. But she has a very infectious laugh."

She was getting used to the way he whirled her amongst the other dancers, and to being looked at by them with an odd mixture of bemusement and admiration. But her head was still spinning. "We have achieved one revolution of the room, monsieur. Which was all I promised."

"I know. But we must talk."

"I refuse to discuss anything in this situation."

"I agree—for that we must meet again. Just now, I have but one question. Will you grant it? Only one?"

"I insist that we stop. After that I'll see."

"Good. There's an alcove free; a miracle." With a quick glance at the Claibornes, who happened to be looking another way, he glided into it and released her. "I'll fetch you some refreshment."

She sat down rather more quickly than she had intended on a velvet-covered sofa and leaned against the gilt back. "Thank you, but I'd rather you stayed here where the palms will hide you. And in precisely one minute I'll make my way back to my friends. Alone."

He subsided in a flurry of pinions. A fine dust, released by the movement, rose gently around him. "Your friends? You told me you had none."

"Is that your question? If so, by your proviso I am not obliged to answer it."

He uttered a sound that was somewhere between an oath and a sneeze, then tore off mask and beak and dropped them on the floor. She had been tempted to smile, but there was no humor in the black eyes that locked with hers. "Here is my question. Why are there no dogs on your island?"

She looked at him in complete bafflement. Then the memory hit her and she sat upright on the sofa. "Do you really want to recall that horrendous episode?"

"That is a question, not an answer."

She looked angrily out at the dancers pirouetting by, then closed her eyes, took a breath and began. "Very well. I don't promise to be edifying. To understand the reason, one has to know something of how things stood between me and my father. How much has Adélaïde told you?"

"Nothing illuminating. Proceed."

"It was after my mother died and before I came to school here, so I suppose I was about nine, when I begged my father to let me have a puppy. The sailors had pets—all kinds, you know, cats, parrots—and they used to take them onboard. He would let them, but he wouldn't let me. It wasn't fair. In the end he relented and brought me a puppy back from a voyage. I called him Pilote."

She managed to stop herself saying just what Pilote looked like and how tiny he was. "I went on the next voyage and I made my father let me take Pilote, but he warned me: if any pets went by the board when a ship was on course, he would never turn to recover them. I took such care of Pilote that I knew nothing like that could possibly happen."

"But it did."

"Yes. We were coming home from a supply run, with no intention of engaging anything, but we ran across an English warship. They recognized the brigantine and gave chase. My father knew we could outrun her, and when all sail was set he cleared everyone to quarters and sent me below. But Pilote got away from me and ran on deck, with me after him. He thought I was playing. He made such a game of it, he was careless and got into the scuppers. I screamed when he went over the side. And I kept on screaming, but my father wouldn't listen. He wouldn't go back."

"Understandable, when—"

She turned on him. "He could have. The English ship was giving up. She'd already gone on another tack. I saw it. I knew what was happening and so did my father. But he wouldn't go back. He had said what he'd said and he would make no exception for me." Her voice sank further. "That was him. That was Roncival." She could still see Pilote in her mind's eye, swimming in the wake of the ship. Trusting. Believing she would save him.

After a second Laffite said, "Don't do that. It makes me want to kiss you."

She shook her head to clear her eyes, and went on. "My father could do nothing with me. I swore at him, before everyone, for the first and only time. Then I ran to the stern and threw myself into the sea."

"*Jésu!* Could you swim?"

"No, not then. So my father had to hove to after all. Someone jumped in and grabbed me and they lowered a boat. Once they'd hauled me in they went back for Pilote as well—against orders, of course. When we came onboard I thought my father would hit me. But he just sent me below. That wasn't the end of it, though. He could see all the sailors were on my side, and he got so furious he told them there was never to be a single dog on the island again. When we got home, anyone who owned a dog would have to destroy it."

"Good God, all over a child's passion."

"We got back and the order went out. The cook decided it was a joke and started sharpening his butcher's knife. But no one else laughed, and the dogs still ran free. Finally my father saw a deputation of men coming along the beach and he knew he had to back down. He couldn't afford that kind of confrontation on our home ground. So he went out to meet them and said I'd begged and pleaded with him and changed his mind. I hadn't: I was refusing to speak to him. I think they all guessed the truth, so they went back satisfied. But no sailor ever brought home puppies after that, and when the pets were gone they were not replaced."

"I trust Pilote lived to a ripe old age?"

"Yes, but we've never had dogs since." She looked at him with resentment. "And I've never told anyone about this, from that day."

His eyes probed hers. "Perhaps you should have."

"Out of a child's passion?" In the same scornful tone she said, "Why did you ask me?"

"Self-preservation. That particular threat of yours I found too ugly to associate with your image. On the other hand, when you threaten, mademoiselle, I have learned to take you seriously. Tonight, I decided our alliance could not go on unless that question had an answer. Thank you for supplying it."

"Alliance." She rose to her feet.

"Yes. We have things to discuss. Expect me."

"I make no assignations with you."

Despite his idiotic costume, despite the late hour and the turmoil of this strangest of evenings, his smile had the fresh openness that it might have had if he were meeting her for the first time, on a sunny morning. "Why not?"

"Self-preservation." She trusted that her own smile, as she turned to leave him, in no way resembled his.

CHAPTER TWELVE

Departures

Later, she lay in bed unable to go to sleep. The governor's mansion was plunged in silence and darkness, without even a vestige of carnival gaiety intruding upon it from the other grand houses in Toulouse Street or from the cool lanes behind. She had on a satinette nightdress that she had almost been too tired to pull out of the trunk, and her hair was loose. She had not wanted her maid to wait up; now that Christina was pregnant, Léonore was careful not to ask too much of her. Sometimes she thought she looked forward to the baby as much as Christina did, for it warmed her to know it would have a home, comfort, two parents. When her shopping was interrupted she had, in fact, been about to search for supplies for the child.

The fire in the grate had sunk and the room was chilly. She pulled the counterpane up under her chin, careful not to touch her ears with it. The sapphires still hurt. She should have left them with Laffite when he first showed them to her in the street; yet she had yielded, not to the compromising gift of smuggled jewels, but to the man himself, to a temptation that left her no power to walk away.

At the ball, she had had no choice but to speak to him, for he had put himself and her at risk to achieve their meeting. She had been forced to distance him from Sophronie, to conceal if she could the fact that the man who daily flouted the laws of the Territory was entertaining himself under the governor's very nose. And her panic and anger had shown him exactly what he had come to find out—that the Claibornes knew none of her secrets.

It was impossible to stop thinking about him. When she closed her eyes, she relived the touch of his hand curved about her waist when they waltzed. Even in her indignation, she had yearned to dance nearer, to let the spinning movement carry her in to him, like a leaf in a whirlpool. Later, when they were alone and he asked his question, she had seen the passage of conflicting emotions across his face and, recalling the brutal, firelit confrontation on San Stefan, she could scarcely prevent herself from sliding against him to banish the memory with a kiss.

She lay with the music of the waltz coursing through her, caught by the swaying measures, and it was some time before she became aware of a quite different tune outdoors—jaunty, insistent, growing louder as the man who whistled it walked down the handsome, echoing street. Then he stopped. Under her window. And the tune resumed, with a wistful quality that she remembered from somewhere. All at once she had it: it was an Irish air that she had first heard on the *Mélusine,* on a hot night in mid ocean, played by Laffite's violinist.

It was a serenade, this time by a solo musician. She flung the covers back and sat on the edge of the bed, rigid, as the endless tune bounced plaintively against the walls outside. She could not let that devil lure her to the balcony. Yet if the household were roused, the servants would be sent down to chase him away, he would be recognized and the governor called.

She found the drapes in the dark, drew them aside, fumbled for the latch, and opened the glass doors and the jalousies. The planks of the balcony were humid under her bare feet and the night air made her catch her breath. With both hands on the rail she looked down, and the whistling ceased. She could feel rather than see who it was, for it was hard to make out his form in the dark, let alone catch the expression on his face as he tipped his head back to greet her.

A sigh reached her. " 'My love falls upon me like roses.' "

"How dare you. Go away."

"It's the title of the song. If you prefer, I've a Sephardic lament."

Her whisper became a hiss. "You must be mad. We've talked tonight. That's enough. I'm not coming down."

"Then I'm coming up."

She gasped and shrank back. The balcony was supported by buttresses of wrought iron that reached down to the pediment of a doorway. She heard his quick run before he leaped, the soft thud as he hit the wall, a scrambling sound as he ascended and the faint ring of metal as he grasped the lowest bracket. From there he used holds in the ornate ironwork to bring him up and over the rail. Before she could register anything but her own fear, he was beside her.

"If the servants have heard, we're done for. And I can promise you, your fate will be worse than mine."

His teeth gleamed in the dark. "First, we must lock your door. And shut the window." He was in shirt, breeches and hose, having left coat and shoes on the pavement. He disappeared inside.

As she closed the jalousies and the panes and plunged the room into blackness, she heard the key turn in the lock, then soft footfalls and the murmur of his voice approaching. "A bed. Wonderful. Ergo, a bedside table. A candlestick."

She was trembling.

He moved to the end of the room and the tiny glow of the last ember in the grate disappeared. A second later, the candle flared and she could see him crouching before it. The dark head, the straight shoulders, the long thighs were limned by yellow light.

He rose, turned and replaced the candlestick by the bed. Then he took two strides to where she stood beside the window. "Forgive me."

He might have meant the kiss to be gentle, but she

could not hold back: the impulse that swept her against him left no breath for gentleness. She clung, her hands clenched in his hair so that his mouth drove down onto hers. There was nothing gentle about the involuntary sound he made as he pulled her body to his. Swept by the same surge that gripped her, his hands slid up her back, his fingers catching in the fine fabric. Her senses swayed, as though he and she were joined in another dance, waltzing on the edge of an abyss. Entwined, they tore themselves through some invisible barrier of raw, stinging air, and plunged into the unknown.

He released her mouth and pressed his cheek to hers, his breath in her hair. "All today. All year."

"It hasn't been a year."

"It's felt like ten."

Her arms loosened from around his neck and he pulled back against them to look into her face. "I couldn't wait any longer. I must leave for Barataria at dawn. I had to see you."

Why? But the answer was in his eyes. Surely it was impossible that a man who looked at her like this could be her enemy.

"You're shivering. Come to bed." He gathered her against him and crossed the room to lay her down. She opened her arms and he sat on the edge of the bed, reached across her and pulled the counterpane over her, tucking it about her so that she lay in a feather cocoon. She watched his face and hands as he lightly untangled her tresses from their soft cage, one by one, and spread them across sheet and pillow. If she could speak, it must be to protest. She said nothing.

"You are different every time I see you. I can never predict." He leaned nearer and slid one hand under her hair, so that his fingers curved behind her neck and his thumb tilted her chin towards his mouth.

The kiss was like a contact with flames, yet she arched towards him, all her strenuous caution abandoned, and the cocoon split open and released her into his embrace. Her gown, his clothing, remained between them, but neither was aware: it was an untrammeled fusion of their bodies, the intimate meeting of skin against skin through the soft sliding of fabric. She exclaimed, and spoke, but in another part of her being, for her lips were given over to a curious hunger, a new dialogue for which they seemed now so devastatingly suited.

At moments he would draw away a little to look at her, so that his eyes caressed her body where his hands had been, and each time she lay back, breathing deeply, bathing in his gaze so that she wondered, with the last of her drifting consciousness, how she would ever surface.

He spoke once, in a whisper, as his mouth descended between her breasts. "Every inch of you is a piece of heaven."

She gasped as his lips touched her, her throat closed, and she put one hand blindly against his chest. With her head pressed back into the bed, she waited for his mouth to travel where his hands, as yet, had only floated with lightning swiftness.

But he trapped her fingers under his own and drew his body slowly away. Retaining her hand, he propped himself on one elbow so that he was reclining beside her. Under her palm she felt his quickened breathing.

"You must manage me now," he whispered. "For I cannot."

She was about to reply, but there was a sudden noise belowstairs. She started and looked at the locked door.

He hissed, "What's that?"

"I don't know. A door closing. Maybe a draft. Everyone's asleep up here, as far as I know."

He released her hand, put his to her cheek to bring her face to him. "For God's sake, what are you doing in this house?"

She shook her head. "What are you?"

He went to speak, then suddenly hooked his arm around her waist and scooped her towards him, plunging his head into the hollow of her shoulder. She was engulfed, aware of the clean linen scent of his shirt, his hair, damp from the night air, the subtle perfume of his skin, stretched taut over the tense muscles of his chest.

Within the urgent pressure of his body, her arms were caught across her waist. She had just begun to realize that she could neither move nor breathe, when he pulled back with a groan and took her wrists in his hands. Bending quickly to kiss her clenched fingers, he rolled onto his back beside her.

His eyes were closed. After a second he said, "We must talk."

Dazed, she stared up into spinning blackness. "I'm afraid so, monsieur. Just where do you propose we start?"

There was a long silence, during which the blissful spell began to lift away from her and the cool air of the night closed in to reclaim her outstretched body.

Eventually he whispered, "Listen." She tensed, thinking he meant he had heard another noise in the house, but he continued. "Two things. First: Oleron y Siqueiros. How well do you know him?"

The chill crept nearer, despite his fingers laced in a warm bracelet around one wrist. She turned her head to study his profile. "Hardly at all. Why?"

"Sure? You've had no dealings with him or his wife? Nothing?" His head turned and the black eyes bored into hers.

Her voice cooled. "No."

"Then I can't figure it out. Something is going on. All I know so far is that they want to keep us apart. They are prepared to go to quite enthralling lengths to make sure you and I have nothing to do with each other."

"Why?"

His eyes were intent. "If you don't know, I certainly don't."

She stiffened. "And what sort of dealings have you had with them?"

"None."

"Then we're not likely to discover their motives, are we?"

"Oh, I shall," he said softly. "The sooner the better. When I find out, I'll let you know."

"Kind of you." He seemed to miss the sarcasm, so she went on in the same tone, "How, exactly? A passing visit to San Stefan?"

He let go her wrist and sat up on the edge of the bed, his back turned. "I told you, I'll never set foot there again as long as I live."

She saw tension in his shoulders and back. The moment thudded by, full of her own desire. She had to put one hand over her mouth to keep from saying his name. She had to push the other one under the counterpane to prevent herself reaching out to touch him. She had so many questions, but she needed a firm voice to put them.

When he swung towards her, his voice was sibilant, almost caressing. "What if I sent a message to your favored inn at Port-au-Prince? The Amiral de Grasse." There was a quick flash of his teeth as he registered her astonishment. "Reply to Saint Philip Street. But promise you'll never sign anything."

"I haven't promised to write."

"You may need to. The second thing"—he took her wrist again and studied her hand, curled palm up on the coverlet—"you possibly know already. You've heard what they call you?"

"Yes, thank you. A fine collection of names, almost as extensive as the ones they call you."

"Did you know that the vulgar tongue has us linked?"

She withdrew her hand. "No, I didn't. Is that what you came to tell me? What makes you think I want to hear?"

"You misunderstand, Lionheart. I came so I could tell you first. So I could swear to you the story is not of my making."

She pulled the coverlet across her legs. "Say it."

"We are credited with a fleet that Edward Teach himself would have given his black beard and liver to assemble. You are depicted with sea snakes in your hair and a voice like Circe's, that has drawn me to a thousand crimes. And when we couple it is on the ocean bed, amongst Spanish bullion strewn with the skulls of the drowned, their eye sockets bulging with emeralds and rubies."

Her expulsion of breath was like a laugh. "My name, if you please."

"Siren."

"Better than Whore."

His eyes flickered, but he persisted. "More potent. There lies your danger. However dark my deeds may be, yours are painted as black as Hades. I am a smuggler, but I am called nothing worse than corsair, which I may take as a compliment if I choose. You are a privateer, but because you are a woman the talk of the Caribbean turns to monsters. Take care, my siren. Take care."

She hauled the coverlet to her waist. Her lips, swollen with kissing, felt stiff, reluctant to pronounce the words. "Isn't it rather late for warnings?"

He shook his head. "I shall always deny any such connection with you. In New Orleans, Barataria, anywhere. After we took the *Hero,* my men enjoyed a little bavardage. But never in front of me. If I hear a syllable spoken, they know what to expect."

"This tender care of my reputation is the last thing I would have expected. After what you have done."

"Believe me, tonight puts you in no danger. Not a soul will know."

"I'm not talking about tonight."

"What then, the fight for the *Hero*? You started that! I agree, it caused damage, but with discretion we can contain it."

"I'm not concerned about my reputation. I'm talking about my life. What kind of discretion can you claim on that issue?"

He shifted sideways to focus on her better. "Explain."

"Do I need to? You know what I mean."

"I can't guess what problems you may contend with, but no doubt you managed to convert the *Hero* into a legitimate prize somehow or other. Or, rumor tells me, you still have her. The tall tales actually serve to obscure the truth. One fateful day a slave ship disappeared like a ghost into the mists of speculation and an English frigate did the same. Who knows precisely whose hands worked the magic? No one."

"Except the English."

His face stilled. "What?"

She overcame an ache in her throat to say, "Except the English. Who were given all the details. Who have also, presumably, been given the exact position of my island, the better to deliver it from a nest of pirates."

"How?" But he had already read her face. An extraordinary rictus crossed his features, as though someone had gripped him by the throat. He got to his feet. "It's not possible."

She lay transfixed by his gaze, her hair flung about her and her hands gripping the coverlet. Exposed, quivering, her skin still tingled with the aftermath of his touch. His eyes opened wider as though he were struggling to see her through thick darkness. She said, "Is it impossible that, having been denied San Stefan yourself, you should decide it might as well fall into other hands?"

His voice was so low it was a whisper. "You can lie there and imagine that. What am I supposed to have done: sailed scatheless into Kingston Town to lay that little tribute at their feet? Crawled arse up to lick the boots of the English, who have sent three of my ships to the bottom in as many years?"

She sat up on the tumbled bedclothes. Her hair fell forward over her knees and she caught the ends in both hands, looking up into a face as hard as bronze. "You have no idea what I've gone through in the last few months."

"No, I had no idea. No notion that you could be with me today, tonight, like this, for such a purpose." He took one step away to stand by the bedpost.

She let go her hair and lunged towards him, supporting herself on both hands. "It's not like that!"

"It's like nothing on earth." He moved again.

She slid sideways, put one foot on the floor. "What are you doing?"

"I bid you good morning, madame." The word was like a knife edge on her bare skin, and for a second she could not move. The man at the foot of the bed took her in with one damning look, as though she were a beggar soliciting him in the street, then walked to the door and unlocked it.

She leaped to her feet. "What are you *doing*?"

He paused, his back to her.

She forgot everything as the words were wrenched out of her: "You can't go like this."

His profile was icy. "We agreed; it's a little late for caution. If I wake the house, I assure you they'll regret it more than I."

He vanished.

She darted to the bedpost, launched herself across the room, stumbled in the soft rug at the foot of the bed, got to the door, which he had left open.

Above the sound of her own panting breath she could hear footfalls departing along the gallery, but she could make out nothing in the dark. Then her eyes became accustomed, just in time to see the tall, black form turn at the newel post and begin descending the top flight of stairs.

So as not to cry out, she put her fingers across her mouth, with a sound like a sob. She felt her way across the carpet runner of the landing, put a hand on the cold rail and looked down. He made no attempt to muffle his departure; his steps were steady, unhurried, audible. He did not look up.

There was no hesitation when he reached the next floor and headed for the top of the grand staircase. In a moment he would be out of sight, but she could reach him if she ran, if she plunged down the stairs after him, caught him in her arms.

Suddenly there was a flash and a voice above her. In the second that she looked up to register candlelight and a challenge, the stairwell below her resolved into empty shadows. She shrank back from the rail, into her room, and half closed the door. Supported against the embrasure, her chest heaving, she listened to the mingled sounds of footfalls, one set measured and relentless, the others nervous and hurried as the two servants went down, shouting.

She heard the bolts of the great door shoot back. A thud as it closed, followed by a bustle on her floor as other chamber doors opened. She pushed hers shut and leaned her forehead against it.

The servants in their turn flung open the front door, erupted into the street. She could follow their raised voices beating up and down the thoroughfare. They did

not linger under her window, whence by now his shoes
and coat would have disappeared.

Returning, the servants were met on the landing by
Governor Claiborne in his nightshirt. Even Sophronie
had been roused, and within a very short time she
knocked on Léonore's door and put her head around it.
"My dear, are you all right?"

"Yes." She pulled the bedclothes to her chin.

"I'm sorry you've been woken. Someone got in, we've
no idea how, but nothing seems to be touched. They are
scouring the house, but we think he's gone. Do not be
distressed. Everything is under control."

"Thank you." Léonore could just see the anxiety in
her friend's face as she began to pull the heavy door
closed. "Good night."

Sophronie's light voice reached her across the chilly
chasm of the room. "Just in case, I think you should
lock this door."

The month of May came and went on San Stefan, and
Léonore did not return to New Orleans to seek Albert
Gallatin, for no English ships had yet appeared on her
horizon, and there seemed no danger from Jamaica. Before she exposed herself to Washington she must have
compelling reasons. Besides, she had found no letter
from Sophronie at the inn in Port-au-Prince when she
made a routine trip to Haiti in April. As it turned out,
it would have been pointless to return to New Orleans
herself: Santo, whom she sent in June on a trading trip,
came home with the information that Gallatin had not
made the voyage down from Washington after all.

Having dredged the city for news, Santo had other
items of interest to recount. Adélaïde Maselari was expecting Pierre Laffite's child in October. Three of the
Laffites' ships, suspected of carrying contraband, had
been impounded by the Louisiana authorities, but the
brothers had employed an ingenious business manager
called Sauvinet who succeeded in having the ships and
cargoes released. Jean Laffite's smuggling ventures involved hundreds of fishermen, seamen and adventurers

who were settled in villages on the two large islands at the entrance to the great saltwater bay called Lake Barataria, south of New Orleans on the edge of the Mississippi delta. He had extended his warehouses in both New Orleans and Barataria. His headquarters were on Grande Terre and he spent most of his time there.

In West Florida, Santo said, the faction that was plotting the overthrow of Spanish rule was arming itself fast. There was money to be made in the sale of weapons to either side.

Santo was deeply excited by all these pieces of information, with the exception of the first. They made him restless, for although he remained keen and adept in the chase after Spanish and English shipping in home waters, his visions of enterprise had begun to extend to a much wider world. But he was no strategist: if ever she broached the future of San Stefan with him, he exploded with ideas, none of which he had quite thought through. If she guided him into looking at alternatives, he grew weary and resentful. In fact the island itself stifled him, unless some bold venture beckoned him from over the horizon. She tried to ensure that it did, with reasonable regularity.

The summer was superlatively hot and wet, which was favorable for the growth of henequen. For the first time, Léonore thought of extending the plantings farther into the swamps. She had a harvest of seeds to be sown for the next season, but the plants, a species of agave, flowered only once every fifteen years or so. To set a lot of new plants, she would need either bulbils of seeds from another plantation or suckers that grew from the rootstocks. Santo was given the mission of bringing these back from the henequen growers on the Yucatan peninsula, and she told him he could take the frigate. She also said that if the farmers were reluctant to sell, he had leave to persuade them otherwise, provided they were paid fairly and only the threat of violence was used, and not the *Hero*'s guns. She pointed out that he had time to accomplish the voyage and be home again for the birth of his child, but he seemed less keen on that than on sailing the *Hero*.

One day in late September, Léonore was bathing in the Anse des Lianes, hovering wide-eyed over the coral and thinking about men and their management. She had told Santo that when he returned he could acknowledge his child and the liaison with Christina. Thus for the first time the mistress of San Stefan was about to throw aside the fiction that had grown up around her since she reached womanhood, and jettison the strange protective covering that was part of her father's legacy to her.

Drifting in the warm waves, she let her mind slip back to the time when Roncival had singled out Thomas. Hardly more than a boy, Thomas had been a man in looks and bearing — strong, tall and with a natural reserve that rendered him silent at the grand table when he was invited to the mansion, and disinclined to regale the men afterwards with what happened when he spent time with Léonore in the salon following the meals. In fact, very little took place, which was what her father had counted on.

It was not until much later that she understood that Thomas was intended to be a buffer between her and the crews, who had seen their wild, passionate young companion turn into the kind of creature over whom rivalries would soon spring up. At the time, her father explained nothing to her, merely asked questions now and then, and it never occurred to her to wonder what he might have said to Thomas.

Meanwhile, she enjoyed the young foretopman's visits. She admired him for his skills as a sailor, pitied him for his social timidity, liked to sit with him and talk of the sea and listen to his slow, considered answers. When he was thinking, and his heavy auburn eyebrows met across the grand orbits of his pale almond eyes, he had the mysterious beauty of a sphinx.

Her father asked her regularly, "Is Thomas behaving himself?" Without thinking, she could always answer yes.

"He holds his tongue? And keeps his hands to himself?" Again yes, though those questions perplexed her.

Then, it seemed, Thomas spoke—only once, but disastrously. The first she knew of it was one morning when she had gone to the careening dock on the stream, to watch the men working on a new prize. She did not notice at first the attention paid her by one of the laborers, but when he followed her into the forest on her way home she began to feel nervous. For he spoke to her in a way no man ever had before: at first insinuatingly, then obscenely and finally with an outright demand. Diverted from the path, trapped in a thicket and with her back against a tree, she heard him tell her just how much he wanted of the inventive favors that Thomas had described to him the night before.

Her attacker did not relish the blows and the screams that followed nor expect the brutal intervention of the workers, who pulled him away at once. Hauled before Roncival, he received a flogging, and the crews themselves would have dismissed him from their company if in his outrage he had not laid blame on Thomas.

She never knew what her father did or said to Thomas in consequence, and she never saw him again, for he left San Stefan on the next voyage. His successors, better warned, behaved without reproach. Underneath, she suffered an obscure sense of punishment, for her deepest hurt in the whole affair had been inflicted by her father. Previously, even at the moments when Roncival had been at his most demanding or irascible, even during the black, unpredictable moods that gripped him after he lost his wife, even when Léonore arrived home from school one summer and found Adélaïde installed in the mansion, her communication with her father, whether in tempests or sunshine, had been utterly frank. His lion cub, she had sharpened her claws by his example. But just at the point where she needed guidance that only a parent could give, clouds rose between them. From then on there had always been questions she did not know how to ask, and problems that he tried to solve only in the most oblique ways.

Léonore swam slowly to the shore and floated on the edge, hooking her fingers into the sand to keep her anchored as she looked over its dazzling whiteness to the green fringe of the bay. The hot air was still. Christina

would have fallen asleep in the hammock an hour ago.
Beyond the ridge, Bernard would be dozing by the path.
Not that such laxity mattered, for the island's security
had been honed to perfection after the departure of Laffite. No one could come now to cause her pain.

Laffite. She rolled over onto her back, feeling the fine
sand shift under her shoulders, the waves tease her hair,
the sun finger her skin through the sleek water. She
spread her arms wide, offering her nakedness to the absent regard of the sky. She was free. Laffite, the only
man who had ever seen her thus, would not be here
again. Surely a matter for relief, not regret.

Eyes closed, she drew a picture: sand, trees, rocks,
woman. To her mind her figure belonged in it as indeli-
bly as the starfish just beyond her right foot, the slender
palm tree etched against blue at the other end of the
beach, the iridescent bay, the great inky splash of the
ocean.

She slipped gently down into deeper water, shook off
the sand, then waded out of the sea to sweep her shawl
from the beach, and padded up the slope.

Christina, not quite asleep, stirred languidly as Léonore walked into the palm grove. The muted light under
the trees gave the young woman's face a greenish hue.
She looked drowsy and unrefreshed as she swung her
long legs out of the hammock and pushed herself upright, smoothing back two locks of tightly curled hair
that had escaped from the knot at the back of her head.
With her arms still raised, she looked up at Léonore
with an expression that bordered on resentment.

Léonore smiled. "I'm getting dressed. There's no hurry."

Christina rose, slowly because of her distended stomach, and hovered about while Léonore dried herself and
put on her clothes. She picked up the shawl, folded it
and laid it across the cushions of the hammock, then
with her hands behind her hips stretched and looked up
through the canopy of the grove, the corners of her lips
drawn back, but not in a smile.

"How do you feel today, Christina?"

"Well, Maître." The low voice held no conviction.

"The heat troubles you?"

"A little. I guess no woman feels much good around this time. Just have to wait until it's over."

Léonore slipped on her shoes, then straightened. "You walk ahead, at your own pace. Take care how you go. There's nothing to hurry for."

Christina gave a nod, draped the shawl over her arm and moved out of the clearing. Léonore watched her as she went, only just resisting the impulse to step forward, put an arm around the fragile shoulders, ask how she could give comfort. It would do no good, however. For the last two months, since before Santo set out for the Yucatan, Christina had become withdrawn. Léonore supposed it was the pregnancy that caused the dull look in her eyes, her muted voice, but she thought it hard that the young woman should suffer so when by contrast the first months of carrying the child had been easy and happy. Christina had had scarcely any morning sickness, even on the trip to New Orleans—which was when she first told Léonore, with some trepidation, about the baby. After that, the changes in her body seemed only to give her an extra glow of health. Before returning to San Stefan, Léonore had told Christina that she could keep her position and, when the right time came, she and Santo could live together in their own quarters within the mansion. Reassured that she and the baby would be protected and provided for, Christina had blossomed. By the time they arrived home she could no longer conceal her condition, but she ignored the servants and the crews when they speculated about where the father might be—San Stefan or New Orleans—and was waiting until Léonore clarified the issue.

Knowing that Christina would have security, Santo and her child, Léonore was perplexed to be deprived of her confidences lately. Christina's friendships amongst the other servants, her lively chatter and laughter, were also suspended; instead she often seemed uneasy, even fearful. Léonore could imagine that a pregnant woman living amongst a pack of brutes like Jean Laffite's men might tremble for herself and her child, but Christina's situation was completely different. So she consulted the midwife in the village about her, but the woman shrugged and said such behavior was not unusual.

Christina had toiled almost to the top of the ridge when the sentry, Bernard, came into view by the candle-nut tree at the turn. "Maître," he called past her, "the *Hero*!"

Léonore's spirits lifted at once. "Is all well?"

"Yes, by the looks. Monsieur Santo is ashore already. Shall I tell him to come and meet you?"

"Indeed, Bernard. Thank you."

He disappeared at a run, but Léonore did not increase her pace. She would allow Christina to be the first to greet Santo as he hurried from the shore, full of excitement and news. To share in his triumphant return would surely revive his lover's hope for the future.

When she got to the top of the ridge she spied Santo and Christina standing together amongst rocks at the foot of the slope. There was tension between them. She saw Christina put her hands on Santo's shoulders, but instead of embracing her, he grabbed hold of her wrists and lowered them. She placed her fingers on his arm, but he pulled back and said something vehement. Then suddenly Christina ran. Across a dry little stream bed, along the stony path towards the bay. She stumbled once while he was still looking after her, but he made no move to follow. Her long arms swung out from her body as she righted herself. Then the momentum carried her forward as she ran on, despite her heavy belly.

Léonore did not move. She stood by the candlenut tree where the old paring knife was still stuck, rusting, in the bark, and watched Santo climb towards her. Beyond she could see the curve of the bay with the *Hero* tranquil at anchor, the more distant figures of Bernard, followed by Christina, approaching the beach, and groups of people on the foreshore. With a new kind of attention, she examined the vigorous man who approached, his bare blond head glinting in the sun, one brown hand swinging the tricorn hat he had just removed, the other hooked into his broad sword belt. He stopped a yard away from her, planting his feet with two audible stamps.

"Welcome back, Monsieur Santo. By your grin, I judge you have what we needed from the Yucatan?"

"My oath, I've more than that!" Clasping the hat before him, he said, "There's another whole cargo besides."

"Where from?"

"An English trader. We ran across her on the way home, in the Channel. Outran her, I should say, and she struck her colors without a puff of resistance."

"Where was she bound?"

"Charleston, New York, then back to Bristol. You've never seen such an assortment of goods—couldn't decide what to choose, so in the end we took the lot."

"And set her free?"

He nodded. "She was a slow old bucket. No good to us."

"I'll remind you, Monsieur Santo, we are taking no more ships at present. Cargoes yes, vessels no. And no lives either, if they can be spared. Any casualties?"

He shook his head carelessly, but there was defiance in his eyes. It was one of his contentions that San Stefan needed a larger fleet, and she knew that every sleek ship that came his way was a sore temptation.

"Don't you want to know what we took?"

"I am waiting with great patience for you to tell me."

When she used this ironic tone with Santo it was usually enough to make him answer sensibly. Today, however, he had a different air about him—pent-up, almost peremptory. Perhaps it was the encounter with Christina that had given his blue eyes their hot, challenging look.

"Fine cloth—linen, good cottons, damask, you name it. Furniture, enough to fill the gun deck, we were fearful of damaging it in the hold. Two boxes of cash from passengers. And, you won't believe, books! Dispatched from London by a company called Rivington, for delivery to the Charleston Library Society, if you please."

"How did they expect to sail into Charleston? What about the embargoes?"

He shrugged. "They were going to get around them somehow, I guess, for the sake of what they carried."

"What else was there? I hope the rest is worth more than books."

"But the books could make us a fortune! I reckon we could ransom them." He forged on. "Back in 1805 there was a Guadeloupe privateer, the *Emerance,* took a cargo that had books for that same library society. They were recaptured and auctioned off in Kingston Town, and the library had to pay dear to get them in the end: more than a thousand pounds sterling. Why shouldn't we pull the same trick?"

"Who would you suggest as middleman, the Governor of Jamaica?"

He looked startled for a moment, then laughed and grinned at her. "We'll get nowhere without taking chances."

"Who were the passengers?"

"A planter from Jamaica setting off for the home country with all his revenue and his possessions. I told him he could claim his insurance on it when he got to Bristol and he looked ready to strangle me. But he was nothing beside the other—an ex-navy captain headed for England too." He broke off to laugh again, slapping the hat against his knee. "He's going home for a desk job, invalided out, for wounds received when his frigate was taken last year. You'd never guess the name of the vessel!"

When he stood straight again their eyes locked, and she shivered. "Don't tell me."

"The *Hero.*"

"He recognized her?"

"Like a long-lost child. I never saw a man so exercised; I thought he would have a fit."

"What did he say?"

"What didn't he?"

"This is no laughing matter!" The tremor in her voice caught his attention. She took a deep breath, trying for calm. "I must tell you, the English have threatened to take this island. It is more than likely they also have our exact position and a good description of our defenses. All because we took the *Hero.* So I would like to hear what this captain let fall about us."

The smooth, tanned skin along his cheekbones flushed. "When was this? Why didn't you tell me, for Christ's sake?"

"I took all due precautions, Monsieur Santo. After that, we could do nothing but wait."

His answer to that was an oath, which he snapped off short with his teeth. His anger, blazing at her out of the blue eyes, had a core of deeper offense.

She closed her eyes. "Tell me, please, what information the Englishman had about us."

"None." Her eyelids flew open and met his overbearing gaze. "He flung every curse at my head that he could muster. He called me every dog under the sun. But he had no idea where I came from—because he thought I sailed for Laffite."

Stunned, she could not speak for a moment. Then: "Did you disabuse him?"

"No, why would I? I identified us as privateers, and gave my name and quoted the letter of marque. It was a fair capture. That's all they needed to know. Beyond that, they could go fish."

"Great God. He has been in the Jamaica all these months. He must have taken part in hearings about the *Hero,* made a report. And all the time he believed it was Laffite who sailed away with her?"

"Yes, why not?" There was satisfaction in his voice. She could tell it pleased him to see her baffled for once. "After all, Laffite captured her in the first place and set them all adrift. It's plain the captain of the *Jubilation* never worked out who we were either."

"No. I see. But I don't understand—it means the English can't have received any certain information about us at all. Otherwise this captain would have heard it months ago."

"You say there was a threat. From where?"

"The English on Martinique."

"How?"

"A letter."

"Did you see this letter?" His voice had become more demanding.

"No," she said slowly. "I was told of it."

He leaned towards her, put a protective hand under each elbow. "I think this is very simple. Someone has tried to frighten you. But they can't. I am with you."

She stepped away from his touch. "Come. Show me what you have brought back."

All the way down the ridge, pretending to listen to his triumphant catalog of the capture, she thought of the letter that the Governor of Guadeloupe claimed he had received from Martinique. Wherever it had really come from, whoever had written it—indeed, whether it had even been written at all—she could not bring herself to care about. What took over all thought and feeling was this final confirmation: that Jean Laffite had never told the English anything about her or San Stefan.

It took hours to unload the *Hero,* stack the cargo in the warehouse and take the precious agave suckers into the shade beside the stream. After that Léonore worked in the crews' kitchen on the beach, supervising the preparation of beef and goat stews, wrapping up leaf-bound packets of newly caught fish for baking, peeling ackee plums for the massive dishes of rice. When her life became too hard to contemplate, she sometimes tried to lose herself in this way, throw herself into the practical task of cooking. Usually she escaped into the kitchen at the mansion, but today she was creating a feast in the village itself. This would be an evening of celebration, to crown Santo's voyage and the return of the spoils.

Santo's position as captain of the fleet had been ratified yet again by success, and the strength of his support on San Stefan could scarcely be greater, so this was also the ideal occasion for the liaison between him and Christina to be sanctioned. If they acted like a couple tonight, under Léonore's benevolent eye, then the new situation and her acceptance of it would be totally clear. Santo no longer needed people to assume he was Léonore Roncival's lover in order to command their obedience. And she herself no longer required a male as buffer between herself and the crews. The events of the last

year had defined the relationship between the mistress
and the inhabitants of San Stefan, and it was one of trust
and security.

Everything went satisfyingly at first. Rum and taffia
flowed freely, along with excellent canary wine that the
English trader had loaded on her ill-fated voyage. The
food was brought out in huge array, accompanied by
music dominated by a Cuban drummer who was a favorite with the keenest dancers. Before her pregnancy,
Christina used to be one of them, and the other women
made her join them. All her awkwardness disappeared
once she started to move.

Léonore watched in delight as animation flowed back
into Christina's long, graceful limbs and her liquid eyes
shone in the lamplight. In the dance, her proud belly
became a graceful part of her sinuous beauty, and it
seemed to Léonore that she had never looked so seductive, nor drawn the eyes of so many men. Except for
Santo's. Christina made it very clear that she was performing for him, but he chose not to notice. Then
Christina called out something to him, raising laughter
amongst the bystanders, and it was then, merely by the
sound of her voice, that Léonore realized Christina was
drunk. Santo scowled and turned his back. He picked
up his rum, looked down the table at Léonore, raised
the glass and grinned. Taken aback, she did not return
the gesture, but beyond him she saw the light go out of
Christina's eyes. The other dancers closed around her
and after a moment she drifted away and sat down
again.

Léonore left the table and walked the length of the
meeting hall to the kitchens. She had told Santo that
tonight was his moment to do the right thing by Christina. What was he waiting for, a public announcement?
After checking on the final dishes she went out the other
side of the building and leaned against the doorpost,
looking out over the beach and the lagoon. There were
people strolling along the water's edge, children playing
on the sand, littler ones gathered at the entrance to the
hall where the light caught their eager faces and the
music issued forth in joyful, turbulent gusts.

Suddenly Santo was beside her. "This is grand, isn't it?"

She looked up at him consideringly. "Not for everyone. What is wrong between you and Christina?"

He narrowed his eyes, looking out at the black lagoon. "Between me and your maid? Why do you ask?"

"You know why; we have an agreement. I promised her protection and I will not go back on that promise. You agreed to honor it tonight."

He turned his head and the blue gaze arrested hers. "Should these little matters be allowed to interfere with what we have, you and I?"

"I don't know what you mean."

He opened his broad hands to the night. "All this. Everything we have worked for together, side by side. You cannot want to change that."

"No, I want to be open about how we stand. There is a confusion in people's minds that has lasted long enough. Now the truth can be told. You have been silent all this time for my sake, and I am grateful—surely you must be relieved that it's over!"

"If you are grateful, why need it be over?" He lowered his voice, so that the workers in the kitchen and the people nearby might not overhear. "We are together; why deny it? You need me. Andrea Santo belongs by your side." He took a step closer, and the back of one hand brushed her arm.

She withdrew it, overcome by cold dismay. Not now. Not Santo. She hissed, "What about Christina?"

He shrugged. "She knows I am devoted to you."

"She is carrying your baby!"

"Is she? How do I know?"

"For *God's sake*. I allow you to live in my house. I extend you almost every privilege, including having an affair under my own roof—and you have the gall to speak of your woman and your child like this. You will acknowledge them both tonight, Monsieur Santo, if you know what's good for you!"

She had raised her voice and heads were turning. She could see anger, arrogance and uncertainty in his face. There was also desire, so naked that she cursed herself

for never having seen it before, so potent that having
him near was like heat on bare skin. She managed to
hold his eye, and therefore saw the tiny flicker that indicated when caution prevailed. The night was not over.
He could wait. Without a word, he turned and walked
towards the lamplight and the music.

It was the women in the kitchen, witnesses to the encounter in the doorway, who had the first inkling of how
that night was going to turn out, but they could never
have guessed that it would rival, in its way, the midnight
scene when San Stefan once farewelled Jean Laffite.

There were signs of trouble earlier in the evening, for
sure. Young Christina got foolish as a fowl halfway
through and ended up sobbing with her head on a table
in the corner of the kitchen. If anyone asked her what
ailed her, she just gave a kind of scream and shook her
head. She looked so pitiful someone got Marie the midwife to take a peek at her, just in case. The baby was
due any day now.

The maître was cheerful and active to start with. When
she busied herself in the kitchen like that she always
reminded the older women of the energetic little girl
who used to work amongst them in the old days—plunging in where things needed to be done, tossing an apron
over the finest of dresses without a care for where powder or juice might stray. And you could always get her
to laugh. Tonight, however, after she and Santo had their
set-to in the doorway and Christina flung herself out of
the hall, she never came back in the kitchen again. She
stayed at the head of the big table, with Philibert on one
side of her and Rigaud on the other, looking down the
board at Santo with a frown line as thin as a catfish
whisker between her eyebrows.

It was something to be part of that night. Everyone
was feeling wealthy. Sure, the council the next day would
decide on the lots to be divided, but the size of them
was pretty easy to work out and it gave an extra zest to
the food and liquor. The dancing set itself into a rhythm
that would go until dawn. There were toasts to everyone
on the Yucatan voyage. Santo even leaped up and drank

to the captain of the English cargo ship and her crew and passengers. "Up their arses!"

In the midst of the laughter someone yelled out, "Never a truer word!"

The maître, looking puzzled, leaned over and put a question to Rigaud. When she heard the answer she stood up and a hush fell. And then it started.

"Monsieur Santo, we'll be hearing your report tomorrow. But I'd like to know just one thing now. After you took that cargo, you let the ship go free?"

"Yes." His voice was as clear as hers, for all he'd drunk.

"You didn't harm the crew or the passengers?"

"No."

"I'm sure we're all pleased to hear that. We are taking goods only. Until the council decides otherwise. So the ship sailed away undamaged?"

He shrugged and stood taller. A fine figure of a man, Santo, and just then full of rum and glory, knowing all the women wanted him and he was the envy of all the men. "Oh, we gave them a parting present. Two rounds of cannon up the backside, in return for their bloody curses."

There was a long pause, and everyone around her stilled. "You fired on them."

He nodded.

"When they'd surrendered their cargo to you and were sailing free in an unarmed vessel, you fired on them. What happened to them?"

"How do I know? Both balls went into the stern; when we last looked she was listing. Maybe they limped to shore somewhere. Maybe they took to the boats." His voice was rising. "Who gives a curse?"

"Every person on San Stefan cares, Monsieur Santo. We are privateers, not murderers. We do not visit outrage on those we steal from. We are after riches, not retaliation."

"We had nothing to fear from the master or that other broken-down old sea dog, whatever he called me!"

"If he was so harmless, why fire on him?" He did not answer at once, and something about the way he looked at her made her voice rise too. "Because you lost your head."

"Did I? Take that line any longer and you can watch me do it now!"

They were staring at each other like two creatures set against each other for a fight, and you could swear there was more to it than just this matter.

"A threat?" Her voice roughened with scorn. "Where is that devotion you offered an hour ago?"

So that was it. Nothing to do with the voyage—this was deep, between man and woman, and Santo's face flamed when he shouted, "God's teeth, I've had enough. You need to be taught a lesson. You'll take me, willing or no. I'll have my rightful place, and no one here will stop me."

Everyone stood and looked at the both of them, open-mouthed. The maître's face was as white as his was red. "You have your place. You are captain of the fleet of San Stefan. Answerable to the council and to me."

"Damn you, I'll have no plaguey whining over what I do at sea. I'll have no poxy ungrateful bitch pocket my gains with one hand and wave a cat-o'-nine-tails in the other. I'll be confounded if I ever take orders again from a woman!"

Her face froze. She nodded to Philibert and Rigaud. They stood up, one on each side of her, and slid pistols onto the table. In that white-hot second, no one had a flicker of doubt whether they were loaded. Then she said, "I take it this is your resignation, Monsieur Santo."

His eyes actually closed with the shock. Then he took a huge breath and held it in while he looked around the hall, searching the faces. You could see his alarm; and that was when it became clear that some men were not present. Whatever had happened earlier in the evening, whatever his ambition might be driving him to, Santo had not prepared for this moment. But she had. You knew for sure that the men who had been missing for the last hour would be at the posts she had chosen for them: on the ships, in the fort, on duty wherever a challenge might be raised.

This time, when he swore at her, he called her whore

and every other filthy name he could dredge up from
the cesspool of his memory, and he cast his eye about
the hall with a look that was so fierce and desperate
there was scarcely a soul could meet it. No one made a
sound to stop his curses, but just the same, not a man
stepped forward to offer him support.

When he had run out of breath she was bone white
and leaning on the table as though she were about to
fall across it. "You are free to go. I am sure the council
will agree that your service merits reward. Your share
of the Yucatan voyage will be taken down to the beach
within the hour. We can ill afford to lose a boat, but
you may take the snow nonetheless. You can invite
whomever you wish to sail it with you—we would not
keep anyone here against their will. As for Christina, I
shall miss her dearly, but she is free to go. She must
decide whether to have your child here, in safety, or risk
leaving with you now."

At this his rage took him over like a mighty wave, so
that he shuddered, and people stepped back from
around him. He drew the cutlass that he always wore
and slammed it into the table. "Go? Christ, damn your
eyes. I go nowhere. Whoever is with me, come lay your
hands on this!"

The maître flinched and staggered back when he
swung the blade, but Rigaud and Philibert caught her
between them and lowered her into the chair. Then
there was a cry, and over by the kitchen, Christina put
her hands over her mouth and sank to the floor with her
back against the doorpost. Santo took in the company
with his fiery stare and registered that no one else was
moving. The people from the household would not look
him in the eye. The men of the *Hero* met his gaze with
a question or a frown on their faces. Another dire interval went by. And he realized he was too late. Whatever
he might have wished and planned for, the moment
was past.

Rigaud took up his pistol and moved to Santo's side.
Others, on a nod from the quartermaster, placed themselves around him to escort him to the mansion. Santo
was so stunned he could scarcely walk straight. The

maître put her elbows on the table and her head in her hands and you could see her shaking.

She stayed there an hour while the hall slowly emptied, and the feast was cleared away, and the snow was loaded and Santo's people went onboard. For there were men who came forward at the last moment to join him, after the talk and feverish whispers out in the night had died away. There were bound to be some. Santo was a rare captain, after all.

As for the maître, it was nothing like the time when San Stefan saw Laffite off the island. She herself did not go down to the beach, and it was Philibert who had the last talk with him, thigh deep in the lagoon, and when he waded ashore he shrugged and would tell no one what was said. There were half a dozen figures in the little snow and a great pile of goods to get in their way as they set sail, but they moved smoothly out under the moonless sky. With Santo as captain, they would come to no harm. You could give him that.

It created a dead, empty feeling that made everyone drift back to the hall, while the sentries on the mansion roof watched the snow lose itself on the ocean.

The maître was still there. She had hardly lifted her head. But she did so when Christina came in. She staggered to her feet in disbelief and then flung out a hand.

"You're staying? You'll let me look after you?"

Christina's eyes were so wild and strange they looked bruised. "He wouldn't take me! Curse you! It's all your fault." She spat at her, then turned and rushed out.

Some of the women made to follow her, but the maître said to let her go. No one knew where Christina got to, for she did not go to her room that night—the very room, they said, that Santo had been visiting in secret since the day he set foot in the mansion.

The council in the morning went as usual, Santo or not, and the booty was divided to the satisfaction of all. Everything was decided and put to rights. But the news, when it came, brought the meeting to a halt.

They found Christina's body on the beach, washed ashore from the gap in the reef, lacerated by the coral but recognizable: the slender limbs, the tight mass of hair, the tender mound under which her child would rest forever. No one could guess what she had believed when she threw herself into the dark sea. She might have thought she could swim strongly enough to reach Santo's boat; she might have cried out and trusted he would turn back; or maybe she embraced the waves in silence.

Léonore Roncival cast herself down on the wet sand and put her arms across the swollen body and sobbed. "Christina! Oh, Christina! He killed you. He killed his baby."

CHAPTER THIRTEEN

❧

The Temple

September 1810, the month in which Christina's child was to have been born, saw the outcome of a struggle in which Andrea Santo had taken a certain wistful interest. After a short, American-inspired revolution, West Florida fell to the United States.

In October, within the shelter and comfort of the house on Saint Philip Street in New Orleans, Adélaïde Maselari gave birth to a daughter, Marie. Pierre Laffite expressed himself delighted with the tiny addition to his flourishing family. Jean, who was absent from the city, sent greetings.

In December, there was speculation about the possible recall of British troops from Portugal and the Spanish border. This would mean less pressure on Napoleon, who still had a sure grasp on his great Continental System. Austria, Prussia, Holland, Naples, Sweden and Russia remained leagued against England—except that the czar, of late, had opened Russian ports to British colonial goods. The United States, holding themselves honorably neutral, were in fact viewed with suspicion and rancor by both sides in the war.

The British attempted to regulate American shipping by commercial blockades and authorized the boarding of any American vessel suspected of carrying English seamen; they also allowed the confiscation of any vessel

carrying goods between ports of any hostile power or
its colonies.

Napoleon in retaliation issued decrees commanding
the seizure of any ship carrying goods obtained or manu-
factured in England, and confiscation of ships involved
with British trade. All American vessels that had entered
French-held ports since May 1809 were forfeit to France.

The Americans were thus damned by the French if
they continued to carry cargoes between English and
United States possessions, and damned by the English if
they supplied Europe. In a fit of outrage they imposed
an embargo at home that left American ships at risk in
harbors across the Atlantic and made the United States
into a nation of smugglers overnight. When this measure
proved to benefit only the grateful ports of Canada, it
was replaced by the Nonintercourse Act, banning all
American trade with England, France and their colonies.

On a fleeting, clandestine visit to Cuba, Jean Laffite
found himself discussing the United States' situation
with none other than Señora de Oleron y Siqueiros.
Mathilde.

The lady was reclining in an overstuffed chair near a
window, from which she had a view of the docks of the
tiny seaport town where they had arranged to meet. The
buildings in the street, like the modest inn, had white-
painted walls, reflecting sunshine indoors that, checked
at the top by a tattered canvas awning, washed in a
bright wave to her feet. Her green gown shone like summer leaves and the light burnished the ivory of her neck
and shoulders and gave a pure illumination to her face
as she returned his look, her full mouth and lazy-lidded
eyes perfectly still, accepting his scrutiny.

He said, "You always make me feel I have just been
received by royalty."

It was true: among her many abilities was the gift of
allowing him to think there were promises yet to be
offered, future favors only she could bestow.

There was a slow, indulgent smile, but she did not
reply.

He was sitting at a table, and his fingers played idly

with things she had let fall there half an hour or so before. A delicate lace fan. Diamond earrings whose facets on this darker side of the room collected only the milky hues of ceiling and walls and the black of his own clothes. A gold locket on a fine chain. When he opened it, there was the faintest movement of protest or annoyance from the figure by the window.

"A beautiful image," he said, "if a little inaccurate."

"Typical of the artist: François Boucher."

"An heirloom?"

"You might say that."

He closed the locket, imprisoning the shimmering colors. "Tell me, will you ever live in France again?"

"You would need to ask my husband." She never hesitated to mention him, and Jean could never decide whether to find this insouciance vulgar or regal.

"What about *your* wishes? You have left nothing behind in Paris that you value?"

"Do you mean property or friends? The daughter of a noble family disposes of nothing that cannot travel. And I assure you, mine has traveled—a great deal of it out of my hands. As for connections: I was a friend of the former empress. Naturally enough, that would be no recommendation to Marie Louise."

"You met Bonaparte himself?"

"I did. One day, perhaps, I shall tell you about it." Her inflection was intended to make him jealous. She almost succeeded.

"What about a return to Spain?"

"Unlikely, while it is in French hands."

"Then you must be encouraged by the latest news from London."

"I might be, if I knew what you meant."

He smiled. "Now that the Prince Regent has one foot on the throne he has decided against a change in government. He's sent his principles to perdition and his political friends into limbo."

"So there's no change in Spain either—Wellington will not be recalled?"

"There seems little chance of it."

"We will rejoice at his victory. But by that distant time we may be well established here."

"In Cuba?"

She looked out the narrow window, her profile pale against the dingy wall. "Who knows? There are so many things to consider. There is the possibility of purchasing land. Sugar plantations, farms, have been suggested."

"These would be large investments for a gentleman who still maintains an estate in Spain."

She smiled wryly as she turned back to him. "And we grow wary of investments in this region. In time of war, it is so hard to guarantee one's returns."

The husband had never been paid, then, for the arms sold to the Spanish in West Florida. He smiled. "Not if you always put your money on the winning side."

There was a hint of pique. "Calculating that is not so simple."

"I agree: I am faced with the problem daily. But there is another option when a conflict is in the balance—throwing in your own weight to help decide the victor."

Either the light changed, or a quick flush came and went on her cheeks. "You speak from experience?"

He leaned back and stretched his legs out under the table. "Here's an example: the United States. Of all countries on the globe, for many decades, America must have had the fastest-growing wealth from trade—until England and France began disputing Europe and the high seas. Now half her shipping is trapped at home by the British navy or on the other side of the Atlantic by the French. So much for the privileges of neutrality—she'd best be at war with one or the other and have done with it. Now"—he leaned forward again—"Napoleon has revoked some of his decrees about trade."

"Meaning more leniency towards American vessels?"

"Yes. But there's a hitch. He has not issued an imperial proclamation or corresponded with the government of the United States. He has only allowed it to be known, to American diplomats, that their vessels can trade in Europe."

"To encourage America to suspend nonintercourse

against France?" Again the flush. He wondered momentarily just what she thought he was talking about.

"Yes. But President Madison ought to take into account that Napoleon's statement has not been confirmed, that the French are still seizing American ships and—perhaps more important—that the English don't believe a word of the announcement. They've been duped by Bonaparte too often."

"But President Madison does believe?"

"It seems so."

"By your reasoning, then, America has found its best ally. Especially since England is the enemy of the United States, even in peacetime. So you think Madison should throw his weight in with Napoleon. Declare war on England, sign an alliance with France, commence supplying Europe."

He shook his head, and she managed not to look surprised. "Think of the manifold advantages of the opposite. Embrace England. Reopen relations with the most lucrative trading partner that America has ever had. Join forces with the most powerful navy in the world. Extend commerce into Europe with the aid of a grateful ally once Napoleon's stranglehold on the Continent is swept away. Possibly, even, acquire new territories in the Caribbean after the war at sea is won. The rewards would be colossal. Those from Napoleon may be mere hallucination."

"And all it requires is a complete about-face. A hand in friendship to the old, hated enemy. A betrayal of everything America stands for."

He grinned at her. "I told you it was simple."

"It would be the death of three quarters of Congress even to hear it suggested!"

"Think what's at stake—the future of a nation, not the health of President Madison's spleen."

"You support sending their principles to perdition."

"I have nothing to do with it. For which I repeatedly thank Christ."

Her eyes probed his. "But you could imagine throwing over your own loyalties in like fashion if the stakes were high enough? What, for instance, about your personal attitude towards Spain?"

Admiration widened his smile as he said slowly, "The emotions I associate with Spain are so deeply conflicting just now that it could be the death of me—or of others—to pronounce them."

She did not smile in return. "Of course, one should choose one's enemies with even greater care than one chooses allies. I am flattered that you followed a little advice I gave you in that regard, on the night we first met."

He remembered. That was the most unpleasant, persistent, irremediable aspect of the whole business: he remembered everything. He found that his fingers were crushing the fine lace of her fan and put it down with care on the table. Looking at it blankly, he said in a voice that he recognized as lacking color, "Your information is remarkable. When I wish to know what is really happening in Havana, my only sure recourse is to come here and confer with my contacts firsthand. Whilst you seem able to guess all my meetings—or lack of them—by divination."

She was amused. "On the contrary, I should have had no idea you were even here unless you had sent me your note. In general, I know nothing of your movements. I have taken an interest in the affairs of San Stefan, however."

The name slid under his ribs like a cool blade. He raised his head. "Why? And how?"

"Why did I caution you? Let me just say that I know the actions of its inhabitants are not well viewed by Spain."

He considered her. It was unnecessary to make the same remark about his own actions. It was likely she would again deflect any direct question about hers. Out of the corner of his eye he could see a pearly sliver of light beyond the half-open chamber door that showed in enticing relief the wave-tossed sheets of the bed they had just quitted. A temporary haven. A battleground. For some time now, it had not mattered which.

"Mathilde." He rose and crossed the room.

On a fine afternoon, Léonore was strolling through the Place d'Armes in New Orleans. At the dockside half

an hour's walk away, Philibert and Rigaud had the cutter
waiting, loaded with supplies. This had been just a re-
plenishment voyage, for which she had exchanged some
more specie. She had not contacted the Claibornes;
Sophronie's magnificent forbearance should not be
pushed too far. Léonore was inclined to think that no
one had yet informed the governor's wife about her true
identity, but she would not overburden such a friendship.

The colorful stalls of the market were aired by a fresh
breeze blowing straight off the broad Mississippi, which
sparkled invitingly beyond the red-brown sails of the
oyster boats lined up on the far side of the levee. The
large stalls owned by the wealthier merchants were fitted
with canvas awnings that gave shade to the concourse
of servants and slaves who came to buy for the households of New Orleans. Other stalls, often owned by
libres—former slaves—were constructed with a few trestle tables and perhaps a slanting parasol or a cotton covering. Few were attended by their owners. The women
who ran them, mostly black, whether wage earners or
slaves, had served an apprenticeship of poverty and re-
sourcefulness that honed their commercial sense to razor
sharpness and gave boisterous invention to the banter
they exchanged with their customers and one another.
The massive square, enclosed on three sides by splendid
French and Spanish buildings of the previous century
and on the fourth by iron railings, the wide levee and
the river, was their own loud, engrossing world.

Léonore paused at a stall that frothed with gaudy lace,
herself festooned by ribbons whenever the breeze gusted
through tall, wooden racks at her side. She looked up
to speak to the seller and recognized a woman who sat
with her back turned at the other end of the stall. She
was Adélaïde Maselari, her smooth head bent, her hands
busy with a red square of cotton on her ample blue lap.
When Léonore spoke to the girl, Adélaïde turned, and
their eyes met in a stare of equal astonishment.

While the purchase was being paid for, Adélaïde un-
hurriedly finished folding the headdress, added it to the
rainbow collection in a low pannier on the ground at her

side, then rose and put a smaller basket over her arm. As
she moved forward she said, "Good day, mademoiselle."

The girl moved respectfully away, but Léonore could
feel that she and the stall holders on each side awaited
the response with eager interest. "Good day, madame,"
she said lamely, interrogating Adélaïde's dark eyes for
a clue to the next move.

Adélaïde glided out. "Will you do me the honor of
taking a walk with me? My residence is not far away,
near the Batture."

They walked towards the levee in silence for a while.
Léonore was lost in perplexity. Did Pierre Laffite have
businesses in the market? If he did, she could not imagine how Adélaïde could have consented to run them—
especially when she must be nursing.

"I heard about your baby. Is she well? And Joël?"

"Yes. You didn't see Joël last time—want to come
home with me now and meet him?"

"Thank you. But why are we going this way? Don't
you live in Saint Philip Street anymore?"

Adélaïde frowned and snapped, "No."

"The Laffites have sold?"

She shook her head and gave Léonore a glance that
looked almost venomous. "Oh no. Pierre Laffite still
lives there. But he's set up a cottage by the ramparts for
the fine, fancy idiot he picked up at the last Quadroon
Ball. And a rare time he'll have, trying to deal with her
mother and her sister into the bargain. He didn't know
when he was well off, curse him for a fool."

Léonore stopped. "He's thrown you off? You, with
a child?"

Adélaïde let out a puff of breath that sounded like a
laugh, then put a hand on her arm to draw her along.
"Don't fret—I made damned certain he gives me my
due. I still get an allowance from him for Marie. Even
though I live with my new man now."

They strolled along the levee amongst the throng of
fashionably dressed gentlemen and ladies, slaves and servants on errands, while Adélaïde recounted with satisfaction the wealth and talents of her present protector,

Juan Alexandro Lugar. She described him with pride as
a *pardo libre* and Léonore felt a pang as she heard the
words. Of pure African blood herself, Adélaïde had
never before expressed a judgment about anyone's color.
In the past, Léonore was sure that the *pardos*—mixed-
race people with lighter skin—would have received no
more approval from Adélaïde than the darker *morenos*.
Yet now she used those Spanish colonial terms without
a second thought. New Orleans, divided by caste and
skin, was tightening its grip on Adélaïde's life.

As they walked in the soft winter sunshine, Adélaïde
told the short and bitter story of how she had been supplanted by a woman called, ironically, Marie—the same
name as Pierre's new daughter. She was young, compli-
ant, and the mother had been "fishing" for Pierre for
months. Marie Villars lived in the cottage he had set up
for her, and at times she stayed on Saint Philip Street
also, with her younger sister, a girl of thirteen.

Léonore knew that sympathy or even interest in the
failed arrangement with Pierre was not what Adélaïde
desired. She wanted instead to show off her new establishment and prove that even though it was in a poorer
quarter of town it was better in some way than the house
in Saint Philip Street. She could not utter enough praise
of her new man, a retail dealer who besides three stalls
in the Place d'Armes also ran a team of a dozen slaves
who sold wares in the streets.

Lugar's house proved to be a long, narrow building
crammed between warehouses in a crooked street near
the docks. Inside, it was dark but lavishly furnished, in
a decorative style that Léonore recognized as Adélaïde's
own. It instantly made the place seem much more hers
than the quarters behind the Laffite shop.

She met Joël at last—a thin, angular child quite unlike
his mother in body and face, who wore a suspicious
scowl and gave monosyllabic answers to both women.
His mother finally sent him outside to amuse himself in
the courtyard. Léonore wondered whether his sourness
was caused by resentment of the baby, who was taken
from a servant and bounced gently on Adélaïde's knee

throughout the visit. Marie had a chubby, nut-colored face wreathed in smiles, except when she caught Léonore's glance, whereupon she pursed up her little mouth and gave a stare of solemn intensity out of her round, thick-lashed eyes.

They drank chocolate, for which Adélaïde had a passion, and ate pecans covered in brittle cane sugar, but for all Adélaïde's hospitable airs Léonore did not find it a comfortable visit, and something whispered to her that it was probably her last. Perhaps it was the sense of finality that made her ask the next question.

"Joël seems a fine boy. And Marie is beautiful. You must be proud of them. I can't help wondering why, in all the years with my father, you never had a child. Were you just unlucky?"

Adélaïde gave a mocking smile. "You don't know better than that by now? No, I chose not to have any child to Roncival. Not unless things changed in that household. So long as you were there, any child of mine would be of no account."

"But how did you manage it?"

The mockery sharpened. "Need to know, do you? I can give you the address of a good healer in Sainte-Marie. She could prevent a whore conceiving if she serviced a whole crew."

Léonore sat back in her chair and put her cup down before she looked over again into the hard eyes. "I sometimes wished I could confide in you, when I was a child. Why did my father make us jealous of each other?"

Adélaïde said, "He couldn't help that; it just came natural. You were always number one wife. I took second place. He said to me once, 'As long as I have Léonore, I have the heart of Marianne.' "

Léonore's gaze fell. Then she took a breath, looked up and said, "What did Jean Laffite do when his brother told you to leave?"

Adélaïde's full lips twisted. "Nothing. Pierre's every whim is sacred to Jean. And Pierre thinks the sun shines out of him. So does the pretty little sister, by the by.

She worships Jean; never says a word, but follows him around like a puppy. She's so besotted they never use her real name; they call her after him—Jeannette.''

Léonore shifted in her chair. "I am afraid I must be going. We are leaving on the tide.''

"We? Doesn't include Monsieur Santo these days, does it?'' Adélaïde chuckled as she rose and handed the baby back to one servant, gesturing to the other to bring Léonore's bonnet. "You know he's with the Laffites now.''

Léonore closed her eyes as she stood up. "I expected it, yes. But no one seems to be able to confirm the news.''

"Oh yes," Adélaïde said comfortably, walking with Léonore down the long corridor to the front entrance, where the stifling darkness recalled the spy chamber in the house on Saint Philip Street. "He took those young lads, Amirou and Dani with him when he left, didn't he?''

"Yes. We didn't realize until the next day. Mirliton is still mourning them—he doesn't believe they went willingly.''

"Seems they did," Adélaïde said as her servant opened the door wide and the light from the street slanted in, sculpting the gleaming contours of her ebony face. "But after a month or two of raiding for no profit they lost a bit of their passion for Monsieur Santo. He didn't like that. So he sold them back to Jean Laffite.''

Léonore gasped. "But they are *free*, Adélaïde.''

"Try and tell Jean Laffite that, why don't you? He's probably selling them off at the Temple.''

"What?''

"He's decided to hold another slave market, down in the bayous tomorrow. Advertised in the *Courrier de la Louisiane,* so they tell me.'' She paused on the threshold. "You must have more questions about Jean. Isn't that why you came here today? There are things I could tell you would make your every hair stand on end.''

Léonore stepped into the street, turned and faced her, examining one last time the voluptuous body, the enigmatic smile. "It was Jean you wanted, all along.''

Adélaïde gave her rare, high laugh. "Doesn't everyone?"

Dominique You detested the bayous between Barataria and the Mississippi. Whether he picked his way towards them from the north with the donkey and mule trains or nosed into their labyrinthine channels from the Lake, the smell of them seemed like an insidious warning issued especially for him. The bass note came from the rich and fetid mud endlessly deposited and reshaped by the river and the tides. Just above it floated the stench of rotted reed beds, the fog of odors that hung about mangrove swamps, the damp emanations of the clinging or drifting plants that clogged the waterways. And at intervals, erupting like shrill alarm signals, a whiff of beached shellfish, a gust of salt from an invisible bank of seaweed, the sharp scent from a smokeless driftwood fire that told of a Cajun hut hidden in the thickets, and watchers who might whisper the smugglers' presence along the breeze and conjure up danger to await them at some blind turning amongst the reeds.

On the day of the auction, Dominique You approached the Temple just before high tide. The bayous, warm and still under the noonday sun, spread out around him like a gigantic, sluggish circulation system that was all veins and no heart. A maze where over past centuries thousands of men had ventured in pirogues, flat-bottomed boats, dinghies, skiffs and makeshift rafts—and many had failed to return. There were no distinguishing features in the narrow, identical channels that snaked amongst the reed-choked islands. Memory only could save a boatman from toiling for hours in vast, meandering circles or from struggling along a promising stream only to find himself alone in a weed-locked lake, where the spike rushes around the dark water made him feel he was floating on a giant eye that gazed up into the indifferent blue.

Dominique, however, had no fear of getting lost. He and the men with him in the narrow Barataria boat held a map of these stretches imprinted in their minds, complete with access and escape routes, and places of am-

bush and concealment. What he hated was the dense
vegetation, higher than the head of the tallest man, that
cut the field of vision to a few yards.

Jean Laffite reckoned it was the artilleryman in him
that suffered. "You just can't bear not being able to take
your range."

"What I can't stand," Dominique used to reply with
a volley of expletives, "is not being able to see!"

Thus he heard the sounds at the Temple long before
it came into view: a low eddy of men's voices punctuated
by the cries of the auctioneer at the top of his pitch, and
the occasional ring of hammer on metal.

The Temple was a long, broad island of spreading live
oak trees, which today held a flock of tents and seethed
with a temporary population of black slaves and the men
of several nationalities who came to sell and buy them.
Unlike most other dryish patches in the bayous, the
Temple was raised a few yards above the water, partly
by natural accretion, partly because it was a shell mound
created by the natives of the region, a place where
oyster, mussel and other shells used to be piled after
feasting, to avoid the pollution of the beds in the salt
marshes. As Dominique's boat drew nearer he could
hear crunching underfoot as well-shod customers walked
about inspecting the merchandise huddled in the shade
of the oaks.

Jean was in the big tally tent, sitting at a trestle table
behind the clerks and looking over the remains of a fine
meal at a well-to-do gentleman in his forties whose large,
observant eyes were narrowed in amusement at something his host had just said. Dressed in impeccable
broadcloth and with a look of contained satisfaction, the
gentleman showed no unease. Dominique, however,
brought up short by the sight, hesitated under the tent
flap as the two clerks in front looked up and gave a
polite greeting.

"Come and join us," Jean said without turning. "Hungry?" He waved away the boy who was clearing the
dishes from the table and sent him off for more food.

Without replying, Dominique walked between the

desks and approached the table, watched by the well-
dressed gentleman, who pulled his chair back and rose.

Jean rose too. "You've perhaps not met face-to-face,
monsieur. May I present Monsieur Dominique You."

Dominique held out his hand without a word and felt
the cool pressure of the other's. There was a bow and a
fleeting smile. "A pleasure. Pray excuse me: I am just
on my way. Let me give you my place at this generous
board. And I must thank my host for a most interesting meal."

Jean smiled back. "Your custom and your conversation, monsieur, will always be welcome. We shall hope
to see you here again."

"You intend to repeat this? I predict you will not lack
for clients."

"We aim to oblige." Jean saw him to the front of the
tent and then came back to the table while the other
strolled away under the live oaks in the direction of the
new wooden landing.

"Bloody hell," Dominique exploded. "Edward cursed
Livingston!"

"Just so. I knew I need not mention the name of such
a distinguished member of the Orleans bar."

"The hound who represented Porter!" The business of
the three confiscated ships the year before had unnerved
Dominique, and despite the Laffites' escape from due
process he still held a healthy grudge against those involved: Captain David Porter of the United States Navy,
who had made the capture; John Randolph Grymes, brilliant young district attorney; and Edward Livingston,
lawyer.

"Someone had to," Jean replied equably. "And explain everything to his client once we slipped free. He's
an intriguing devil to talk to."

Dominique applied himself to a dish of mud crab and
rice. "What's he spying here for? Did he ask where we
got the slaves?"

"He'd scarcely expect any answer to that. He's quite
prepared to accept the fiction that they're from the Territory. Bought one himself, as a matter of fact."

Dominique looked up. "Why?"

Jean shrugged. "Goodwill? I suspect he thinks we may need a clever lawyer one day. Or perhaps one of his own slaves ran away and joined the insurrection last month. There were over sixty executed, after all. A good many buyers this afternoon will be planters from upriver, searching for replacements."

Dominique looked dubiously out at the blacks crowded under one of the larger trees nearby. "Let's hope this lot don't get to hear about that until they're off our hands. They say the ringleaders were all straight from Africa and right out of their minds."

"Off their heads more like it, poor bastards. They've stuck half a dozen on stakes downriver for the buzzards to pick at."

Dominique stopped chewing in surprise. "You don't approve?"

"No. Nor do you."

The tone was such that Dominique returned philosophically to his meal.

Later they walked down to the wharf to see whether there were any further customers arriving, but most of the traffic was outward, in flatboats that would take the buyers and their purchases inland towards the river or along the serpentine route Dominique had just navigated, to luggers awaiting them in the Lake. The auction was progressing merrily behind them and one of the overseers came up to report progress. Thus Jean, with his back to the water, missed the unexpected arrival.

Dominique caught sight of Léonore Roncival the moment her boat rounded a promontory of bull-tongue rushes and glided towards the jetty. His heart jolted with resentment about his cannon—one day he intended to get them back. Then he felt suddenly anxious for Jean. Which was absurd, for of all men Jean was the least likely to let a woman under his guard.

She had not seen them yet. He had leisure to study the golden hair caught up by two bandeaux, the easy stance of her light body, clad in sprigged muslin. Her bonnet and a soft cape in some shiny fabric lay on the thwart beside her and now and then an eddy of light leaped off the water and rippled across her smooth skin. She had a beauty that caught fire in an instant, at a word, at a gesture, on an impulse from within. Even now, sitting erect and scanning the shoreline, she gave off sparks that drew the eyes of every man.

Except Jean. Who surely had this thing under control anyway. After the insane relinquishment of the *Hero* there had been, as far as Dominique knew, only one meeting between them. Pierre had told him about the episode at the smithy—bizarre, and without a sequel. Jean had not said a word about the woman since, even when Andrea Santo turned up and petitioned to join them. Santo claimed he had left San Stefan of his own accord, but Barataria gossip told a different story: he had gotten one of Léonore Roncival's maids pregnant and in a towering fury she had turned him off. No one had heard Jean comment on that, either, even Pierre.

Considering her as she made ready to land, Dominique could not banish nervousness. It was a pity Pierre was not around; he had always known how to handle Jean, right back to the days when they were children. Dominique remembered Jean's agony when their mother left, without warning, without a word of parting for her youngest child. The boy's grief had been in proportion to his worship of her: raucous, prolonged, like that of an animal in pain. Only Pierre had known how to rescue him, to guide him to silence and acceptance. And only Pierre had understood when she turned up all those years later and Jean had kept that silence, directing towards her the cold mask that should have prompted her, by its sheer horrifying contrast, to remember the mercurial, open responses her littlest boy had always offered her. Only Pierre fully comprehended why with Jean and women, from that earliest, crucial time, it was all or nothing.

The overseer left them to return to the auction ring and at that moment she stepped ashore. Jean turned as if by instinct, and Dominique, inches away, could not mistake the reaction. His face blanched, so it made his profile look like a crude cutout in black and white. Then he took in a long breath and his color returned.

She saw them, hesitated a fraction and then advanced. She had expected the meeting; she was prepared. Best to leave them to it.

"Alexandre."

He halted, with a kind of tender shock. It was the first time in a decade that either of his brothers had used his real name. Looking at the bleak profile beside him, he saw that Jean was unaware of having spoken; the plea for him to stay had come from a region beyond words. So he stood his ground and watched her approach. Jean must have already decided—with this woman, it was to be nothing.

Her men stayed on the dock and she came up to them alone. The bonnet and cape hung loosely from one hand as though she were about to take a stroll in some woodland glade. But her face displayed frigid politeness, and underneath it was an emotion that struck Dominique as contained horror. She did not look at the slaves and buyers crowded under the nearby trees.

She stopped in front of them and produced the merest sketch of a curtsy. There was a shudder in the smooth skin of her throat, above the breastbone, as though she was trying to force herself to speak.

Jean nodded, but did not bow or inject any courtesy into his first words. "What are you doing here?"

"A fine greeting to civilized company. I am sure that Monsieur You, who has enjoyed the hospitality of my house and eaten at my table, can come up with a better."

"Mademoiselle." Dominique bowed. "We are honored, of course. How may we serve you?"

"I am looking for someone. Two people, in fact."

Jean said at once, "Santo? He's not here."

She flinched slightly. "Where have you sent him, then?"

The response was level and, to Dominique's surprise, exact. "Treasure hunting."

"Really?" She was talking in small rushes, her brain otherwise engaged. "Where?" Then he could see her think of San Stefan, and the sea-colored eyes snapped open in alarm.

Dominique said roughly, before Jean could torment her more, "The Shoals of Heniagoe."

The relief was so great she laughed and turned her smile on Jean with a trace of bravado. "So he talked you into that, did he? I'm sure he omitted to tell you who navigated the last time he was there. It certainly wasn't Andrea Santo."

Dominique cursed under his breath and muttered to the side of his brother's face, "Then he'll never find it in a month of Sundays."

Jean said nothing, but held her eye. It was as though she read his next thought, and it made her catch her breath.

"Oh no, not Dani and Amirou. He's taken them with him?"

Dominique's "No" was overridden by Jean's cold, "And who might they be?"

Dominique looked at him in surprise, and she sneered. "Of course I can't expect you to have the slightest idea. Your former slaves, the ones who chose to stay with us on San Stefan. They left lately with Santo, and he's rewarded them by selling them into slavery again, or so I hear. I've come looking for them. Would you care to give me a tour of your merchandise?" Her horror showed again as she pronounced the word.

"No I would not." It came out as though from unendurable pressure, with such intensity she took a small step back. There was a quiver along Jean's temple that Dominique mistook for a second as anger. Then the voice came back under control. "It is too hot to keep you standing in the sun. Pray come into the shade, madame."

As they walked up the slight incline to the nearest tree, Dominique thought seriously of wandering off and leaving them alone. The tension in the air came from great turbulent volumes of the unspoken, which would remain so if he stayed around. But Jean gave him a look that ruled out escape. So he extracted his short clay pipe from his pocket, excused himself to the lady and walked away a little to smoke and watch the activity on the water, within hearing distance meanwhile of everything they said.

She had more courage than Jean. Within seconds there was a quick intake of breath, then, "I've genuinely come about the slaves. I could not be sure of meeting you. But I determined that if I did I would say something."

Silence. Dominique had no need to turn to see the uninviting smile.

"Last time we . . . I once accused you . . . That is, you inferred an accusation on my part. I have since discovered I was wrong. I apologize."

"That's quite unnecessary. I just added it to the list."

"So you do not accept my apology for it."

"While the catalog remains so long? But I am not implacable. If you wish, you may receive absolution for the lot in one fell swoop, this instant."

"By saying what?"

"By leaving. Now."

A pause. The voice quivered when she said, "Not until I have what I came for. Are Dani and Amirou here?"

"What on earth do you want with them?"

"I want them back on San Stefan. They chose to be with me, and that choice was snatched away from them. They deserve another."

"And what if they decide not to go with you?"

"Decide? Don't you try that with me! You stand surrounded by the most miserable creatures on earth, whom you drag here to be inspected like animals. Dani and Amirou's lives were ruined by bastards like you. Are you going to tell me where they are, or do I have to walk right through this place of torture to find out?"

"Madame, I did not capture these people from their villages in Africa or whip them to the coast in chains. I did not purchase them from the Arabs and then keep them in dungeons until the ship arrived. I did not cram them belowdecks and bring them through hell to be worked to death in Cuba. Save your contempt for the Spaniards I rescued them from."

Dominique blew out a long thread of smoke and watched it dissolve in the warm, still air. Jean never explained.

"I'm not going to debate that with you."

"Why not? You're afraid to have some of your cherished notions overturned by reality?"

"No, I'm afraid of you." Her voice broke off abruptly, and Dominique could feel her consternation as she resumed. "That is, afraid of what you are."

"How *can* you be?" The passionate reproach silenced her. After a moment he continued. "It is you, you make this unbearable, not me. What can I do?"

The pause was so long this time that it was impossible for Dominique—exasperated, full of apprehension—not to turn. They were not touching but gazing at each other, oblivious of everything else. Dominique could not see much of Jean's face. Hers, upturned towards him, quivered with tension and she was biting her lip.

"You can sell me Dani and Amirou."

"You came to buy them?"

"My money is perfectly good enough for you." There was no color in her cheeks, but the scorn was creeping back into her voice.

"How could you imagine this? You may have the little beggars. You persist in casting me as your enemy. Test me then. Tell me what you want—it is yours."

She stared at him, the jewellike eyes wide in shock. "I cannot just ask you for them. Because . . . there is no equivalent I can give you in return."

"Would you bargain with love?"

She swayed backwards, put out a hand blindly to the tree trunk. Then she cast one bewildered glance around her at the whole pullulating mercantile mass of the Temple, seeing nothing until her eyes locked again with her interrogator. "This is *love*?"

Dominique could not see Jean's expression, so he was unable to tell whether he took the change on her face for revulsion. But he replied with instant mockery, "You'd like a public demonstration?"

With a quick movement she broke the gaze, pushed herself from the tree and took three paces past him. She turned, standing still under the shade, her eyes like blue sparks. "I should like you to tell me where they are."

"It seems little to ask, in all conscience." Dominique

now received the benefit of the hard, ironical gaze. "Monsieur You, can you give us their whereabouts?"

Baffled, annoyed, Dominique recited at once what they both knew. "Barataria. On Grande Terre."

"Thank you." Only Dominique saw the tension with which Jean turned to her again. "You are welcome to them, free of charge. I shall give orders that you are to be received at any time. Simply moor out of range off Grande Terre, dip your colors and you'll be given a signal to send a boat ashore for them."

For an odd moment, standing alone on the dappled shells in the shadow of the vast tree, with the shimmering bayou behind her, she looked like a wistful girl in a painting. Then the picture fragmented: the figures on the jetty moved as her men realized she was about to depart, and she looked down, folded the cape more neatly over her forearm. The curtsy and the quiet "Thank you," were directed to both men.

When she turned away Jean did also, striding off so abruptly that Dominique had to hurry to catch up. Jean ignored him and everyone else, his face closed, his gaze fixed as though on some distant and inevitable disaster.

They reached the tally tent. Finding it empty, Dominique could not repress the explosion any longer. "Bloody hell. You could have told her. You never paid a peso for those two—they joined us like rats off a rotting ship."

"So she'll find out. If she comes." He stopped short in the middle of the tent, looking around as though he had forgotten where he was.

"I wouldn't count on it."

Jean looked at him, dazed, then said, "Can you manage the rest of the afternoon?"

"I suppose. Why?"

"I've got to get back." He said to one of the clerks who was running back in, "Curtis. Now."

"Why?" said Dominique, trying to banish the twist in his gut.

"So I can tell those two little bastards that I paid for them."

CHAPTER FOURTEEN

Sheba

Dusk lasted just long enough for the cutter to draw near the passage into Lake Barataria and for the Roncival colors to be readable by watchers onshore as Léonore had them hoisted to half-mast. From amongst the houses and low trees on the island called Grande Terre, a man emerged with a lighted lantern. He stumped down to the beach with it, swung it from side to side in front of him in three lazy arcs, then put it down on the sand. Léonore ordered the colors struck in reply and, as the boat was lowered, the lantern bearer walked back up the beach again and disappeared.

The last light faded out of the sky as the boat pulled for shore. A cool breeze blew towards the island, where lanterns and lamps were being lit one by one in the huts amongst the clustered palm trees. Her sailors behind her in the cutter, looking landward as the color sank from the sky and was rekindled in the warm rooms of Barataria homes, would feel melancholy for a moment, as bereft as outcast men doomed to ride the ocean forever. She was glad she had ordered an especially hearty meal to keep them occupied during the wait. Then she forgot them.

They were met by Curtis and four men, who materialized out of the bushes as soon as her boat touched the bank of shells, exposed at low tide, that bordered the slope of the beach. Her own men, in whose faces she had

seen a covert longing for land as they rowed in, considered Curtis and company warily as they helped her to
step dry footed ashore. They remembered Curtis, and
their thirst for conviviality died the moment they met
his oily, sidelong look. When she asked them to return
to the cutter and await her signal, they were not unwilling to go. At sea, when the *Fantôme* communicated with
the *Mélusine,* there had been talk, drink, cards and dic-
ing that still provided anecdotes to while away nights on
San Stefan. But this encounter, on the fringe of Laffite's
stronghold, set up warnings they were not inclined to
ignore. Suddenly, the prospect of wandering around
Grande Terre with the maître did not seem tempting. If
she was of a mind to go it alone, so be it.

Curtis bowed and greeted her, as surly as she remembered. After dismissing her men she pulled the velveteen
cloak across her traveling dress and lifted the hood, then
stood waiting in silence.

He had not used her name. He turned, saying, "Would
you kindly follow me this way, mademoiselle?"

The crunch of shells under her feet reminded her of
the Temple. This was another piece of madness, struggling up the beach behind the man who had once nearly
cost her San Stefan, and whom she had deprived of two
fingers and an incalculable treasure. Yet she pushed on,
letting the tall, dark-clad form walk in front of her, and
followed by the others, none of whom she could recall
from previous encounters.

She could have asked for Dani and Amirou to be
brought down to the beach and then left at once. Laffite
had told her she could have them, which meant there was
no need to see him at all. But she followed Curtis without
a word, driven by an impulse too deep for thought.

He was leading her down paths that wound through
the scrub, skirting the houses and the sandy lanes where
a few children still played by the light of lamps that
shone through uncurtained windows or across narrow
timbered verandahs. So far she was being allowed to
remain anonymous. Possibly the people of Grande Terre
were never to be told of her visit. Curtis was the perfect
escort, for he would scarcely relish admitting that he had

been the one chosen to welcome her ashore. Perhaps she should give credit to Laffite for such discretion. Perhaps she should give up trying to think.

For this meeting, she was leaving all considerations about San Stefan, strategy or commerce behind her. She was coming to Laffite as a woman to a man. Whether he would understand that or not remained to be seen.

She walked behind Curtis through a grove of skeletal trees hung with Spanish moss. A spongy bed of leaves gave gently beneath her feet, and the smell of damp earth rose into the air with the rustle of her passing. She glanced up through the bare branches and found stars hung amongst the soft clouds of moss. And suddenly, on a breath, the night opened around her like a secret garden, into whose paths and pavilions she was stepping free and unprepared.

They came out of the trees. There was a promontory ahead, occupied by a single house, neither large nor new, with a tiled roof and a verandah on all sides. From a slight rise it commanded a view of the Mexican Gulf, in which her cutter twinkled like a firefly.

The curtained windows of the house glowed crimson. There was no fence around the bare ground. No gateposts, no sentry.

When they reached the verandah, Curtis's boots on the boards sounded like blows on a taut drum. He knocked twice on the door and waited, intent, without looking back at her. The sound from within must have been very low and brief, for though she was not far from the threshold she did not hear it. Curtis, bowing, opened the latch and motioned for her to step onto the verandah and through the door.

A white-plastered hallway with a polished wood floor. Closed doors on each side with candles in sconces above them. Ahead, heavy curtains encrusted with beads under a painted timber arch. The instant the front door shut behind her the curtains were thrust back with a sound like shells swept by a wave, and Jean Laffite stood with his arms across the entrance to the well-lit room beyond, a tall black cross on a golden ground.

They looked, without barriers. She felt his gaze on her

like a firm, smooth caress. Her eyes spoke to his in a language she had never learned, yet which came to her as easily as breathing, so that it vibrated soundlessly in the narrow capsule of air between them.

She stepped forward and his arms fell. The curtains swung inward with a grating sigh and he turned side on and held out a hand, palm down, for her to slip her fingers into.

He led her through to the inner room, his hand clenched hard at first and then holding hers with a less painful clasp that sent warmth coursing up her arm, seething into her chest and throat.

She stopped and looked at his face with the same concentration that she had devoted to it during the intense moment on the *Mélusine,* but this time the deep, black-lashed eyes were open on hers and there was no mirror frame about the head, just a gilded haze shimmering on the rim of her vision.

A smile widened his dark pupils, radiated to the fine skin around the eyelids, extended smoothly up over the tanned forehead.

She raised her free hand and placed her thumb across the gap between the black eyebrows. He let her complete the gesture as her thumb traveled over the brow and her fingers slid into and tangled with the thick, wavy hair.

The smile reached his mouth.

She said, "You have no frown lines."

"They are drawn on my liver instead."

"I call that unfair."

"So do I."

She took her other hand from his and put it to his temple so that she held his face between her palms. Then her fingers drifted down his cheeks and neck onto his shoulders. "And this is my welcome. I have a scramble through thornbushes to your closed door with the least agreeable animal in the universe, and you can produce not a rug to my foot nor a douce syllable to your greeting."

"Forgive me." His arms slid around her waist, under the cloak. The kiss, containing not a vestige of apology, riveted her lips to his. He did not claim her body—his hands on her back communicated a tense, deliberate restraint—but the kiss took her across a hot threshold that she had been seeking since their very first cataclysmic embrace.

It was she who broke it, releasing his mouth and resting her forehead against his shirtfront. His warm hands left her back, and she felt his fingers at the clasp of her cloak, over her breasts. He pushed back the hood, allowed the cloak to slide off her shoulders to the floor.

He crooked his fingers around the nape of her neck, bent his head so that one temple rested against hers. The whisper penetrated her like a shaft of keen air. "I have never allowed myself to believe that you would set foot here. If I had predicted, you could have come like the Queen of Sheba."

She drew back, interrogating his eyes. "And what, apart from my black ancestry, makes you liken me to her?" She held her breath.

The innocent smile reappeared. "Your fabulous beauty. Your even more fabulous wealth."

"And how do you resemble Solomon?"

"I specialize in cutting babies in half." As she pulled predictably away his hand tightened on her neck. "Dear God, let us act for one night as though we were alone on earth."

He understood. But she still said, "How can I?"

"Are you afraid? No need. Let me show you."

He stepped away, bent to sweep up the cloak and throw it on a chair, then took her hand again. The room they were in occupied the whole front of the house, and the French doors on the seaward side were unlatched. He pushed them open with one hand and with the other arm around her waist drew her onto the wide verandah.

"Behind us are a few hundred rogues well housed and dubiously occupied who would rather be filleted and roasted in hell than come within my purview tonight. There are no attendants here: queen that you are, you never had such a servant as I shall be. Before us is the Gulf. Tell me now if you see anything that threatens you."

For a moment she could see nothing at all beyond the

edge of the verandah. The light from the room, spilling out across the worn boards, capturing moths and smaller night insects as though in a fine net, made the world outside appear dark as a cave undersea. He guided her to the rim of the light and stood with his arms crossed over her midriff, trapping both hands in his.

His breath stirred the hair on the top of her head. "Tell me what you hear, then."

Waves brushing across shells as the tide turned. The whispering breeze through trees farther down the slope in what must have once been a garden, for the scents that eddied up towards them were those of fig trees and lavender. Far to the right where the long island stretched out into the darkness, a dog barked, answered immediately by another. A man's distant voice, raised in admonishment, trailed off into a laugh. Along the path to the beach where she had landed, beyond the moss-smothered grove, there was the faint sound of someone whistling.

She swayed back, leaned her head on his chest, opened her eyes wider. The dark swathe of ocean drifted into view, bordered in front by an apron of bare earth, a black fringe of low trees. Her limbs relaxed. Her legs felt as though if he moved away she would fall. He did not: the grip became more possessive. Abandoned against him, she imagined his hands rising to her breasts. On an intake of breath, she shivered.

"Come inside. And we can forget it all."

There was the touch of a hand under one elbow as he led her through the doorway again. Then she stood in the center of the room watching as he pulled shutters across, fastened the French doors, drew the curtains. She snatched a glance around the room. It was spacious, neat, well furnished. There were in fact rugs to her feet, should she want them, two comfortable sofas, a long, polished board like a refectory table laid at the far end for two.

He remained by the doors, the fingers of one hand twisted into the curtain. "You'll stay?" Before she could answer he went on. "I'll have Dani and Amirou brought to you before dawn and you can sail at first light. I promise. Or take them now. As you wish." A pause, during which his hand released the curtain and returned to his side. The easy, assured stance was as she always saw it in her dreams, but the eyes were different, vulnerable.

She did not need to tell him the two lads had very little to do with why she was there. She did not need to ask for any further signal to be sent to the cutter, which was ordered to wait indefinitely at sea. She needed only to take three steps into this man's arms.

He said, "You'll have a meal, at least?"

She could not possibly eat. She shook her head.

"A glass of wine?"

"Thank you."

He went to the buffet near the table, where beverages were set much as they had been on the *Mélusine*. There was no mirror above them here to show her the expression on his face, but she had seen it already and knew it to be the image of her own, despite the high contrast of her fairness and his Gypsy looks. The strongly drawn contours of his brows, his straight nose and firm jaw remained delineated by magic, for beneath them it was as though the bones were softening, being worked into another shape by an overwhelming force. A wordless force that sapped every attempt at conversation, made a mockery of every polite gesture.

She approached softly from behind him and he stilled, an outstretched hand on the neck of a decanter. She put one hand on his shoulder and ran the other down his arm, over the narrow black sleeve, the brief margin of white silk. His fingers opened and hers slid over the back of his hand to divide and capture them. Their hands tightened in a confused sensation of heat and cold—the warmth of their skin, the cool, hard glass under their fingertips.

She said, "No, after all."

"No to the wine?" He did not move.

"Yes."

He gave a quick laugh, then turned and caught her to him so strongly that all breath and thought disappeared on an annihilating wave and she was flung against him, one hand tangled in his hair, the other clutching his coat. He lifted her off her feet so that she hung upon him as though on a rock in raging surf, and her lips parted and drove down on his with a sound like a drowning cry for help. He let her slide down the length of his body so that she felt all of him—sure, safe, compelling. And meanwhile the kiss sang in her head, sent another message to her throat and breast, promising not smooth seas but the violence of a coming storm.

His arms around her waist, holding her curved into him, he kissed her cheek, her ear, her neck.

She tightened her arms around his head. "All year."

His voice was muffled, pent up. "It's not a year. Not until carnival time."

"You shouldn't have left me!"

"Then you shouldn't have come." He pulled free enough to put a hand to her forehead, push back a strand of hair that was drifting across her eyes. "For I tell you, Lionheart, tonight you go nowhere."

She sought his mouth, and with eyes open she witnessed the room dissolve around her, until there was only the gold and black of his face and hair, then a bright haze under her eyelids. Her hands were flat against his chest, creating an inch of space between them bridged only by their lips.

She could hardly stand. She managed to disengage herself from the kiss, to sway back a crucial fraction and brace herself once more.

It was her last chance to accept where she stood and what she was choosing, before the breaker curled and tumbled and swept her under.

"Have there been—?" She halted, called on her dignity. "I don't want . . . confessions. I just want to know. When I leave—how soon before another woman is here with you?"

His eyes blazed. "Never. As far as I am concerned, there have never been any women on this island." His arms gripped her painfully. "Until tonight." Then he smiled. "Come with me, and you will see a bedchamber as bare as Stylite's pillar. Find me a trace of the female in it, locate but a hairpin between the floorboards, and I'll give you the whole tribe of Grande Terre to command, blackguards, women and whimpering brats included."

She submitted to the hand that placed itself in the

small of her back, steered her towards the beaded curtains. Her voice quivered. "Two hairpins give me the *Mélusine,* and leave to toss Monsieur Curtis from the crow's nest into the Gulf."

The curtains parted and they stepped through one of the doors. He laid his hand on the latch, but she looked over her shoulder. "Whose is that room?"

The smile reappeared. "Jealous. Thanks and praise be, she is jealous." Then, catching her expression, he took both her hands and held her palms on his temples so that they framed the coruscating eyes. "Look. Do you realize what this means to me?"

"How can I? Tell me."

"Life and death, madame." After a long moment he released her, turned and thrust open the door. "Life and death."

It was a wild, sweet journey, and she noticed neither the room around them nor the bed they voyaged in, though there was a candle close beside it, by the light of which he had undressed her and then himself, before he beckoned her onto the billowing white sheets.

For a long time there was no speech, the discoveries provoking wordless sounds that fluttered in her throat as though she were finding a new way to breathe.

His hands explored for the first time in all the places where she had longed to feel them, and then returned, reclaimed, found untaught pleasures. She could not hold back; she had no reason to hold back, especially when her own joyful ardor caused in him pulses of surprise she had never expected to provoke.

His hands cupping her breasts, his mouth poised between them, he whispered, "Say my name."

Her arms slipped under his, hooked him closer. "Your first name?"

"Yes."

"Is it your real one, though?" She slithered under him, slid her hands lower, testing him.

He shifted, placed his hands below her waist and raised his head, with a laugh that was like a groan. "Say it."

She enlaced him with her legs, felt again the jolt of his surprise, then the reaction coursed through her so strongly it came out on a sigh. "Jean."

For a moment she thought he was about to accomplish what she thirsted for, but he simply lay against her and began caressing her again, accompanying the slow, tantalizing glide of skin against skin with whispers of reassurance, of protection.

Her head pressed back, eyes closed, she said on a faltering breath, "Do you chatter on like this with other women?"

He stilled in her arms. "Don't ask such questions unless you want true answers."

"The truth, if you please." She clenched her teeth.

"Very well. With other women I am as silent as the deep."

His tongue, his mouth, encircled one nipple. Quivering, she managed, "Why this delightful loquacity with me?"

He moved so that he was poised over her, his gaze sweeping her body and returning to her eyes. "Because you are the reef. On which the wave must break."

She closed her eyes as he allowed his weight to descend upon her with slow care. His elbows framed her shoulders and his whisper stirred her hair. "When you are with men, do you speak?"

She gave a quick sound of protest, but he held her still, his fingers wrapped about the crown of her head. He had ceased to breathe.

"Yes."

His grip tightened. "And what do you say?"

"Only their names."

He let out his breath between his teeth. His fingers slackened and his forehead dropped to the pillow beside her. "Tell me. I want to hear them all."

Her hands, bolder than before, ventured between them, sowing havoc, but she prolonged the pause until exquisite impatience began to undo them both. Her eyes sought his, then opened to the depths. "All the men with whom I have ever lain, all the men I have ever touched and held like this, are called Jean."

The black eyes sparked. "Léonore." He moved, and

brought her inexorably to the knowledge of pain, the promise of ecstasy.

There was no sleep, though in the morning she lay curled with her back against him and her head in the crook of his arm, almost dozing. Birds had begun to wake, but she ignored their voices, concentrating instead on the soothing, regular sound of waves on the beach below.

Gray light seeped in, through a gap in the curtains at the high window, across the floor of the corridor, which she could see through the open door. The candle had long burned down and, being of fine wax, had disappeared in its own incandescence, leaving an empty silver candlestick. Beside it was a tray with the remains of the fruit and wine he had brought her during the dark hours when they decided, laughing, that enough meals had been missed to warrant brief attention.

Pale, bare walls. A walnut desk in the far corner and two high-backed chairs. The bed: wide, lofty, with a rampart at the foot and a giant scroll of wood rising behind the bolsters, Empire style.

The sheets, by turn rumpled, damp, twisted into fantastic seascapes, now covered them both to the waist. Her hair, flung across her shoulder and over her breasts, tickled her chin, and she moved a hand languidly to draw it down.

The hand was caught and carried to his lips, and he kissed her palm. She turned irresistibly and aroused again the already familiar, the astonishingly unexpected, in his response.

Afterwards he turned her so that they lay as before, and raised the drift of hair from her neck. Quiescent, she sank farther into the bed, her face half-buried in the pillow.

With one finger he followed the delicate tracery of the hummingbird tattooed between her shoulder blades. "When was this done?"

"When I was a child. Do you like it?"

"A beautiful image. Painfully accurate. How could you bear it?"

She twisted, catching his arm under her shoulders. "You are shocked."

One eye closed in a slow wink; the other smiled. "By you? Forever, I imagine."

She examined his face. Shadows of the endless night around his eyes. Tousled hair falling over one ear, the tip of a loose curl just touching his cheek where stubble extended down to the blue line of the jaw. The mouth, full and tender now with kissing, but often, in repose, as severe as that of a Greek statue.

Outside, the birdsong ceased abruptly. After a pause, during which she read in his eyes a dread that matched hers, human voices began, far off, to raise a busy murmur. Almost break of day.

The hollow that yawned under her ribs was so disastrous she cast herself forward and clasped him fiercely, her mouth crushed to his breastbone. She took a deep breath, drinking in the smell and taste of him, then pulled back, slipping from his arms to sit up and clench the sheet around her waist.

By the time their eyes met again she could tell that he too was trying already to teach his muscles, his nerves and skin to navigate out of the mighty surge that had swept them against each other all night.

Her throat ached as she spoke. "What will you do today?"

"Have the lads fetched. And Curtis to see you off. Prepare to depart myself."

"Where do you go?"

"Wherever trade takes me." He caught the change in her eyes and reached out to put a hand on her knee. The warmth stole into her through the sheet. "You really want to know? North regularly up to Natchez, along the coast as far as Pensacola one way and Bayou Teche on the other."

"Where were you going to take Dani and Amirou?"

"Nowhere. They want to go and join the militia in New Orleans, the Free Men of Color. I've told them they'll have the roughest of coats to their backs and barely a centime in their pockets, but they have dreams of martial splendor."

"Free?"

"Indeed. They came cheap to Grande Terre. A month in the company of Santo was enough for them to plumb the inch and a half of his fine strategic intellect. They did not even give the Bahamian venture a second's consideration."

Through the thrill of astonishment, she registered a nuance. "You don't expect that voyage to succeed."

"No." He took his hand away, sat up against the bolsters, one arm along the polished wood at his back. She took a last look at the finely muscled, straight shoulders, the hard chest on which the marks made by her teeth in their first encounter had left only the faintest white lines, like the traces of a minuscule sea insect on a scallop shell.

"Why send him, then?"

"An object lesson. I have a great covey of Italians in Barataria, some of whom share Andrea Santo's endearing characteristics."

"Damn Santo."

"Santo be damned." The free hand lunged, captured hers. "Where do you go?"

"Home, for the present. I cannot neglect my enterprise any more than you can."

"Then we must settle when next we meet. On the last day of carnival there is a ball at the Sellières ballroom. I have already promised an old friend, General Humbert, that I will go. Undisguised. Tell me you'll come. You must be masked, for safety. And in turn I promise a rendezvous afterwards that Sheba herself would not have scorned."

Her fingers were burning. "We'll see." She took them away. But remained poised within inches of him, coy to the waist in the ruined sheet, brazen above within the cage of her hair. When she took a breath, it was like inhaling smoke. "You said I could ask you anything."

"*For* anything." But there were as yet insufficient barriers in his eyes.

"I am asking you, then. If there is anyone else."

A squaring of the shoulders along the dark line of the bedhead, a daggerlike response. "No."

She drew back, to the very edge of the mattress. Around her on the floor was the chaos of their clothes, and beyond them the uncluttered path she must soon take to his front door. "Swear to me."

He did not quite realize. He was still able to smile. "On what? The Holy Book is not ready to hand."

Desolation threatened, but her voice did not falter. "On your mother's head."

His lip curled. "I should prefer my father's. If I knew him." Then as she slid sideways, one foot on the floor to take her out of reach, he moved suddenly, knelt to take her face between his hands. "This is solemn."

"Yes."

"Ask."

"Swear to me, then, on the heads of your unborn children."

He caught her in an embrace that twisted and hurt her neck and shoulders and the whole upper part of her body, but in that raw moment his voice tolled like the purest bell. "There is no one but you, as God is my witness, and on the heads of my children."

Her cheeks flooded, and she tore herself from him and with the same movement yanked a great swathe of the sheet from the bed, to stand festooned like a carnival figure with the soft cotton folds pressed to her eyes.

After a moment, she looked around for her buried garments.

He rose from the side of the bed, pulled her slowly to him so that she rested, blind, with her forehead against his throat. He whispered, "You break my heart. Every time. How long does this go on?"

"That's what I came to find out."

CHAPTER FIFTEEN

~⚬~

Masque

Dani and Amirou sailed to San Stefan with Léonore. They still wanted to join the Free Men of Color in New Orleans, but they were prepared to wait until she went there herself. Meanwhile, they had decided to confer with Mirliton on San Stefan; it was in fact the old man's martial recollections that had given them a taste for the militia in the first place.

Since she had the lads onboard, she took the cutter to the Shoals of Heniagoe on the way and anchored over the wreck of the *Barbadoes*. They did not encounter Santo or any other rivals and had one successful dive before the conditions became impossible. It cheered the crew, and provided a slender excuse for the return voyage to New Orleans in a few weeks' time.

To avoid observant eyes she chose to do the cooking most days, letting the usual cook amuse himself fishing. This pleased no one, except at meal times. They met no likely prey on the way home, for which she was thankful. Every fiber of her body turned her away from action into a thrilling, dreamlike state. She could stand at the chopping block doing nothing for half an hour at a stretch, reliving sensations that were more real than the heat of the iron stove or the scarred wood under her fingers. No one could fail to notice.

Sometimes she overheard the seamen talking. One day, after a long, contemplative silence, one said, "Do you think she's pregnant, maybe?" Stunned, she held her breath, but the only answer was a snort.

She could not be pregnant. She had learned in one night with Jean so much about lovemaking that she already regretted the need for his withdrawal, and was ready to seek out Adélaïde's recommended healer in Sainte-Marie, to discover what precautions a woman could take. She planned the visit without a flicker of shame—then blushed in secret, because she did not blush before the world.

There were moments when he seemed to be physically beside her, his warm lips on her face, his intense whisper in her ear, and each time she released her pent-up breath on a sigh.

There was no one to talk to; there never had been. Anyway, she wanted no dialogue but his. Her venture into his territory had been as unprepared as his invasion of San Stefan, and as fraught with danger, but she dreamed that somehow they had twisted a cord between them that would hold, no matter what distance or destiny dealt to them both.

He had refused to let her go unless she promised to be at the ball before Lent. In return he had answered all her questions about his life in Barataria. He led her into the mysterious other room and she found it crammed with trunks of books and clothes. He was having another house built in front of the old cottage—two-storied, with a terrace, "well fortified, like another place I know." The possessive kiss that followed these words threw them together in equal violence, equal dread.

When Jean Laffite walked into the Sellières ballroom it was packed with a noisy, turbulent crowd already infiltrated, on this last hectic night of carnival, with pleasure seekers whose ambition it was to enter the next bleak month deliciously prone, under the influence of neat spirits and a hot, sprawling body encountered on the dance floor. There were, of course, other classes of revelers present, but few of the well-bred kind who had graced the ball at the French Exchange the year before. The room was equipped with a splendid bar that ex-

tended from the edge of the floor down a mirrored wall
to double doors leading onto a side street, through which
only men entered and left. Jean, arriving at ten o'clock
with General Humbert, steered his friend to a spot near
the dancers and leaned his elbows on the bar to examine
the room. She was not here. He was glad: he owed it to
her to be early.

The general, according to their tradition, bought the
first drink. *"Salut."*

Jean savored the white rum's penetrating scent; then
both men emptied the small, narrow glasses. With the
fumes filling his head he turned his back on the crowd
to order the next, and anticipation shivered up his spine.
She was unlikely to step unaccompanied through the
main doors, far down the opposite end of the ballroom.
When in New Orleans she claimed—and got—the honors due to a lady of society. She would arrive in the
midst of some elegant group. She had said it would not
be the governor's, thank God: Claiborne and his wife
would consider the Sellières far too raffish. Then she
would let him know how she could be extricated.

Off the edge of the floor, a few yards away, was a
paneled doorway through which four gentlemen issued
into the room, laughing. He put one hand flat on the
bar. "That room, there."

"A cardroom, monsieur. You're looking for a game?"

"Keep it free."

"I'm not sure we can do that, monsieur."

He lifted his hand to expose the banknote underneath
it. "Keep it free."

He turned to give the general his glass, and when he
glanced over again he saw that the door to the little
room was shut and a black, liveried attendant stood im-
passively beside it.

He had not wanted the general to hear the exchange,
but after a few minutes his friend looked sidelong, winked
and said loudly, "Impatience! It's a handy spot, but is it
comfortable? How are you going to take her, against the
wall or on the table?"

Jean looked at him in disbelief and caught beyond the
general's gray head a raking glance from a bystander.

He ground his teeth: he should have noticed how much damage the general was doing with the wine at dinner. This kind of asinine vulgarity made its rare appearance only a few times in the year, when the general had to be prised from Thiot's Café and carried, waving and shouting, through the back streets to his quarters behind the Hôtel de la Marine.

He could find no reply that would not be an insulting rebuke. He simply shifted to the general's other side, edging him farther along the bar and screening him from the men behind. Most of them were young, nattily dressed, passably drunk. Subdued by the lack of response, the general devoted himself to admiring the women, bowing graciously to some and being favored with an occasional nod.

Jean watched the passing whirl of skirts, silk hose and dancing pumps and saw instead the rooms he had had expensively prepared upstairs in the narrow dwelling two streets away. He hated inns, so he had hired a house. For a week. His heart beat strongly as he reminded himself: don't tell her. If she granted him only a night, she would never know with what foolish care he had arranged this encounter.

His eyes on the doorway, he reflected wryly that earlier on he had considered allowing the general to address a few words to her. Jean Robert Marie Humbert, venerable repository of a glorious past: major general in France's revolutionary armies, brilliantly victorious in the Vendée, wounded at the Danube in 1799. After which he had been given a third of the French forces in Santo Domingo and led them right into the teeth of Toussaint L'Ouverture's slave revolt. Where Dominique, fighting under Humbert and alongside their uncle Beluche, had gained his magic touch with artillery, before the French crumbled and Humbert consoled himself by going back to France and taking a mistress, Pauline Bonaparte. Whom he had left, mercifully, somewhere in Brittany after his definitive rupture with Napoleon and before his flight to New Orleans.

Jean smiled and laid a hand on the other's shoulder. Despite his talent for indiscretion of every kind, he was a mentor, under whom more than one Laffite had served. It could be said that General Humbert was really all they had by way of family credentials. Nonetheless, he was not going to let him address her tonight.

Eléonore de Rochambeau, pupil of the Ursulines. Her claim of nobility, her carefully maintained friendship with Sophronie Claiborne were touching, spectacular, doomed—though he need do nothing himself to destroy them. He had battled an almost intolerable ache of impatience today, to prevent himself from interrupting her movements about town. He knew that her phantom ship with its indigo sails had glided up the river yesterday to moor at the docks, but he did not know what Léonore's business might be, nor even where she had lodged on her first night. He knew where he wanted her, however, for the second.

The general began to comment on the ladies ranged on the other side of the room while Jean pretended to listen, seeing her face instead, at the moment when she made him swear there was no one else. Thereafter, all that had reconciled him to her leaving Barataria was the urgency of writing to Mathilde. Which he did the instant Léonore sailed.

Usually he enjoyed composing letters, but this one was so problematical it had taken all day. He had based the proposed rupture on reasons of policy—the delicate situation with regard to the husband, the señor's noble loyalty to Spain—but the truth shrieked through every line. He calculated that Mathilde, if she considered herself about to be supplanted, would fly like a fury in the other direction. He would have her eternal enmity, but he need never confront her again. The only thing he regretted was that he had completely failed to discover what she was up to with regard to San Stefan.

"By Jove, have you seen that dark-haired Venus near the doors?" Jean looked over as the general continued. "Only one word to describe what she's wearing, eh?"

Catching sight of a fine form beneath almost transparent muslin, Jean said, "Diaphanous."

"Diaphanous? A wisp!" Despite trouble with his consonants, the general was more than audible.

Jean said in a lower tone, "I grant you, she does make herself something of a target."

The general laughed. "Nipples at fifty paces!"

A loud, arrogant voice behind them said instantly in English, "The gentlewoman to whom you refer is a friend of mine."

Jean turned without haste. One of the young fellows. He said evenly, "Not a relative? My felicitations."

The others laughed, and the challenger's face turned red. Amongst them, however, was a newcomer, taller and older than the others, who said gravely, "She is a cousin of *mine*, sir."

Cursing inwardly, Jean assessed the rancor in the man's glance, then noticed that beyond him again stood Edward Livingston. He nodded to the lawyer and received a level, cautionary look in reply, then examined the other man again. Well dressed, with an intelligent air and no hint of the braggart—but he would not stand for any insolence in front of the youngsters.

Jean put a warning hand on the general's arm. "My friend's eyesight is not what it was in his military days. Any offense was unintentional, sir. Pray excuse us."

The general took his arm abruptly away, and one of the younger men voiced the same surprise. "I never heard such a havey-cavey reply! Are we satisfied with that, by thunder?"

The older man, to whom this was directed, looked quickly from Jean to Livingston, who was walking round the group to the general's side, with repressive intentions. The man was irritated at being put on the spot, but not ready to back down. "I should prefer a specific apology for the language, gentlemen."

Jean looked over towards the doors in a vain hope that the bold young lady in question might have disappeared. Instead he was riveted by the sight of Sophronie Claiborne sweeping in with a large group. Amongst whom, in a splendid red-and-gold gown and the black mask flashing with brilliants that she had worn at the French Exchange ball last year, was Mathilde de Oleron y Siqueiros.

"Damnation."

He had said it aloud. The result was instantaneous. "Damn *you*, sir, if you think that's an acceptable reply!"

Jean's attention snapped into focus. The gentleman, his face rigid beneath the fashionably curled brown hair that fell over his brow, was gazing at him with an anger as genuine as the rising excitement of the young men around him. Without being ruffians exactly, they were of the kind whose favorite contest would involve fisti-cuffs, if not an outright brawl. Though not, one hoped, in a ballroom. The gentleman, on the other hand, dealt exclusively in affairs of honor. Cursing again, unheard this time, Jean decided on action before Mathilde could look across and spot him.

Stepping quickly to the gentleman's side, he said, "May I know your name, sir?"

"Raines."

"May I have a word with you in private, Mr. Raines?"

After the merest hesitation, Raines allowed himself to be ushered away from the bar, out of earshot of his belligerent friends, to a spot near the door of the card-room, where the flurry of dancers provided a screen.

Jean observed him closely, for he had recognized the name. Marcus Raines was a wealthy linen merchant and a member of the Legislature. Unlike the majority of Jean's complacent customers, he was a vocal supporter of Claiborne's pleas for an end to smuggling in the Terri-tory. He also had a taste for sport and the company of young men, and was a crack shot.

"And your name, sir?" The older man's voice and manner were unbending.

"Allow me to first give you my friend's. General Jean Robert Humbert, of whom you will have heard." Unfor-tunately, the general himself could be heard like a clar-ion at this point, expressing another loud opinion to the bar. Jean pressed on. "I'm sure you'll forgive an indis-cretion by a man who has both his age and a certain amount of liquor operating against him tonight."

"My quarrel is not with him, sir. I should be glad to be told your name." Then Jean saw the light of compre-hension rise very suddenly in the man's eyes. The gener-al's identity had just penetrated, along with a helpful recollection of his friends and associates. In addition, the gentleman's gaze had met the admonitory look that Edward Livingston managed to shoot through to him across the giddy movement of a waltz.

Smiling, Jean knew his own name was no longer needed. It was equally unnecessary to inform the gentleman that he had never been touched in a duel, by either sword or bullet. "I am not in the habit of apologizing on behalf of my friends, or for the company I keep. But I repeat that no offense was meant, and I should be glad to close the matter here and now."

He held out his hand. Raines hesitated another few seconds: he was no coward, but nor was he foolish enough to be provoked into a duel simply to impress his young companions. He gripped the proffered hand.

Watching Raines walk back to the bar, Jean gave a quick sigh. It was not over; he would have to extract the general, but he would not leave this place before Léonore arrived.

The waltz ended, and the couples began to disperse like colors gliding off to the edges of a giant prism. And he caught sight of a figure walking in a straight line through the drifting crowd. Her steps, graceful and with avid purpose, were bringing her in his direction. Mathilde. Erect, gloriously attired, with the black veil brushing her fine shoulders. As she drew nearer he could see that this time there was a mask underneath as well, velvet covered and concealing the brow, nose and cheeks. Beneath the brilliants, there was just a hint of her full mouth and a smooth scroll of golden hair behind the neck.

He walked forward and bowed. She half extended a hand, then slowly drew it back. He had sworn to himself not to touch her, and it chilled him to think the woman for whom he had made that silent pact might even now be entering the great doors across the ballroom. He looked and could see only Sophronie Claiborne gazing their way.

His voice, miraculously, was steady. "Madame."

She was very still. If he had not known with what

venomous anger she was now possessed, he would have
thought her thrown into uncertainty by the greeting.

He glanced swiftly towards the bar, where vehement
conversation was still going on. Livingston, however, appeared to have it under control. "We can't talk here."
He looked across the ballroom. The devil grant him
enough time. "A word in private." The music began
again. Another dance was about to form. With a sweeping bow he indicated the door to the cardroom a few
steps away. In the bustle, it was possible no one would
notice them retire.

The woman at his side glanced up at him as though
about to speak, then followed his gaze towards the bar,
where Livingston had at last managed to maneuver the
general away from the others. Without a word she glided
to the door and waited for him to open it. Under his
stare, the lackey took one step aside.

He was inches from her as he reached past her to turn
the latch. He inhaled her perfume, felt with a shock how
easy it would be to slip a hand over her bare skin under
the veil as she stepped through the door. The entry into
the room had the delicious timing, the sweet promise
that he had planned—except for the woman who turned
and considered him from behind the mask. Her beautiful
mouth was tremulous, her gloved hands were clasped
before her as though to contain her quivering body.

Despite everything, he almost felt sorry for her. With
his back against the door he reached out and stripped
off veil and mask.

Earlier in the day, Léonore had been taken by surprise while buying a carnival mask. Sophronie Claiborne
spied her from the front doorway of Feversham's and
walked in to accost her.

Once the greetings were over: "How long have you
been in town?"

"Since yesterday."

Sophronie was looking especially beautiful, in a cambric gown of forest green with scallops of gold around
the hem, a pelisse fastened up to the high neck with

tiny gilded buttons, and an elaborate turban. Two older women, who had entered with her and were examining ribbons farther down the counter, looked drab by comparison, despite their elegant gowns and expensive merino capes. Léonore gazed into the liquid eyes and saw a hint of disappointment that touched her.

Sophronie spoke kindly, however. "Do you stay long?"

"Probably not. Which is why I have not contacted any friends, as yet."

Sophronie gave a quick glance towards the other two women and lowered her voice a little. "Audubert and I are making a party to the French Exchange tonight: should you like to come?"

"I'm afraid I can't. I already have an engagement, at the Sellières."

Sophronie brightened. "We can take you on, after the Exchange. Much more amusing. Where do we fetch you?"

Léonore stared at her, nonplussed. She had mentioned the venue only to put Sophronie off. "But you do not frequent the Sellières, surely? I did not think your husband would approve of it."

"William is not coming," Sophronie said airily. "But Audubert is—so if we need any protection we are perfectly provided for. In fact, where you are concerned he could hardly ask for anything better!"

Léonore shook her head. "I must tell you, I am meeting a friend at the ball. I am unlikely to be leaving it with you. And it is the kind of meeting that . . . would put Audubert's nose completely out of joint. I should rather not take the risk of offending both of you in one night."

Sophronie's eyes sparkled with curiosity, but after a moment's thought she put a hand on Léonore's arm and said, "If your having secrets offended me, you would have seen the last of me long ago. I know there are things about you that you might once have confided to a friend, but you would prefer the governor's wife not to know. But will it hurt to concede me a little of your company tonight? Do come to the Exchange. Then we

shall take you to the Sellières and stay for just a single
dance. And to avoid awkwardness I promise not to invite Audubert. Will that serve?"

It was impossible, and probably unwise, to resist, so
Sophronie's carriage arrived at the docks to gather her
up at nine o'clock. Her friend was staggered to see a
gentlewoman dressed with such splendor emerge from a
trading vessel, and amused the company with specula-
tions about how Léonore managed onboard ship. No
amount of laughing correction could convince her that
the cargo hold was not at least half taken up with dressing room and boudoir.

They danced and ate supper at the Exchange. True to
her word, Sophronie did not let on to Audubert about
the later appointment and, when the party's carriages
made their way down crowded Condé Street towards the
Sellières, Sophronie and Léonore rode alone in the first.

As they drew up outside the brilliantly lit portico,
Sophronie gave her a long, considering look. "I am
about to let you go. But I have a request—that one day
soon you talk more frankly to me about what you are,
what you do. The time may come when you need me
more than you realize. Do you comprehend me?"

Léonore reached out and touched her hand. "I do.
And I thank you." She just managed not to say more.

After an instant, Sophronie gave a sigh, then a smile.
"Very well. A few turns about the room, and I shall
leave you in peace."

They entered the ballroom at the head of a large
group of ladies and gentlemen whom Sophronie had collected up when they left the French Exchange. Léonore
knew none of them and could summon no interest in
them. She was overwhelmed instead by an anticipation
that robbed her of breath as she paused on the edge of
the dance floor and looked around the ballroom.

She saw him at once. He was amongst the dancers at
the far end, watching a gentleman walk away from him
towards the bar. He was dressed as usual in black, his
white cravat ablaze under the bronze chin, within the
high collar. He was clean shaven! And alone, for the
moment. He looked after the other man in stony irrita-

tion. Then he turned his head her way, almost as though he knew already that she was there.

The music stopped, and in that very second she made her decision.

She began to walk directly towards him across the crowded floor. Sophronie had asked for a frank message: this was it. Her friend could not follow her on this slow, blatant procession, for half the people in the room must know the identity of the man she went to meet. It was time for Eléonore de Rochambeau to step definitively out of the Claibornes' world and make her choice clear. And her choice was Jean Laffite.

The couples continued to disperse as she glided amongst them, the ladies' colorful gowns looking like a windblown field of lilies. Her eyes were fixed on his face. The smooth skin enhanced the handsome perfection of his features, in which she could read his exact reaction—a powerful mixture of shock and admiration.

It was inconceivably bold to approach him like this: Jean Laffite's scarlet woman, advancing uninvited to claim him. The hem of the dress glowed red at the foot of her vision and the veil before her eyes drew a billowing film across the room. She felt for a moment as though she were moving through a thundercloud, with shafts of lightning shooting from the brilliants sewn into her veil. It was a march of possession. *This man is mine, whatever storms surround us.*

He understood. He made no move to retreat; instead he took a few paces towards her. The moment when she came to a breathless halt before him was so intense she could not speak. She put out a hand, then drew it back. No greeting would do but a kiss, and she could not give it from behind the clinging mask and veil.

He looked equally tense. "Madame."

She almost smiled. When he had said it for the very first time on San Stefan, it had been meant as an insult. Since then, through many permutations, it had become a subtle joke that no one but themselves could possibly understand.

He indicated the door behind him, and a thrill of relief and desire took her through it and into the small room beyond, an alcove equipped with card table and chairs, empty of players. She turned to him as he closed the door, able to breathe again, to take in his nearness. She looked up into a face frozen with apprehension.

He swept back her veil and, taking the mask at each temple, lifted both up to let them drop to the floor behind her.

Instantly, his head drew back and he gasped as though she had shoved a knife under his ribs. Shocked almost into terror, she shuddered, and her eyes searched his contorted expression. It was a grimace of extreme surprise.

She took a deep, wild breath. When she let it out, the words almost choked her. "Just who did you think I was?" She watched him struggle for composure, his face so distorted it looked like a stranger's.

"Léonore——"

She gave a savage laugh and took a step sideways. "I was the last person you expected! How many more have you got lined up?"

"It's not like that. Listen——"

"It's like nothing on earth." The rage and grief made her voice shake. The impulse to escape was so strong she felt as though she were fleeing from death. He put out a hand and she shrank farther back, hunching against the wall with one hand on the door. "Get away from me. There is nothing you can say. You have done enough."

He was saying something, reaching out. To escape the lie he was about to utter she tore open the door and burst into the ballroom. He had an appointment with someone else—let him keep it, and spare her his denials.

There were dancers seething about again; the music of a fandango was just striking up. She kept moving. He was behind her, she could hear his tense breathing, then his quick words. She walked on, into a circle of couples.

"Listen to me."

His hand touched her wrist and she whirled, breaking the hold, sending a man and woman reeling away from her. "Leave me alone."

His eyes glittered with what could have been anger.

Ignoring the scandalized couples, oblivious of a tight group of men who suddenly detached themselves from the bar and began to approach, he said, "For God's sake. Let me talk to you."

"Keep away, if you value your life." Rage scoured through her voice. He genuinely never seemed to realize what he did to her. And she was a fool to expect that he would.

The men were upon them, but he advanced again. She began to retreat within the dancers, who were being swept around her now under the frantic impulsion of the fandango.

A dark-haired gentleman said to him, "There's been enough of this behavior tonight," and laid a hand on his shoulder.

Jean shook it off savagely and took another step towards her. The others circled, placing themselves in the way, and with those last dire words ringing in her ears she turned around, cannoned into another couple, recovered and strode towards the other side of the floor.

There was a scuffle behind her. No blows, just low words spoken with venom. She walked on. He was bound to break free and follow her, nonetheless. The other edge of the dazzling, spinning crowd was approaching. He was not yet at her back.

Sophronie advanced. Amongst her group, on the fringe, figures stood like statues, sheer enjoyment on every face. He had not yet crossed the room. Sophronie was with her, an arm around her waist, ushering her towards the others. "Are you all right?"

"No."

"I have just been told who that man is. What on earth is happening?"

"I am leaving. Will you take me? Quickly, before he catches up."

Sophronie took a wide-eyed glance down the ballroom. "He's not coming this way. He's leaving, walking out, past the bar. He threatened you? Wouldn't we be safer here than outside, for heaven's sake?"

He was going, then. He had given up already. "Please

help me. Please let us go now." Getting from the ballroom to the portico, dismissing the inquisitive friends,
awaiting the governor's carriage, was a continuation of
the nightmare. The blood pounded in her ears like pur-
suing footsteps, making speech impossible.

"You look ill," Sophronie said sharply.

The carriage appeared. There were plenty of staring
bystanders, but Jean was nowhere to be seen. She got
in with Sophronie, who said, "You must come home
with me."

Léonore shook her head as the vehicle began to move,
then gave one sob and covered her eyes. After a moment she forced herself to say, "The ship, if you please."

"What has happened?"

She closed her eyes, sick to the heart. "It's too . . .
I can't."

"If he has offended you, something absolutely must
be done. I wonder if I could tell William?" Sophronie
beat her hands in her lap. "That man Laffite is the bane
of his life—if I tell him, he'll be forced to act at last.
But he won't like it, there's the rub. Laffite has sailed
free from every trap William has devised so far. He
wants to hit him with the full force of the law. But this
isn't the cause he's looking for."

Léonore's voice still shuddered. "No, I beg you. I
want nothing done. You don't understand: I brought this
on myself. I cannot speak of it. And never to your
husband."

Silence fell, and Léonore wept in little gasps, with few
tears; the shock of loss kept them at bay. How astounded
he must have been on Barataria, at her plea for him to
love only her. What scorn he must have felt behind his
glib promise. What a fool she had been to imagine even
for an instant that his passion was anything like hers.
He held her cheap. He was quite prepared to risk losing
her, for he had taken no precaution against any other
woman turning up at the Sellières. He found her arrival
a surprise and an inconvenience and made only the
briefest attempt to stop her going. It was true that he
would have made things worse by prolonging the scene

in the middle of the dance floor, but he could have followed her and tried to talk to her privately. Instead he
had let her draw her own conclusions, and drive away.

With a jolt, the carriage reached the docks. She got
out, assisted by the groom, then turned to summon a
good-bye, only to find that Sophronie was descending
too.

"Let us walk a while." Sophronie put a hand through
Léonore's arm and began pacing along the margin of
the levee, as though it were the most ordinary thing in
the world for two ladies to take the air by the river
at midnight.

"That's better. I needed a breeze to cool my head.
Now"—she squeezed Léonore's arm—"time for plain
speaking—if you cannot manage it, I can." There was a
pause, nonetheless. "In case you do not think tonight
warning enough, here is what I know of Jean Laffite.
Apart from his manifold crimes, there are the usual stories about women. Lately a very singular one has come
to my ears, and it is being made much of in New Orleans. There is an outlandish rumor about a woman who
roams the high seas to make her assignations with men—
Jean Laffite amongst them. She is a beauty known as
the Siren, and they say she is a brigand and smuggler,
like him."

Numbed, Léonore simply waited for her to go on.

Sophronie shrugged. "Idiotic, of course. Siren, indeed!
If there were any such thing as a woman pirate now-
adays she'd be as appalling as the trollops of the past,
Anne Bonny and Mary Read—no stays above or restraint below, and mouths like privies. It's all Louisiana
romanticism: the truth has gotten caught up with ludicrous fantasy. For there is some truth to it. I have it
through the Spanish in New Orleans."

Léonore looked below them at the *Fantôme* riding
peacefully on the flood-high river. The watch, recognizing her, went below to rouse Rigaud. She took a last
look along the levee. No one came rushing to prevent
her from sailing down the Mississippi to the sea.

Sophronie put a gentle hand on each shoulder. "My
dear. I don't know what this may mean to you, but you

must be told. He does have a flaming affair going with a woman. She has hair of Titan gold, they say, as bright as his is black. She lives on an island to the north of Cuba and has a husband often absent. There is no doubt about her origins or her Christian name—she is a Spaniard, and her name is Matilda."

CHAPTER SIXTEEN

Bandit

When Jean shook off Raines, the young men moved to stand shoulder to shoulder, blocking his path. Hissing an obscenity, he made to move between them, but two things happened: another youngster grabbed him by the back of his coat, and Raines spoke again.

"Your behavior to women is unspeakable, sir. You must be taught a lesson."

"And you're the idiot to try it?" She was walking away without a backward glance.

"At your convenience."

"Done." He could not do her the further injury of chasing her across the floor. "Livingston, you'll be my second?" He met the startled eyes of the lawyer. "Well?"

"If you wish, certainly, but—"

"Arrange it, if you please." She had reached the sheltering arm of the governor's wife. "Dawn, at The Oaks." He switched his gaze to the red-faced leader of the young men. "You. Outside, now."

They all grinned, baring their teeth like a pack of mongrels. She was with the governor's wife, hesitating by the doors, about to leave. He had minutes only, to get it over and race around to the front before the carriage left. "Let's go."

Livingston and Raines stayed where they were, hardly knowing how to begin their thorny conversation. The young men crowded around Jean in excitement as they passed the bar. He snarled at the general to stay put, and something in his face made the old man obey. One minute.

Out the bar doors, too smoothly for anyone else to guess what was going on. Around into an alleyway, where many a contest had been held before. A circle formed. The red-faced youngster pulled off his coat to reveal a heavily muscled, stocky frame.

Jean too stripped to his shirt, but would waste no time rolling up the sleeves. Two minutes.

The murmurs around them hushed. They faced each other across a couple of yards of hard-packed earth between stone walls, one of which was pierced by a window set high in the scullery behind the bar. The light slanted out, dirtied by the dust of the street, with motes and mosquitoes spinning in the beams.

The youngster circled. Thick thighs, a low center of gravity. Strength, perhaps even speed, but what the hell. Three minutes.

He stepped in, took a wide, haymaking swing, and missed. Toppling forward, he left the other a gleeful second to effect a brutal uppercut with the right hand. Jean fell into it, then twisted his body in the last split second and clipped the other's shoulder, accelerating the young man's movement as he rocked back with his own weight. There was a slithering crash and a smothered, collective laugh as the youth's heavy body connected with the legs of the bystanders behind.

They both fell, but it was Jean, still counting in his head, who finished the calculated move first and was waiting, poised in a crouch, when the other began to pick himself up out of the dust. Confused and angry, the young man let his gaze drop as he rose. His knees were bent, but he was on his feet when Jean delivered the blow. True, annihilating, on the point of the chin. Jean felt a crack, as it connected and took all the skin off his own knuckles. The youth's head snapped back and he arced right into the position he had occupied the moment before. Except this time he was there to stay. Three and a half.

Appalled silence. Then one or two bent to examine the prostrate man. Jean picked up his coat.

"Christ, he's dead."

He took a step out of the ring. He had broken the jaw, that was all—his own stinging hand would be in worse shape if the blow had snapped the neck.

Next, when they saw that their humiliated friend would live and was even coming round, rage overcame them, and he could feel the pack turn towards him again. Let them growl: later he would fight them one by one if need be, but he must get to the carriages now.

He was almost at the end of the alley when the first man attacked, leaping against his back and flinging an arm around his neck. He broke the hold without turning and took two more quick steps towards the street. There he would leave them behind. They had enough pride not to be seen brawling five (six?) against one in a public thoroughfare. His own anger had gone, replaced by what he expected to see when he reached the portico—a red dress disappearing into a carriage. Four minutes.

The blow on the side of his head came from something like a sail boom swinging in a storm. He never knew what they picked up in the dark—wood, however, not metal, or he would have been dead from the force of it. As it was, he was down on one knee and hand, blinded. He never got up. The second was a kick in the ribs, but he went with it, dragging the man's ankle so he hit the ground on the flat of his back. The others, impeded on that side, moved to beat a frantic tattoo on the other. He protected his head for a moment, considering, then lunged up in a tackle around someone's hips, gaining a few feet but bringing them both down. The man twisted under him. One hand on the throat, a quick rap on the nose that sent blood pouring, tortured his flayed hand and made them both grunt. It was the only good blow he got in. Next second two of them hauled him off and someone else doubled him up with a fist under the ribs. He was on the ground, breathless, and the serious business began.

Oddly, the red dress blazed in his mind throughout. He found he could breathe after all, because two of them at least had on dancing pumps. He was learning to look forward to the contrast when they connected. The punishment was mostly inflicted from his ribs down, and the piece of timber did not make itself felt again. Smashed into the dirt, teeth set, curled up within the cage of his arms, he tried to keep counting.

Then it was over. "Here's Livingston!" There was a scuffle around him, a ragged withdrawal, footsteps retreating.

The side of his head where the timber had swung had already swollen enough to close that eye. With the other he watched fleeting shadows disappear into the dark at the end of the alley. He stretched out his legs, revised the idea, rolled onto his back. Above him, Livingston and the general loomed aghast, as though he had fallen from the mainmast to the deck. He closed the eye again.

"Good God, man."

"My friend." The general knelt dramatically.

"Have they gone?" Talking made him feel sick, but at least his voice worked.

Livingston said, "Disappeared, all of them. Damn, I had no notion they'd do a thing like this. Would to God I'd come out earlier."

"No. The carriage."

"Of course, I'll have mine fetched. General, look after him. Excuse me a moment."

Six, seven . . . he had lost count. Ten minutes, perhaps, since she turned and left him. The general's anxious face swam through a crimson haze; he reached up and grasped his shoulder. The old man's voice trembled. "Anything broken?"

He shook his head: a mistake.

The general put a hand under his elbow and heaved. "Can you stand, do you think?"

He sat up and promptly demonstrated that for the moment he could not even speak. The spasms over, he leaned on one hand, inhaling shallowly, every breath like knives.

When Livingston returned he managed to say to him, "The governor's carriage."

"What? It's left. Here's mine. General, help me raise him."

He got to his knees. "No. Thank you. I have to follow them."

"In this state?" Livingston examined him critically as he stood swaying with one hand on the general's shoulder. "We're taking you home. Where to?"

The general, sober under the shock, replied for him. "Saint Philip Street."

There was a crowd now, standing in the pool of light outside the bar. If he moved forward and propped himself against the vehicle the performance would be less public. The first steps were wrenching, the last a painful stagger, and he ended up bent over with one shoulder against a wheel, retching again.

He heard Livingston's cool incisive voice. "There'll be no duel tomorrow. I shall have to consult Raines's second."

"No duel!" The general's tormented roar filled the alley. "When Raines unleashes that rabble onto one man? I'll fight him myself, the cowardly bugger."

"I don't think we can blame Raines for this. It's not the kind of satisfaction he's looking for."

Breathing carefully, Jean lifted his head, moved to fit his shoulders against the paneled side of the vehicle. "I'm obliged to you, but I fight my own battles. With, as you see, spectacular results. Shall we go, gentlemen?"

Edward Livingston was not surprised to be kept waiting when he returned to Saint Philip Street in the chill dark hour before dawn. He was shown into a parlor that had curtainless French doors leading out onto an unlit courtyard. Pierre Laffite kept him company over two shots of bourbon whilst both of them, striving for some kind of conversation, were tensely attuned to movements in the rest of the house. When a piece of iron fell and chimed on cobbles somewhere in the nether regions, he jumped and Pierre Laffite cursed. The man looked shattered, sleepless. When his mulatto woman appeared at the door he rose at once to her silent summons and left the room without apology.

The first day of Lent. Sackcloth and ashes; the march

towards doom. Nonetheless, having had all night to think it through, Livingston harbored no regrets about seconding Laffite. Strictly speaking, his first concerns should be his own standing and reputation as a lawyer, but in a town like this the secret knowledge that he attended the meeting would do no damage to either. New Orleans would see him not so much as Laffite's ally as an impartial witness determined on fair play—the role he had already filled in the ballroom.

He had laid all his other doubts to rest during a conversation with himself as devil's advocate, conducted in the small hours. To begin with, he could not really fault Laffite for accepting the challenge. When the general first offended Raines and his companions, Laffite had sought reconciliation in gentlemanly fashion. The others' interference on the ballroom floor had been provocative, and the young men's actions after that were contemptible. There could be no outrage over Laffite's electing to fight. As for the man himself, he was on the way to being one of the wealthiest merchants in New Orleans and he could be seen as a powerful figure in the local scheme of things. Did that necessarily make him the kind one rubbed shoulders with in public? The answer was a qualified yes, given the polyglot structure of what the city chose to call high society.

Laffite was reputed to transact most of his business outside the law—but nothing against him had ever stuck. And, as Claiborne himself always said, if you aim to govern people, you must understand them first. He smiled at the recollection, placing no bets on the governor's likely chances.

The regrettable business at the bar and on the ballroom floor had dragged the reputations of two women in the dirt—but the outburst over the unnamed lady whom Raines claimed as a relative had been obliterated in everyone's mind by the contretemps that followed. And, on the second occasion, what was a gentleman to do when a magnificent woman swept straight across a room to greet him: turn his back on her? Repudiate her before the multitude? Laffite had compromised her by closeting himself with her—but she had acquiesced in that.

Livingston took a sip of the bourbon, remembering his first good look at her as she darted from the card-room into the throng. In face and figure, one in a thousand. Impossible to guess what the precise link was with Laffite, but speculation had sizzled around the ballroom the second she left with Mrs. Claiborne. Impossible for her to do anything then but leave town, which it appeared she had already done, employing a Mississippi pilot to take her ship downstream in the night. Eléonore de Rochambeau, occasional guest in the governor's mansion, unlikely now ever to return. He felt a twist of regret, wondering at the same time what was going through the vitals of the man he was about to accompany through the dark streets outside.

Like all duels, this one was defined by the unexpected and riddled with ambiguity. The challenge had contained Raines's threat to remodel Laffite's attitude to women, but the issue had become blurred since—by the shabby attack in the alley and the contrasting splendor of Eléonore de Rochambeau as she glided unharmed from the encounter under the aegis of the governor's wife. When Laffite took up a pistol today, it was as though he defended her right to free movement, his own right to meet her without vicious interference. Paradoxically, it seemed that Laffite rather than Raines was the man most determined to keep her name unsullied. Indeed, no one would dare to openly couple it with his after this morning's meeting.

He looked up to see the man at the doorway, and rose. The results were, as he had himself remarked, spectacular. The swelling on the injured side of the face had gone down, but angry bruising stretched from temple to jawline, undisguised by sideburns or mustache. The eyes, black as unlit coals, held no animation as the greetings were exchanged. Livingston just touched the other's right wrist, since the hand was neatly bound with gauze. There was no hint of the more extensive, hidden injuries except his overcareful stance and his evident impatience to quit the house. His energies were clearly not going to last more than an hour or two.

There was no one in the street when they left, and

the whole household came to the door. Pierre Laffite's emotions were an embarrassment, and Livingston found himself turning away from the sight of his principal captured in full fraternal embrace, afraid for the man's composure. The women coped better, until the carriage moved off, whereupon the younger girl, picking up her cotton skirts, ran forward with a shrill, desperate cry.

"Come back to us! Come back."

The window was down, and Laffite lashed out, his voice brutally clear in the cool air. "Get inside."

She faltered, stopped, and tears started from her eyes. Seized by pity, Livingston watched her turn and rush through the open doorway. As the silent group fell back out of sight he could not help catching Laffite's gaze, though he was aware of the disapprobation in his own.

It struck him that the smile he got in return was cruel, though one had to take into account the distorting effect of what the ruffians had done hours before. The voice held no feeling. "I've upset her. Again."

Livingston did not comment, recalling what Pierre Laffite had said—that the women had looked after his wounds when he was first helped into the house, but later, when his messenger came back from the docks to say the lady's vessel had sailed, they were sent out of his room and he tended himself.

Laffite shifted uncomfortably on the seat opposite and rested his head back for a moment against the lining of the coach. "I'll have to offer her another gift. Though to do her credit the little thing's not in the least acquisitive."

In this callous mood, the next question might as well be blunt. "What are your intentions this morning?"

The smile reappeared, slow and ironic. "Take care, sir. I invite no complicity."

Livingston went cold inside; the implication was unmistakable. "I am obliged to put the question."

"Then I shall give you a philosophical rejoinder, quotable to boot—fate will decide between us, on the field of honor."

He felt a stirring of annoyance. "And what are your dispositions, should it go against you?"

"Everything can be referred to Sauvinet; he handles my affairs in New Orleans."

"With respect to your family—"

"I repeat, Monsieur Sauvinet is your contact."

He swallowed, summoned his driest tone. "Mr. Raines's second is a gentleman named Arden. He has told me that Raines had no knowledge of the attack upon you. I saw him quit the ballroom by the main doors directly after his conversation with me, and I believe him on that point."

"It is of no consequence."

"You are at least certain of meeting a man of integrity, sir."

"An irrelevance, even if true. That is not what either of us is there to prove."

Silence again. His own view, also irrelevant, was that dueling never proved a thing, and as a method of settling disputes was so far inferior to the due process of the law that it stood in his mind more or less on the level of a cockfight—down to the avid betting that sometimes accompanied it. There were undeclared issues between these men, deeper than the brief arguments that had flared in the ballroom. It was hard to know what impelled Raines to the meeting, but a fair guess could be made. As for Laffite, the impulses were perplexing. Whatever they happened to be, a bullet through one man's body or the other in the next half hour could not be guaranteed to resolve any of them.

He was curious about the event, though, for the good reason that he had never officiated at a duel in his life. And nervous, in a way that reminded him of the first time he had defended a client in a New York court of law. He had been well instructed, but he had been confident only of going through the forms, not of achieving his youthful ideal, which was to serve the course of justice. As it happened, he had gotten his client off the charges, whilst strongly suspecting that the man was guilty. It had been an unforgettable lesson. He hoped Raines did not imagine that a righteous man with a gun

in his hand would make any more skillful a duelist than
the villain he thought he was facing.

The carriage halted and he looked out. They had
reached The Oaks, the copse of widely spaced trees outside the city where countless duels had taken place. He
was relieved to find the scene devoid of spectators: the
only figures in the dawn-lit clearing were Raines, Arden
and another man, presumably the doctor Arden had
agreed to bring. He laid his hand on the flat mahogany
case of pistols at his side and looked across at Laffite,
who had not moved. The smile on his face contained a
certain proportion of self-mockery, which made Livingston uneasy. He would prefer not to second a man who
held his own life cheap.

They descended with care, Livingston because he carried the case of pistols, Laffite from stiffness. The others
in the distance turned and fixedly watched the two approach. Laffite stopped twenty yards or so from them
and lit a cigar, then waved Livingston on. Both gestures
grated slightly on the lawyer, and as he walked onward
with dignity he reflected again on what New Orleans
society might think about his acting as friend to a notorious bandit. Last night, in the tense atmosphere of opposition, things had gotten to a point where the duel
became inevitable, and he had admired the way Laffite
handled himself throughout. This morning, he was suddenly afraid of having stepped into an error.

The impression did not last. His faith in his own judgment was restored at once by the opening comment from
Arden: "We are glad of your presence, sir. It is a relief
to be sure that matters will proceed by the book and
under proper direction." He then introduced the doctor
and the three men began their discussion.

While they spoke, Livingston glanced at Raines,
dressed in sober, dark brown broadcloth, who in turn
was staring across the clearing at Laffite. The expression
on Raines's face confirmed his own guess about
motive—Raines considered not just Laffite's actions, but
the man himself, as an offense. Raines had taken up the
role of crusader for respectability, the scrupulous guard-
ian of social privileges. Despite surrounding himself with

somewhat brutish young men, Raines had no doubt that when he took a weapon in his hand he would be fighting as an irreproachable gentleman against an upstart.

Looking across at the upstart in question, Livingston wondered at Raines's air of security. There was nothing of the common about the tall figure strolling about under the trees, trailing behind him the slow smoke of his expensive cigar. As usual, he wore his impeccable clothes as though he had been poured into them. The black coat was of the elegant cut one might wear to a morning visit and he had under it a black-and-silver waistcoat offset by the gold chain of a fob watch. The skin-tight gray pantaloons set off the lean hips and long line of his thigh, and in sole concession to the morning's business he wore Hessian boots, which shone like mirrors as he paced about. If Raines could not catch the hint of cold iron under that suave exterior, he was a fool.

Livingston opened the box for the inspection of the pistols and the others handled them respectfully. They were Laffite's own. He was reputed to be a connoisseur: if so, these must be the jewels of his collection. The smooth lines, lent by the Forsyth percussion lock, gave the pieces a more sinister, deadly look, despite the delicate inlay of mother-of-pearl on the polished butts. They were so rare that Livingston suspected Laffite had ordered them directly from the maker in Scotland—or else taken them from some very rich and unlucky British traveler.

He looked at his principal again, wondering how a man might feel at the prospect of being blown out of existence with his own treasured weapon. At that moment Laffite ground the cigar out under his boot and looked across, an alert readiness in his face and stance. He had fought quite enough duels to know that the preparation ought to be over with.

The task of placing the opponents and giving directions was allotted to Livingston. Arden had a brief word with Raines while the doctor retreated to stand not far from the other carriage, which was pulled up under a tree. There was still no sign of any spectators: Livingston

thanked Arden for his party's discretion and received
the same appreciation in return.

Livingston walked slowly to the center of the clearing,
beckoning both men as he went. It was to be a clean
contest, then, with the minimum of witnesses. Stark
and solemn.

The dewy circle of ankle-high grass, the bare branches
of the trees that overreached the glade were bathed in
milky light from an overcast sky. No birds sang there,
and the hush felt eerie to Livingston as he asked the
opponents to shake hands. Laffite stretched out the
bandaged right hand and after a second's hesitation
Raines took it. The lawyer winced inwardly at the pressure on the flayed knuckles but there was no change in
Laffite's expression.

The men stripped off their coats and gave them to
Arden, who draped them over one arm, then held out the
loaded pistols. Laffite stepped back a pace, leaving the
selection to Raines. The merchant looked uneasy, and Livingston wondered what sort of effect the violent bruising
to the other man's face, the injured hand, might have on
his conscience and even his confidence. Especially as Laffite was now freeing his hand. He unwound the bandage,
rolled it up and inserted it at the waist of his pantaloons,
under the waistcoat, then stepped up and calmly took the
remaining pistol. Livingston saw in the battered face the
hint of irony that he had noted in the carriage. This man
did not after all hold his own life cheap—but it was an
open question how much he valued that of his opponent.

Under orders, they turned back to back. Laffite's profile was unmarked on this side and the black hair, swept
back from the brow, lent a contrasting purity to the
smooth skin, the strong nose and firm lips.

To pronounce the next words, the lawyer had to overcome an obstacle in his throat. As the men began to
pace, a bird cried sharply in a copse of trees beyond his
carriage, causing him an instant of sheer panic.

They stopped. He raised the handkerchief high. They
turned. The little square of linen drifted delicately from
his fingers into the still air.

When the shots rang out as one, birds flung themselves shrieking from the trees and the air seemed to quiver with the impact. The breath shuddered in Livingston's lungs and his sight blurred, so the figures at each edge of his vision wavered as though both were about to fall. But only one man toppled. The torso rocked back under the concussion, the pistol dropped from his hand, and Raines crumpled to the ground.

There was a dreadful instant, during which he failed to move again, then everyone except Laffite rushed to his side. His eyes were closed, the head was flung back, one leg was crooked under him. The hand that had held the pistol lay open on the grass, the empty fingers curled, motionless. Blood was soaking the shirt in a bright stream. The doctor fell to his knees beside him, made a swift examination, shook his head and raised shocked eyes.

Livingston wheeled to get away, then made himself turn back. "Can you manage? Is there anything I can do?"

Arden looked at him, white faced. "No. We shall leave as soon as possible. I suggest you do the same."

Livingston turned on his heel, picked up the pistol and walked over to Laffite, who was donning the coat that Arden had dropped in the grass. He raised one eyebrow at the lawyer.

"Through the heart. Instantaneous." The other nodded and turned towards the carriage. It struck Livingston that almost the only time Laffite had bothered to look at Raines was when he aimed his weapon to kill him. Through a wave of revulsion he said, "Thank God he has no wife or children."

There was no answer. They entered the carriage in silence, and Livingston gave a sharp order for the return to Saint Philip Street. The coachman pulled away with a jolt, and Livingston saw Laffite grimace for the first time and grip the edge of the swaying seat.

As they drove, it gave Livingston a certain obscure satisfaction to see the effort it took to keep the other upright and to observe the clenching of the teeth that created a tight ridge along the jawline, the uneven breathing, the struggle behind the eyes that made their surfaces dull, metallic.

When Livingston grew weary of the silence he summoned up his most detached tone, addressing this time the alabaster profile. "It would interest me, off the record, to know why you agreed to fight him."

The pale lips hardly moved. "He got in my way."

CHAPTER SEVENTEEN

─❦─

El Santo
Rosario

The Peak had a loneliness that she was used to—clean, clear and unalterable. While her father was suffering his last illness and Adélaïde had taken her turn at tending him, Léonore had often followed the passage from the roof to the tower and scaled the path to the summit. There she would spend half an hour alone before descending the same way or strolling down the slope where they twisted the henequen ropes, then back through the gardens and along the beach.

In the house, it had been a bitter time. For more than a year, Roncival had indulged in longer bouts of drinking, which had disguised a deterioration of the lungs. When the disease caught up with him, it sent him into fevers and delirium, which were a torment to him and to his nurses. In his lucid periods, he reproached Léonore for the failure of plans that he had never seriously attempted to carry out—to install her in a creditable home on one of the French islands.

Her father had died with all his dreams in ruins, except that of wealth. Even on that score, for the last weeks of his illness he refused to speak to her about the fate of the island or the possessions he left behind him. It was not until two days before his end that he sum-

moned her, sent Adélaïde from the room and told her
the state of the Roncival fortunes. It was the knowledge
of this last conference that had made the people of the
island ready to aid and listen to her when he died; and
it was largely what had kept most of them loyal to her
since.

Today she sat on smooth rock with her arms about
her knees and her back to the sun, gripping the handle
of a parasol that leaned on one shoulder and created a
pool of shade around her feet. The summer heat struck
across her lower back through her muslin dress, while a
steady breeze ruffled the fringe of the parasol so that
the blue arc of the sky rippled with silken filaments.

Her own dreams had lasted a much shorter time than
her father's, and unlike him she had been aware from
the first how fragile they were. It ought not to have
surprised her that Jean had lied about the other women
in his life. Or that, when she forced him to swear she
had no rival, of course he had sworn—on the God he did
not believe in and the children he hoped never to have.

It was not so much the knowledge of his lies that
crushed her at the ball, as the moment when he whisked
her into the private room and took off her disguise. She
reviewed his haunted look as she reached him on the
dance floor, his deep tension, the control he exercised
over his voice. He had stepped forward not to continue
some casual flirtation, nor to test his power over a recent
conquest: far worse, the person he thought he was meeting had a special power over him—and that was why the
unmasking shook him to the depths.

The woman must resemble herself very closely, in
height and figure, and in what he could have seen of her
face and hair. She remembered trying on mask and veil
in Feversham's, just before Sophronie turned up. In the
mercer's mirror, the color of her hair had been discern-
ible under the black gossamer. Did she have what one
might call hair of Titan gold? More or less.

"No!" She said it aloud, bent her head and pressed
her face to her knees. No. She would not torment herself
with this unknown woman any longer. She must stop
fighting what she could not change; she must cease going

back again and again over the same ground and reliving that scene. She had done the right thing then: walked away. She had refused to hear him, spurned any idea of excuses. For she had known instantly that there was only one explanation he could give: "I thought you were the woman I love."

Yet if he had followed and tried to speak to her again, she would have listened. The desperate impetus that sent her flying from the ballroom could not have carried her onward if he had made an attempt to reason with her; she would not have been able to deny him a hearing. But he had not pressed for one. In a single instant, with one catastrophic gesture, he had lost her—and he had made no move to get her back.

She raised her head and scanned the ocean that lay spread out before her like a gigantic piece of ultramarine crepe, wrinkled but unmarked from the rim of San Stefan's perfect reef to the horizon. Except in the north. She shifted position, laid her hand on the spyglass she always brought to the peak, gripped the parasol between her knees and raised the instrument to her eye.

A smallish vessel. Too far away to identify, but certainly not the *Fantôme,* at present on a run to Port-au-Prince. Even as she watched, it changed tack to head towards the island. A rush of wild expectation brought her stumbling to her feet; the parasol rolled away, and she had to bend to snatch it up before it floated off the summit on the breeze. Then she stood with it clamped between her hands, trying to crush the hope out of her heart, reminding herself of Jean Laffite's hard promise never to revisit San Stefan. He would not come searching for her. Never again.

Someone was visiting, nonetheless—beating against a contrary wind, which gave the islanders ample time to conceal their arms, their possessions and their readiness. The *Hero,* much larger than the absent *Fantôme,* drew too much water to be hauled right up to the careening yard, but with the masts unstepped she could be warped far enough into the stream to be hidden by the trees. To disguise the function of the warehouse, long fishing nets were draped on frames erected before it on the beach, and a few women and older men sat about in the sand mending them. The cannoneers on the roof kept their heads below the parapet, and those assigned to the shore batteries crouched on mats amongst the bushes and whiled away the time with card games. Most of the men were off on the *Fantôme,* but the home squad, well drilled by Rigaud, had no doubt of their ability to defend San Stefan.

Léonore had a chaise longue brought out onto the sunlit terrace and relaxed in it, waiting. She had changed into an afternoon gown of apricot silk with embroidered panels at the sides and a filmy covering over breasts and throat, gathered into a choker of pearls. Her fine straw hat, festooned with gauze and feathers, had a sweeping brim as ample as the parasol she kept folded by the chaise. She told herself she was dressing for her own sake, not for Laffite. At last the vessel drew near enough for its colors to be identified and the call came down from the tower to the mansion. Spanish. She bit her lip.

She looked out over the calm waters of the lagoon, following the darker line of the channel to where it snaked out through the gap in the reef to the fathomless waters beyond. The sloop, which the lookouts said was now approaching on a northwest tack, was not yet visible. It could do them no harm when it came into view. Thanks to the reef, not even a ship's boat could land on San Stefan, except by navigating the dangerous passage into the lagoon, and the rest of the island afforded no targets that could be bombarded from the sea. The village and the mansion, protected by the curved arms of the bay, were out of range even from a man-of-war, so the only way they could be attacked by artillery was if a ship succeeded in slipping by the battery on the point. At low tide, as now, no vessel larger than their own cutter could pass through.

In her father's day, few ships had ever paid San Stefan a visit. An old mate, the privateer Boursier, sometimes called in to take on water. If curiosity brought strange captains into home waters, Roncival often chose simply not to return their signals of greeting and waited until they gave up and sailed away. If they insisted on trying to put a boat ashore he used to send out a pirogue and have the visitors brought swiftly through the entrance, knowing they could never remember the tricky maneuvers into the lagoon. If they wanted water, he sold it to them. If they sought anything else, he told them that the island furnished only just enough for the people's humble wants. No one believed him, but it discouraged return visits.

How had this particular Spanish vessel arrived—by accident, or design? Léonore felt a momentary chill when at last it glided into view. A Bermuda-rigged sloop, sailing under mainsail only, armed with what looked like half a dozen four-pounders on deck, and as many swivel guns. Minutes later, it hove to with the big triangle of canvas flapping in a strong wind. She raised the spyglass again and inspected her, but there was no name visible on the curve of the planking and no figurehead under the bowsprit—only a carved decoration that looked like two lines of wooden round shot joined by a rough-hewn crucifix. Spanish privateers operating out of Havana fancied sloops, for their speed.

Within minutes a longboat had been lowered and was approaching the reef. There was a single passenger in the stern, holding a speaking trumpet: across the distant boom of the reef and the gentle wash of the lagoon she caught a tinny, pathetic sound as he called towards the shore. She gave the order for a pirogue to be sent out, and leaned back in the chair. They had sailed over the horizon and directed themselves so confidently towards the island that it was foolish to hope they had come upon it by hazard. This was a mission, driven by parties who already knew something about her. She must find out as much as she could about them.

When the pirogue had threaded through the reef she trained the spyglass once more on the visitor in the stern. Thin, straight-backed, wearing a chapeau de bras trimmed with gold and a russet coat with enormous revers, the guest also sported a wide silver sash decorated with a showy star—whether it was a military or civil order,

Léonore could not guess. But with a jolt, she recognized
the gentleman himself. Don Julio de Oleron y Siqueiros.

While he landed and was escorted up the beach towards the mansion she remained where she was, struggling against alarm. She could not work out why; she
had met him only twice, in the most anodyne of circumstances, yet there was something personal in the sense
of threat he evoked.

She heard the rap of his heels on the stairs. When his
long, inquisitive head appeared above the stone coping
of the terrace and she swept forward to greet him, she
had the notion of taking part in an evil parody.

"Mademoiselle de Rochambeau! How delightful to
meet you again in such a setting."

As they went through the formalities she wondered at
his use of her adopted name. If he had discovered her
home base, he must know her true family, her activities.
He was playing games. She could not work out whether
this childish tactic made him less or more dangerous.
Laffite, when he came marauding, had done it with
naked blades and plain speech. She felt an absurd twist
of the heart at the thought.

She decided not to invite him indoors. He was a man of
elaborate courtesy, most comfortable in hushed, luxurious
rooms. She would oblige him instead to parley with her
in the barbaric glare of the sun. She invited him in under
the colonnade, where a low marble table was laid with
cordials and trays of refreshments. He pretended to like
it, admiring also the prettily ordered beach, the position
of the house, the terrace's exposure to the health-giving
sea breezes. So far he had said nothing to the purpose.

She disposed herself comfortably on the chaise longue.
"I am curious, señor—to what do I owe the pleasure of
this visit?"

"I come as Emissary Plenipotentiary of the Crown of
Spain, mademoiselle. Havana sends me to address you,
for the good of Cuba."

She leaned back, took a sip of barley water, and considered him. It was idle to point out that the crown of
Spain rested at present on the head of Napoleon's

brother. Or that no emissary could possess the "full powers" of an ambassador. "Cuba?"

A small bow. "Since we last met, I have taken up residence in Havana. It is impossible for me to refuse if my countrymen turn to me for help—they esteem that my past efforts for Spain fit me to promote her interests in these far lands." He waved tapering fingers towards the open sea. Following the gesture, Léonore examined the sloop, which was hovering beyond the entrance, having failed to find anchorage in the offing.

"What is the name of your vessel, señor ?"

"El Santo Rosario."

"The armorer being the captain-general of Cuba, I collect?"

He nodded. "Juan Ruiz Apodaca, from whom I bring a message, mademoiselle. The captain-general asks—"

Her question drowned his. "And how does madame your wife enjoy Havana?"

The thin lips were compressed. "Tolerably. She would like us to settle somewhere for good, and I should like to oblige her. But while frontiers are so unsure in this little world, how can I draw my own with any confidence?"

"How indeed?"

"The captain-general, however, owes it to Spain to allow no such uncertainty in her dominions. Which is why he has asked me to raise a number of points with you, mademoiselle."

"He should be clear on one, at least. This island may have been named by Spain long ago, but it is French territory."

"I am afraid that is not what our official records say."

"No? With respect, that is none of my concern."

"It should be, mademoiselle. Consider the insecurity of your position. Even if France genuinely held territorial rights to San Stefan, of what use could that be to you at present, when there is not a single French base in the Caribbean? You are placed in the most dangerous isolation, and should there be reprisals against any of your . . . enterprises or activities, to which country could you turn for protection?"

She smiled and began to rise. "That, señor, is why we

of San Stefan place such importance on self-protection."
She put her feet to the marble paving, rose and moved
into the sun, pacing slowly by the table and examining
him sidelong. He studied her with a superior expression
that held a certain wariness. "You would not be sitting
here now unless I had given you an escort into our harbor. This island is impregnable."

"Except to those who know the passage."

She moved in a wider arc, her eyes turned towards
the lagoon. It was true that now there were expert seamen abroad who had snatched that knowledge to themselves and who vowed no loyalty to her: Baudard, Curtis,
Santo. Laffite. She shivered in the hot sun and glanced
back at the hidalgo. What could any of them gain from
betraying that knowledge to Cuba?

He rose and joined her at the balustrade, taking in
the view of the beach with an appreciative eye "A
peaceful scene. Has it occurred to you how much more
secure you would feel if your family were to come under
the aegis of Spain? Let me propose this to you: Cuba is
interested in using the island as a depot and water supply. The captain-general would also like to send a team
to reinvestigate the gold mines." He raised a hand to
forestall any interruption. "We have reason to believe
one of them could be profitably reopened."

Curtis was the last person to have a good look at
them. Curtis? She took a long breath. "The mine that
used to yield the most gold is also the most dangerous.
It was closed when five miners died. Their bodies are
still there."

"Proof that much greater expertise is needed—something Havana could readily supply. And that is not all
you are offered. Imagine becoming the custodian of San
Stefan under an administration that would ensure the welfare of everyone here." He motioned towards the village
and she wondered if he had any idea that the *Hero* was
hidden beyond. And whether he knew that her latest
prizes had come from a Spanish trader.

"I hate to disappoint your captain-general, but if I
could ever imagine San Stefan under any administration
but my own, I should not be applying to Spain."

"Where, then?" There was a harder tone in his voice. "Not England—she has even more reason than us to deplore your actions. England would extend no benefits to a pirate. My wife and I lately played host in Havana to an unfortunate victim of yours, mademoiselle. The captain of a British frigate whose life has been twice threatened and whose livelihood has been destroyed by you and your henchmen."

"Slander, señor? You disappoint me." She leaned over the balustrade and signaled the escort to come up the steps. "I felt when we first met that your conversation was unlikely to hold my interest. You are ill chosen as an emissary."

He stiffened. "I could have come seeking reparation, mademoiselle. The captain-general was inclined to take a combative line, but he was persuaded to employ conciliation first. Persuaded, in fact, by my lady wife, who reminded us that we are dealing with a person who makes claims to gentility."

The escort came through the gate and held it open for the guest. Léonore managed a tight smile. "I am obliged to the señora. Convey my compliments to her."

"It is my duty to warn you that the captain-general will view your attitude with grave displeasure. Personally, I regret your failure to see reason."

"And I regret your failure to offer it, señor. I wish you a safe journey."

Jean was laughing. He had been playing cards for hours and it was absurd that he continued to win, especially since he had started the games only in order to ease the tension following the afternoon's council of war, at which some of the delegates, notably the most vocal Italians, Gambi and Chighizola, had turned sour and uncooperative. He had had his own way, but he could see everyone needed cheering up, so he had turned the affair into something of a carousal, during which the card play got going. Now he had won yet again, and the whole group was looking at him from the other side of the table with exasperation and brooding Mediterranean envy. Standing amongst them was also a little girl who looked no older than four, holding tightly onto her father's hand.

Jean laughed again, scooped the piles of money towards him across the table and picked out a sovereign. The girl's eyes grew as round as the coin when he placed it in her palm. When he nodded dismissal, the father turned at once and the child was led out through the door, intent on her treasure. She was dressed in a white gown, and a corner of the woolen shawl draped over her shoulders brushed the shiny new floor behind the heels of her little shoes. She was the picture of neatness, but her long black hair was tangled at the ends; they had gotten her out of bed to bring her over and cut the cards.

"He took his time fetching her," growled Gambi.

"They had to row her over from Grande Isle," Chighizola said, as Jean stood up and began to sweep the offending cash off the edge of the table into bags. "No good looking for the hand of an innocent on Grande Terre!"

The pack of cards was still in the middle of the table. The play had gotten so nasty he had decided to declare the next game the last. The Italians had looked murderous at the idea of his retiring with all the spoils of victory, so he had declared a final round. It ended up being between himself and Gambi, so he had suggested a simple cut of the pack, black or red, winner take all. Gambi had been given the choice and picked red. By custom, only a neutral person without reproach could cut the cards, so they had all sat there getting more and more out of sorts, drinking and waiting for a moody half hour while someone went off to fetch the child.

When she arrived, her timid face had been in such contrast to the scowls and darting glances around her that he was almost afraid to address her in case she screamed and ran away. She had responded to his quiet command, however, and put out a smooth little paw to take a few cards off the top of the pack. When she turned them over, there was the six of spades.

He was lining up the money bags on the table, still

grinning to himself, when someone said, "We should have gotten a nubile virgin to do it. At least we could have had some fun with her afterwards."

Andrea Santo's voice said, "A virgin in Barataria? We could wait a thousand years!"

His hands, his whole body stilled as he remembered.

It had happened in the old house, now dismantled. In a candlelit room that no longer existed. On the bed where he could still see her sometimes, her gaze so profound that he had been able to watch the movements of apprehension, longing and abandon rise and glow in her eyes. The drowning moment when at last he knew, and took, her virginity.

He rose abruptly, walked to the cabinet where he kept the cigars, turned his back to the room. Now everyone was laughing but himself. There was still an odd edge to their mirth however. It was the first time he had invited any of them to the new house, and he had expected them to be happier about it. Suddenly, he wanted them all out.

He took a full box out of the cabinet and put it on the table. "Help yourselves. Will you join me in a last glass?"

Eyes brightened; this indulgence was rare. The box emptied fast, and there were murmurs of appreciation.

Curtis held a cigar to his ear and twirled it expertly. "Thanks, Bos. Rolled on the thigh of a virgin."

Chighizola turned and gave a guttural laugh. "There are virgins in Havana?"

Someone else laughed. "Not if Curtis can help it!"

He walked to the open French doors, lit his own cigar, looked out at the moon dipping and riding in the Gulf swell. Directly below, the waves crashed in and sucked at the banks of shells. He had done well to build this house in front of the old one; it brought him nearer the voice of the sea, and the terrace gave him a view of the beach, the ocean and the channel between the islands.

"To virgins."

He turned. The voice was Gambi's. The look the Italian shot him through the circle of raised glasses was unpleasant, but he could read nothing specific into it.

Louis Chighizola, otherwise known as Nez Coupé, looked permanently sinister, having had his face remodeled in a saber duel. Jean glanced at Curtis, who was looking at the table, then Santo.

Santo tossed back his bourbon and quickly poured another shot. "And here's to experience. If you asked me to choose between them, I could tell you a tale of experience that would make your virgins look . . ." He trailed off, and everyone laughed. Santo's grand statements always came unraveled.

"Foolish?" Jean ventured.

Santo rose. "As to that, there is a tale I could tell."

Jean dropped his hand, clamped his teeth onto the cigar and took one step back into the room. He held Santo with a look, his stomach cold and his intentions clear.

A second flicked by, then Santo dropped his gaze. With an almost inaudible "Good night, then," he turned and left, the other Italians following with the same bad grace.

In a few minutes, the room was clear except for Dominique You, who shook his head. "A bad evening, altogether. They're sore as hell and they don't like your latest strike plans for along the coast. They're going to spend the rest of the night firing each other up. You know that, don't you?"

"Let them."

"Want me to stay?"

"No. Get along with you."

It sounded brusquer than he meant, but his brother just got quietly to his feet and picked up his hat and sword.

As he reached the door, Jean said, "You remember school on Martinique?"

Dominique turned, startled.

"There was a boy used to spend a lot of time with you and Pierre. Félix something. His father was overseer on a plantation near Mount Pelée. You remember the name of it?"

"The Cascades."

"That's it. And the owner?"

"A French marquis. Name of Richemont, I think."

"What else can you tell me?"

Dominique shrugged. "Nothing. Pierre is the one to ask. He was more friendly with Félix than me. Why?"

"It's just—I recall him saying something about one of the daughters. That she ran away with a ne'er-do-well and the family cut her off." He took a breath to manage the next sentence. "I wondered whether that might have been the woman from Martinique who married Roncival of San Stefan."

Dominique shrugged again. "Could be. But there's a story that her mother was black, which alters the picture. Not likely the old lady was a marquise!"

Jean stared. "Why didn't you tell me?"

"You never asked."

After Dominique had gone, Jean paced the terrace while the table was being cleared and the place set to rights. He remembered her joking words, in the main room of the house he had now razed to the ground. *My black ancestry.* Said with a smile and a hint of challenge.

There had been a thunderstorm in the afternoon that cracked over the island like a flail, flattened the sea under gouts of rain and dropped inches of water to lap against the low stone parapet of the new terrace. When the sky had been washed clear and the tiles shone again in the sun, tendrils of steam wreathed themselves amongst the surrounding cabbage palms. Even now under the high moon, moisture was still in the air, soft on his face, carrying the scent of gardenia from two venerable bushes in the grove that had been spared in the construction of his fortress. Here, the gardenia flowered all summer and into autumn. The rain-fresh petals brushed against his mind, easing open the gates of memory.

Her perfume was laced with gardenia; it was like her always to wear the most luxurious, expensive essence. He should have recognized it at once when she glided up to him in the ballroom. He should have realized that the impulse to slide his hand over the smooth shoulders, to lean across and brush his lips against the veiled cheek, was in response to the body he had already touched

and known with every fiber of his own. Not Mathilde's.
Never Mathilde's.

Even now, standing in the dark all these months later,
motionless and hollow with the thought of it, he could
not believe his error. She was the same height as Mathilde, but that was an insane excuse. Léonore's figure
was finer, her hair a brighter gold, her eyes a more intense blue. It was not so much the gown, the veil and the
mask that had obscured these differences from him—it
was his own bitter idea that Mathilde had come to the
ball for confrontation and revenge. He had been blinded
by his own impatience to shake her off before Léonore
arrived.

Alone in the dark, he could also feel exactly how un-
quiet the island was. No bed tonight. He went back inside and made a few preparations, which included
bolting the back door and putting a man on the verandah at each side. If anyone wanted to talk to him, they
could come up the beach to the terrace. He lit a tall
flare at the corner and then reclined in the hammock,
one boot on the tiles, one eye on the silver track of the
full moon over the sea.

The waiting gave him an occupation of sorts. Something to stop him from following a constant urge to write
to her, attempt an explanation. Only a fool wrote such
letters to women. His first to Mathilde had been a huge
miscalculation; there must not be another.

When they came they were holding torches, and the
flames shuddered amongst the cabbage palms. A small
group, but there was a shadowy, larger one behind, gathered in expectation. By now they would all know of the
clash around the table and how he had steered the meeting his way. His leadership in Barataria had built gradually, almost on its own, through his steady management
of the practical and others' acceptance of the commercial
benefits he won for them. It was strange to come up
against this jealous opposition that the Italians harbored.
But not surprising. Some such moment, after all, had
been bound to come.

He rose, walked back inside and picked up one of his
pistols from the table.

When he came out again and stepped past the hammock onto the well-lit front portion of the terrace, he
saw that Gambi had appointed himself as spokesman.
He was standing with legs stiffly apart, his square, stocky
figure and shock of gray hair making him look like an
actor in some drama, called upon to play the grizzled
Roman general whose advice would save the state. He
ruined the effect at once with his rough Calabrian snarl.

"You thought to dismiss us, but there are things you
can't shuffle off with a few smooth words. You wouldn't
hear us out at your table—so we'll have our say now.
Where all can witness, by God."

He looked at the others, drawn up around Gambi and
scowling watchfully at him in the glow of the torches.
All armed, and all able to meet his eye.

Under the long, oppressive silence, Gambi cracked.
"And you think you can get away with saying nothing
to us? You don't know what you have to reckon with,
then. We've had enough. You can't just snap your fingers and expect us to go along with every cursed plan
you come up with. It's us that run the risks and take
thought for the rest when things get hot. The lads behind
us can trust Louis Chighizola and me—what faith should
they have in you, that takes the profit and won't listen
to the men who risk their necks for Barataria voyage
after voyage? Who do they want as leader, you or us?
Give them a choice—a real choice, and we'll soon see!"

Gambi's voice, hurled into the chasm between them,
had swelled to a strident oratorical roar. His cohort drew
closer, and the line of the shadowy host beyond began
to waver, as men shifted their feet and turned to each
other.

"You'll give us an answer, by Christ, here and now.
You'll be ruled by the men who ought to be the leaders
in Barataria, that you've held down these last months
and will be held down no more. This is it, Jean Laffite—
time to yield to us."

It was Andrea Santo who stepped forward, on a nod
from Gambi. He was stripped to the waist, with a pistol
stuck through a bandolier that slanted from shoulder to
belt, and his bare chest shone in the torchlight. He held

a cutlass at his side and there was a grin on his hand-some face. With the avid crowd behind him, and all the bold words said for him by Gambi, he glowed with more confidence than he had ever shown since arriving in Barataria, even when he displayed his most conquering airs, or indulged in his infernal boasting.

There was a rumble of voices in the shadows and Santo raised his head higher, like a stallion sniffing the wind. In two seconds, he would be leaping up onto the terrace.

Jean did not alter his position, for he was standing full in the light where all could see. He simply extended the pistol and fired.

Later, he remembered the faces. All of them, in a stark frieze, and Santo's features melting in shock as he took the bullet in the throat.

Santo's knees gave and he fell. Before the blood had even stopped pumping, they all knew it was over. As soon as they bent to carry the body away, Jean walked back inside and closed the doors.

CHAPTER EIGHTEEN

~

Fury

Early in December, Léonore's cutter was leaving the
Yucatan Channel, heading into the current that
swung up northeast around the Gulf towards New Orleans. Since she had decided on the voyage while in
Port-au-Prince, it had made sense to choose the route
that ran south of Jamaica and Cuba, but she was not
after prey in these busy sea roads. Even if she had happened to be in the *Fantôme* or the *Hero,* she would have
had no thoughts of plunder, for this was an impromptu
mission to meet Albert Gallatin.

She had just been to Port-au-Prince for powder and supplies, and put up at the Amiral de Grasse, on her first visit
for many months. She had tried to keep her voice normal
as she made her usual inquiry about mail, but she could
not control her features when the innkeeper told her there
was a single letter waiting for her, which had arrived several days before from New Orleans.

When it was brought to her room she took it with
shaking hands, then sat and studied the superscription
for a moment before breaking the seal. She had never
seen his handwriting. Clearly she had a bad memory for
anyone's hand; the letter was from Sophronie Claiborne.
Only the final paragraphs sank in.

> *I feel sure that someday you will tell me just where
> your island really is and allow me to write to you*

*direct. In the meantime, I hope these gleanings of
New Orleans gossip amuse you. I have one last
piece that only you can judge the importance of.
The secret lady with the initial "M" whom I mentioned to you has broken off relations with a certain
gentleman, they say. Could it be because of the encounter witnessed at a certain ball? You will recall
something we heard once in a Congrève play at the
Théâtre St. Philippe: "Hell hath no fury like a
woman scorned." But I can make no guess as to
the consequences between him and her.*

*I promised to let you know if Albert Gallatin in-
tended a visit. He does, and it will be soon. He
plans a tour down the Mississippi, leaving Philadel-
phia for Pittsburgh in December. How long he will
stay here is somewhat vague, as he must expect to
be asked at any moment to enter the lists on behalf
of his country. You have no doubt heard the latest
from Washington. The debates in Congress are wild.
You know me, of course, I am all for peace. And
friendship. Which I send you with heartfelt good
wishes. Sophronie*

She knew what her friend meant about the recent
Twelfth Congress. President Madison himself had accused England of "hostile inflexibility in trampling on
rights" and the war hawks had pushed for measures to
strengthen the United States' preparations for war. As
the debates continued, a general mood emerged that the
national honor was at stake, and peace with Britain was
becoming incompatible with patriotism. Sophronie had
told Léonore that Albert Gallatin had the trust of President Madison, and if negotiations had to take place before or during war with England, it was likely he would
be named in the American deputation. She must see him
before he was posted overseas.

Léonore consulted first with Rigaud and Philibert,
since one of them needed to manage San Stefan while
she was absent—the respite the Spanish had given them
since the visit of their "emissary" could not last much
longer. Rigaud volunteered: older and more experienced

than Philibert, he was a gifted sailor and would make the trip back with two of the men in a pinnace that they bought on the spot in Port-au-Prince, taking most of the essential supplies. The islanders were to wait an indefinite time for her return, with no excursions, keeping their total firepower for defense.

It made her nervous to be sailing the little cutter close to the shores of Cuba, sneaking past Havana like the thief she was. Standing one day in the stern she looked towards the coastline, hazy on the horizon, and wondered about the motivation for Cuba's sudden interest in San Stefan. As Jean Laffite had long ago pointed out, it was natural for Spain to imagine it could reinstate its sovereignty over the island. But why now? Was the exchequer in Havana really greedy enough for gold to begin delving in the ruined mines of the peak? Could they genuinely want the island as a revictualing post, when they had the harbor of Santiago de Cuba not far distant on their southeast coast? Since the rapprochement with England, they might well like to offer San Stefan as a station to the British navy—but it was far too tiny to serve the fleets that operated from Kingston Town in Jamaica, only days away. No, the whole tenor of Oleron y Siqueiros's talk had suggested not acquisition but revenge. She had stung their shipping too often, and now they had been outraged at the story from one of their new allies, the *Hero*'s former captain, robbed a second fatal time by Santo. They could not attack San Stefan, but on the high seas their vessels would have orders to challenge and capture any of hers.

One thing she could not work out was why the hidalgo had been so willing to join in the bid to claim her heritage for Spain. She had the strange feeling the wife had influenced him to do so, perhaps even urged Cuba's captain-general to send her husband on the mission of vengeance. The hidalgo had said his wife was eager to settle somewhere—did she imagine them both leading the occupation, taking over as seigneurs of a tropical island?

It was Philibert who saw the vessel first. Single masted

like the cutter, low and sleek, it was following them on a course that would intercept theirs from the southeast.

The cutter was already moving at her best rate of knots in a steady wind. After twenty anxious minutes they had left the shadow of Cuba behind, but the sloop was still in pursuit, and gaining. Léonore put on a cloak and kept out of the line of observation from the rear.

She left everything to Raymond Philibert. He had impressed her on this trip with his initiative. He was younger than herself but had been well trained as both navigator and sailor since he left Guadcloupe to join the French navy at the age of twelve. He was a thin, active young man of East Indian blood, with alert brown eyes and a nice turn of invective if men did not at once leap to his commands. The crew respected and even liked him, and the twenty men on this voyage moved smoothly under his orders to get every ounce of speed out of the cutter.

She studied Philibert's sharp, dark profile as he raised his spyglass again. There was a quick compression of the thin lips. "Spanish."

"Is it the sloop that came in the summer; *El Santo Rosario*?"

"No, but it could be her sister, judging by her speed and arms. I can see marines on deck. I'd say we're outnumbered around two to one, and I don't like the size of her forward guns." He lowered the spyglass and turned to her, his gaze level. "If she makes a challenge we must consider yielding. They'll strip everything off us, but the odds are they'll set us free again."

"Not if they know who we are."

"I wasn't suggesting we tell them!"

"Any captain from Havana is bound to guess. How many women ply the Caribbean in nameless vessels that are fully armed and manned?"

He gave a bitter smile. "True. But I don't like our chances if we take them on."

"I fear it's that or we all rot in a Cuban prison until they execute us. I regret this, Monsieur Philibert. Kindly pass that on to the men, if you please."

They hauled into the stern the piece that had the longest range, cutting a new opening in the gunwale to set it up on the best angle for firing from the quarter. When everything else was in readiness for action, Philibert came to her again.

"Maître, have you thought that we could yield but keep you safe hidden? We could claim we don't know San Stefan from Hades and we operate out of the Yucatan."

"I did think of it—but it would go worse for you all if they found me. I suspect there is a Cuban bounty out on me, and I've no idea whether the preference is to take me dead or alive. I could hail them when they come in range and give myself up—" He exclaimed, and she overrode him. "But it's not just me they want, it's San Stefan. There's no hope they'll let you sail home once they have me."

"God's death, they'll not lay a finger you."

Philibert walked away and gave his orders to the quartermaster. None too soon, for seconds later the sloop sent a warning shot splashing into the waves a few yards to starboard. They were within range.

The task of their big aft gun was to knock out the sloop's mainmast and kill the pursuit, but it was not going to be easy. Their lightning response to the sloop's challenge tore a hole in one corner of the other's triangular mainsail, which raised a cheer from Léonore's crew but did not seem to slow the sloop's progress. Thereafter the guns of both vessels fired almost without intermission.

Despite the cutter's lack of size, she was usefully armed, and there was no concern about powder and shot—in fact they had taken on a great store of gunpowder in Port-au-Prince. In these circumstances it was a serious risk, and Philibert ordered wet sacks draped over the barrels as protection from flying sparks from their own guns or exploding shot from the enemy's.

The moment the cutter was hit, Léonore quivered as she had done the first time onboard the *Fantôme*. The shot tore through the rigging just above her but brought down neither yard nor canvas, and she managed to stay in her place near the steersman. Smoke poured over the deck on the wind, stinging her eyes, but she could see and hear clearly enough when the next ball crashed by, and she swung around to watch it shred the ratlines to starboard and plunge on into the sea. The Spaniards were aiming high, to cripple the cutter, not to sink her. They had capture in mind rather than summary execution. Yet she tasted her own fear, acrid at the back of her tongue, and she was seized by a very clear idea of what it would be like to die.

Then the port bulwark burst open, and timber, metal, chains and shot hurtled across the deck before her eyes, scything down everything in their path. Screams erupted, and amongst the rubble and smoke were thrashing limbs.

Behind her, Philibert shouted, and there was another roar from the rear gun, but she ran forward, plunging into the melee, calling the names of the gunners. She stepped on someone's hand, slid in a patch of liquid, righted herself against the gun and looked down. The corpse beside her, to which the hand belonged, lay headless in a pool of blood.

She was sick at once, one arm flung over the cold body of the gun, her stomach wrenching as though an iron fist pummeled her under the ribs. Doubled up, convulsed with horror, she was still heaving helplessly when strong black arms grabbed her from behind and swung her off the gun and into the shelter of the bulwark.

The gunner deposited her on her knees and thrust her head down. "For God's sake, Maître, stay put."

When she could unbend a little she looked up, her whole body shaking. The gunner was back with the others, trying to move the dead and wounded, and she made herself count them as she staggered to her feet. Five mutilated, two dead. There was a lad lying motionless nearby: in her panic, she could not bring his name to mind. She had killed him, but she could not remember who he was.

She wiped her mouth with the back of her hand, moved forward and crouched beside him. She felt the pulse on his neck: he was alive. Then she heard a whine from behind her and nothing could stop the terror that made her pitch forward across his body and bury her face, screaming, in his bloody clothes.

There was a rushing sound, a shriek of tortured timbers, and the world split apart. She was thrown out from its center with a speed so dizzying that when the impact came it was like hitting a wall at full tilt, and it was only with her last flicker of consciousness that she realized the dense mass was water, folding around her head in a solid black wave.

By Christmas, the Claibornes had still not received Albert Gallatin at the governor's mansion on Toulouse Street. For a number of reasons, Sophronie found this end of year a somber and melancholy time, and her husband became so concerned about her depression of spirits that he recommended she take the carriage to visit friends out of town.

Without much enthusiasm, she decided to pay a call on the Duplantiers, who had a plantation upriver, beyond the district of Sainte-Marie. As she was driven from the levee down a short avenue towards it one afternoon, she ran a critical eye over the manor house. It was single-storied, like most other "châteaus" along the Mississippi, but with generous proportions and a screened verandah. Surrounded by its stables, coach house and other amenities, it made a handsome enough picture in the midst of a luxuriant park.

There was activity going on in the buildings when she descended from the carriage, and the front door took so long to open she began to fear the house had been deserted for the business in the rear. At last, however, an old servant appeared and assured her that Madame Duplantier was at home and in the drawing room. As she crossed the hall behind him, another servant burst into view from a corridor and went quickly up to him with a muttered question. Sophronie, impatient of delays and inefficiency, simply walked past and thus reached the drawing room before him. Through the wide doorway she could see Hortense Duplantier seated near the window, and the tall, dark figure of a gentleman standing between the curtains with his back to the room. He turned, and Sophronie came to an abrupt halt.

The old manservant chose that moment to shuffle in and announce her. Hortense Duplantier twisted around at once, startled, and rose quickly from her seat, while the gentleman stepped away from the window so that the light fell on his face. The first and only time Sophronie had seen Jean Laffite, it had been across a vast room and he was clean shaven. By contrast, this man had a mustache. She knew him, nonetheless.

Hortense Duplantier, to do her credit, handled the situation well. If she had had warning, Laffite might have been swiftly escorted out the other door, but it was too late now for anything but prevarication. It was unthinkable for a lady of quality to force the governor's wife into company with the pirate of the Gulf. It was also important to deflect attention from whatever illicit activities were going on behind the house.

"Madame, what an enchanting surprise! It seems to be my day for the most welcome of visitors. May I present to you a friend of my husband's who has just traveled down from Donaldsonville? Monsieur Noël, Madame Claiborne, the wife of our esteemed governor."

He moved forward and made a low bow, to which she nodded while she sized him up. Smooth skinned, immaculately dressed, unruffled by the hostess's disarray. Being renamed for the season appeared to amuse him, and his black eyes held veiled laughter as he let his gaze travel over her in a single appreciative sweep. The set of the mouth under the dramatic black line of the mustache was firm and serious, however, and his tone when he spoke was respectful.

"This is an unexpected honor, madame. In all my visits to this city I have had no more than distant glimpses of you presiding over the polished crowd. I am as staunch a republican as the next man, but I find it pleasing to think a queen rules over New Orleans."

She held his gaze speculatively. "I am as fond of flattery as the next woman, monsieur, but you exaggerate. Only my husband dares try to rule here, and I am the last one to envy him the task. As for society, good company has a natural objection to being presided over. One aims merely for a little mutual tolerance."

Hortense Duplantier indicated a chair, and when Sophronie and the hostess were seated he took the sofa opposite, his eyes gleaming with interest.

"How apt, especially when it comes to New Orleans. I have met travelers quite bewildered by its diversity of tongues, traditions, tastes. But you are too modest about your own powers. You introduce into this society more than mere tolerance."

Hortense Duplantier cast a despairing look at the two people who had just taken over her drawing room and decided that they would not be leaving it in a hurry. "I must say, madame, I agree: your soirees are always of the most fascinating . . . May I suggest you both remain for dinner? We eat early today, in half an hour. My husband does not join us, I'm afraid: he is not expected until this evening."

Sophronie accepted and then watched Laffite as he made his polite thanks. She could see no debate going on behind the black eyes, but the situation was surely problematical for him. The longer he stayed in her company, the more compromised they would both be if the encounter became known. On the other hand, the activity in the outbuildings could well be connected with a delivery of goods, ferried across the Mississippi and now requiring safe storage and payment. If he had a contraband shipment in hand, he must intend sticking around until the business was settled.

Besides, he appeared to be enjoying himself, as he waited for her reaction to his last compliment.

"You forget that I was born in the Territory, monsieur. However many factions may try to divide it, I am at home here."

"But do you not sometimes find that rather an annoyance? If petitioners want to approach the governor they must do so by appointment, but to beg for your notice they need only accept one of your generous invitations."

"True, but guests cannot feel it right to importune me in my own house."

"You mean you have them all under civil regulation.

I wonder if you know what an achievement that is? I wonder if you realize the fascination that a certain kind of beauty exercises: how unconsciously a fine eye invites confidences, or a particular grace confers a feeling of being listened to and understood. There is always the risk that petitioners may become like suitors—easily self-deceived."

It was a rare, subtle style of flirtation, in which Sophronie very seldom had the chance to indulge. She gave the remark serene consideration before replying, "Then they must look to themselves, for I am not bound to clarify every issue that comes before me. In fact, I often find the most useful thing to do is to leave ambiguities unexplored."

"You see what I mean?" He turned his head to smile at the hostess. "Here is tolerance of an ingenious kind."

He had a courteous ease of manner that astonished her, considering the circumstances, and an alertness to every turn of her conversation and mood that was a compliment in itself. At dinner, she found herself responding to his adroit speeches and his presence. He dedicated himself to her, without meanwhile neglecting their hostess, who was gradually being reconciled to having yoked together the two most unlikely guests she would ever have at her table.

At the same time, Sophronie felt a growing discomfort, to which he seemed oblivious. When they talked of New Orleans notables, the name of Edward Livingston came up, but she saw nothing in his face to betray any memory of the ball. Yet he could not have forgotten that she was there that night; he would know that she had seen the lawyer stand in his path to allow Eléonore to make her escape. To Sophronie's sensitive perceptions, it seemed that their talk constantly touched on things that recalled her friend, and she began to feel them like thorns that snagged the conversation, halting it for a second, during which she had an unhappy temptation to pronounce Eléonore's name. Despite the complete lack of concern on his face at those instants, she had an intuition that the same thorns caught in his flesh too.

She might not have said anything, finally, if Hortense Duplantier had not been called away. At the end of the meal, Sophronie mentioned that she would need to set out shortly to reach the city before dark; just afterwards, a servant came in and murmured a few words to the hostess. Neither of the guests had any trouble guessing that the problem centered around what was going on in the storehouses to the rear, but the lady rose and gave an almost convincing apology about "domestic concerns" and left the room with the servant, no doubt inwardly cursing both her absent husband and Laffite, for the latter remained at the table looking quite unperturbed.

On the instant, Sophronie gave way to the guilty antagonism that had been building up in her all afternoon. She remembered the night when, for the first and last time, she had seen Eléonore shed tears. She looked into the charming face before her and realized she could not leave without injecting something genuine into their dialogue.

"When Madame Duplantier returns, I must thank her for a very agreeable meeting. I have been sad lately. This afternoon has been good for me."

He should have been warned by the different tone, but it was with his usual suavity that he said, "You have had troubles recently?"

"Yes. A few days ago I learned that I have lost a dear friend."

She said it looking directly into his eyes. She had no idea whether it was her own intensity or a radical response on his side that effected the change, but in that split second the encounter moved into another dimension.

He said nothing and she was obliged to continue—this time, with a shiver of trepidation. "She was on a voyage to visit me when her boat was intercepted by a Cuban vessel. There was a challenge, then an exchange of fire."

"Who?" The interruption was brutal.

"I believe you knew her. Eléonore de Rochambeau." The face before her changed again, blurred. She decided not to look at it. "A shell hit the magazine and her boat was blown to pieces. There were no survivors."

Silence, pounding in her head like a drum. He made

a sound, and she looked up. Her words had hit him like
a blow in the solar plexus: his eyes were wide and the
breath had been punched from his lungs. He believed
her, absolutely and without reprieve. In that naked instant it was as though she could read him like an ana-
tomical study, with every nerve displayed.

He wrenched back the chair from beneath him, lunged
to his feet and stood staring at her with the impact of
her words contorting his features.

He said something that sounded like, "Excuse me,"
turned blindly and left the table. The door beyond, that
led to the morning room, closed behind him.

Immediately after it clicked shut, she heard a thud
that reverberated through the floorboards under her
feet. She sprang up, then stood with her hands clasped
before her. She cast a wild look around the dining room;
she was alone. And so was the man she had driven into
the next room. Probably this was the moment to leave—
but she hastened forward to tear open the door.

He was just inside it. On his knees. She closed the
door and leaned against it, gripped by a quivering emotion that was almost fear. She could not see his face, for
he was bowed over with his wrists pressed hard against
his temples, and she could not be sure that he had even
heard her come in.

She moved, bent low, put out a hand without daring
to touch him. "Monsieur."

He gave a long gasp and recoiled, as though her voice
burned him. She saw his face.

The words burst out of her: "I'm so sorry! I had no
idea." There was a slithering of silk as she sank down
before him, put a hand on each elbow. "Forgive me. Let
me help you. Can you rise?"

His eyes had been tightly closed, but at her touch they
opened on hers with a look of horror that made her
catch her breath and recoil in her turn. He got up,
swayed, put one hand on the back of a chair to recover
himself, then took two paces to another and sank into it.

On her feet again, she looked at the bent head. Tears
washed into her eyes in a wave of overwhelming pity
and she cried out, "I never imagined."

His voice was partly stifled by his hands. "You *knew her*. What else could you imagine?"

"She told me nothing. It was all guesswork on my part. I never dreamed that you . . . All I knew was that you had hurt her somehow."

Unable to speak, he shook his head. She went timidly to sit at the end of the sofa near him, afraid to look at his half-hidden face, to see the way his shoulders began to shake, and to hear the quick intakes of breath as he succumbed to the devastation she had just dealt him.

Despite her own tears, she tried to keep her voice consistent and gentle. "Please forgive me. If I had known, I would never have lashed out at you with such news. I loved her too; that is my sole excuse. I would give anything for it not to be true. But it is. We have it officially." She stopped, took a decision. "My husband would disapprove of my letting anyone know this, especially you. But how can I deny you the facts?"

She fixed her gaze on the floor, so as not to see the tormented struggle that went on beside her. He still could not speak.

"There has been a communiqué between Cuba and the governor of the Territory of Orleans, so I am afraid I am about to make you party to a state secret. I must simply trust you. I must charge you never to pass on anything I am about to tell. Just today, thinking over it myself, I had some ideas about it that . . . I cannot be sure, but it is a message that perhaps hides as much as it reveals. They insist that Eléonore was killed in the attack, but—"

"Great God. You can do this, and then try to offer me *hope*?" He took his hand from his face and sat back, fighting for composure.

Roused, she spoke rapidly, still not looking at him. "The communiqué was from the captain-general of Cuba to my husband. It was a protest, accusing me of trying to set up a secret meeting between the occupier of the island of San Stefan and the United States Secretary of the Treasury. The captain-general warned my husband in the most insulting terms to keep his wife out of diplomatic affairs, and stated Spain's claims to the island. He went on to say that a pirate vessel from San Stefan had been intercepted in Cuban waters and challenged. It retaliated at once, the Cuban vessel was forced to defend itself and the San Stefan cutter was blown apart and sunk with all hands."

He said through his teeth, "Then how did they know she was onboard?"

"They found my letter to her, suggesting the meeting—so they knew exactly where she was going and why. The better to humiliate my husband, they enclosed a copy of my letter in the package, which arrived here the other day. He put it into my hands, with suitable reproaches. Every word was there. If they found my letter floating in the wreckage, it must have been in a watertight box. If they could pick up a box, they could pick up a person. My letter may even have been on that person—and she may have been alive at the time."

He made a sound between a sob and a laugh, and got to his feet. "Just how likely is that?"

She bowed her head and clasped her hands in her lap. "I don't know. If she were dead, why take so much trouble to forestall any United States interest in San Stefan? It would be much more expedient to simply move in and occupy it. If she were alive—"

"She would be in prison in Havana."

She raised her head, forced herself to look at him. "Yes. Now I have told you all I know. It is the least I can do."

It was like seeing another man. It was as though the handsome features, remolded under intense pressure, had congealed in a new, indefinable form. When he spoke, his voice too was rendered ugly by revulsion and grief.

"Thank you, madame. Excuse me. It is time I took leave of our hostess. I bid you good day."

He made her no bow, turning before she could reply and going back through the doorway to the dining room. She closed her eyes. His hollow footsteps on the polished floor sounded as uneven as those of a man walking to execution.

CHAPTER NINETEEN

Havana

Juan Ruiz Apodaca found his guardianship of the Ever Faithful Isle a source of pride, variable rewards, and perplexity. It was true that Cuba was not such a crucible of revolution as Buenos Aires, Venezuela, Bogotá or Peru, and collaboration between Peninsulars and Creoles was so far pleasant enough for two Creole deputies to attend the *Cortes* at Cádiz and voice support for Ferdinand VII, captive in France. The upheaval caused by thousands of refugees from Santo Domingo in recent years had been surprisingly beneficial, since they had revitalized Cuba's sugar production; and he was confident of the loyalty of the new militia, the Cuban Volunteers. But there was nothing enviable about watching over the security of what had been Spain's major base in the Caribbean, whilst the blockade of Europe was decimating the country's export of cigars, the planter aristocracy were terrified that the *Cortes* at home might be about to abolish slavery, a number of wealthy Creoles were avid to cut Cuba right away from Spain, and there was the haunting doubt as to what territories England might covet as a reward once Wellington reestablished Ferdinand on his throne.

In comparison with worries like these, deciding what to do with a prisoner from a tiny, obscure island might seem of slender importance. He gave it some thought this morning, nonetheless, especially since he was receiv-

ing a visit from Señora de Oleron y Siqueiros. He sat
sipping his favorite mixture of coffee and chocolate in
the spacious drawing room on the first floor of his residence, and reflected how regular her calls had become
of late, a habit he relished, since she was one of the
most seductive women he had ever met and she did not
always choose to bring her husband.

"Don Julio is well?"

"Yes." The blue eyes held a faint smile. "I have
scarcely thanked you sufficiently for choosing him as emissary to San Stefan."

He smiled carefully back, knowing that he had her
gratitude for the pension he had granted, and possibly
even for the husband's absence on the voyage.

"Did he go with you to the prison this morning?"

"No, I was there but a moment. I went simply to deliver some clothes I have had made for Mademoiselle
Roncival and to recover the ones I lent her at first."

"I hope she appreciates your unstinting kindness. You
found the patient fully recovered?"

"I am told she has almost regained her strength, but
not her spirits."

"You have not seen her?"

She shook her head. "That would be hypocritical. I
abhor her way of life, her crimes and her associates. I
look forward to her coming to trial for acts of piracy
against Spain, and to seeing her stripped of her vessels
and removed from San Stefan. Legally and morally, she
must be taught a sharp lesson. I took an interest only in
her *physical* welfare after the outrageous attack by your
man-of-war."

Her voice was a little unsteady on the last few words,
and he looked at her with interest, then said, "It was
merely a sloop, not a warship. The captain's intention
was to take the crew and vessel whole and entire. The
shot that hit the magazine was most unlucky." She had
been horrified at the result of the bungled capture, and
while the prisoner lay close to death had sent her own
physician and a nurse to tend her night and day. Told
that Léonore Roncival was certain to die, the captain-
general had chosen to assume this as a fact when he sent

his warning to the Governor of the Territory of Orleans.
Since then he had not discussed his policies with the
hidalgo and his wife, nor had he made either of them
privy to Sophronie Claiborne's letter, a passage from
which slipped into his mind as he sat observing the beautiful woman opposite. "You mention her associates—do
you have anyone particular in mind?"

"I do," she said coldly. "From Spain's point of view,
she could scarcely have chosen worse. She is in close
collusion with Jean Laffite of Barataria. It is well known
that he has used San Stefan as a station for his raids on
Spanish vessels."

"Well known? You learned this from whom, exactly?"

She gave a hard smile. "From a reliable informant.
But no one who could be used as a witness against Laffite or her. Other means are needed to break that foul
alliance; I rejoice that you and the public prosecutor
have found them."

He put down his cold cup and signaled to the servant
to pour his guest more coffee. She declined it, however,
and rose to leave.

As he bowed over her hand, Apodaca said, "We are
now building the case against Léonore Roncival. I have
called for the advice of a very learned gentleman, who
is daily expected from Santiago de Cuba. Don Luis de
Arango, a specialist in the law of nations."

Her face froze. "But surely—your prosecutor has it
all in hand. He assures me you will have the power to
exile her from San Stefan and seize it for Spain. What
else can this Don Luis propose?"

He shrugged. "Execution?" He noticed her sudden
pallor and said at once, "Señora, forgive me. I should
never speak so before a lady. Let me say only that I
shall welcome Don Luis's opinion and I shall not act
until we have sifted the whole issue."

As she left the room, he detected a mighty effort on
her part to readopt the cool insouciance she usually displayed when their prisoner was being discussed.

Apodaca did not expect his public prosecutor to be
very keen on the invitation to the more widely qualified

Don Luis: officials in Havana were jealous about the case and were likely to resent his consulting someone they considered to be a pure academician. Don Luis, who had never bothered to visit Havana, lived as a virtual recluse in Santiago de Cuba, but had a formidable reputation in the Caribbean.

Don Luis was a scholar and a gentleman, who had gone home to Spain for his education and made a brilliant success of his law studies in Toledo. He had never practiced, having ample private means and no need of a career in the courts, and having early chosen international law as his field. After ten years in Europe he returned to the family mansion in Santiago de Cuba, where from his vast library he corresponded with learned men all over the world and published an impressive series of books. He was a luminary of the Royal Economic Society of the Friends of the Country, and a distant relative of Francisco de Arango y Parreño, the first syndic of the *consulado* that had represented Cuban interests in Madrid since the 1790s.

When the gentleman was announced that afternoon, Apodaca felt a strong curiosity, for he had never met him either.

His first reaction was surprise. He had expected to see a man of mature years, with a slightly faded look caused by his indoor existence, and a studious manner. But the gentleman was considerably younger than he had imagined, and his face had a healthy color set off by a neat imperial and curled hair of a short, fashionable cut. The only sign of neglect in his attire was the coat, which was shiny with age and looked rather as though he had slept in it—but he had after all just arrived from his journey, and the clothes he wore beneath were of fine quality and in the first taste.

The gaze was direct, even a little disconcerting, and the accent was pure Castilian. "Excellency, my apologies for the delay. I had hoped to reach here yesterday afternoon."

"Not at all. Pray be seated and allow me to offer you some refreshment. I appreciate your coming to see me straightaway, but we must not tire you. Let us discuss this tomorrow instead, if you prefer. After all, the prisoner can wait!"

His guest frowned and sat down. "What state is she in?"

"Barely recovered, but fit enough to stand trial."

The lawyer had been brushing a thread off one knee of his tight pantaloons but his thick-lashed eyelids flew up at this. "She was in danger?"

"Yes. I explained that in my last letter." Apodaca observed Arango's fastidiousness with hidden amusement. It seemed pointless for the man to concern himself with the nether garments when his coat was threadbare at the elbows and, now that he was seated, rode halfway up his forearms. Years of hunching over his desk at home must have made him the despair of his tailor.

The guest gave a flick of his fingers to wave away the manservant who was offering drinks. "Would you be so kind as to recount the affair from the beginning?"

"Gladly." He made the story brief and was interrupted only once by Arango.

"What caused the captain of the sloop to challenge the cutter? Did he know that it was from San Stefan?"

"Yes. One of his lieutenants was aboard *El Santo Rosario* when Don Julio de Oleron y Siqueiros made his visit to the island. The officer recognized the vessel—it had been in harbor at the time."

The guest's dark gaze was iron hard. "I thought you were going to start at the beginning. But there is another beginning to this story. What visit to San Stefan, and what was its purpose?"

Irritated at having to repeat information he had already given in his correspondence, Apodaca took a deep breath. "Our emissary was told to make it clear to Roncival that we know where she is to be found. And also what she has perpetrated against Spanish shipping. It was a mission of intimidation that did not achieve its purpose." He then returned to the destruction of the cutter, the sloop's sweep past to see what could be picked up, the retrieval of a few items, amongst them the sealed box containing the letter from Madame Claiborne.

When he got to the moment when Léonore Roncival was spotted unconscious in the water, her body draped over a piece of broken timber, his guest rose abruptly to his feet and began to pace the floor. Apodaca glanced up and the lawyer gave him a veiled look devoid of apology.

"It aids reflection. Pray continue."

"There is little more to say. She was revived, with great difficulty, and for several days it was uncertain whether she would live. She was cared for by a physician recommended by the Señor and Señora Oleron y Siqueiros. She has now recovered, though there is lingering damage, as much mental as physical."

The lawyer's eyes had widened a little. "You have seen her yourself?"

"No, that is quite unnecessary."

Arango came to a halt between the silk curtains of a wide window and faced him with a look of stern inquiry "What else did you find in the box, apart from the letter?"

"A large sum in banknotes."

"In what currency?"

"American dollars."

"Pitiful. Did anything in the wreckage provide evidence of *any* of her activities, on this voyage or in the past?"

"No. But the letter—"

"I should like to see that, if you please."

"I have already told you—"

"If you please. Since it appears to be the only useful item we possess."

Apodaca unlocked his desk and handed it over. His guest stopped his annoying maneuvers, sat down and read it, his firm lips set in an inexpressive line, the eyes downcast. From what Apodaca could see, the letter seemed to take some of the stuffing out of him for the moment. It was folded and slipped into his fob pocket.

"Don Luis, that is the original. So far we have made

only one copy, which was sent to the Governor of the Territory of Orleans."

"I shall return it in due course. Now, to business." He put a hand on each impeccable knee and raised the beautifully shaped black eyebrows. "Before we discuss the trial, I must know the outcome you desire. That is why I am here: not to tell you about the law, but to hear from you exactly what you have been trying to achieve. The law, Excellency, must not dictate in this matter. Think of it as your servant."

For the first time, Apodaca began to be cautiously glad he had unearthed this gentleman from his library. "Let's be clear about Roncival. Her plunder of Spanish vessels is an unholy inconvenience. The alliance with Laffite on our back doorstep is damned infernal cheek. But what I won't have is her truck with America."

"Explain."

"For the last few years the Caribbean has been an area of unrest, revolution and war for every country except the United States. I don't need to tell you how tempting it is for that nation to take advantage of the uncertainty. Witness the loss of West Florida. We know that only two years ago the government was being urged to annex Cuba. And this year we have had an American secret agent going the rounds." He was pleased to see Arango sit up; at last he had told the man something he did not know. "We have learned his name and can guess his business. William Thaler. He was frightening planters with what would happen if the *Cortes* abolished slavery or Great Britain decided to turn history back and reclaim us—ruin and invasion, from either or both of which we could be neatly rescued by the benevolent United States."

He paused a moment, eyeing the lawyer with despondency. "Madison's belligerence towards Britain makes the situation even more threatening. The United States is looking north to Canada with a hellish ambition it has not shown since the Revolution. What it sees on looking south, I shudder to think. I don't care how small San Stefan may be—I will not countenance its becoming an American base."

"Then why did you forewarn Roncival by sending your emissary to threaten her?"

"My dear Don Luis, I sent him to report on the island's defenses, about which we knew nothing. The captain of *El Santo Rosario* tells me it is impossible to force a way into the lagoon and pointless to set up a blockade—the island is self-sufficient. I was uncertain how to proceed until she very fortuitously played into our hands. Now that I have her, I intend to have San Stefan. That is the purpose of the trial."

"I see." His guest rose and began to pace again, his long legs measuring out the parquet floor. "You realize that a conviction against your prisoner for piracy, no matter how heinous the crimes, will not legitimize your annexation of San Stefan?" He gave Apodaca a quick, keen glance. "Legally and diplomatically, the issues are unrelated."

"I do, thank you. Nonetheless, I have a certain bargaining power with the prisoner. She may well prefer Spanish rule to a hangman's noose."

"On the other hand, she may ask herself how you propose to assemble enough evidence against her. From what you have said, any witnesses to her acts of piracy and any booty from her crimes are one and all on San Stefan. Which as yet you do not hold, and which you have no certainty of conquering. You could only hope to gain anything from this trial if you made it known to the world. And it would be embarrassing to lose it in the international arena."

"She has mounted any number of attacks on Spanish vessels under our very noses!"

"Her captains and crews have. But I understand that she has never been seen on the offending ships."

"No, but—"

"Then you must prove the connection. And all possible informers of that kind are on San Stefan."

"We have the woman herself, damn it!"

To the captain-general's relief, the lawyer took a chair. "Precisely. I have a proposal. I shall visit her and see what can be done to extort a confession." He gave a harsh, uncharacteristic smile. "I am not unversed in these procedures. If I fail, which is not impossible, I would recommend that you give up a trial in Havana." Against the captain-general's instant protest, he held up one well-shaped hand. "Escort her back to San Stefan, use her as hostage to gain control of the island and hold her there, in her own residence, under permanent arrest."

About to explode again, the captain-general suddenly realized the genius of his guest's strategy. No trial meant no effort and time spent in raking elusive evidence together. No trial meant that neighbors would be unaware of his moves against San Stefan until the Cuban administration had been put in place. As far as United States interference was concerned, Havana had complete freedom of movement—for, thanks to his own initiative, Léonore Roncival was officially dead. There was no need to announce her recovery, if at all, until she was on the island.

"You are confident we could keep her under arrest indefinitely?"

"The wheels of litigation revolve slowly. In international disputes, they may take a decade to turn an inch."

For the first time in days, the captain-general allowed himself an unguarded smile. "Interrogate her whenever you choose, Don Luis, with my blessing. But take care: she is reputed to have wiles of her own. They call her Siren."

The smile he got in return held not a vestige of the scholarly. "Excellency, leave her to me."

The Bateria de Santa Clara outside Havana was named for the Spanish governor who had had it built late in the previous century. The high curved terrace, spiked with cannon, was edged by a stone parapet looking out over the sea. Behind and below the massive rampart were the magazines, armory, stores and living quarters of the guards and gunners. And in a low-ceilinged corner so far from the sound of shot and shell that it seemed carved from the bedrock of the bluff, was the little prison, containing recesses set side by side like stone pigeonholes, used as cells for soldiers on detention.

Apodaca had chosen the Bateria because he preferred
to hold his prisoner in an outpost rather than within the
city. Its lonely position was convenient if he should need
to transport her elsewhere—a ship could load up and
leave harbor discreetly and moor off the Bateria to receive prisoner and escort from a longboat sent out from
below the ramparts.

It was many days before Léonore could piece together
where she was and what her captors might intend. Battered and bruised, and with her lungs and head on fire,
she drifted in and out of consciousness under the care
of a strange man and woman who seemed to have materialized from the sickening ocean swell that figured in
her memory. Then came the misery of complete recall,
and she lay weeping for hours, thinking of Philibert and
all the companions who had been blown apart with the
cutter. She owed her own life to the young man whose
warm, breathing body she had clasped as a shield just
before the fatal shot tore its way through to the barrels
of gunpowder.

They had all died for her sake; and in this time of
anguish and loss her love of San Stefan seemed like torture rather than a comfort. Ever since Laffite had invaded her island she had known how vital it was to her.
And with no family left, she had made its people her
own. The unique tribe that they formed together was
her strength and her responsibility—and she had just
failed them. It was as though her whole identity were
thrown into question.

She was not ill treated. The stone cube that housed
her might ooze a little moisture from its walls, but the
mattress they had laid her on was dry, and a table and
chairs had been provided for the use of the two people
who came to tend her. Eventually she grew strong
enough to be escorted several times a day to the empty
cell next to her own. Water was brought to it and there
was a bench with a ewer, jug and towels, a covered
bucket and one change of clothes.

She was not badly fed, either, but she had no interest
in food and still less in resistance. She could not even
summon any resentment against the guards, for they

were not the men who had blown her friends to pieces,
nor were they likely to be her executioners if she was
convicted of piracy. The cutter's little crew had been
annihilated because of one person alone—herself—and
this knowledge hurt more cruelly than her injuries.

When she reached a dismal plateau where she could
bring herself to think about the future, she rather expected to receive a triumphant visit from Oleron y Siqueiros, especially after she was told by one of the
guards that the care and clothing she had been given
were supplied by him and his wife. Neither came, however, and she guessed that they would be unlikely to be
curious to see her until her trial. As for the proceedings
themselves, no one had explained when they were to
begin.

The first visit, therefore, was startling. The only fore-
warning she had was the sound of other footsteps following those of a guard down the corridor, outside routine
hours. The men paused on the other side of the thick
door and the panel slid back. She was allowed candles,
two of which she always kept burning on the table, and
by their light she could see the face of one of her jailers
looking in.

The chain rattled on the other side and the door
swung inward. The men entered together, jostling in the
doorway because the visitor had pushed ahead of the
soldier. She gave a cry, staggered up from the bed where
she had been sitting and put a hand on the table to
steady herself. The man in front, advancing on her with
an iron gaze that made his black eyes seem like hooks
thrown out to grapple her soul, was Jean Laffite.

In that split second he came to a halt, raised both
hands as though to adjust his high collar and very
quickly, unseen by the man jammed behind him, touched
one forefinger to his lips.

Then he stepped aside and the jailer announced in an
aggrieved tone, "Don Luis de Arango."

She was leaning over the table, openmouthed, her
eyes trapped by Jean Laffite's, which now reflected her
own anguish.

"Señorita." He gave a stiff-necked bow and said in

Spanish, "I am directing the case for the prosecution."
As she shrank away from him he continued. "I have a
few questions. If you will be good enough to sit down."

Bewilderment distorted her face and voice. "What are
you doing here?"

He lowered his voice, but she heard the tremor of
effort in it. "You will allow me to explain. Pray be
seated, señorita."

She sat, because she was incapable of doing anything
else. "And why should I talk to you?"

"Because I have been sent by the captain-general of
Cuba. Whose duty it is to decide your fate." He nodded
to the guard, pulled out the chair on the opposite side
of the table and stood staring at the man until he sham-
bled back through the doorway and pulled the door
closed after him. Then Laffite sat down.

As the chain clattered against the outside of the door
he darted one hand across the table and crushed her
fingers in his grip. He said in an agonized whisper, "I
thought you were dead."

She pulled her hand away. Over his shoulder she
could see the opening in the door where the guard's avid
face had reappeared.

Her heart swelling in shock, she dropped her gaze, bit
her lip and stared speechless at the table. If he was going
to do this, she had no idea how they would manage.

"I shall begin with the simplest of questions. Do not
be afraid, señorita."

She raised her head. The guard could see her face,
but Laffite had no need to conceal his. There was an
unbearable contrast between the burning questions in
his eyes and his smooth, clear interrogation.

"May we conduct these preliminaries in Spanish?
Then I may judge whether you should be granted an
interpreter for your trial."

"As you wish." Her fluency could not match his, but
avoiding French might help her to treat him as a
stranger.

He said, "What is your state of health? How do you
feel?" She looked at him in disbelief, then heard his
desperate whisper. "*Lionheart, answer me.*"

"You mean, am I fit enough to stand trial? Barely, but then there is no basis for one. My cutter was fired on and sunk, on a peaceful voyage. I demand to be returned to San Stefan and I also demand reparation."

He leaned back, closed his eyes, pressed thumb and forefinger to the bridge of his nose. He looked tired, driven, and she realized he was unequal to this task unless he had her cooperation. She straightened her back, composed her face and managed not to look past him to see how the guard was appreciating their little drama so far. There was nothing to do but follow Jean Laffite's lead and take the consequences.

"I am waiting for your answer, Señor de Arango."

He collected himself, leaned forward slightly, his hands on this thighs. His clothing looked as though he had been traveling in it for a week. The sleeves of his threadbare coat scarcely reached below the elbows. He said, "You fired on a Cuban vessel after it had issued a challenge in due form. Yours was sunk in legitimate defense, as will be shown at the trial."

"The captain of the cutter did not act under my orders—he reacted as he saw fit. He is dead, at Cuban hands: it is not up to me to defend his decisions and it ill becomes Havana to condemn them."

"You claim you were merely a passenger in your own vessel? Come now, señorita, your activities on the high seas are notorious."

"That is for you to prove. I demand to know the charges. I shall then inform my attorney-at-law."

"You really think you can find someone to take the case for the defense?" He injected scorn into his voice, while with eyes full of compassion he examined her face, her body, the bare cell around her. "Whom exactly do you have in mind?"

"I thought of Edward Livingston."

He was genuinely taken aback. "Of New Orleans? You know him?"

"Only by reputation."

He made an attempt at recovery. "You have a touching trust in American goodwill, señorita. As evidenced by the correspondence with Mrs. Claiborne."

It was her turn for unpleasant surprise. Sophronie's letter. They must have recovered her box. She closed her eyes, seeing words that were now engraved on her mind. "A certain gentleman. A certain ball."

His voice continued—steady, insistent, audible to the guard outside. "I must tell you, Mrs. Claiborne's statements in that letter were ill informed. She seriously misrepresented the state of affairs."

"Which state of affairs?" But there was really no need to ask. She could see from his look that he was not thinking of Albert Gallatin.

"You mustn't believe her. You must let me . . . As soon as . . ." He had to rise from the chair to stop himself from going on in this dangerous vein. She watched him nervously as he walked over to the door, where he turned and faced her again, his voice steely. "The truth is that you cannot expect to receive assistance from any quarter, least of all America. You cannot defend yourself against charges of piracy. Your best course is to make a full confession and throw yourself on the mercy of the captain-general. I have his permission to discuss terms, and I do not think you will find them ungenerous."

During the whole speech he held his left hand low, where it could not be seen by the guard. With the thumb turned down.

She took a shaky breath. "I refuse. I demand my release and reparation for the loss of my vessel and crew."

He advanced, leaning close over the table. "I shall give you a few more hours to think this over. I am sure that by tomorrow you will have changed your mind. *Trust me.*"

At the last whispered words, tears rushed to her eyes and she raised both hands to hide them. "How can I?"

With a stifled exclamation he wheeled, strode to the door and struck it once with the side of his fist. She could hear the guard fumbling in his haste as he unfastened the chain and slid it ringing through the bolts outside. The door opened.

He glanced back, said, "Tomorrow," as though he were spelling out her doom, then marched away down the corridor without waiting for the guard.

CHAPTER TWENTY

~⟡~

Mermaid

The ocean was profound, seething in Jean's ears. She was luring him again outside the reef, far below the coral, her long tail snaking within the tendrils of her hair, all her brightness leaching into the water as she sank, always just beyond his reach. The body turned like drifting seaweed, and as her pale eyes met his the head floated free and the severed torso and tail began their eerie spiral to the seabed, fathoms down. A slow current caught her long locks, as transparent now as trailing filaments of jellyfish, and they eddied up and over her face, hiding the bloodless lips, the drowned eyes. He called her name and it issued from him in a gout of indigo ink that dissolved silently in front of his face; then water surged into his mouth in a choking wave.

He woke sweating and coughing, and reared up from the sheets to take huge gulps of air. He dug his fingers into the mattress and pressed his forehead to his knees, aware of his raucous breathing in the still room, of sleepers he might waken in the dark residence. He stayed like that, bowed and panting, until the undersea images began to ebb away. Then he flung off the sheet and stretched out again.

Seeing her at last had made no difference to the horror of what he saw in his sleep, and finding out she was alive had failed to stop the nightmares that began on the voyage over, before he slipped into the little coastal town where he usually made his clandestine landfall. That instant of wild relief had given way to the desperate concerns of her illness, her imprisonment, the frantic research to uncover Havana's intentions, the urgency of intercepting Arango.

He had never felt the slightest fear of confined spaces before, but in the afternoon, seeing her trapped like a frail, wounded creature in the dark warren of the Bateria, he had been seized by a suffocation so overwhelming it was as much as he could do not to try breaking out with her, there and then. He had to get her out. Before Apodaca met someone who knew Arango, before he himself was recognized.

He had retired early to avoid being hauled gaily before the whole of the captain-general's acquaintance, including no doubt Oleron y Siqueiros. The exhaustion he had pleaded was genuine: since setting foot in Cuba he had hardly slept and his dreams had been as terrible as his waking anxieties. He had to keep reminding himself that Arango, no matter how angry and ingenious the little man might be, would find no way to circumvent the banditti who watched over him. And he must force himself to adhere to his own plans, guard his tongue. What on earth had possessed him to tell her he knew about the Claiborne letter? If there had been any good reason for that, he could not remember it. He had felt sick to the heart when he read the words: *the secret lady with the initial "M."* Could Léonore guess? Did she already know?

He sat up, tried to think. If she had guessed about Mathilde and himself, if she knew Mathilde was her persecutor, would she have consented to receive the ministrations of doctor and nurse, wear the proffered clothes? Impossible.

He rose, went to the window, unfastened the shutters and looked out. Havana before dawn. Silver light showed him an empty square surrounded by elegant buildings drawn with smoky indistinctness against a pale opal sky. He must be gone by afternoon.

Léonore was told nothing when they marched her through the corridors of the Bateria and up to the ter-

race in the afternoon. She was blinded by the strong
light at first, and things came into focus gradually. A
group of infantry, standing in double file along the parapet. The sweep of coastline beyond, then the harbor entrance, and Havana within its bay, basking under the
bright sun.

She made herself examine the soldiers. They were
armed, with rifles. She stared at the captain who had
led her escort up from below. "What is this? I demand
to know."

He said, "Kindly step forward, señorita," and gestured
towards the far end of the terrace.

She obeyed, filled with dread that in a moment she
would be made to turn and face her executioners. But
the captain stayed by her side and gestured again, this
time towards the sea. The three masts of a ship came
into view, then the vessel itself—a frigate that she did
not recognize, flying Spanish colors, its deck bristling
with troops. Directly below, a longboat was tied up at a
square stone jetty, accessible from a steep stairway leading down the ramparts.

"I bid you farewell, señorita. The captain-general has
made arrangements for you to be transferred to San Stefan
and held there in custody. Allow us to escort you onto the
San Pedro. It is commanded by Captain Estrada."

She stood with one hand on the stone wall and stared
down at the frigate. It was low in the water, evidently
well loaded with stores, weapons, men. Large enough to
carry everything necessary to set up a Cuban garrison
on her island. Well enough armed to mount a significant
bombardment when it arrived, if the guns could be
brought to bear on mansion and village from within
the lagoon.

Even before setting eyes on Captain Estrada, she
knew exactly how he expected to find his way through
San Stefan's reef. The idea stiffened her back, brought
her clenched hands to her sides. If he was keen on this
voyage, she would not tell him that he was making it for
nothing. Torture might await her at the end of it, but at
least she would be heading home.

All the time she was descending the steps with an

infantryman behind and before, she thought not of
where she was going but of Jean Laffite. There was no
sign of him, just as there had been no mention of his
visit, nor anything to confirm that it had actually happened—and in retrospect it had a dreamlike improbabil-
ity. Against all odds he had made it untouched through
the hostile port, penetrated the prison, by deceit or brib-
ery or both, and left unrecognized. She had not been
able to tell whether he had the slightest hope of helping
her; but there was one stark message to be read in his
eyes—he had come to her through unimaginable risks
for the simple reason that he had not been able to stay
away. The feelings that had coursed through her when
he seized her hand and whispered those covert words
had swept aside all the painful resentment she had harbored against him for so many months.

Henceforth she stood in a new relation to him—a
much more perilous one, for she had no idea how he
could have found out that she was alive and in Havana.
With no survivors from the attack, who could have let
slip the news but the Cubans? Amongst whom he
seemed to walk without fear of detection, speaking a
Spanish so pure and fluent it might have been the language of his upbringing.

On the jetty, a bundle of her belongings from the cell
was tossed into the longboat. Then she was handed in
by a lieutenant, and the sailors pulled for the *San Pedro*,
leaving the soldiers behind. She sat in the bow watching
the massive sea walls above her recede, keeping her face
closed so that no one could guess the lingering horror
that her dark prison inspired. She breathed the salt air
deep into her lungs. Even if she met death when she got
home, it could not equal the nightmare of lying in that
dark stone coffin in the Bateria.

By the time Jean left Havana he had developed considerable respect for its captain-general. This gentleman
of indolent appearance achieved prodigies of action once
he was convinced that the prisoner should be moved,
and summoned up the necessary manpower, equipment
and vessels within hours.

Don Luis de Arango was supposed to sail on the supply ship that went with the frigate and be deposited at Santiago de Cuba on the way to the island, there to concoct Havana's legal case for its treatment of Léonore Roncival. Jean had spent the early morning convincing the captain-general that these moves were urgent, making himself extremely unpleasant in the process and uttering a nasty series of complaints about the inconvenience of coming to Havana and his detestation of the capital, which he could not wait to escape. When he boarded the supply ship in the harbor, Apodaca was relieved to see him go.

As the little vessel waited in the offing for the *San Pedro* to emerge from the vast shadow cast by the Bateria, Jean staged an irascible conversation with the captain, which resulted in his being ferried across to the frigate and welcomed, with some surprise but no objections, by Captain Estrada. He requested an interview with the captive and made no attempt to conceal his impatience when he was asked to wait until the ship got underway and the routines for securing a prisoner onboard were properly in place. Upon inspecting the cabin allotted to him, however, he pronounced himself satisfied and stayed in it until the captain gave permission for him to examine Léonore Roncival.

He paced the floor or stood staring out the porthole. The wind and ocean conditions were favorable; this delay was not. He watched with nervous attention the way the midwinter sun slanted onto the wavetops. Every creak and groan of the ship's hull around him told him things he did not want to hear concerning the distance that might be covered by nightfall.

At last the message came and he was taken to the deck above and shown to a cabin in the stern quarter, which he judged to be near the captain's. It had two advantages of position: the devil grant one did not cancel out the other.

There was an armed guard on each side of the doorway. The usual kind of door, with no lock, opening inwards. The usual kind of cabin for a first officer: portholes too small for even the slimmest body to pass through, oiled wood floor, sparse furnishings. He made himself observe them, forced himself not to look towards her where she stood to his right, waited in breathless silence for the latch to fall behind him.

Then he turned and met her wild gaze. He opened his arms and she rushed into them, her forehead and palms hitting his chest in passionate collision. There was a second of intense shock before he felt her hands slide around his waist and she abandoned her body against him. He made the embrace and his whispered reassurances tender and gentle; and meanwhile desire shot through him, shaking him so profoundly he had a flash of panic that it would undo them both.

"Señorita." He managed to say it loudly and steadily enough for the listening guards. "I trust you are comfortable."

Still pressing her to him, he ran coaxing fingers along her temple. She was trembling, but after a second she drew her head away from under his chin and said in low but audible tones, "If I am, it is no thanks to the captain-general of Cuba."

He took her face between his hands, smoothed back the tangled hair, gazed into the iridescent eyes. "You are mistaken. Your welfare is of the greatest concern."

Her voice trembled. "What proof do I have of that?"

He could not help kissing her. It was another hot collision that lit a blaze in his head and body and lost him the grip on timing that he had been so determined to keep.

When he pulled back she laced her fingers together behind his neck and tried to tug him farther into the cabin. He shook his head and planted one heel against the door. If he could not part his body from hers, no one must come in.

"Since we voyage together, I thought we might take this opportunity for a little civilized conversation." His hands caressed her breasts through the fine gown, the bare skin above silky under his fingertips.

She inclined her head and half closed her eyes so that her lashes, much darker than her loose crown of hair, fluttered on her pale cheeks. "What makes you think I shall listen to you?"

"This." When his lips followed his hands she gave a

choking sigh, but though he feared it might have been
heard, he could not stop. In desperation he slid to his
knees, flung his arms around her and pressed his face
into her to muffle his own response. The words he might
have poured out to ease her suffering and his own
swelled inside him, pent up, smothered by her lithe body
and enveloping hands.

He felt her voice vibrate through his head and chest.
"What does this mean?"

He summoned thought, drew back and clearly said,
"A promise."

She arched over him and gazed down into his face,
her own suffused with a warmth that made the turquoise
eyes shimmer like melting ice. She could not speak.

He took the chance. "A promise that you will be
safe." Then with slow care he mouthed one silent word
into the charged air between them: *tonight.*

She saw, understood, gave a smile that was so tremulous he could have wept. He clasped her again, and as
his mouth descended and explored, she managed to go
on speaking, to spin and extend a gossamer veil of protest that disguised the way she shivered under his touch.
Above his head he heard the case for the defense uttered in a series of fluent rushes, amongst which were
the words "France," "heritage," "title," "sovereignty,"
while all the time she was surrendering to him in an
ecstasy of release that moved him beyond anything he
had known.

He would never have believed that he could give so
totally and still remember that if he were to walk away
afterwards the extreme of pleasure must be all hers.

When at last her words fragmented and caught in her
throat and her breathing turned to chaos, he rose swiftly
and snatched her up in his arms. She was still quivering
when he stepped away from the door.

He took a deep, unsteady breath. "I believe I understand you, señorita. We must talk further. But I should
not tire you. Permit me to support you to a chair."

He yearned to lay her on the bunk instead and to cast
himself down there with her. But he placed her on the

solitary chair, made himself release her after only one violent kiss, and stepped back.

All the meaning was in his eyes. "I shall return this evening, when you have rested and given the situation your most careful thought. Consider the point you have gained: you are returning home under our protection. Consider the advantages of cooperating with Cuba once you reach there. When you speak to me tonight, I hope it will be in a spirit of confession. I guarantee, that is by far your best course."

She must reply, or he would not be able to tear himself away. Collapsed in the chair, however, she looked for the moment so fragile that he had the painful idea that he had weakened her, and that anything he planned for the next hours would be beyond her strength. When she finally spoke, he was not sure her words even carried across the cabin.

"Very well, señor. I await your visit tonight."

He walked out between the attentive guards with his mind and body on fire, but they let him pass without a flicker of suspicion.

Léonore's sleep was dreamless for the first time since her capture. It was so deep in fact that she did not stir when the evening meal was brought to the cabin; she woke to find it ready on the little fold-down table, the tray covered by a napkin that gleamed white by the flame of a single candle.

It was dark. She rose from the bunk, stretched, and looked out through a porthole. The swell was peaceful and regular, and there was just enough light to see how steadily the wind ruffled the surface. Her usual sense of time had deserted her, and it was impossible to guess the hour. She sat down at the table and lifted the cloth. She must eat, to give herself stamina for whatever Jean had in mind.

Jean. Who had circumvented reality in a moment so dazzling it had the force of a dream. Who had made a promise that she accepted with no more resistance than she had offered to his lips and hands. She waited for him with a resolve that would not alter even if they

faced death together on the other side of the cabin door.
Transported, restored, pulsing with expectation, her
body felt capable of answering any demand.

When he was announced much later, he had the same
tense manner as before, and it did not disappear when the
latch fell behind him. He was still dressed in the threadbare
coat that must belong to the real Don Luis de Arango,
but under it he had a close-fitting shirt with no stock at
the neck. He wore breeches and hose without a waistcoat.
In one hand he held a soft leather document case with a
long strap; after greeting her he opened it on the table.

"I have taken the trouble to draft a confession for
you, señorita."

"What?"

"It contains a number of points. Before we broach
them, I am sure you would like to read this. Pray be
seated. And take your time."

When he drew out the sheet of paper she glimpsed
inside the case a coil of light cord and a brace of pistols.
But in answer to her look of inquiry he simply touched
the butt of one of them and then gestured towards the
paper, which held only a few lines.

She was seeing his handwriting for the first time.

> I know you can swim, Lionheart. But can you stay
> in the water with me tonight for an hour or two,
> perhaps longer? Tell me now.

She looked up and nodded.

> We argue. You become angry, then distressed,
> then you have a kind of fit, whereupon I call in
> the guards. When the first gets near enough, you
> produce the pistol and command his silence. Mean-
> while I take care of the second. The captain is on
> deck: we leave through the stern lights in his cabin.
> Trust me. This is love.

She read the first sentence with incredulity and the last
with a stab of recognition, remembering her challenge
at the Temple and his bitter, sarcastic reply.

He was only a step away, observing her so intently she felt he could guess her every response. But there was relief in his face when she raised her eyes and smiled.

He held out a hand for the paper. "You understand my suggestions?"

"Indeed. I am astonished you have the effrontery to show them to me." She ripped the paper up, crushed the pieces together on the tabletop and then put them in his outstretched palm.

He gave a sudden laugh, badly disguised as a cough. "Permit me to open the glass, señorita, and let in some fresh air."

As he walked to the porthole she extracted the pistol he had indicated from the case and held it in her lap. Then she took a deep breath and tried to assemble some ideas.

"What on earth makes the captain-general believe I would confess to crimes I have not committed? If he is going by your advice, I can only assume he is an idiot."

At the porthole, he flicked his fingers and the white scraps of paper spun out and away into the gloom. "You have not met him. You should be relieved; the captain general is not merciful when it comes to piracy."

"He is not aware of the due process of law, either. This is outrageous. I am attacked, robbed and imprisoned, held without a single charge being laid against me—"

"Cuba is preparing its case as we speak, and I must warn you that you live and breathe solely because of our care and respect thus far."

"And you call yourself a lawyer? What kind of twisted ideas are these? Unbelievably perverse! I refuse to say another word to you."

"Calm yourself. You will find us reasonable if you consent to—"

"I consent to nothing! I demand representation, I demand my release the moment we touch San Stefan, and I demand that you get out of my sight this instant."

"Señorita, I—"

"Get out! I can't bear it. I can't stand it a moment longer. Take your filthy paper— Abominable— Impossible—

No!" She rocked the chair so that it scraped on the floor, and injected such violence into her cries that the little cabin echoed with them.

Hastily taking up the other pistol and holding it behind his back, he strode to the door. When he pulled it open she caught sight of the guards' faces turned towards her. Giving way to inarticulate frenzy, she flung herself back in the chair so that her bosom risked being exposed by the taut gown and tossed her head from side to side, all the time holding the pistol concealed.

Through her clamor she heard Jean say, "Do something! How am I supposed to manage her like this?"

Heavy steps came towards her. Through her lashes she saw a bulky figure looming, his face uncertain, his rifle pointing to the floor.

Another step. She sat bolt upright and extended the pistol to within inches of his heart. "Not one word. Lower the rifle, slowly. Now."

He was transfixed. There was a crack, and the other guard subsided under a vicious tap on the head from Jean's pistol, was caught and deposited neatly on the boards.

"Now," she said again, desperate to keep the man's attention as Jean reached back and silently pushed the door shut, then advanced.

It was messier than the first encounter, for her guard, crouching as he put the rifle on the floor, realized rather late that it was not in their interest for a pistol shot or a shout to be heard. He twisted to protect himself and gave a cry that was trapped just in time by Jean's hand as he flung an arm around his neck from behind. They struggled, stumbled, then from an awkward angle Jean used the pistol butt again; there was a ghastly crunch as the other man collapsed.

She leaped to her feet, Jean grabbed her pistol and stuffed it into the bag, then seized her wrist. "Quickly."

There was no one in the corridor when they emerged and shut the door behind them. He led her swiftly in the dark to another door. There was faint light shining through the crack beneath it, but he opened it without hesitation and pulled her through.

All along she felt a tremor in his arm that communicated itself to her wrist. When he let go, she realized it was laughter. He clasped her close for a second, his breath tickling her ear as he whispered, "I never guessed you could come so gloriously undone!"

"Just don't try me again."

They moved in unison. He jammed a stool against the door while she ran across to the lead-light windows in the stern of the captain's cabin, pushed out the lowest panel and fixed it open with a long iron catch.

Jean flung one end of the lanyard once, twice around the beam from which the central lantern hung. He murmured, "Off with the dress and put it in the bag."

When she was stripped to chemise and drawers, he took the other end of the lanyard, which was already knotted in a slack noose, and dropped it over her head and shoulders, then lifted it so that it caught under her armpits.

"It will bite, my darling—I could find nothing else. I'll lower you, then follow. Enter the water as neatly as you can. For God's sake, don't slip free until I join you."

In a few seconds she was being let down over the stern, her hands and feet busy trying to negotiate the hull without making a noise against the rough planks, her mind filled with fear and regret. It would only take the captain to lean over from the quarterdeck above, it would only need him to return to his cabin or one of the watch to notice the marines were gone from outside the other door, and they were done for, both of them—shot trying to escape. She should have snatched one last kiss. Acknowledged the debt of love, in case Jean had spent his life to save hers.

She gritted her teeth against the cool shock of the water, and hung on to the top of the noose as the wake took her and dragged her straight out into the open. She bobbed backwards in the slick patch of water behind the stern, breathing shallowly with her mouth wide open, the flurry of her movements impossibly loud in her ears. Then with a jerk the rope came to the limit of its length and she had to lock her jaw over a gasp of pain.

She made a little bow wave of her own as the *San*

Pedro towed her through the black water. Then Jean, wearing neither coat nor shirt, swung out and onto the rope and she was being drawn back again towards the stern. He glided down hand over hand until he was poised above her, holding a knife in his teeth and with the leather bag slung across his chest. He lifted the flap, drew out one of the pistols and slid down farther so he could hand it to her carefully by the barrel. Then with a slither he was in the water, and the loaded line began to drift back with the current, ready to draw taut again and expose them both to any observers above.

He took the knife in his free hand. His body was molded to hers by the moving water; his mouth was a fraction of an inch from her ear. "Keep the pistol dry." Then he slashed through the lanyard and cut them free.

When the cruel pressure on her back and underarms ceased, Léonore sank at once, but she held the arm with the pistol aloft, feeling a cold wave rush up her arm to the wrist, dampening the butt and the heel of her hand.

With one strong scissor kick she was up and breathing again, treading water, trying to find a rhythm that would allow her to keep silently afloat, with the one hand above the surface. The waves were high, and for panic-stricken seconds she could not see Jean. Then the swell dipped and she realized he was three yards away, making no effort to approach again. He must have dived and resurfaced at a distance on purpose, to reduce their visibility from the *San Pedro*.

It was so dark in the water she was frightened. The only light came from the stars, and the night would have seemed pitch-black if she had not been able to make out the darker shape of the *San Pedro* against the sky. The fear of being spotted, of floating like a practice target in the sea, of feeling a bullet slice through the waves into her body, gave way to the terror of losing Jean.

She kicked frantically, circled, searched through the gloom. He was nowhere. Then with the smoothness of a sea creature he surfaced beside her. He tossed the hair behind his ears and his white teeth gleamed at her in the dark, his finger across them spelling silence. Sound traveled so clearly over the waves that they could still hear the creak and tug of the *San Pedro*'s sails and the chuckle of water under her keel.

He struggled to open the bag at his chest, slid the knife into it and hauled something out. It was a wine skin. Treading water, he took out the stopper, put his mouth to the skin and blew it up. When it had ballooned to its full capacity he rammed the stopper back in, swam to her and gripped his hands over the top of it and let his feet descend so that he could hang his weight on the float. Then with another grin he pushed it to her, exchanging it for the pistol.

A keen look towards the invisible ship and horizon, and he hissed, "All right?"

"Yes. What next?"

He gave a soft laugh. "You wait to ask me now? Brava!" He paused.

She was becoming accustomed to the temperature of the water, to the slow rocking of the waves, but she could not bear any more silence. "There is a ship, I presume."

"Dominique's, in point of fact. The *Tigre*."

"What is it doing, quartering the coastline? With a view to discovering us by Easter?"

"Having observed us ranging along the coast and kept a discreet distance behind, it has been gradually closing in since nightfall."

"How do you know?"

"I know Dominique, and he has his instructions. Besides, I glimpsed the main topsail at sunset, stalking us from the west. He's about, Lionheart. Somewhere."

"So we wait until we glimpse another sail?"

"I'm hoping it will be easier than that. I promised to be off that infernal tub by nine, if we had to take the captain with us to the bottom. From nine thirty, there is to be a torch at the crosstrees of the *Tigre*. High enough not to destroy visibility from the deck. Bright enough to give us their position."

"And the pistol? We have but one shot."

"True, but there's a flare down the tube—a pitiful

makeshift one because that was all I could manage, but it need only go up a few yards. And there's the whistle you've got dangling from the float."

She dredged a sleek little cylinder of jet out of the water.

"Try it."

She blew, produced a few bubbles. Blew again with greater force and energy. Nothing. The dreadful silence closed in further, tightening its tentacles. Even in the dark he saw her expression, put out a hand to her wet cheek.

"It makes no sound for us. But Dominique's pointer can hear it. Belair—he's sailed on the *Tigre* for years. He can pinpoint that sound within a radius of two miles."

It took hours. For a while they exchanged the float occasionally to relieve each other's strength. Then he refused to take it. The water was tepid enough to keep their blood flowing, but there were cool eddies that triggered bouts of shivering in Léonore. At these times he would glide up to her, wrap himself around her from behind and give her the warm protection of his upper body while kicking so that her weight alone was supported by the float. He had recognized her new fear of the vast oceanic silence, and for the rest of the time he floated lazily near her on his back, talking of many things: villages on Barataria where the fishermen and smugglers made their homes; sorties among the bayous when they sent out decoy boats to lure the customs patrols away from the real shipments; expeditions inland to riverside towns like Saint Louis that she had never seen.

He said nothing about how he had found her, what he had done in Havana, what his dealings were with Arango and Apodaca. That was all too raw, too recent, to be built into the life raft of words he was offering her.

He saw the sails first, swam up to her and put the whistle to his lips.

Her teeth were chattering, but she said, "It's too soon!"

"No, they're close. I should have seen them before. I was too busy spouting."

He blew constantly, and at last Léonore spotted the

vessel's change in tack. When it was near enough, he pulled the trigger of the pistol and against the million odds they had each laid for failure it went off, sending up a flare like a sputtering firecracker that bathed them both in a crazy radiance for about ten seconds before fizzling into the waves. Also against the odds, it made them both laugh.

It was enough. A longboat from the *Tigre* was soon within shouting distance and there was scarcely time for the wonder of relief before they were between the sweeps and the sailors were hauling them inboard. There was hot rum in the boat, and blankets; Jean flung two around Léonore before he donned his own, then sat with her on the thwart, holding her tightly.

He spoke only once as they were rowed to the *Tigre,* in a murmur that penetrated as deep as the fiery liquor. "Tell me this is love."

She turned in his arms and buried her face in the hollow of his neck.

CHAPTER TWENTY-ONE

Gallatin

It was late afternoon on the last day of the crossing. They would be at Grande Terre just after dawn the next day, but Jean had no wish to arrive. He had no desire to be anywhere but in this cabin, which Dominique had vacated with good grace and hidden misgivings, and which he and Léonore had scarcely left since.

In this time of thrilling intimacy, they talked endlessly. He had told her almost everything about the night of the ball, except the name of the woman she thought of as her rival—while vehemently insisting that she was not her rival and had never been. Léonore cried when he told her about what happened in the darkness outside the ballroom. It was as much as he could do not to tell her about the duel. He recounted as undramatically as possible the impromptu meeting with Sophronie Claiborne and all he had done since. She was horrified at the way he had heard the announcement of her death.

There were many painful moments. He handed her the letter from Sophronie Claiborne, unreadable now from its hours in the water, and watched her throw it into the sea. When they talked about it, he could tell she was tempted to demand the identity of the lady with the initial "M." But she had too much pride. And surely to God he had proved to her now that no other woman existed for him.

She was asleep, lying in the crook of his arm with her

hair spread over his chest in a bright fan. The only vestige of her ordeals in prison and ocean was this tendency to succumb to tiredness now and then. She would snuggle against him like an exhausted child and doze off with absolute trust in his nearness. He would lie motionless for hours, listening to her quiet breathing, filled with wonder and a terrifying sense of her fragility. Of the delight she gave simply by lying beside him.

She stirred, brushed one hand across her eyes to free her hair, drew back to look at his face. Reading it with ease, she murmured, "Only one more night."

"Alas."

"What shall we do with it?" She was only half joking.

"To begin with, Dominique has asked us to take supper with him." She put her forehead on his chest to hide her expression. He lifted a lock of hair aside. "We are his guests, you know."

Her voice was muffled. "Also, there are things to discuss."

"Yes."

She raised her head again. "Where do you think the *San Pedro* is now?"

He accepted the change of subject. "Havana."

"I certainly hope so. There was no point in their going on to San Stefan. What an embarrassing report they had to make when they got back."

"Apodaca must have felt equally chagrined when Don Luis turned up."

"I should have liked to see Captain Estrada's face when he met the real man. I wonder if he gave him his coat back."

"I don't give a damn." She looked surprised, and he tried to smile. He was never going to tell her the reason for his enmity towards Arango: the lawyer had been set on a brief trial and swift execution. "He was famous for wearing that putrid garment every day of the week. He just about burst into tears when I hauled it off him. I think he cared more about losing that than being hogtied by my men."

She wriggled so that she was lying on her side, her head on his shoulder and one arm across his chest. "We shouldn't waste time talking about them. Tell me more about you."

He closed his eyes, leaned his head back in the pillow. "It is my understanding, mademoiselle, that you have explored everything there is to find."

"I'm not speaking physically."

"What a pity."

"There are huge unexplored tracts. Your family. Where you were born and raised. It's not fair: you know all about my childhood."

"Do I? Very well. Which version would you like? The children of the Revolution, the foundlings of Guade-loupe, or the brave Cajun family dispossessed in Canada who came south to struggle in the Delta?"

She sighed. "Why do you lie so about your past?"

"I don't know," he said truthfully. "It's a ridiculous compulsion, like juggling eggs."

Her voice was flat. "You're not going to tell me."

"I was born in Port-au-Prince, one of eight children. My mother found the youngest of us somewhat supernu-merary and left us in the hands of a relative, Oncle Re-nato, who took us to Martinique and sent us to school for a while. Beyond that we're largely self-educated. He and one of my brothers are military men by experience, the rest of us lean more towards commerce."

That was all he would tell her, and she knew it. He wondered whether she would protest, as most women did. She let the silence lengthen for a while, then raised her head again and ran one finger down his cheek and around his chin. The tip grated on the stubble, which had grown since he shaved off the imperial. "As a matter of fact, I know a way to juggle eggs. My mother taught me. You make a hole in each end of an egg and blow it in the usual way. Then you pick off the shell very carefully to leave the inner skin intact. When it's collapsed it's small and flat, like a little piece of paper. You put it on a springy surface, a battledore racquet, say, and bounce it up and down until it fills with air and becomes a beau-tiful white egg again. You can make it disappear in a flash by catching it in your fist and palming it between your fingers. Magic."

He ran his free hand around her waist and slowly up her spine until his fingers rested lightly between her shoulder blades. "Tell me about the hummingbird." She could not draw back—because of how he held her and because of his confidences, which she knew he had not wanted to make.

Her head subsided onto his shoulder again. After a moment he let her roll sideways to lie with the back of her neck over his forearm, her body stretched out along his flank. "I was eight. I was going to be a sailor when I grew up, so I had to have a tattoo. I knew no one would agree with the idea, but I managed to trick our best tattooist into doing it. I convinced him my father had given me permission. Now that I look back, it's a miracle that Mirliton—the tattooist—ever agreed, because I think he was in love with my mother. Mind you, everybody was." She paused again. He was already sorry he had asked, but perhaps it would help exorcise the pain that seemed to lie behind the simple words.

She went on. "The hummingbird came from her. It was my favorite image of hers. That's why I wanted it."

He drew his arm slowly from under her neck, sat up. She glanced at him absently, then fixed her eyes on the cabin roof again. "She had a gold locket that she always wore. It was given to her by her father. I loved it; it was one of my great treats to get her to open it for me. There was an exquisite miniature inside it. I thought it was the most wonderful picture in the world."

He slid from the bed, began to put on his clothes. He moved about the cabin quietly, so she did not stop.

"Her father, my grandfather the marquis, commissioned it from a friend of his called François Boucher. He was a marvelous painter, apparently, but he lived back in France and I'm sure he couldn't ever have seen a hummingbird in his life. So it ended up being a rather fantastic creature, a riot of contrasting colors. My mother adored it, from the first moment she saw it. It was her most precious possession. She was wearing it when she sailed away from San Stefan, a few days after my tattoo was done. My hummingbird is correct to the last feather, but I'd much, much rather see hers again."

She raised her head, looked startled to see him by the door. He managed to say, "Excuse me. I've a word to say to Dominique." Then he shut it behind him.

On deck he chose the spot farthest from anyone else and leaned on the gunwale. The waves crawled below and he closed his eyes. It was like seasickness.

He remembered the rendezvous with Mathilde at the little inn on Cuba, her quick movement of resistance when he opened the gold locket. The iridescent, vividly painted bird inside it. His own condescending remark about Boucher's flight of fancy.

He pictured Marianne Roncival sailing away from San Stefan, determined to leave her husband, who perhaps had already turned into the moody, domineering man Adélaïde had described to him with such resentment and longing. Marianne, the mother of an eight-year-old child, who must have been consumed with hatred of her existence if she were prepared to let Roncival and her little daughter believe she had gone to the bottom of the ocean. He pictured her as he now knew her, traveling to France under another name, making the brilliant, wealthy marriage with which she intended to wipe out the memory of San Stefan. Until she was widowed, and then met Oleron y Siqueiros and dared to go back to the savage scenes of her youth.

He opened his eyes, tried to calculate. He had learned from Pierre that the Marquis de Richemont's youngest daughter was seventeen and pregnant when she defied her family and fled Martinique with Roncival. Mathilde, now in the prime of her magnificent beauty, looked in her mid-thirties—but she could easily be a little older.

And there was the resemblance. The catastrophic resemblance that had set off the hellish events at the ball. How had her daughter never recognized her? He ran a hand over his face: he was not sure how often or how closely Léonore had seen Mathilde. But there had been at least one ride in a carriage together.

From the moment she returned, Mathilde must have sought information about her daughter. Spied on her, perhaps with her husband's knowledge and help. And learned that Léonore had taken up Roncival's hated trade.

He narrowed his eyes against the setting sun. Mathilde had kept absolutely faithful to her new identity—so why this constant interest in the child she had abandoned? With a chill, he acknowledged that Mathilde had first approached him after she became aware he was linked in some way with her daughter. There was a possibility, distinctly unflattering to himself, that she had done so to get him away from Léonore. To save her child from a man only too similar in her eyes to the one she had deserted in such spectacular fashion years before.

Then there was the threat that had been passed on to Léonore through Guadeloupe, supposedly from the English. Could that have been concocted by Mathilde herself, to put Léonore off the supposed alliance with himself? He shook his head, struck the gunwale with the heels of his hands. No return of motherly devotion could explain the subsequent events. Oleron y Siqueiros's eagerness to undertake the San Stefan mission, first proposed by his wife. The Cuban claim to the island, the unprovoked attack on Léonore's cutter, the vicious determination to achieve trial and execution. If she was her mother, she was also her jealous rival, her worst enemy, her most implacable persecutor.

Out of the corner of his eye he saw Dominique's pointer scramble up out of the companionway and sidle towards him, its claws clicking on the deck. Where Belair appeared, Dominique was not far away. He cursed and turned to go below. To the woman he had snatched from death. To the child who must never hear that her mother lived, nor learn her present name.

Léonore tried to enjoy the lavish meal at which Dominique You presided that evening, but it was difficult. Jean Laffite's stocky, powerful lieutenant trusted her no more than he had when they first met, and the fact that he found her attractive did nothing to diminish his wariness. He was an excellent host, nonetheless: proud and fond of the *Tigre* and her armaments, supremely at home in his sleek ship of prey.

The first time they had sat at table together seemed aeons ago. This evening he made much more effort to talk, perhaps because Jean was unusually silent. He began by asking her questions about Havana and the Cuban fleet. Jean looked at him with disapproval, but they were practical questions that she could not resent, and oddly enough it was some relief to be able to speak of her captors in purely military terms. The conversation turned to the Bateria and its engrossing array of cannon, and she could see admiration in You's glance as she proved how much she had been able to record in the midst of mortal danger.

With a smile that showed he did not expect frank answers, he went on to talk about San Stefan. She wondered whether he still resented the loss of his thirty-two-pounders, and waited for him to mention them. He asked instead about the magazine.

"Monsieur Laffite was right," she said. "It's in one of the old mines." Then added, "But the treasure is not on the island."

Dominique You's eyes brightened. "Why not?"

"Because we're not silly enough to leave temptation too close to hand. The islanders see the treasure as their insurance. And it's all the more secure for being buried where only the Roncivals can touch it."

Dominique narrowed his dark gray eyes. "The Yucatan?"

She smiled. "Rather too far away to be handy, don't you think? No, I visit the Yucatan only to buy crops."

"Campeche?"

"Don't waste time speculating," Jean said dryly to his lieutenant. "The Roncival treasure is rumored to be in more places than Blackbeard's."

She smiled. "There was a young man in San Stefan once who believed he'd heard something useful one night when my father was drunk. He stole a snow and left in the dark—we all thought it was the end of him. Next thing we heard, he'd dug up half a coffee plantation on La Gonave. My father laughed for a week."

"You're welcome to inspect the treasure on Grande Terre when we sail in," Dominique You said with casual pride. He winked slowly in the way Jean sometimes did.

"Imports are up lately and the warehouses are full. So are the barracoons."

There was a movement of impatience from Jean, which she ignored. "You're still dealing in slaves?"

"Still? It's our richest trade—better than all the rest put together."

"You're mistaken if you think I'd want that infamy paraded in front of me, Monsieur You. Where are the slaves housed, Grande Terre or Grande Isle?"

"Both."

"Then I'll not set foot on either."

"But I thought—"

Jean cut in. "I am escorting Mademoiselle Roncival to New Orleans. Whether she stays over in Barataria on the way is entirely up to her."

She looked at him. He had said it coolly, and his face was unreadable. So far this had been a voyage of bliss that still possessed her, so being in a strange cabin, having a table between them, already seemed a painful disjunction, which would hurt more if he began to speak coldly of what was closest to her heart. She had wanted to land on Grande Terre, to see his new fortress, to have the walls of his home around her for just one night. He did not look as though he remembered that, or cared.

Dominique You broke the silence. "Why go to New Orleans?"

"To pay a visit to my banker. I have a fancy to possess more than one gown to my back, and I must seek the means to return to San Stefan. Also there is an appointment I decided on some time ago, which I am anxious to keep."

Jean said swiftly, "You still want to see the gentleman from the north?"

He was warning her not to mention the name before Dominique You. But his tone also revealed disapproval.

"I have no other choice. The sovereignty of San Stefan has been brought under scrutiny and I must act before someone else does. Again."

"Why choose the United States? Why choose any nation? My God, when I look about the Gulf, I see no power deserving of a shred of respect or allegiance."

"That is a fine, independent stance that I can only applaud, Monsieur Laffite. Just the same, you operate from United States territory."

He grinned at her, but his eyes were hard. "Not so, mademoiselle. Barataria belongs to me."

She caught Dominique You's glance. He said, ignoring Jean, "I do not quite understand your dislike of trading in slaves, mademoiselle."

"*Dislike?* It's very simple to explain. I believe all men and women are born with equal rights. Slavery is an evil violation of those rights and should be abolished."

He blinked. "I see. Then it must be difficult to know what to do if you happen to seize a slaver. But we can help you. In future, why not pass the cargo on to us? I'm sure we can strike a deal acceptable to both parties."

He obviously knew nothing of the abhorrence with which she had concluded the long-ago bargain over the slaves on the *Jubilation*—she had done it only for her crew, because failing them would have meant losing San Stefan. She stared at him, then took a deep breath. "Let me tell you a story, Monsieur You. My grandmother, Ayisha, was a quadroon." She said the horrible word with contempt, and he sat back. "She was a slave. She escaped from Martinique and went to France to seek her freedom. She was married there, to an aristocrat, the Marquis de Richemont. Despite her black ancestry, the marriage was sanctioned by the most powerful man in France at the time, the Duc de Richelieu. He also upheld what she did when she returned to Martinique—she freed all the slaves on the plantation. My grandmother still lives, and the black people who work with her have been free for fifty-five years. My mother and I inherited her convictions. If you cannot credit that I hold them on principle, Monsieur You, believe them to be in my blood."

With the lines of difference so clearly drawn across the table, the rest of the meal could not be comfortable, and Léonore became miserably aware that the opposition might well remain when she and Jean returned to the cabin.

Perhaps he feared so too, for they were scarcely inside when without a word he turned and kissed her, bringing her up, startled, with her back against the door, then arousing her with a violence she had never yet known in his arms. Trapped, panting, she responded deliriously to his plunging hands and kisses, her own fingers wound into his hair. Pressed hard against him, she felt him gather the enveloping gown, tug it to her hips. She flung her legs around him and as they rocked against the door they both let out a sound that was lost in the groan of the timber at her back.

So far, despite the fact that everyone on the *Tigre* knew what went on in the captain's cabin, they themselves had maintained some discretion. Tonight there was no control, no consciousness of anything but their own desperate need. When he took her, still coupled, to the bed, she abandoned herself to every sensuous lesson his body had to teach her and at the same time brought him into a realm that admitted of no restraint.

As a castaway, she no longer had any of the prophylactics the healer at Sainte-Marie had passed on to her, but she had still kept account of the date. Snatching her breath atop a great surge of desire, she tightened her legs around his waist. "Stay with me. It's safe."

His words caught in his throat, then burst out in a hoarse rush. "You're sure?"

"Yes."

They clung, cried out, were swept away.

Albert Gallatin, Secretary of the Treasury of the United States, was fond of New Orleans, in ways that his acquaintances in Washington would have found hard to understand. Having been brought up in the Calvinistic clarity of Geneva, he might have been expected to deplore the chaotic impulses seething beneath what Lousianians were pleased to call society, but it intrigued his analytical mind.

He enjoyed falling back into his native French again,

though the city's cosmopolitan atmosphere caused him fleeting moments of homesickness for Europe. He came with a sense of purpose, also, for he had been as good as assured that when war was declared on England (certain) he would be asked in the event of American victory (dubious) or defeat (possible) to help negotiate peace on behalf of the United States. And in the bargaining that would ensue, he had very little doubt that the fate of New Orleans would be one of the matters under debate. Strategically, the great southern port, through which all the produce of the West issued, was of more importance to the country than Washington itself, and it presented a most seductive temptation to the English. He had acquaintance and business enough in New Orleans to justify his present visit—he also had a curiosity to view again the priceless emerald in his adopted country's necklace of ports, the gem it could least afford to lose.

His hostess, Madame Claiborne, was an intelligent commentator on what went on in the city. He and she were united in considering America appallingly unprepared for war, and he had to be very careful not to alarm her when they talked about the navy. Land forces were supposed to have been more or less provided for by the army bill passed in January, but a navy bill introduced at the same time had been defeated by a margin of three votes, despite the Hawks' impassioned arguments for the immediate strengthening of the defenses for New Orleans.

One morning he was sitting downstairs in the breakfast room being served coffee when his hostess walked in. She and her husband had evidently eaten earlier, for Claiborne had already left the house and she was dressed to go out. After sending the servant out of the room and chatting a moment while she pulled on her gloves, she said, "Have you a few minutes to spare for a visitor?"

He rose again. "You are expecting a guest? But—"

"There is no need to move, monsieur. I mean here, in this room, alone. I intend the conversation to be of benefit to you, since you are in New Orleans to collect information. You will find this person interesting."

He sat down again. "Who is it?"

"An old friend of mine. Who stands in . . . a most unusual relationship to me. Some weeks ago I thought she had been killed in horrible circumstances, but yesterday I received a message from her and we had a most happy meeting. In the old days, she used to be welcomed openly in my house, but now the times are such that that is no longer possible. She has undergone severe trials of late, and lived under the threat of death, all because of her situation. Which is one that only a diplomat of your knowledge could hope to understand. May I bring her to you?"

He gave a startled nod, and she glided from the room, using the servants' door that led towards the kitchen. He rose, tossed his napkin onto the untidy table, tugged at his waistcoat and glanced down at his apparel. Neat, irreproachable, of a blue-gray that his Parisian tailor had kindly pointed out as ideal for any gentleman whose complexion tended towards the sallow. Good enough at any rate for so unorthodox an introduction.

She entered alone. The door opened, closed at once in the servant's face, and she took slow steps through the room to fetch up on the other side of the table. She wore an emerald gown of finest merino that showed off every contour of her perfect figure. He was aware of a wide, unflinching blue-green gaze framed by burnished gold ringlets arranged across brow and temples. Her full, beautifully sculpted lips did not open or smile.

He actually stammered. "M-madame."

She brought her ungloved hands to her midriff and dipped her body in a slight curtsy, holding his gaze meanwhile across the littered tablecloth and the remains of his breakfast. "In this house, I am known as Mademoiselle de Rochambeau."

He bowed, belatedly. "Albert Gallatin. At your service, mademoiselle. Would you care to sit down? I am afraid this is scarcely—" He began to move around to pull out a chair, but she did it herself and was seated by the time he got to the corner of the table.

He retreated, glanced along the board. "Coffee? I would gladly pour it myself, or call—"

"Thank you, no. And pray sit down. I promise not to take up too much of your time. It is infinitely kind of you to see me."

"Not at all."

"Monsieur Gallatin, for two hundred years my family has lived on the French island of San Stefan. It is tiny, very easy to defend and has a small harbor of no interest to the navies that occupy the other more useful ports of the Caribbean. Until recently we were privateers, operating with letters of marque from Guadeloupe. But Guadeloupe is now English and the British navy has greatly increased its activities in our waters. There has also been a direct threat to us from Cuba. One of our cutters was attacked off Havana and blown up, with the loss of everyone onboard. Except myself." Here for the first time in the extraordinary recital he saw a quiver in the firm lips. "I was imprisoned, and they tried to take me back to San Stefan to invade it and hold me under permanent arrest. They were prevented from doing so, and as you can see I am free to return home. But we hold no letters of marque, which makes us pirates, liable to retaliation from any quarter."

"You expect Cuba to attack again?"

"I have no idea. But now"—she gave a little shrug—"Havana is fully aware how difficult that would be. And Captain-General Apodaca must also have woken up to the fact that I have . . . allies, who might make an invasion more difficult still."

"Why are you in New Orleans, mademoiselle? To consult with those allies, or to seek others?"

She gave a gentle, appreciative smile. "Both. I have just passed a crisis, but I fear there are more to come. I hope you will not mind my asking you a few simple questions."

He bowed again.

"Do you think war is inevitable between America and England?"

He nodded.

"In that event, will the British navy be much more committed in the region even than it is at the moment?"

"Undoubtedly."

"Do you estimate that they will make use of Havana as well as Kingston?"

"It is more than likely."

"Monsieur, however the tide of war turns, I'm afraid the outside world has caught up with me. Dispute over San Stefan has just begun, and I must think about how I would wish it to end. I will not yield to Spain or England. France can send me no assistance. But there is a nation, at present neutral, whose privateers are the envy of all the maritime powers. I should like to know: what are my chances of one day operating with a letter of marque from the United States of America?"

He sat back. "My word. What you ask is a little out of my sphere. You must allow me time to explore the matter." He examined her, unable to keep the wonder out of his expression. "May I ask with whom the Navy Department would deal if it were possible to issue the license?"

"With me. As representative of the company of San Stefan. Our fleet consists of two ships at present and would never be more than four; the harbor is not big enough."

He said rather faintly, "What else can you tell me about your enterprise, mademoiselle?"

She drew a folded piece of paper out of her sleeve and handed it to him. "I am giving you the coordinates of my island. There are some other figures also. The number of inhabitants and the jobs they perform. Our industries. Our resources. It is only one page, but it reveals more than anyone outside San Stefan has ever known before. I trust you to keep this absolutely to yourself while you consider it."

He searched her face. "It seems to me, mademoiselle, that you imagine the United States might take some . . . strategic interest in your island. Yet you tell me it is tiny. And there are other powerful claimants. What advantage could our country gain from involvement with San Stefan?"

"Perhaps none at present, but you are on the brink of war. When it is over and negotiations begin, you will eventually reach the stage when concessions are being offered. You have a much clearer idea than I of what will be on the table. But there will be territory under consideration. Canadian, for instance. At that stage, the negotiators can find it useful to have some small concessions to demand or offer. Indeed, such trading can even break a stalemate."

He allowed his admiration to show, then frowned slightly. "I think I take your point. In all fairness, I must make another. If you permit me to consider United States' interest in San Stefan as a bargaining counter with England, you must admit the possibility of its being played to our advantage but not to your own."

"Thank you for your directness, monsieur. I am prepared to take that risk."

He looked at the paper in his hand. He did not need to read it to know how little it would tell him, and they had come to no agreement, given each other no guarantees. Yet he was prepared to proceed—because of where he met her, and also because of the steadiness of the clear turquoise eyes that gazed into his from the other side of the table.

He rose. "This remains a private conversation. In fact, as far as the Secretary of the Treasury is concerned, it never took place. Unless it becomes expedient for it to have done so."

"I understand. I am grateful." She extended her hand.

He took it and brought it to his lips. Her smile held a hint more of confidence and hope. He supposed he must consider that as his reward.

Jean had said he would wait in a cabaret at the next crossroads and watch out for her, but when she walked around the corner she found him already in the street. He was not alone. As she drew nearer, with uncertain steps, she suddenly realized who the other man was.

"Monsieur Rigaud!" She reached him almost at a run.

"Maître!" He took and pressed her outstretched hands. "What joy. Monsieur Laffite just told me."

"What are you doing in New Orleans? How did you get here?" She looked past him to Jean, who stayed a few paces off.

"You have no notion what it was like, waiting. We thought long and hard, and took a vote. We picked New Orleans first, since you were headed here. The *Hero* stayed behind, fully manned night and day. I came with a skeleton crew in the *Fantôme*." A crooked smile lit up his square, copper-colored face. "Mirliton told me to hoist the blue sails and they'd bring you home."

Her eyes filled. "I wish they could bring more than me."

He patted the hand he still held, then let it fall. "I know. Monsieur Laffite told me."

"You had no trouble from the customs?"

"We brought no cargo, and I said we were collecting supplies. They searched from stem to stern, but let us through."

"Praise be. Is all well on San Stefan?"

"Yes, never fret. The tide's right, Maître. Shall I make all ready?"

She looked at him through a mist of tears. "Thank you, Monsieur Rigaud. Thank you with all my heart. Tell the crew. I'll follow you."

He clapped his boot heels together, replaced his hat, turned and just touched his hand to the brim of it as he strode past Jean and away down the street.

She wiped her eyes, walked slowly towards Jean. He did not move or change his ironical expression when she stopped before him.

"They came looking for me!"

"So it appears."

"You have no idea what this means to me." He turned in the direction of the river and gave her his arm, and she began to walk by his side. "It means home is still home."

His only reply to this, while he looked up and down the street: "Shall we walk, or take a cab?"

She tightened her fingers. "Let's walk."

He looked down at her. "You tire so quickly still. And there is rain coming. You can catch the scent of it rolling down the river."

"No, I can't."

The noises of the street crept in to fill the silence

between them. The hollow sound of their boots on the banquettes, the clatter and grind of horse-drawn traffic, the rattle of other footsteps, other people's voices. She slowed her pace further. The longer it took to reach the docks, the longer she could breathe the same air as he did, inhabit the same warm space. They had agreed to part again because their separate commerce left them no other choice—but still she wished home could one day be where he was.

"This wearies you." Before she could answer he continued. "You have nothing to say about whomever you just saw?"

She shook her head, thinking not of Gallatin but of the brief, emotional reunion with Sophronie. She remembered her friend putting her hands on her shoulders and looking fearfully into her eyes. "I thank God I told Laffite what I knew about you. But never in my life have I hurt anyone so much. I cannot forget it. Eléonore, that man loves you. Take care."

She glanced at him. His profile was as icy as it had been when he slipped from her arms on a black carnival night long before.

She looked ahead, took a sighing breath. "I must go back to San Stefan. You know I must."

During all their last, magical hours, they had pretended it was not about to happen. He had found a house, not far from the ballroom of the Sellières, where they could be alone. Only once, in bed, had he made an oblique reference to what was to come. He had lain back and drawn her slowly over him so that her body rested on the length of his; then he ran smooth hands up her arms to take her wrists.

"Cover me. Cover my eyes." She obeyed, bent to kiss him, but he said, "I have had your image from the second we met. Speak to me. I want your voice."

Today she held her tongue as they walked the loud streets. She bit her lip when the levee came in sight, and stopped dead in the midst of the traffic when she glimpsed the *Fantôme* riding at anchor beyond the docks, the dark hull trapped in the sleek brown vice of the Mississippi.

Jean put an arm around her waist and steered her to the other side of the thoroughfare. They paused next to a massive pile of logs that screened them from the docks but not from passersby. She took no notice of what was happening around them and glanced instead at the darkening sky. "You're right. There's a storm coming."

At that very instant it struck. Lightning and thunder crashed in one fell visitation: there was a flash that lit up everything around them with white fire, and a sound as of a gigantic canvas being ripped from end to end. She screamed. Even in shock she saw him with absolute clarity, stark black and white in the vivid lightning, not a muscle moving as the thunderclap shook itself to pieces. Then he swept her into his arms and held her.

She clutched him, breathless. Her bonnet had fallen down her back and with one hand he undid the choking ribbon, caught the tumbled ringlets back from her temple. His voice was harsh in her ear. "What future is there, when I will not set foot on your island nor you on mine?"

She shook her head and tightened her arms around his neck. "We can be together. We are together. You and I . . . are voyagers. We migrate. I am only going south for winter, like the hummingbirds."

"I don't accept that."

She pulled away, rescued her bonnet before it slid to the ground, twisted the ribbons in her hands. "Very well." She closed her eyes. "You once said I could ask you for anything."

"Oh, God, Léonore, don't ask me that."

She opened her eyes, but he avoided looking at her. "Why? What would happen?" When she could not bear the silence any longer, she said in a shaking whisper, "Tell me what would happen if you stopped dealing in slaves."

He grimaced, gave a short, incredulous laugh and rounded on her. "You know as well as I. It is out of the question. For hundreds upon hundreds of reasons. All of whom would turn to insurrection in a second, at a mere word."

"You will not even consider it? For my sake?"

"*Jésu*. Surely you of all people must realize. They would not be a dozen at my door this time, they would be a thousand."

Her heart went cold. "You have had opposition?"

"When do I not? Last time they used your Santo as a spearhead."

"What did he do?" Her voice faltered.

"He's dead."

He was watching her closely and she had no chance of concealing her reaction. Ambitious, foolish, brave Santo, maker of babies, breaker of women, gone forever. She had no need to ask who killed him.

She took a step away and turned her head to the river. The longboat from the *Fantôme* waited at the quay. She could see the sailors in their faded oilskins and shiny hats. The handles of the oars and the neatly painted gunwales were dirty white against a backdrop of muddy water made leaden by the lowering gray sky.

Her hands were caught. Her fingers twisted inside his and she said on a sob, "Will you promise to think? At least?"

"Of you? What a question."

She could not look at his face. She lifted his hands, crushed her lips to them, wetting each with her tears, then tore herself away and ran. Down to the quay, stumbling and crying.

It was not like the other departures: once she was on the water she looked back and watched him the whole time. He did not move from where she had left him. He stood straight and severe as a sentinel, and his hands were at his sides, one holding the wide hat, while the curtain of rain swept at last down the river. It was only when her ship was about to glide out of his sight that she saw, through the merciless downpour, the black ellipse of the hat raised high in farewell.

CHAPTER TWENTY-TWO

❧

Bayou Lunaire

In London on May 11, 1812, the English prime minister was assassinated as he entered the House of Commons. When it was known across the Atlantic that the prime mover behind the British navy's persecution of American ships was dead, the public celebration was so gleeful it was as though the murderer had struck a vengeful blow for America's maritime trade and her damaged national pride.

Negotiators like Albert Gallatin hoped that the readjustment would grant time for the English to consider opening more conciliatory discussions with Washington. But London stuck to its two major goals: destroying Napoleon and controlling the oceans. Wellington, with his great adversary on the march into Russia, was beginning his costly but relentless drive towards Madrid and the liberation of Spain. At the same time England refused to change its policy towards impressment: constantly short of men for its warships, the navy intercepted American merchant vessels and extracted from them by force any "British" sailors aboard them, so that more and more bitter clashes occurred at sea. On land, though, England was obliged to throw all her resources into the struggle against her worst enemy, Napoleon. She did not really want war across the Atlantic as well.

Meanwhile, everything was being said in Congress to move the United States towards it. America's right to export its goods wherever it pleased must be defended. The English were suspected of stirring Indians to insurrection in the northwest, and congressmen kept talking about invading Canada. On June 1, President Madison sent a message to Congress that gathered together all the American grievances against England, placing impressment at the top of the list and ending with a full account of the weighty sins that England persisted in committing and that meant "on the side of Great Britain a state of war against the United States, and on the side of the United States a state of peace towards Great Britain."

On June 4 Congress voted in favor of war. Then the bill was passed to the Senate and approved. On June 18, Madison signed the declaration of war. On June 23, as it happened, Britain's hostile maritime regulations were revoked. A move that came five days—or, arguably, several months—too late.

In July, all of Europe expected Napoleon to be victorious in Russia, but Wellington meanwhile managed to turn the tables in Spain. The crushing blow to French forces was the Battle of Salamanca: on August 12, Wellington entered Madrid in triumph.

In the same month, Léonore was in Haiti on a visit to the sisal plantations on the island of La Gonave, accompanied by Mirliton and three of the women who looked after the henequen plantings on San Stefan. Most of the crew returned to the *Fantôme* at night, but the rest of her party stayed at the Amiral de Grasse, taking up every chamber in the hostelry.

Almost the moment she arrived she was handed a letter that had come in a few weeks before. This time she recognized the writing, and her heart pounded. She broke the seal and read it there and then, taking a few paces away to a window so that sunlight fell directly on the single sheet of paper and none of the others could glimpse her expression as she read. There was no greeting or signature.

Where are you? You have wrought havoc—all my compass needles point south. Any longer and I shall lose bearings completely. But first a warning. Havana has not been discreet: indigo sails on the Mississippi are now out of the question. On the Gulf, by contrast, they are more welcome than the summer sky. Come soon, in the heat. Come so I can take you to a place in the bayous where the moon at midnight burns like the sun. Come now.

Next day she was walking through sisal fields with Mirliton and two of the women who ran the San Stefan plantation, Consuela and Maïté. Meanwhile the third, Doudou, was standing under the thatched roof of a shed two fields away, watching the workers operating the combing machines and trying to assess whether San Stefan needed more modern equipment or could muddle along with what they had.

The plant that the growers of Haiti cultivated for export and local rope making was *Agave fourcroydes,* different in some respects from the two agave species that grew on San Stefan and in the vast swamps of the Yucatan and Cuba, but similar in the formation of its long, fleshy leaves, which had spines along the margins and a punishing needle point at the tip.

"Do you think we should be growing sisal?" she asked the others.

They were at the edge of a field that had lately been harvested, and the swordlike leaves, their cutting edges stripped off, lay draped over rows of wooden hurdles, the exposed cores already turning yellowish in the sun.

Mirliton ran a fingertip across some of the fibers and squinted at Léonore from beneath his faded forage cap. "The quality is fine. Worth buying. But I don't think the finished ropes will compare with ours."

Maïté, who was in charge of the plantings on San Stefan, said, "The workers here, they tell me most of this goes out of the country raw. The owners, they let the manufacture go by the board more than a little. They're not shipping that much rope—the cargo's fiber, most often."

Léonore said, "That means less competition for us, while Haiti is trying to raise her cordage exports to where they were before the revolution." She caught the sharp eye of the San Stefan harvest overseer, Consuela. Consuela was a tall, thin woman with an aquiline nose, who wore a brown headcloth tied in many layers over her tightly curled hair; the way she stood and held her head always gave her a look of fastidious pride. Léonore asked her, "Can we learn anything from the way they harvest here?"

"They're faster than us. Doesn't surprise me, considering who we've got working back home." Consuela gave a disdainful sniff. "But they're not so careful." She touched the fibers. "Can't get fine slivers if you damage these when you strip them. Can't get smooth ropes if you don't make fine slivers."

Léonore began walking slowly back between the rows towards the distant figure of the overseer. "We'll buy. I leave the quantity to you, Mirliton. Consuela, you and Maïté can pick the quality."

She wanted to increase San Stefan's export of cordage, and the quickest method was to buy in sisal fibers to augment their island harvest, along with any new techniques that Haiti might have developed in recent years.

"Can we have a shipment ready by the end of the month?" she asked.

Mirliton looked surprised. "Not with this lot! But sure, with what we already have—half a cargo for the *Fantôme*. You're bound for New Orleans?"

"Yes." She took a breath. "But we can't sail up the river. Cuba has named me for a pirate and San Stefan for a nest of banditti. If we show our noses in the Mississippi they'll be convinced we're smuggling something. At the least they'll charge us prohibitive customs dues; at the worst they'll impound the ship. The war makes it even more risky—they might confiscate the cargo as a security measure. I've no mind to make the United States Navy a gift of our cordage."

"What can we do, then?" Maïté said.

"If I'm branded a smuggler, I might as well act worthy of the name. We'll anchor the *Fantôme* in the Gulf at the mouth of the Bayou La Fourche and take the cargo in pirogues up to the Mississippi. Then float it downriver to our best customer in Sainte-Marie, west of town."

There was a stunned silence. Then Consuela said, "Jean Laffite's territory is right about Bayou La Fourche, Maître. You plan on getting his say-so when you sail by?"

"I'll discuss it with him, certainly. There may be an even better route, up through Lake Barataria. We'll see."

Jean, Dominique and Pierre were in the dining room of the big house on Grande Terre, with maps and papers spread out on the table before them and wreaths of cigar smoke drifting along the high ceiling.

Pierre stabbed a forefinger at the top of the largest map, which Jean had just unrolled. "Upper Canada has thousands of American settlers. Wouldn't that make it easy for U.S. troops to move in?"

Dominique shook his head. "There's no saying which way the Indians will jump."

"And England controls the lakes," Jean said. "Unless the U.S. Navy can—"

"What navy?" Dominique said with a grin.

Jean shrugged. "It's hard to judge which is in worse shape: that or the army. But if they are to move troops into Canada, there are really only three places where they might challenge the English. The Detroit peninsula." Then his finger moved eastward. "Or here, between Erie and Ontario."

"Niagara?" Dominique said. "I don't envy them that approach."

"And here." Jean's finger stopped at Montreal. "But the first assaults are almost bound to be back over in the northwest."

"Nothing for us to worry about, then. The English will be too busy up there to bother us." Dominique caught Jean's eye and sighed. "Unless they decide on a bloody blockade."

"Who needs a blockade when all America's fighting ships have been ordered to stay in port?" Jean rolled the lower part of the map right out and they all looked gloomily at the eastern seaboard.

Pierre said, "Most of the privateers got free before the ban."

"Sure," Dominique replied, "but they operate in the North Atlantic. Won't they stay there, with the choice of prizes they've got now?"

"I guess." Pierre shook his head. "If we're looking at sea power, America hasn't a show of putting any vessels in our waters."

Jean laid his hand across Cuba and spread his fingers out over the Gulf towards the great curve of shoreline from the Floridas to Mexico. "Which gives the English free cruising here."

"With extra battleships?" Dominique said.

Jean shook his head. "No point. Mind you, there'd be every reason if they were sending troopships in to invade."

Pierre grinned. "Then we've a while to wait. The English won't have any forces to spare until Napoleon's on the run."

Jean looked up, keeping his hand flat on the map. "You're not forgetting Wellington, I trust? The way he's cleaning up Spain, they could be shipping veterans our way by next year."

"To do what?"

Dominique picked up a silver paper knife from the table. With delicate care for the surface of the map and the tabletop underneath, he balanced the fine point and held it poised in the chosen place with a fingertip.

"Indeed." Jean continued dryly. "In the words of Thomas Jefferson, 'There is on the globe one single spot, the possessor of which is the natural enemy of the United States. It is New Orleans.' If they took New Orleans they'd have the whole of Mississippi-Missouri in the palm of their hand. It's a far greater prize even than Washington."

When he raised his hand, the map rolled up again with an eager rustle and sprang against the blade.

On the sunny morning when the *Fantôme* reached Grande Terre, the San Stefan company were not permitted to land. Léonore ordered the colors dipped as before, but there was no answering signal from onshore and no movement amongst the trees and dwellings on the point, though their presence was surely being reported to whoever was in charge of the island. There was nothing to do but wait.

And to wonder. Whether Jean was in residence. Whether his invitation had been anything more than a fancy that had come upon him in the heat of the night. It read like that: produced under the influence of some heady concoction like the *petit guave* they served in bars and houses of ill repute. She wondered whether it made sense for her to consult him about smuggling the cordage, and to thus allow her enterprise to touch his. Perhaps she should be keeping her desires and her commerce separate. Her crew meanwhile were avid to go ashore and take a look at Laffite's stronghold. They approved of the consultation with the Baratarians, and there had not been a single dissenting voice to the expedition itself. They trusted her, they were with her, more strongly than ever. The loss of their friends and the cutter, her absence, which might just as easily have wiped the name of Roncival from San Stefan, had won her their ultimate respect. She had been to hell and returned; they knew what that was like.

She had discussed the future with the council and they were cautiously enthusiastic about the notion of privateering under the U.S. flag. Six weeks before the declaration of war against England, the Territory of Orleans had become the State of Louisiana. In June, Congress had given permission for letters of marque to be issued to privateers willing to pursue British vessels. Only one of the Baratarians had apparently taken up the offer so far: the Laffites' "uncle," Renato Beluche, with his four-gun schooner the *Spy*. He had captured an English merchant vessel and claimed her as a prize, while Dominique You, raiding without a license as usual, had seized another.

Léonore's men were just as quick as she was to see the advantages San Stefan might draw from the war. They had also agreed, however, that it was rather too early to figure out who was likely to win it. It appealed to them instead to try a little low-risk smuggling under the noses of the officials to whom they might later apply with more legitimate proposals.

There was a pleased murmur when at last a party showed itself onshore. At once Léonore saw Jean amongst them; he was wearing the familiar black, and a wide hat shaded his face.

He sat in the stern facing her as six sailors pulled towards the brigantine. Léonore tried to keep her face expressionless, her mind clear. Her whole body yearned to give him a lover's greeting, but none of her crew expected such a reaction—this was business.

Aboard, he stood looking at her for a moment with an eloquent smile, before bowing and then taking a quick glance around the deck. "Well met again, mademoiselle. I see that everything about you prospers. I would say you are even more beautiful than ever. If that were possible."

"Thank you, monsieur. I hope prosperity continues to attend on you?"

"With more regularity than I deserve. To what do we owe the pleasure of your visit?" He included Rigaud in the polite question, but his eyes returned irresistibly to her.

"We would like to discuss a commercial matter. Perhaps we can do so onshore?"

He considered for a moment, tapping his hat against his thigh, then said easily, "I have other visitors that you have expressed a preference not to encounter, mademoiselle."

Her heart sank. "In the barracoons?"

"Precisely. I regret—on both islands."

"You might have arranged this better. Or not issued the invitation."

He did not miss the inquiring looks from her crew, who knew nothing of his letter. His answer was mild. "We have no power over when and where such captures are made. Monsieur Curtis brought in an unexpected prize just two days ago." When she said nothing he raised his eyebrows and said in a carrying tone, "But that will not prevent the men of San Stefan from coming on land, I hope? Rest assured we have more than enough accommodation, and we are not too busy to offer you good entertainment, day and night."

He left her no choice, for this offer was exactly what the crew had been hoping for. "Thank you. I—"

"Done." He spoke to Rigaud. "Allow me to pilot you through the channel to safe anchor in the Lake. Then we can discuss business. First things first."

With Jean's longboat trailing behind, the *Fantôme* was expertly guided between Grande Terre and Grande Isle to a mooring amongst the Barataria craft on the calmer waters in the lee of the islands. The crowd of vessels took Léonore's breath away as they came within view. She had never doubted Jean's power, but the evidence before her was compelling. If the Americans or the English brought a naval force into their waters, this was a fleet they could not afford to meet in anger. Jean was tactfully immersed in conversation with Rigaud and the quartermaster, and had no need to look her way to know the awe that struck the people of San Stefan when they took in Barataria's navy, the warehouses along the Lake and the bustling activity around the landing places on the shoreline.

She was contemplating it all in silence when Jean reappeared at her elbow. Without turning she said, "I don't see the *Tigre*."

"Dominique took her out not long ago and captured a vessel with a great swag of whiskey aboard. It played hell with someone's navigation, and the *Tigre* went down on a shoal." At her quick movement he said, "No lives lost. Very few wits recovered." He was quite audible to the few members of the crew standing by as he continued. "Monsieur Rigaud tells me you are considering two routes, Bayou La Fourche and inland from the Lake."

"Yes. Do you have a recommendation?"

"From the Lake. I'll guide you."

"The customs?"

"They're not in the area." He caught her expression and continued. "We have it on excellent authority. There's no risk to speak of."

"And what shall we owe you for the favor, Monsieur Laffite?"

He shook his head. "On a first run? We'll consider it as an investment in future trade. Your cordage is no competition for our merchandise. We'll give you a safe conduct for this shipment. If there happen to be more, let's discuss them when they arise."

It was even easier than she had imagined. Months before, this very smoothness would have made her suspicious, but not today. The arrangements were simple: her men were to be welcomed ashore, leaving a small watch on the *Fantôme,* and she was to accompany Jean in the longboat.

"Where? For how long?"

"To the place I promised you. We return tomorrow morning." He read her face and grinned broadly. "I'm holding you hostage for the good behavior of your crew. Or vice versa."

The bystanders laughed, and she could not help smiling back.

The rowers took them swiftly to the eastern shore and into the dense, winding channels of reeds. Léonore, calculating distance and direction automatically, recognized without trouble where they turned farther northward, and just how far from the open lake shore they traveled. Yet all the time she was most conscious of Jean, who sat in the stern with her. His brown, well-shaped hand lay on the thwart next to hers, and it would have taken the smallest of movements to brush it with her fingers— but she did not, while six pairs of eyes raked up and over the two of them with every sweep of the oars.

Farther into the maze, the men shipped the blades, turned and propelled the narrow boat with paddles. Then the boat reached a dead end. At each side, the thick, high stems of bull tongue rushes formed a barrier that grew straight up out of the shadowed water from a depth she could not guess at. One of the sailors glanced back, and on a nod from Jean all six drove their paddles deep and gave a few mighty thrusts to send the longboat shooting at the rushes. Scraping and squeaking against the hull, the vegetation swayed and parted, just enough to let the boat slide through on its own momentum. The thicket was scarcely a yard wide. As the foremost pair of sailors dug their paddles into clear water again, the longboat glided out onto the hidden bayou on the other side.

It was a haven. A long, broad stretch of blue water kissed by the sun at the center, streaked on the other side with dark green under the shade of overhanging trees. On the edge of a clearing was a little crescent of sunlit sand.

Jean was watching her. "Here we are. Bayou Lunaire."

She turned to him. "Why is it called that—because of the beach?"

"I named it when I came across it last year. Lunaire because of the moon, what else? Tonight you'll see why."

The sailors turned, took the oars again and pulled for the beach. Looking along the length of the bayou, Léonore could see that the channels at each end were too narrow even for a pirogue.

He read her thoughts. "Yes, it's the ideal refuge. We've hidden here more than once when the customs are on the prowl. We come through at a different spot each time to avoid smashing an entrance in the rushes. So far so good."

The boat swung stern-on to the beach, and he vaulted out into the shallow water. "You must not get those shoes or petticoat wet. Permit me." He lifted her out in one smooth movement, and she had just presence of mind to hang on to her parasol, which was all he had allowed her to bring.

Her feet had scarcely touched the sand before the boat pulled away. She looked at Jean in consternation, but he smiled.

"Never fear. This place provides everything."

She followed him up the beach towards the trees. "Overnight? What do we eat? What if there is a thunderstorm? Have you noticed what I'm wearing?"

He turned. "Every stitch. If that muslin were any

more transparent I should have had mutiny on my hands before we crossed the Lake. As it is—look here."

He had thought of everything. Behind the trunk of the largest tree were two large wooden cases, presumably ferried over while the *Fantôme* was being piloted into the Lake. He opened one and left her to examine the food and equipment while he undid the other. There was a waterproof tent, which he put aside. Instead he stretched a striped, fringed fly between two trees, arranged a rug on the ground beneath it and threw onto it a pile of oriental cushions. There was also a generous shawl from India, woven with silver thread.

She left him to the unpacking and wandered away into the grove, to return barefooted. The island was tiny, mere feet above the surface of the water at its highest point, but crowded with thick-leafed trees.

He stopped what he was doing, put out a hand and led her down to the miniature beach. She dug her feet into the coarse sand, let the water lap over her toes, then turned and slid her hands around his waist.

"We're totally, really, completely alone."

"You noticed." He gave her a flattered smile.

"For the first time."

"Except for the midnight swim in the Gulf."

She shivered and tightened her grip. "I hope you haven't been picturing any repeat of that horrendous exercise."

"On the contrary, I think of it often, with a certain slippery relish. But you're right: we can't swim here. For reasons that lie directly behind you."

She tensed, but just managed not to turn. "What?"

"Alligators."

She squeaked, jumped, cursed, and he scooped her into his arms and bore her up the beach, laughing.

The moon rose late that night. They lay waiting for it, languorous, sated, intensely awake. Warmth from the bank beneath them radiated up into their flimsy cave, the air as soft as the shawl spread across their naked bodies. Léonore had leaned against him and slid one hand to his inner thigh where it was crooked over hers. She could scarcely feel him breathing, and they made no sound or movement to disturb the deep, slow respiration of the night—the sea's whisper through the reeds, the regular caress of shallow waves on the sand.

When the eastern rim of the sky turned pale, the frogs along the bayou, which had been practicing crescendo and diminuendo all evening, closed a thousand throats in an instant and fell silent. A burnished disc sprang up behind the rushes, creating a frieze of the tight, vigilant heads, and suddenly all the night creatures began to shrill again in unison. The moon rose, spilling brightness over the surface of the bayou until it washed right across and from end to end, sending silver eddies into the farthest channels.

It was as dazzling as a new day. And at the same time the colors of the night around them took on a new intensity—the dark fretwork of leaves above, the umber crescent of the beach with the scarlet pinpoint of the fire where they had cooked their meal, the vast waterways behind and before, smudged with islands that were charcoal on fathomless black.

She gazed. "The moon's not quite full." It was as though a hot blade had pared an ounce of silver from below. "I should have come two days ago."

"Days! Months."

"But you and I coincide."

"Like this we do."

"And elsewhere. In other ways. Even when we are apart. Otherwise you would not have brought me here."

He assented with a soft sound in his throat. Lying transfixed, Léonore absorbed a shining certainty. For the rest of her life, whenever the moon rose flawed yet utterly perfect, and made the wavetops flare with slow fire, she would remember this night.

It was like swallowing quicksilver: swift, penetrating and final.

She moved her head to tuck it closer against his jaw, keeping her eyes on the shimmering bayou. Where their hot skins met she was aware of a smooth sheen of mois-

ture between them. A moment later the shawl slipped
off her with a sound like a muffled sigh, and he let it
fall beside him.

Her hand moved at last, slid inward, became part of
a tide that swelled through them both. When he rose
above her he had the moon over each shoulder. When
she looked farther up she saw how its luminescence
spread above the trees, masking the sky. Her head
tipped back over the cushions and she glimpsed a star,
far off over the dark lake, trapped in a close bracket of
leaves. Then it flickered, leaped and darted beyond sight.

When she eventually got to Sainte-Marie, the customer bought the whole cargo. She allowed him to have
it at just a fraction less than the usual price, while taking
every precaution to keep him from guessing that it was
smuggled. If he did so after her departure, she expected
him to reflect that the risk and cost of hauling the cordage to him by secret means offset the margin she gained
by not paying customs duties. Which was only just.

Since she was in the district she made a visit to the
healer, who examined her and pronounced her in bloom-
ing health. She was not surprised; every atom of her
body thrilled with undiluted happiness.

Jean had taken the same house near the Sellières,
where they could be together for two more nights. When
his business in the city was over, he would take her back
the way they had come, with the little company of men
who had brought the merchandise through.

When she left the healer's she had one of the men
with her, to carry packages and accompany her about
town, always keeping a few paces behind. Dressed as
she was in the finest of clothes, she would draw attention
if she strolled about or rode in a cab without a companion or a manservant to accompany her. There was a slim
chance that she might be recognized. But she would not
give up her old freedom of the streets.

Just outside the healer's she ran into Adélaïde Maselari. She was not alone either; in her train walked two
black women carrying baskets on their heads—making
a delivery, perhaps. Léonore faltered and stopped, and

Adélaïde smiled in her slow, familiar way. "No need to ask why I find you here! And no need to guess who you're seeing in town. How are you?"

Her own voice sounded nervous. "Very well, thank you."

The full lips were compressed a little. "No doubt you've been to the smithy and know all the news?"

"I have not."

"That Marie Villars just gave Pierre another daughter. Rose, they call her. So Jean's keeping you to himself, is he? Doesn't matter. They'll hear every scrap about you by the end of the day. There's nothing Jean does that Pierre doesn't know of, and same the other way. That whore's sure got her hooks in Pierre. And the little sister still has her tongue hanging out for Jean. I'd clutch him pretty hard while you can."

Léonore considered her, trying to stifle unease. "You never used to counsel me when I was a child. These days it's not only far too late, it's irrelevant. Don't take the trouble, if you please." She moved to pass on.

Adélaïde placed her hands on her ample hips. "You think I give you warnings only when it suits me as well? Damned right. But that doesn't suck the sting out of them any. So listen to this. His woman was back in town the other day. Alone: left the husband in Havana. It was just a visit. Didn't seem a lot of reason for it unless you call Paris gowns a reason, and she sailed for Cuba again yesterday. She'd be mad as a cut snake if she knew she'd just missed him."

Léonore froze. It was several seconds before she remembered to breathe. When she did, the air was redolent of the heady sandalwood perfume Adélaïde always wore and that always reminded her of her father. She swallowed, composed her face and managed to say with rigid indifference, "Who are you talking about?"

"The magnificent señora, Mathilde de Oleron y Siqueiros. She's gone home, like I said. But there's no telling when she'll be back, is there? And next time he might be here, and you almost certainly will not. As I said, make the most."

With a rustle of her full satin skirts, Adélaïde walked on.

CHAPTER TWENTY-THREE

～≈～

Traitor

It was dark. She had dismissed her man and was standing alone in the street outside the house. Part of her brain seemed to have been seared away by what she had heard in the afternoon, but the worst was remorselessly clear.

It all fit. The physical attributes that the faceless woman shared with herself. The initial "M"—if only she had known the señora's Christian name. Yet even Sophronie Claiborne, who was astute and much more copiously informed, had missed the connection. Her friend had seized less than half the truth: the name was not quite Matilda; the lady was not a Spaniard, but married to one; she lived not on an island off Cuba but in Havana itself.

It all linked together, like pieces of fabric sewn with white thread, every seam tracing the way to the same dire conclusion. The grand lady's inexplicable hostility on the day they met. The deliberate distancing since, which explained why she had not approached with her husband at the first carnival ball. Léonore ground her teeth as the memory struck her: Jean had not come to her side that night until the Oleron y Siqueiros couple had departed. Had it amused him, stimulated him, to have two rivals in that ballroom at the same time? And where else had he enjoyed executing his intricate dance between the married sophisticate and the naïve younger woman—in the street? *In Havana?*

It all made fatal sense. The relentless persecution, with the cuckolded husband as the agent. Jean had known about that all along. With a few words, at any time, he could have explained to her why Mathilde de Oleron y Siqueiros was her enemy. But he had not spoken. And by concealing that knowledge, had left her vulnerable.

It all hurt, like knives through her flesh. The humiliation of being kept in the dark. The way every encounter with him, in retrospect, was contaminated by the other woman—the clever, experienced, mature gentlewoman whom Louisianians admired as much for her fabulous beauty as they did for her high·standing and her social skills, and who obviously exerted as much seductive influence over Jean from Cuba as she had when they used to meet and conduct their affair in the same city.

She stood staring at his house from the other side of the street. The lights were on upstairs, but they might have been lit by the servant he had hired to look after the place. She had no idea where he was, how he had occupied the afternoon, whether he had yet returned. Up until this moment, such questions would not have occurred to her—they were the worries of wife, mistress or lackey. She and Jean had met so violently, clashed so strongly, been joined to each other so powerfully that she had come to feel that they belonged in another, unique sphere.

Idiot. She was a woman; he was a man—and therefore capable of treachery. She gazed on, dry-eyed, quivering with tension. The night breezes by the Mississippi were not as warm as the balmy air that lay over the waters of the Gulf. The brick wall behind her felt cool under her palms. She could not cross the street. Tonight or ever. All she could do was push herself upright, turn away and take a few steps to the street corner.

She rounded it—and walked straight into a man. She would have collided with his chest if he had not grabbed her shoulders. She gasped: it was Jean.

"Where do you think you're going?"

She looked up, saw his face, closed her eyes. She could not answer. After a second, he opened his hands.

"So you were leaving. Without a word." His voice was deep and steady.

She was a few inches from him, unable to move. She said dully, "How long have you been here?"

"Long enough." There was an enormous silence, during which she kept her eyes averted. Finally he said in the same tone, "You have heard something you do not like."

She murmured, "Let me go," and took a little step to the side.

"You have heard something. And you choose not to face me. Why don't you have the courage? Because you think I might not be able to explain." He moved, to see her more closely. "Or because you are afraid I can."

She looked into his eyes at last and cried out, "I am not afraid of you!"

He said at once, "Then come into the house. You can tell me what this is about."

It was the very coldness and control in his voice that made up her mind, stirred a fury in her that she hid from him by turning her back. "Very well."

They crossed the street, the servant opened the door to them and Jean instantly sent the man home. Then he led the way upstairs.

The night before, she had believed her whole happiness resided in this house. He stood in the middle of the little salon, apparently at his ease, his pose relaxed. But he hid his hands behind him.

There was no keeping the agonized question back. "Just how many women have you had here?"

His gaze was quite level. "One."

"And why should I believe that?"

"I have never lied to you."

"Don't you dare say that! I know better. You lied to me when you said there was no one else. On Grande Terre. When—"

She choked on the words and could not go on. He cut in immediately. "That was no lie. I made the decision before you set foot on the island. I told myself—if you came, there could be no one but you from then on."

Her voice vibrated with scorn. "A very *contingent* decision, then, wasn't it? Which you could undo just as lightly."

"It was an oath. Which I have never forsworn."

"You could have betrayed me with her before the week was out. She was not far to find. What could be easier?" He said nothing, so she said through the ache in her throat, "You know who I mean. I can name her, if you will not. Mathilde de Oleron y Siqueiros."

There was no denial. It was the name he had expected to hear. Tears flooded her eyes as he said deliberately, "I have not seen her for more than eighteen months."

She turned, forced the tears away, calculated, wheeled back towards him. "And when did this sordid tale of adultery begin? Before or after you first met me?"

"After." Watching her face, he said very low, "Don't ask such questions unless you want the truth."

"Before or after the first time you kissed me?"

"After."

"Was it   "

"For God's sake! I wish I had never met her. I wrote to her the day after you came to Grande Terre. She knew she would never see me again, unless she sought me out. And she has not."

"Why should she, when you have unlimited access? Considering that you seem to move in and out of Havana at will." His eyes widened in disbelief, but she went on, "How do I even know whom you were with when I was in the Bateria?"

He moved so fast she jumped and cried out, as he took her upper arms with a violence that jolted her from head to heels. "Say that again."

She bit her lip, closed her stinging eyes. Sick with shock and sorrow, she could not speak.

"Say it again and you will recognize it for an abomination. I broke with her in the clearest terms possible. As for Havana, God spare me from ever enduring that again." His hands, tightening, jarred her again. "Look at me."

Her lids opened, and she gazed into his burning eyes, wondering how she could ever have thought them black. Despite the punishment of his hands, she waited.

"This is the man who saved your life. What have you to say?"

"It's true. But why?"

He took his fingers from her flesh as though it scalded him. "Why indeed?" He took a pace away, turning so that she saw him only in profile, and continued savagely. "So you could repudiate everything I have done or said. So I could throw away any chance of ever getting into Havana again."

"Then you did visit—"

He rounded on her. "Yes, I have contacts in Cuba who are just as damned unreliable as that kind of informer anywhere. Yes, I used to go there regularly. I can't see myself doing that any longer, can you? Having imprinted my features in the mind of anyone of importance in Havana. Having made fools of their commanders and kicked Apodaca where it hurts most—in his cursed Spanish pride."

She crossed her hands, held on to her upper arms where he had hurt her. "I do know how much it cost you. I have thanked you in every possible way. But how can I trust you now?"

He grimaced, walked away from her, then turned to face her when he reached the table. There was a long silence. At last he said, "I concealed nothing. You have known since last year that there was someone before you—but you chose not to ask me about her. Now that you know her name, does it make so much difference?"

"Yes!" she cried. "Of course it does. If you don't realize that, then you never loved me. If you don't know why I hated her and you the moment I heard it, then you are not a man."

His voice and his face went cold again. "Who told you?"

"Adélaïde, who knows what jealousy is. She wanted to hurt, and she succeeded—I believe her."

"How can hearing a name make you believe that alley cat and call me a liar?"

"Ask yourself. Ask yourself how you would feel if someone could give you names from San Stefan."

He went pale. "What are you saying?"

She forced herself to go on. "But of course no one can do that. When you killed Santo, you removed the one informer you had."

He remained still and erect, one hand gripping the edge of the table, the knuckles white. "This is beneath you." His voice shook and she recognized menace as well as anger. "Don't do it."

"Don't do what? Challenge you, or act like you, when I am betrayed?"

"Ah!" It was a harsh sound, expelled involuntarily as he moved again, to the window. The effort for control was visible in every feature.

She stared at him in outrage. He was guilty, yet he behaved as though she were in the wrong. He had hurt her atrociously, yet there was no understanding at all, much less any regret. She had come to him for explanations, and he had just forbidden her to speak.

The pain tore at her stomach. "I can't bear it. There's no point."

She walked blindly away from him, put a hand on the doorknob.

"Léonore." She was pulled up short by the hostile voice that reached her from across the room. "You've called me a liar, but believe me, this is in earnest. If you walk out that door, don't expect to come back."

She broke then, with a wild, inward cry that became a shriek so high it strangled her. She collapsed against the door, her mouth open and her eyes shut tight, helpless under an onslaught of tears. She slammed her palms on the door, gasping for breath. Then the pain swept through her again. Next moment she was on her knees, her hands clamped over her face to muffle her sobs.

She heard him say something, come towards her. Then he flung himself down and crushed her in his arms. "My heart's darling, forgive me." His fingers on the back of her head pressed her face to him, and his voice vibrated as though her grief penetrated his chest. "Don't go. Forgive me."

With her hands trapped against her ribs, she could hardly breathe, yet inside she felt as hollow as a cavern. Gradually, however, under the broken murmur of his voice and within his strong embrace, she managed to quell her shuddering and her tears. When he realized, he loosened his arms, but only a little.

"Forgive me." He kissed her forehead, her ear, her neck. With each kiss, tears started from her eyes again. But she was silent.

He raised her, led her gently to the ottoman and made her lie down, then stretched himself beside her. She placed her arms as before, tight against her midriff, encircling the empty space that had been carved out inside her. He held her, caressing her hair and her back, whispering endearments. She recalled another time when he had held her tightly and said, "This is love." She knew now what that meant. She was learning.

She tried to speak, then stopped. But at her movement he drew his face away and she looked up at him. His expression shocked her—it was as though pity and despair had stripped him to the bone, and the white face made his eyes glitter with frightening intensity. On instinct, she pulled back.

"No!" He gripped her shoulders with both hands, shaking his head. "Don't." Then to her astonishment he buried his face below her breasts and said again, as though the words were wrenched out of him, "Don't leave me."

Her hands closed over his head, her fingers tangled in the thick hair. She pressed his face to her body and an extraordinary sensation coursed through her, as though she were shaken by a swift, raw buffet of air. She was on the edge of a high plateau, with no idea where she was going.

A weird kind of exultation distorted her voice. "Do you *want* us to be together?"

There was a great intake of breath; then he said her name. It was like a cry for help. He raised his head and crushed his lips onto hers.

They made love as though they were falling, and might land anywhere, in a strange world. She wondered, in brief snatches, whether he realized that she had become a foreigner, to him and to herself. Yet at the end she lay still, seized by a terrifying sense of peace. They lay entwined, in a vast silence filled with utterances their bodies had just exchanged in a new, unknown language.

When they got back to Grande Terre, this time she went ashore. Jean assured her the slaves had been removed, and offered to take her on a tour of the island. She read the intention: she would be invited, on the way, to view the empty barracoons and to ratify that he spoke the truth. She told him she knew the layout of Grande Terre already, for Dani and Amirou had drawn her a rough map of both islands. The conversation took place before others, and he kept his voice as bland as hers in reply. Within his house, it was different.

There they were alone and he took her through every room. "You have no idea how long I have waited to show you."

She knew. She could have told him exactly how many months, weeks and days. His way of bridging the abyss between them was to talk. Hers was to assent with her lips and her intellect, while her heart wandered elsewhere, crying in the wilderness.

The garden was momentarily touching. It was amazing that he even had a garden, for she remembered the bare expanse around the old house—the one that had vanished, like their first night of love. There was an ancient fig tree near the beach and a hedge of lavender, which she recalled scenting on the sea breeze as they stood on his verandah, eons ago. There was also a grove of trees to one side, studded with gardenia bushes still in bloom. The moon was hidden behind thin clouds, but by its dim, filtered light the flowers glowed like minor stars against the dark bank of foliage.

He picked one of the gardenias and touched the white, satiny petals to his lips, then held it out for her to drink in the scent. She approached, inhaled, took it from his fingers. He was standing very close to her, darker than the glimpse of sea behind him, not speaking now. She had an impulse to press herself against him, lose herself in him, to go beyond thought, beyond misery. But there was no getting away from the unspoken questions: which were the gestures already familiar to another; which phrases were already secondhand?

He put an arm around her and led her back inside. She kept the gardenia in her fingers, a tiny fallen star caught in midair between heaven and the hard earth.

The main room was beautiful—spacious, lavishly furnished and with the glass doors and shutters thrown open to let in the perfumed air. She put the flower on one of the rosewood tables, strolled to the threshold to glance out onto the terrace.

He said suddenly, "Léonore, we must settle this now or never." He took one step towards her. "There is no man my age without a past. If you cannot forgive me that . . ."

He did not go on. She had never seen him at a loss for words. It moved her, but her answer sounded bitter. "It's not a matter of forgiveness. I used to know very little about these matters, but experience is a swift teacher. Forgiveness is not the point. She is the point."

"Ask me then," he said, sitting down on one of the chairs. "Ask and get it over with." Then, before she could even summon breath, he said with his eyes burning into hers, "There was no love. I had none for her, and if she is capable of loving a human soul, I should be astounded beyond reason."

"Then why?"

His gaze dropped. "I told you how it began. She was intent on separating me from you. I thought there was something behind it, but I never found out what."

"How disappointing for you."

He put his elbows on his knees, his hands over his eyes. "I warned you against her, every step of the way. The cursed thing was, I never got a hint of the worst she might do to you. And once I broke with her, I had no inkling at all."

"You *discussed me*?"

His hands dropped. "No! Your name was never mentioned between us."

"And the hidalgo? The other side of this sorry equation?"

He shook his head. "He cannot know, or I would be a dead man."

"As simple as that?"

"One of them has an informant amongst my people. It could be anyone. Curtis." He shrugged. "Though he wouldn't touch me; they'd have to hire someone else."

She stared at him. "And you let such things go on?"

He rose, impatient. "I have a thousand men, as near as damn it. Can you imagine commanding allegiance from this mob of hell-bent animals by anything but the basest appeal to self-interest? Curtis, who should rightly be called Curtiz, by the way, has family and a common-law wife in Havana. He is permitted to pay them the brief little visits that neatly suit him, just whenever it happens to suit me. Curtis is loyal and will remain so—for one reason. He has no imagination; he will never be able to conceive of anything better than what I offer him. And in all modesty, nor should he."

Silence fell again. She had nothing more to say. She put her arms across her midriff and he saw the gesture and approached.

He took one of her hands. "You have to know what you mean to me. I would sooner die than lose you."

She was still looking out into the night, and the forceful words felt like a series of concussions on the side of her face.

When she did not turn he went on. "I nearly died in New Orleans, in the street. Watching you decide to walk away. She is nothing. You are everything. I will prove it to you by any means you choose. Name it, I will do it."

She faced him, and with her hand still in his, looked straight into his eyes. "Find a way not to deal in slaves."

The grimace might have been shock, anger, self-mockery. Then he tipped his head back. "I'll try. If I stay alive, I promise to try. God!" He repressed another exclamation. Then he looked at her with the beginning of a smile. "Anything more?"

She said it then, leaning her forehead against his heart. "Love me."

He flung his arms around her. "What else?" His voice shuddered. "What else do I do?"

It was a kiss of such passion that she abandoned resistance and stepped with him, unburdened, into the abyss.

In November the federal government decided to try recouping some of the customs dues denied to the Treasury by the smuggling operations in and around New Orleans. For years Governor Claiborne had been sending complaints and pleas to the capital, deploring his Legislature's lack of interest in preventing the illegal import of slaves and the untaxed entry of a stupefying inventory of luxury goods into the Territory. Washington in return had waited, without much conviction, for the governor to exert the right influence himself and get the local forces to take care of the problem. Finally, fuming under the added expenses of the war, the administration reacted. The U.S. Army was authorized to man strike vessels with a company of dragoons and to lead them into the likely areas of coastline on a dedicated campaign against illegal importers.

No one was at all surprised, least of all the Baratarians, when a flotilla began regular forays in their vicinity, over the Lake and in amongst the bayous and trembling prairies around it. The soldiers took to patrolling the waterways at dusk, and after sunset on moonlit nights, ready to dart after the swift pirogues sent out from Grande Terre or Grande Isle, hoping with each new chase to snatch a rich haul of contraband, with the ringleaders red-handed onboard.

Pierre turned up in November and stayed in the big house. It amused Jean to see how the atmosphere changed when his older brother was around, for Pierre had an odd domesticating influence. Dominique happened to be away, and when Pierre accompanied Jean to inspect the stores, or stood talking to the women who prepared the meals, the tempo of island life shifted. The days seemed longer. There was time to talk about food, or at least for Pierre to talk about it. They lounged about in the saloons, stopped in the lanes or at the washing pool to talk with the women. There was a chance for the place to seem like home. Which, on an island seething with hidden conflicts, was just absurd enough to be dangerous.

It all worked out fine, however. Jean was thankful for the way Pierre managed to occupy every moment. He was grateful for his being in the house, where meanwhile there was another presence to be felt in every room. He could allow himself from time to time to be distracted from his obsession. To be diverted from the ache of knowing she was gone, of wondering when next they could meet.

The day Pierre chose for his return to the city was also perfect for getting the next boatloads off. The sky was a steely gray with a promise of drizzle. The clouds lowered in the late afternoon and visibility had deteriorated by the time three of the larger fishing boats, carefully loaded in the Barataria anchorage, moved out over the Lake in the usual formation and began to ply the shrimp nets.

Jean was raking the shore when Pierre, beside him, said uneasily, "I can feel them hovering."

Jean lowered the glass. "I'm not so sure. But we'll find out soon enough."

The new ploy was to take one of the fishing boats far up the Lake, then send off not one decoy but two, within fifteen minutes of each other. The first pirogue would dart northward; the second would veer off into an inlet. More than enough to occupy the army's boats, which would have to reveal themselves in pursuit, since they could make no speed within the concealing vegetation.

Dusk was falling, but not too soon for them to see the two-pronged maneuver completed in the far distance. The pirogues blended swiftly into the water margins, unmolested. All that moved over the Lake were a line of ducks wavering across in the west, and a lone cormorant, flying in to roost for the night, skimming over the wavetops with a strong, regular beat of its black wings.

They swung the fishing vessels close inshore. Ten pirogues, already packed with merchandise neatly waterproofed and well lashed in, had only to be slid out from under the spare nets piled on deck and lowered on the landward side. They dropped into them, two men apiece, and sped to shore through gathering darkness and a gauzy curtain of rain.

Strung out, with Jean in the front and Pierre in the second pirogue, they hugged the line of reedbeds, traveling fast with the aid of the rising tide.

It was not until they heard the first shot that it all began to go wrong. It was way up in the northern reaches of the Lake: a challenge to the farthest decoy. Jean looked back over his shoulder. Everyone was paddling except Pierre. Jean shook his head at his brother, bent and took up his stroke again. The best way was through clear water—they might never have to dive into cover if the military remained distantly occupied.

The only annoyance was the breeze, blowing as usual off the Lake and masking any inshore sounds. It grew fresh and chilly. Then between gusts he caught an unmistakable combination of sounds, less than a mile ahead—more than one voice, the knock of wood on wood.

At his gesture, all the pirogues veered off, each into the first available channel. He had signaled a wide swing around the oncoming vessels. It was now hard, slow work. In their channel were two pirogues, his own and Pierre's. He cursed inwardly; Pierre had strength for short bursts, but ever since his illness he had lacked stamina. Jean had intended this to be an easy haul, for his brother's sake. It was not a lucky night.

Then shots rang out to the right. Then shouting, the clash of blades. There was no way the dragoons could have approached in time from the position of the first challenge. They had sent one force down the shore while another lay in wait. The only way now was between the two.

Twisting, he gestured to Pierre. A little farther on they swung north through tall reeds that sighed with the breeze and drowned the frenzy of their paddles. With haste, they could make the Bayou Lunaire. Together they held the best of the cargo; they could ditch it under

the trees and slip back to see what could be done about
the ambush farther inland.

It was easy. They penetrated the last barrier at speed.
It was ironic; the first time he had been back here since.
They scudded like sleek water birds across the bayou. His
pirogue kissed the beach first and he sprang onto the
sand. All at once it seemed too quiet, the blackness of
the encircling trees too dense.

His own man was hauling the pirogue up, the others
had just touched the sand. He drew his sword, turned
towards the trees. A movement. He sprinted straight towards it to get out of the open, calling a low warning as
he ran. One shot, let off out of sheer panic, whipped by.
He veered towards the flash, there was a whine and the
other man had just enough time to meet the sword with
his own.

His arm jarred, he planted his feet, parried and then
thrust. Behind him there were running feet on the shelly
bank. The big soldier before him feinted, danced away.
Four against a shadowy host.

"Look out, they're everywhere!"

There were no further shots; the fighting amongst the
trees was too close. Now his blood was up. He would
have liked it to go on longer. Except for Pierre.

It lasted until there were three against him, their eyes
glinting like sparks behind the whirling blades, and he
backed against a tree trunk. Except that it was a soldier,
who throttled him with one brawny arm and did something with the other that resulted in a searing flash of
light and a roar in his ears that obliterated everything.

CHAPTER TWENTY-FOUR

The Cabildo

The crown jewel of the Place d'Armes, the Cabildo, used to be the seat of the old Spanish government. It was aristocratically ornate, with an imposing entrance that now led into the grandest jail in the southern United States. Behind the white facade were marbled corridors, vast bureaus and frescoed halls reposing in majestic splendor. Beneath these were the damp quarters allotted to those awaiting trial for felony, murder, insurrection and crimes against the state.

The cell assigned to the brothers Laffite was a stone cube rather larger but no more welcoming than that once occupied by Léonore Roncival in the Bateria. The furniture was considerably less comfortable: a single wooden bench against one wall, which Pierre occupied while Jean paced the flagstone floor.

It was his first hour, his first night in prison. It took a certain adjustment, an effort of perspective, complicated by Pierre's exhaustion and unspoken fears. Pierre hated closed spaces—a result, perhaps, of the long period when he had been confined to bed, after the apoplexy that had distorted one side of his face and cost him part of the sight in one eye. When they were thrown into the cell, Jean had to avoid looking at him in a conscious effort not to sink again under the helplessness of those weeks after Pierre was struck down. The bleak interval while he recovered. The horror of knowing that in some respects he never would.

He kept pacing.

In the gloom, his brother was a hunched shape on the bench. "Do you have to do that? It can't do much for your head."

"My head's fine. I was stunned for a second, that's all. Stunned and shocked: their swordplay isn't bad, but they fire like peasants on a rat hunt. God help the U.S. Army if the English ever do get down this way."

There was another pause.

"It's getting light," Pierre said resentfully.

"We can't expect Sauvinet to accost them at the crack of dawn. He'll be here soon, no question. And we'll be out by the afternoon."

"You're sure they'll post bail?"

"Wouldn't you? It's revenue they're after." He gave a quick laugh. "With that and the cargo, it might be all they ever get."

The resentment was still in Pierre's voice. "I'd like to know just how the hell they did it."

"They've had weeks to work out that they needed smaller boats. So they commandeered some."

"It was a goddamned classic pincer movement."

"It was a lucky strike." He peered to see his brother's expression. "What? You think someone told them where to wait for us?"

"Maybe."

"Balls. There's not a creature on Barataria who wouldn't rather cut his own throat. These last few months, I've never seen them happier. They're spewing silver and shitting gold. Even Gambi's laughing, and if you can achieve that you could get a cackle out of Job."

He kept moving.

It took Pierre a long time, but inevitably it came. "Do you think it was a good idea to let Léonore Roncival see so much of Grande Terre?"

"Clearly yes, since that's what I did." Something stopped him, and he leaned his back against the wall. It was tiredness—he never got angry with Pierre. He relaxed, crossed his legs.

"Was it wise to take her to Bayou Lunaire?"

"It was . . ." impossible to put into words. Almost impossible to describe the timbre of it: something like a deep-toned bell, struck once, over still water. Despite the string of disasters since, he could put his head back and close his eyes and recall every moment, pure and unaltered. His mind began expanding into that limitless, moonlit space, and he forgot Pierre had spoken.

The whole night. The next day, before the catastrophe. When they arrived at the house near the Sellières she had given him a present. A beautifully bound, slim volume from a shipment of books she had intercepted on its way to Charleston. It was a first collection, published only the year before she captured it, the product of "hours of idleness"—appropriately enough, since the poet was an English lord. He had laughed at her for seizing a prize and finding only literature. She had tried to take it back from him. Then he caught her around the waist with one arm and flipped the thing open, holding it out of reach to read something at random in a silly voice—it was a piece of bravado about drinking wine from a skull. Then he laughed at her offended face, and kissed her, and promised to read the whole effort.

To please himself, after she was gone he would have done no more than glance through. But to please her he read it thoroughly and learned one piece by heart for next time. It was six stanzas long but irresistible, being about a woman with exactly her coloring and what the poet called her "wild.reality."

He would not have minded having the book now. At least he had the poem. Willing Pierre not to interrupt, he started it in his head.

> *Remind me not, remind me not,*
> *Of those beloved, those vanish'd hours,*
> *When all my soul was given to thee;*
> *Hours that may never be forgot,*
> *Till time unnerves our vital powers,*
> *And thou and I shall cease to be.*

Can I forget—canst thou forget,
When playing with thy golden hair,
How quick thy fluttering heart did move?
Oh! by my soul, I see thee yet,
With eyes so languid, breast so fair,
And lips, though silent, breathing love.

Pierre said, "I don't understand. It's not like you." A pause.

Jean cleared his mind in one savage sweep and opened his eyes.

"This woman. Commercially, it's a bloody fine balance, but to my mind the scales just tipped to San Stefan. As for you—well, look what happened over Cuba. She gets into the most massive trouble and you move heaven and earth to get her out. It would be awfully nice if she could do something like that for us now. But I can't quite see that, can you?"

Another long pause. If Pierre could have read his face he probably would not have gone on, but the cell was still dark.

"All right. I know the rest is your business. But she comes and goes just exactly when she pleases. And as she pleases. I don't get it. With every single solitary one of the others, it's always been you that walked away."

"Well, I suppose there's only one answer to that."

"What?" Pierre shifted nervously.

"This one's different."

Bail, predictably exorbitant, was paid up by their New Orleans manager, Sauvinet, without the slightest hitch and the trial was set for November 29.

Despite their weariness they strolled about town a bit before going home. They ran across a few friends, like Bernard de Marigny, whose conversation proved as natural and commonplace as usual. When Jean tipped his hat to Edward Livingston's brother-in-law, Davezac, he got a broad grin from across the Place d'Armes and the suggestion of a wink.

They decided to avoid Saint Philip Street until the trial and went to Pierre's cottage by the ramparts. After

Pierre had spent a while consoling Marie, they held a conference. The decisions were not difficult. There was time before the trial to get the New Orleans affairs in order. There was not a shred of a suggestion that anyone could or would have a go at Barataria. Pierre would stay in the city. Jean had the task of consulting discreetly with Edward Livingston and, if necessary, even more discreetly with the district attorney, Randolph Grymes. He would then go back to the Lake. They left open for the moment the question of whether both or either of them would turn up at the trial.

The women were anxious; Marie was inclined to loud bursts of tears, the mother fussed around the new baby with an air of long-suffering reproach and the sister was wide-eyed and very still. Jean had no time for Marie, but the other had always appealed to him. A shy girl when she first arrived in the household, she was now a lovely young woman who by some miracle still held the fresh, frank look of a child in her honey-colored eyes.

Before he left, he had no problem getting to talk to her alone, since in the normal course of events it was something she was constantly angling for and never got. She would not sit down, but stood before him with a smile trembling on her soft lips as she said, "Don't you worry about your brother, now. We'll look after him."

"I have no doubt of that. I want to talk about you."

There was a quiver in the tender skin around the eyes. "We can cope with trouble. Don't pay us any mind."

"I mean *you.*" As the consciousness penetrated he said deliberately, "You're not bound to share your sister's problems. What your mother does is up to her as well. If she suggests you move house, if you want to do that yourself—stay with relatives, perhaps—that is your choice. You have every right to consider your own reputation."

"You think I'd desert you?"

"No. But I'm begging you to seriously consider it just the same. Things are bad here, and they're going to get worse."

"I don't care."

"You should."

"Why?"

"We are soon to be prosecuted. Whether we are convicted or not, from now on you'll be linked with a household of criminals."

"It makes no difference to me."

"Listen. Remember this—order, if you like—over and above anything Marie or even my brother may say. Do not ever try to protect us, or to help us, if by doing so you would harm your own future. Do you understand?"

"I would never betray you!"

"You are too young and too good to suffer for our sake. I forbid it."

She looked mutinous and close to tears. He was not getting through. She hated being thought young.

He drew nearer, lowered his voice and said gently, "My dear. I shrink at the thought of your making any sacrifice for us." She looked up. Her eyes began to glisten and her lips parted. "If you came to any harm, I should regret it."

She whispered, "It would make you unhappy?"

"Very. Will you promise to think about this?"

She nodded and her mouth trembled. She sighed something he did not catch and her wet lashes squeezed shut. He turned and quitted the room, leaving her to the relief of tears.

By Christmas the story had gathered considerable detail, and in this form it spread from the Floridas to the Antilles and beyond. The Laffites had been ambushed, arrested and thrown in the Cabildo, and their whole cargo of contraband, the richest they had ever tried to smuggle across the Mississippi, had been confiscated. They were released on colossal bail and the trial had been set for the end of November. But it had not taken place because they never turned up for it. Before they made themselves scarce they were seen about town, as bold as you please, dining, talking and drinking with all their old cronies, including wealthy planters like Pierre de la Ronde and de Marigny.

They also showed up for a party at the Hôtel de la Marine in honor of General Humbert, who was celebrat-

ing his birthday in habitual fashion, no exaggeration
spared and plenty of *petit guave*. After the toasts the
general stood up to reply, and banged his uniformed
chest and waved his saber about and had a fair bit to
say about his glorious past. Then he got maudlin and
started moaning and groaning about the depths he'd
fallen into and what low company he was forced to keep.
No one thought to stop him until he came out with the
bit about pirates. He said that he, who used to be a
hero for France, was reduced these days to the company
of pirates.

Everyone froze. The Laffites stood up. The general
stopped short in the middle of an elaborate obscenity
and then began to weep. Jean Laffite walked up to him,
and everyone shrank back. But he put the old man's
head on his shoulder and a hand on the back of his
neck, and when the general was recovered a bit they led
him home. And no one had seen Jean Laffite since.

Léonore felt sick when she heard it; she went away
and sat down alone, on a wooden bench at the edge of
the lagoon. No matter how short Jean's time in prison
might have been, she could not help equating it with her
own ordeal in the Bateria. Whatever might have happened at General Humbert's party, she could not think
of the man without disgust, remembering the hideous
events of the ball at the Sellières, set in motion by
Humbert's drunken belligerence. Jean's account had
been terse, but there had been no mistaking the distaste
and bitterness in his voice as he gave it. As for the final
insult, only she knew just how deep that would have
gone. It was impossible not to recall his face when she
named him pirate after the raid when they first met.

As Léonore sat watching the water lap on the shore,
a little girl came up to her: the daughter of Nelly, who
used to be a friend of Adélaïde. The three-year-old
played about Léonore's feet for a while, tolerantly
watched by an "aunt," who sat on a chair outside the
kitchen, preparing okra. Because of the danger of the
lagoon, Léonore had asked that someone should always
be onshore to keep an eye on the children, whether
working or not. It was a task coveted by the pregnant

women, for it gave them the chance to sit for a few hours under the eaves of palm fronds, gently supervising the little horde of other people's children and imagining their own amongst them in the near future, with the same bright eyes and clear limbs under the clinging film of coral sand.

Léonore felt the child's touch on her knee and looked down.

"I've got my hands."

"So you have." With a fingertip she gently pressed the dimples at the base of each plump finger. "All soft on this side." She turned the little hands over. "And all smooth on this side." She tickled the palms until the child giggled deep in her throat and snatched them away.

They rose and walked slowly along the beach, coming across finds of shells that Babette held out in earnest contemplation, while Léonore compared their ridged and multicolored surfaces with the child's suave dark skin. They created an unconvincing Peak in the sand, which Babette lost interest in sooner than she did, and Léonore was permitted to examine a bracelet made of mother-of-pearl, the gift of Babette's papa. She recognized it as a trinket from the last capture—an English ship encountered in the New Year—and was touched by the thought of the man taking out the links to adapt it to his daughter's tiny wrist.

On the way back Babette began to lag behind, so she scooped her up. A plump arm went around her neck and the solid body settled against her. The lagoon, the bay and the inlet took on a new aspect, aligned against a round cheek fringed with sweeping lashes and shaded by tufts of red-gold hair.

All at once Babette threw out her free hand, index finger imperiously extended. "Papa!" The sailor came towards them from the corner of the refectory, arranging his face into that of a man aware of just where his daughter had been for the last half hour. He had something of Santo's appearance, with the addition of good humor. He took the eager Babette from her with a grin. "Her mother's fretting."

"Of course."

Babette held her fist an inch from her father's nose and demanded unrealistically, "Look, look. Shells." She spoke in English, for her mother Nelly was a former slave who had escaped from Jamaica.

He replied, "Come and show them to Maman. Say good-bye to the maître."

Babette glanced at Léonore vaguely and then twisted in her father's arms to look over his shoulder towards the kitchen. When he turned and walked away, however, she leaned her head against his mop of fair hair and gave Léonore a big, possessive smile.

Léonore strolled back along the sand towards the house. The sailor was clever with his hands and excelled at scrimshaw. It had more than once crossed her mind to ask him to make something for her to give to Jean; but she could never think what. A conch shell with a cameo scene of fighting ships for the mantelpiece? A carved coral ring—when he had the purest of gems to choose from?

Their gifts to each other so far had been bizarre. She had received from him one stolen diamond and two rare sapphires; she had given him poems by a gentleman who would probably write no more. He had saved her life; she had abandoned any expression of resentment about his past.

She climbed the steps and went inside. It was too breezy to laze on the chaise longue under the colonnade, so she reclined in the salon with a copy of the *Assemblée,* the indispensable ladies' magazine that cataloged the latest fashions from Paris and London.

She was also at leisure to consider the other news that Rigaud had brought to her from his last call in Port-au-Prince.

In the summer and autumn following America's declaration of war, it had been prosecuted on three fronts.

In the west, there was an attempt to take the Detroit peninsula from the English, but by the end of August the entire American force had surrendered, handing over considerable military equipment, including an armed brig, and Michigan was declared reannexed to Britain without a single British life being lost in the campaign.

Meanwhile, a succession of American commanders attempted assault on the heights of Niagara and failed, with 958 men taken prisoner, while another assault party was beaten back from Fort Erie. In the northeast, an army of 6000 headed north for Montreal, but the local militia flatly refused to press across the frontier. America's single ray of hope was that American ships had secured control of Lake Ontario, for the winter at least.

At sea, U.S. frigates in pursuit of convoys on their way to England achieved some spectacular successes. Encouraged, the Navy Department formed three squadrons and threw more resources into ship building. By the beginning of 1813, however, the British reply was only too clear—lest the Americans become "insolent and confident," their burgeoning sea force must be kept in harbor. The ports of New York and Norfolk were sealed, and Boston was subjected to the most vigilant blockade.

Henceforth, if America were to wrest any power in the North Atlantic from the British navy, it had not the remotest hope of doing so without the aid of privateers.

CHAPTER TWENTY-FIVE

Madame Lunaire

The Bayou La Fourche was as tricky to navigate in its way as the swamps of Lake Barataria or the brown turmoil of the Mississippi. But the three little craft that had been brought from San Stefan on the *Fantôme* made good progress up the long waterway, guided by a young man named Wallace from Baton Rouge, who had spent his early years by the Mississippi, working on the tow-paths and roads that linked the settlements on both banks of the river. He was to get the party to the head of the Bayou, where they would hire mules to carry the cargo to Donaldsonville. No one objected to looking for customers in the upriver town; on the contrary, they were all eager to try rivaling the Baratarians at their own game. San Stefan had been rich in prizes in the last few months, with no outlet for its surplus goods. The Laffites took contraband as far up as Natchez—why shouldn't they?

They had paid a courtesy call at Grande Terre, of course, on the way. A fair while after their signal, a longboat had put out from the point with Captain Curtis onboard and, like the surly fellow he was, he held the exchange with the maître without even rising from his seat in the stern. Jean Laffite was at sea, with Dominique You; Curtis didn't say where and the maître didn't ask. There was no invitation for the crew to come ashore. Even from the faces of the seamen at the oars you could

see how much things must have changed in Barataria
since the raids. They used to lord it in the place as
though it were their own free territory—now they had
the look of men besieged. Curtis was near enough to
rude in his replies, but then you couldn't call that a
change. The maître was as cool and crisp with him as
he deserved, but left a polite greeting to Jean Laffite,
which he said he would pass on.

You would never have guessed that the meeting disappointed her, except that she went below straight afterwards, without a command to Monsieur Rigaud, who
had sails up and the *Fantôme* away before the longboat
touched the island again.

When they got to Donaldsonville, Léonore left the
business proceedings to Rigaud, aided by Wallace, who
had relatives in the town. They contacted one or two
people whom she had met and traded with in New Orleans and paid a fee to use two stalls in the market,
which opened the next day, in which they could offer
the smaller items and a few of the fabrics for sale. The
quality pieces were to be shown privately to select customers, who were given to understand that the merchandise had arrived in barges, from depots in the north. It
was supposedly being sold off by merchants eager to
convert their stockpiles of goods into gold, given growing
anxiety about the war effort. The shopkeepers of Donaldsonville wisely did not probe for further information.

Wallace and Rigaud escorted Léonore to the best hostelry, but she was annoyed to find that there were no
rooms available and she would have to put up at the
Old Oak, which stood on marshy ground at the edge of
town. The inn yard was muddy and the two-storied
building had sagging eaves that gave it a crouching, apol-
ogetic air. The ancient tree after which it was named,
now a blackened stump with one limb, had been used
as a gibbet in the past.

From the commercial point of view her visit promised
to be favorable, but everything else made her miserable.
She was tired, damp and lonely. There could be no
greater contrast than that between her coral island gir-

dled by bright ocean, and this sluggish, fetid town sprawled along the river, breathing fever and discouragement.

She gave no name when she ordered her accommodation. As the gig in which she had arrived from town drove away, the innkeeper examined her and the young crewman standing behind her with bafflement. "We have an apartment available upstairs, madame. There's room for your maid also, when . . ."

"I shall be staying two days at most. I do not require a maid. You have a place for my groom?"

"Of course. Come this way, if you please. And we are to make arrangements for Madame . . . ?"

She drew a purse from her muff. "I prefer to pay in advance. What do I owe you?"

He was so busy calculating the expenses on the way upstairs that he made no further attempt to learn her identity.

The rooms were clean and reasonably well appointed, but dim. She turned to him. "This is surely not your best apartment?"

"I regret, madame, the larger one is already occupied. It also gives on to the road—I think you will find this one quieter. Would you like me to look into it, nonetheless? I do not know when the gentleman is leaving, but if you wish me to—"

"Thank you, this will have to do for now."

When he had bowed himself out, leaving her meager baggage in the middle of the little salon, she sat straight down on a chair by the window. But it was just as mournful looking out as in. Beyond the yard and lean-to stables was a strip of land planted in cabbages and beans, flanked by tupelo trees and swamp cypress. She could see where the road out of town, which led past the front of the Old Oak, disappeared amongst the tall trunks.

On San Stefan she had the friendly comforts of home and a score of occupations to seize her interest and divert her mind, but in this melancholy place there was nothing to distract her from the deepest sense of separation. She had begun to trust in the strange spell that drew her and Jean together across the leagues of island-studded ocean. Their encounters, whether marked by violent collision or by their own mysterious form of bliss, had seemed driven by fate, inevitable. This time, however, she had sought but not found him.

Listless, she rose and unpacked. She decided to order up hot water for a wash, but there was not even a bell-pull in the room. Opening the door and stepping out onto the landing, she was aware of a bustle downstairs and was about to raise her voice to call the innkeeper when a door opened at the far end of the corridor.

She turned as a man stopped halfway through the doorway in stark surprise, his hand on the latch, the light behind him. She could see no more than his tall shape and the gleam of his eyes; but at once a hot, giddy rush filled her chest and throat and she darted towards him. He moved at the same instant: the door swung closed behind him, he strode to her with open arms and they came together in the darkness with the shock of thunderclouds meeting in a storm. The embrace was fierce, painful, electrifying.

He broke the kiss and the whites of his eyes flashed against the black pupils and lashes. "I'm dreaming."

"You're here." She pulled his head down to hers.

When she released his mouth he pressed his temple hard against hers. His voice vibrated in her head. "I go mad without you. It's impossible."

"I'm here." She wound her arms tightly around his neck. "At last."

He took her back with him two steps, reached out and reopened the door. "Let me look."

Pale daylight from the room spilled over them as he stood with one foot propping the door open, both hands on her waist. She leaned against the frame, face tilted up towards him, her shoulders thrown back and throat exposed. It was a gift of her whole self, and he read the gesture so completely that he was spellbound, unable to speak or move.

They missed the footsteps as the innkeeper mounted to the landing, and they started when his voice reached them from the head of the stairs. "Oh! Excuse me, sir. Madame."

For a second, Jean's face froze. But he kept his eyes on Léonore and the next moment said to her, "I had no idea you would arrive so soon, my darling." Then he flicked a glance at the other man. "Why did you not inform me my wife was here?"

There was a pause, then, "I beg your pardon, but madame gave no such instructions."

"Never mind. You can move the luggage in here later. I'll call you." With a hand on the small of Léonore's back, he ushered her into the room and shut the door. His arm slid farther around her waist as he said very low, "What name did you give him?"

"None. Just as well."

"Now it is Madame Lunaire."

She smiled and raised her eyes, unable to keep the joy and confusion out of them. "Does he know who you are?"

"I don't know. I don't care. It's the first time I've stayed here, and it will be the last."

"This place is appalling, isn't it?"

"It was."

She twisted in his arms so that she could slide hers around his neck. "What are you up to?"

"Business. You?"

"The same. I called at Grande Terre on the way. Why weren't you there?"

"Because I was here." He emphasized the point with kisses. "As you. Adorably. Remarked."

Her hunger was so great all further words dissolved in her head before she could say them. They moved towards the bed, and she heard him laugh at the quick frenzy with which she flung her clothes off as she went. She lay down, her eyes devouring him as he reached for her. From then on he was wordless too, all their exchanges being much less articulate, far more potent, than ever before.

It was dark outside. There were two lamps in the room, their light diffused by a mosquito net that was gathered up into a ring suspended near the ceiling. Stretched out beside him, propped on one elbow, she trailed a forefinger from the rough point of his chin down the length of his throat, along the breastbone, onto his firm midriff and stomach to where a silky margin of midnight hair disappeared beneath the sheet. His breath caught, his hand trapped hers and he shivered.

She relaxed her fingers and looked with fond satisfaction at his face, which showed the same exhaustion that she felt. The eyes were closed, the lashes forming long shadows against the bronzed cheeks. The thick hair that clustered behind his ears was damp and a fine sheen of moisture lay on his neck and in the hollow of his shoulder.

Sprawled together on the storm-tossed bed, they made a picture of spent passion, of strength subdued; but she had learned in the turbulent passing of the hours that even in their deep, rare intervals of repose, desire burned just a fraction beneath the surface, capable of arousal by a brush of the fingers, a half-breathed murmur.

She slipped her fingers from his, subsided onto her back and stretched her legs out under the sheet. She remembered lying thus in the chilly bedroom at Sophronie's, long ago.

She had to ask, get it over with. "When do you go back to Barataria?"

"I'm heading north first, to Natchez."

"Is it safe? The Creek Indians, the Red Sticks. No one can tell what they'll do next. They seem to be able to put war parties in a dozen places at once."

"I heard tell they're operating farther east. There are troops chasing them, anyway, led by Andrew Jackson, who's a pretty seasoned Indian killer." He turned his head to look at her. "What, are some of the locals worried? No one's said anything to me."

She shook her head slightly. "One of my men knows these parts; he comes from Baton Rouge. He has a healthy respect for Indian warriors, especially the *batons rouges* themselves."

"He's out of date; Jackson will need to go looking beyond the Alabama River."

"Well, Wallace is going to talk to what he calls the 'Kaintucks' tomorrow. So we'll have the latest news."

He turned his head to look at her. "Wallace?"

Damn, she had not been thinking. "Yes."

He raised himself on one forearm and looked at her more closely. "Red hair and a grin like a demented rabbit?"

She nodded.

"Wallace. *Jésu!*" The tone was genuinely aggrieved. "Where the hell did you pick him up?"

"Rigaud took him on in Haiti. I've no idea how long he'll stay; I gather he's a bit of a rover . . ."

"No he's not. He was three years with me, and most of that time he was raking in five hundred dollars a month like the rest of them. He's a lily-livered, ungrateful parasite." He lay back again, brooding.

It struck her then, for the first time, just how severely the Holmes raid and the threat of prosecution might have harmed him and his enterprises—she was so used instead to imagining, and frequently resenting, his incredible successes. The figure of five hundred dollars took her breath away.

She gazed at his profile. "Do you know the name of everyone in Barataria? Even people like Wallace?"

"Can I afford not to?"

She took another breath. "Tell me what is happening in New Orleans."

"Over what?" He met her look and grimaced. "The trial? In our absence all they can do is keep postponing it. They're not empty-handed, however. The penalty's been twelve thousand so far."

She gasped. "You've paid it?"

"Evidently, or I should not be free to go skulking about the countryside like this." He caught the expression in her eyes and gave her a half smile. "Fret not, my darling, it was a mere drop from our giant melting pot of gold. Though there were moments when I considered applying to you for a loan from the Roncival treasure."

It was a joke, and against himself, but it disturbed her. She put up a hand to caress his cheek and an intoxicating wave of tenderness made her say, "Aren't you going to ask me where it is?"

His eyes narrowed and he said at once, "Where?"

"La Gonave."

The left eyelid flickered closed and he considered her skeptically. "Your father guffawed at that: what about the young man who sneaked off there on a wild-goose chase and dug up half a plantation?"

"He picked the wrong half."

He laughed, flinging back his head so the sound filled the room. Then he collapsed back on the bed and took her wrist in fingers that quivered with his mirth. "Brilliant." After a while, when he had subsided: "I wish I could have met your father."

She was silent.

He slid his arm under her, drew her close and kissed her forehead. "If only I had; if only I had known you when I was younger. Imagine. Things might have been different."

She shook her head, but he persisted. "Don't you ever daydream? I never used to. Now I do it all the time."

She pressed her lips to the line of his jaw. "I do, but it hurts."

"It can't hurt now." His grip tightened. "Not while we are man and wife." She gave a quick sound of surprise and protest, but he continued swiftly, "Yes, we can make that so, for as long as we are here together. Why not?"

Because to pretend now was an admission that it could never happen in reality. But she was afraid to say so.

He murmured, "Madame Lunaire."

Rigid against him, she said, "Don't make fun."

"God." He drew his face away a little, his fingers along the line of her chin, and gazed into her eyes. "You are my one treasure on earth. You are the only wife I shall ever have."

She looked at him with agony and longing. "If only. But it's impossible. We can't even make promises to each other. How can I expect you to give up selling slaves when your whole trade hangs in the balance? How can I abandon San Stefan when both the English and the Spanish turn against me?"

"What has happened?" he said quickly.

She shook her head. "Nothing. Yet. They have the war to think of. But—whatever we may dream, everything drives us apart."

"Lionheart, is this a dream?" He caressed her until she began to quiver in his arms. Then he lifted her so that she lay along the length of his body, her breast against his. He reached down and drew the soft, worn sheet up until it was draped over her head, and he held it to the mattress on each side so that it enclosed them like a veil, a second shelter within the translucent tent of netting around them.

His arms spread in surrender, his eyes compelling her, he said without mockery, "I take thee, Léonore."

But she lowered her head and whispered, "This is blasphemy."

"It is no blasphemy against love. Say it."

With her hands on his chest she raised her upper body, her knees digging into the mattress, her feet curved into his hard thighs. Warmth stirred through her, invading her breasts and throat as she said on a sigh, "I take thee, Jean."

He closed his eyes and tipped his head back as her hands slid between them with exquisite sureness. He did not lift his arms, nor touch her lips except when she leaned over in a cascade of hair and commanded the deepest of kisses. The sheet fell around their hips, she began to move in more elaborate cadence, and still he lay with his arms spread, his eyes glittering through half-closed lids and his lips drawn back from his teeth so that she could hear his ragged breathing. His skin grew hot, and shuddered under her hands, and she shifted into a kind of frenzy, possessed and possessing.

When she reached the edge of endurance she lunged forward, dug her fingernails into his shoulders and said between gasps, "Is this your idea, monsieur, of consummation?"

The sound in his throat was like a laugh. "It's all I can manage, madame."

Whereupon he gave himself the lie, as his mouth and hands claimed her breasts. Then his arms locked around her waist and he rose to meet her in rapturous, shattering response.

Next morning, over breakfast, they argued. It started with America.

He said, "I take it you haven't applied for a privateer's license from the Navy Department?"

She shook her head and poured herself more coffee from the jug the waiting woman had left.

"Why not? I thought you wanted a rapprochement with the United States."

"Only on my terms."

"Unattainable. All you could hope is to prevent the devils encroaching too far. Small chance, now you've talked to Gallatin."

She sat back, annoyed. "What do you know about that?"

"Not much, except for the glaring fact that he's Secretary of the Treasury, with a sworn mission to wrest the greatest profit for the States out of this war. And an unholy affinity with Secretary of State James Monroe, the most acquisitive statesman the country has yet produced."

"Then it will rejoice you to hear that my relations with America are just as ambiguous as yours."

He stood up. "I imagine not." He prowled over to the window to look out on the road. "Unless there is a warrant out for your arrest."

She said to his cold profile, "Am I to take my cues from you, all at once? It makes no sense. Our circumstances are totally different. I have a motley bunch of a hundred people who have only just managed to mold themselves into some sort of community. I have a tiny island that my family has occupied for generations. When the world begins to take notice of me, when great nations think of invasion, I have nowhere to run; I must stand and defend my own. Whereas you have a very mobile navy of a thousand—the largest in the Caribbean and the Gulf."

"You're saying you need allies and I need none?

Thanks for the consolation, but there are other ways to scuttle my precious navy, and your friend the governor is beginning to wake up to them."

"He is not my friend! I have no friends anywhere, thanks to you."

He turned to look at her then. "What are you talking about?"

"Before you came to San Stefan, I was still trying to decide what to do. I wanted us to be self-sufficient, but I couldn't think how. We had the physical means of survival but no income—we could not go on like that. Then you struck, and exposed San Stefan completely, and I was left with a single option. To build up our forces and go back to the only trade we knew. And so I made enemies all around me. Who are stronger and more vicious now than ever before."

His eyes flashed under the black, drawn brows. "That's a cursed ingenious excuse for a life of piracy! So it's my fault! I see it all now—no doubt I am to blame for my own losses into the bargain: nine lives, two cannon, a fully armed frigate, and however many of my men you care to seduce away, beginning with young Wallace."

"When I say 'enemies' in that context, I am not thinking of you!"

"Nor when you say 'allies.'" He moved away from the window, pacing the floor. "What is wrong with the French? Why do you not turn to them? France must be your best source of security. That is where your natural loyalties lie."

She shook her head, twisting the table napkin in her lap. "No. For all the interest Napoleon has in our part of the world, we might as well be off Tierra del Fuego. And how much help could the French be anyway—now they've been smashed in the Peninsula and decimated in Russia? I tell you, after the atrocities that army committed in Spain I have no loyalty left for the French, natural or unnatural. They are being led by a monster. Far better America than France—at least it is still a republic."

He stopped pacing. "With a greed for territory that makes Bonaparte look like a petulant child. They want the Floridas: they as good as have them. They want Cuba: one day they will take that too. If they want San Stefan, *mi amor,* they will not treat with you, or even flirt with you—they will swallow you whole."

"Don't you speak Spanish to me!" Her voice shook. "Given your touching concern, let me explain my strategy. Such as it is. You are right about the Floridas and Cuba—they are objects of desire. San Stefan is not: it is minuscule and produces nothing. Its only value to the United States is as a pawn in the war. The only value to San Stefan is this—when the war is over, if the U.S. has been seen to notice the island, it will be thought of as an American protectorate, whether it obtains that diplomatic status or not." She raised her head and caught his penetrating gaze. "You are right about the magnitude of the United States. That is what I am counting on. They are too big to have any genuine interest in San Stefan, and too powerful for any other nation to contest their influence there."

"You are playing with fire."

"Don't I always?" With a muffled exclamation he began pacing again. When she could bear it no more she said, "What about you? If the English bring an invasion fleet to the Gulf you must make some choices too. You hold the back door to New Orleans. Will you let the English through Lake Barataria, or side with America?"

"I don't know." He stopped and turned to look at her. "All I know is . . . whatever battles may come, wherever they occur, I could not endure us to be on opposing sides." He came closer. "To avoid that, I would break faith with any nation on earth."

His eyes blazed, demanding a response. She laid her hands on the table, paralyzed.

After a second he moved back and sat down on the chair at the end of the table. She stole a glance at him. He was sideways to her, one arm resting on the chair back, his elbow bent and his fist pressed to his lips. He looked as grim and glowering as before, but his skin at the hairline was pale and there was a contrasting flush along his cheekbone. A moment before, she had seethed under his superior assumption that he must be the one to give her advice; now it felt as though the positions of power were reversed.

"Monsieur Lunaire." His startled eyes met hers. "I trust you have not forgotten our promises, spoken or not, for I can give you every word. To have and to hold. For richer, for poorer." He put out his hand; she took it, rose and stood before him. "In sickness and in health." He pulled her down onto his knees and put his arms around her. "From this day forward. Until—" The breath was crushed out of her by the strength of his embrace.

He said into her hair, "I hold to every oath. I'll even give up the slaves—God and the heavenly host assist me, for the Baratarians will not." He drew her hair back from her face. "You realize I must wait. If I were to broach it now, there's not a soul who wouldn't call me insane. No one would countenance it, least of all my brothers."

"Brothers?"

He smiled into her eyes. "Pierre and Alexandre—that is to say, Dominique You. He is the eldest."

She looked at him in amazement, then murmured helplessly, "Do you have any further confessions about your family, monsieur?"

"Yes. There are Spaniards in the background. Hence the non-French spelling of our name." He took her face between his palms. "None of that matters. To hell with it; what do we care who is for us or against us? We are one. Let no man, no country, put us asunder."

CHAPTER TWENTY-SIX

Lady

In May 1813, Albert Gallatin left the United States with Senator James Bayard, both named by President Madison as peace commissioners and bound on a two-month journey to Russia, where they were supposed to persuade the Czar Alexander into mediating between America and England over the war. After a week at sea Gallatin had to admit to himself that the signs were not favorable. The most that Bayard seemed to have going for him were his good looks and his reputation as an able lawyer, and he was not destined to be an ornament at the Russian court: his table manners were rudimentary and his conversation unswervingly practical. Gallatin applauded Madison's choice of Bayard from one point of view, however, as the appointment by a Republican president of a congressman from the opposition party, it was a laudable attempt to balance the mission. In fact Bayard was not only Federalist but had actually voted against the war.

After dinner one afternoon, the senator picked up a paper from the table in front of him and waved it at Gallatin. "I was sent a lot of this kind of thing, just before we left. Other men's eloquence. Are we supposed to be flattered that they lend us words? Here's someone who thinks I'll turn War Hawk if I read his own grand statements. Listen to this: 'To me, it appears that the Author of Nature has marked our limits in the south by the Gulf of Mexico, and on the north by the regions of eternal frost.' I can see the czar looking a little frosty at that, can't you?"

Gallatin said, "It's irrelevant; it's not the focus we've been given. The focus, indeed the *condition* of peace, is that England abandon impressment."

Bayard cheered up and began talking of the recent American successes in Canada, while Gallatin listened without enthusiasm. "We've burned down the Canadian capital, after all," Bayard concluded. "You can't mean more business than that!"

Gallatin sighed. "The president believes that we shall be bargaining from a position of strength, and it is our duty to put that as convincingly as possible to Czar Alexander. I wish only that we had some indication that England will accept his offer to act as mediator."

Bayard stared at him. "Good Lord, it's a foregone conclusion, surely. Else why in the name of fortune are we taking this perishing trip to Russia?"

On a blazing July day, Jean stood at the corner of the Place d'Armes surrounded by a pungent aroma of fish. He and Pierre had come across the river in an oyster boat, and while his brother headed off in the direction of the ramparts, Jean had hoisted a tray of shellfish onto one shoulder and walked across the levee and into the square as though making a delivery. He was clad in duck trousers, a thick cotton shirt discolored with grime and fish scales, and a large rectangle of blue canvas, one end of which lay between his shoulder and its burden, while the other was draped over his head to shield him from the salty water slopping about in the wooden tray. That and the long, drooping mustache he had recently cultivated were disguise enough from the casual eye, but he hoped no one would come up and try bargaining with him for the fresh produce. He was waiting only for the Free Men of Color to move out of the way before he crossed the square.

Sixty-four men of the battalion, a full company, were drilling at present on his side of the Place d'Armes where the high iron railings divided it from the levee.

Despite their ill-assorted uniforms they made an impressive sight, being well trained, well armed and proud of it. He had no trouble picking out Dani and Amirou amongst them, as their uniforms were identical—nor did he have any trouble guessing who had given them the extra money for their fitting out and the purchase of their .69 caliber Springfield muskets. Otherwise the battalion commander personally paid for most of the men's equipment, so they could scarcely run to a summer uniform; but the former Baratarians had managed one step towards it with their nankeen pantaloons. These flashed white beneath blue coats that were faced with red, fastened with brass bullet buttons and cross-belted with white worsted tape. The two young soldiers wore their collars turned up, under new sky-blue shakos with plates that shone so perkily in the sun that they put Jean in mind of little practice targets.

He would be able to tell her that two of the men she had filched from him were alive and well and dressed in the latest of military fashion. Which made him wonder whether she still had Wallace, the bastard.

As soon as the company marched out of his road he went across the square, giving the more fastidiously dressed idlers a wide berth and ducking farther under the malodorous canvas when he noticed familiar faces in the throng. And all the while he kept looking for her, his heart knocking with the rhythm that had started up as the oyster boat began to punch its way across the Mississippi.

It was absurd, of course, to think he might catch sight of her. Although she did not have quite the same reasons as he for concealing her presence in New Orleans, she would be no more likely to stroll openly about the Place d'Armes than to call on the governor's wife. Those in the city who remembered Eléonore de Rochambeau did so with doubt and suspicion. There was an outlandish story from Cuba that she had once been found onboard a vessel that was preying on Spanish shipping— though she gave her name as Roncival. There was a rumor that on her previous visits to New Orleans she had brought contraband up the river. And the rest of

the gossip concerned her connection with himself. Yet it
had spread mainly among the lower echelons, through
whatever the common run of the Baratarians knew or
guessed, and tended to be discredited by the upper
classes. Amongst these, where speculation existed, the
gentlemen were discouraged from voicing it by Edward
Livingston and the memory of the duel, and the ladies
feared the fatal displeasure of Sophronie Claiborne, who
always spoke of her absent friend with unqualified
approval.

Given the uncertainty of the tales about her, and the
status of her allies, there was even a possibility that she
might reestablish herself in society. His mind stumbled
over that crucial question: would she ever choose to do
so? She had revealed no indication either way, of late—
except for her decision not to apply for a privateer's
license. Reason told him that she was simply reluctant
as yet to enter into any official relations with the United
States. But his heart shrank from another idea: that she
was concealing her enterprises from New Orleans because she could not help coveting a place within it—a
place that would be denied her if she were known as the
purchaser of a license, let alone as a privateer herself.

Meanwhile she had agreed to meet him in secret, to
slink along the back streets as he was doing now, to the
same house he always rented. That is, if she was in town
at all, for the arrangement had been made months before. She had been due to revisit Donaldsonville and
had agreed to come downriver to New Orleans, arriving
on the same day that he made it up from Barataria.

It was more complicated this time, because he had his
brother to look out for. Despite Pierre's desperate need
to see Marie, he was too nervous ever to stay more than
one night in New Orleans—and when Pierre moved,
Jean moved too. His greatest fear now, though he never
voiced it, was that Pierre would be caught and arrested
while he was alone. And thrown in prison alone. Thus,
whether the blow fell in the city, the island or the lake,
it must fall on them both. Which meant just one night
with Léonore. If she came. After which she would take
a ride down the Mississippi to the sea, where the *Fan-*

tôme would be waiting for her—provided it had run the
British blockade, which had been more or less in place
since May.

She had suggested they rendezvous in Donaldsonville
or Barataria instead, but he had put her off both; the
first because of Pierre, the second because he could no
longer rule out full-scale invasion of his headquarters
by militia. The Legislature remained inactive, but the
governor was looking more dangerous by the week. He
could not expose her to those risks. And then there were
the English, who if they struck against the American
coast might well choose wealthy and strategic New Orleans as their prime target.

Given his appearance, he had arranged to arrive at
the house before her. The servant who opened the door
reeled back, then had to struggle to keep a straight face.
"The lady is not yet arrived, monsieur."

Jean slung the tray down off his shoulder. "Here, put
this in the kitchen. For dinner, have someone open the
oysters and cook the crabs. Fill the half barrel in the
backyard so I can wash. I'll be down in a minute." He
stripped off the fishy garments and dropped them on
the floor. "Take these out the back and sling them on
the woodpile."

The servant, averting his gaze politely, gave the rags a
slit-eyed look of distaste. "I'm to burn them, monsieur?"

"Good God, no. Just give them an airing."

Despite the suspense and the discomfort of trailing faint
marine emanations through the rooms, he could not resist
inspecting them at once. They were as he had ordered. He
came to a halt at the threshold of the bedroom, which
was full of flowers, also as ordered—gardenias, which
flung their fragrance at his head and gave him the sensation of being caught around the throat with satin ribbons
steeped in perfume. He leaned against the frame of the
door and closed his eyes. At once, acute and transfixing,
came the idea that if she did not come he might never
see her again.

Downstairs he banished the grime, the decorative
scales and the mustache. Upstairs again he donned fresh
garments and stood at the window toweling his hair.

Thus he saw the sedan chair as it was carried along the lane and set down before the door. The gloved hand that pulled back the curtain and grasped the edge of the opening so that she could step out. The green-and-gold turban with the plumes sweeping back from an elaborate knot over the brow. When she tilted her head to look up at the house a diamond in the center of it sparkled like her eyes.

He drew back just in time to prevent her seeing him. Standing out of sight at the head of the little staircase, he could hear a shuffle of shoes as the chair was borne away, three knocks on the door, the servant opening, his greeting and a hiatus while her baggage was deposited in the vestibule.

Her murmur was too low for him to catch anything but the melody of it. But the servant was audible enough: "Monsieur is upstairs. Shall I announce you?"

A second later there was her light, hasty step on the stairs, an impetuous intake of breath and her voice calling his name, low and musical. He stepped out and caught her by the newel post, spinning her so far they nearly fell into the void—but she laughed, in a delighted peal that penetrated his chest and head. Her happiness enveloped him like sunshine. But even as he kept her alight with kisses, his throat ached with the words that must soon be said: "This may be the last time."

It was next morning: before dawn, but after the hour when he had said he must leave. Ruthless, consuming, she had delayed him beyond the limit, to the time when the sickle moon was beginning to pale before the threat of the coming sun. Now he had slipped from the bed and torn back the curtain to make her see.

She looked at him instead. She wanted to remember every contour, every nuance of light and shade, the planes of his chest, the lines of his thighs. She sat up and drew over her knees and breasts the sheet that was still warm from his body. "I don't understand. I don't agree."

"Yes you do. Must I say this a thousand times? No-where is safe for you just now but San Stefan."

"I don't care."

"That's a lie. You will not abandon your people, any more than I will sneak away from mine. I've told you, the English are on the move. The only position you can reliably defend is your island. We cannot risk trying to meet again, anywhere, for the forseeable future."

"Just because they attacked Dominique You last month—"

"Yes. Because. With a frigate, at the mouth of Bayou La Fourche. Next will be Barataria, which rules out both of them as far as you are concerned."

"We can meet here."

"No. I have no idea when I shall be coming to the city again."

"Port-au-Prince."

"My darling, this state is at war with me and England at the same time—can you imagine me risking a trip to Haiti, with all hell about to break loose?" He took his shirt off the back of a chair, flung it on, then moved to the door. "I have to go. Spare me. Don't come down."

She was out of bed with the sheet bunched around her, too close for him to be able to turn his back on her. "I don't accept."

"Lionheart—" He put one hand over his eyes.

She took two steps, placed her fingers around the raised wrist. "Promise me one thing, then: if it all becomes impossible, if everything catches up with us, come to me. Come to San Stefan. My home is yours; we can stand there together, against the world."

His hand dropped so quickly her fingers parted. His eyes bored into hers. "Are you mad? The only way I could ever revisit that place would be feet first. I gave my word: I'll never go back." Aghast, she recoiled, and the slight movement woke a new tone in his voice. "You really don't understand, do you? Anyone else, subjected to what you dealt to me, would have returned on the morrow and hurled one stone from another until there was not a man, woman or child, not the vestige of a structure, not a stick left standing on your island. To this day, no one in Barataria can fathom why I did not do it."

For a second the shock took her breath away. Then she cried out, "You accuse *me*!"

He bowed his head, said between his teeth, "What is done is done. We cannot alter it. We can only go on."

"Where?" She was so beside herself now she stamped her foot on the floor. "Where? You are shutting every door against me!"

He half turned from her, his voice low and desperate, his face in shadow so that all she could see was his dark profile. "This is no time for argument. Let me go."

A flood of tears gushed into her eyes and choked her throat, but she flung her back against the door to confront him and managed to wrench out the distorted words: "You have never loved me."

His hands descended on her and she was shifted aside with a speed that left her shaking. "Stay out of my way."

She screamed and punched him in the face. It was the hardest blow she could deliver, but it glanced off his cheekbone without changing his stance a fraction. Then he seized both her wrists, forced them behind her back and pulled her helpless against him.

He buried his face in her hair. For a moment he could neither speak nor control the short, painful breaths that almost drowned her voice as she said his name again and again.

He let go of her wrists, and she held him with all of her strength, her mouth open, while all the words of sacrifice and possession, all the eternal vows, tangled in her throat.

He forced her arms from his waist and kissed her hard on the lips. Then he let her go and put his hand on the door. "When this is all gone by we'll be together. Nothing will change us. Nothing—whatever happens. Remember."

Later in July, Albert Gallatin arrived in St. Petersburg to find that the czar was absent from the city, so he went sightseeing.

In August, Wellington drove the French forces to the northern limits of Spain and half the French army fled across the border into France.

In September, the American navy gained control of Lake Erie; along the rest of the Canadian border, how-

ever, the opposing armies' trifling territorial gains remained more or less equal. In the same month, at
Moravian Town, the Shawnee chief Tecumseh fell at the
hands of victorious Kentuckians.

In October, the British began the invasion of France.
On the third of the month, one thousand of Andrew
Jackson's troops annihilated two hundred Red Stick warriors in the heart of the Creek homeland. On the four-
teenth, in the swamps near New Orleans, a company of
dragoons took possession of a schooner from Barataria
carrying contraband. Jean Laffite led his men on a counterattack; they retook the vessel and its contents and
escaped into the marshes, leaving two wounded dragoons behind them.

Next month, Governor Claiborne had a proclamation
posted at prominent spots about the city. It concluded
thus:

I, governor of the State of Louisiana, offer a reward of five hundred dollars, which will be paid
out of the treasury, to any person delivering John
Laffite to the sheriff in the parish of New Orleans.
> Given under my hand at New Orleans on
> the 24th day of November, 1813
> William C.C. Claiborne

Two days later another notice appeared in the same lo-
cations, much to the amusement of the citizens of New
Orleans.

I, Bos of Barataria, offer a reward of five thousand
dollars, which will be paid out of my treasury, to
any person delivering Governor Claiborne to me
at the island of Grande Terre.
> Given under my hand at Grande Terre on
> the 26th day of November, 1813
> Jean Laffite

CHAPTER TWENTY-SEVEN

Brothers

There were four in conference in the fortress overlooking the Gulf: Jean, Pierre, Dominique and Renato Beluche. The others had been thrashing things out for some time while Jean listened, too intent even to smoke.

"If they were planning to attack us soon, I'm sure I'd have picked up on it." Oncle Renato tapped the fingers of one large hand on the table. "But we've dealt without a hitch so far. That's the advantage of having a license. I don't give a curse about the bit of paper, but they do. It makes all the difference. It makes us legitimate."

"It makes *you* legitimate," Pierre said, "as long as you declare the prizes the way they want. It doesn't do a bloody thing for the rest of us."

"No, Oncle Renato's right," Dominique cut in. "It gives our friends in the state an excuse to support us— and what the hell does it matter whether they do it in public or behind closed doors? So far, there are plenty of gentlemen in the Legislature who need us as much as we need them. Look at the arms run to Mexico—not a man of them has pulled out of that. I'm still handling it for them and I'm still 'My dear Monsieur You.' "

Pierre persisted, "But Claiborne's putting more pressure on them now. He has to. He's running scared."

Oncle Renato laughed. "What isn't the man scared of? The Choctaws and the Creeks, the English, and now he's gotten it into his head that slaves are about to take

New Orleans by storm. The only thing he's not pissing himself over are the Spanish, and that's because Jackson's prowling about by the Floridas."

"It would have been handier for us if Claiborne did fear the Spanish," Pierre said. "If the United States had included Spain in the declaration of war, all our captures would have the sanction of the government."

"The sanction of the Republic of Cartagena is good enough for me," Dominique said cheerfully. "There's no point in getting the shits about the feeling in New Orleans."

Jean leaned forward. "It's time we decided on action. What to do if they plan to attack, what to do if the English arrive, how we keep on trading in either event." They all looked at him expectantly, then sat back without a word. He took the time to light a cigar.

"We'll know well in advance if Claiborne's lot are coming for us from New Orleans, and they won't try it without a large force. Before they get here we must move the main corps and all the merchandise and ships we can to Isle Dernière. I'll stay there with Pierre, who'll look after the construction—we'll need more buildings if that's to be the new headquarters. Dominique, you'll remain in command here with a few hundred men. If they come and you can see there's no show against them, blow up the ships that are left, set fire to everything else and get out. Any questions?"

There was a stunned pause, then Renato Beluche growled, "What about me?"

"You're the eyes and ears at sea from now on. We have to know well in advance if there's an English fleet in the Gulf. We'll put someone in Jamaica and another in Havana and they'll keep regular contact with you."

"We're not suspending voyages?" Dominique asked in alarm.

"Not yet."

"And if the English come," Pierre said, "what will we do?"

"If they attack, we hold them off. If they want to parley, we listen to what they have to say and make a decision."

Pierre shrugged, dissatisfied, but he knew Jean had no intention of trying to second-guess what the English might discuss. He said quietly, "And how do we go on trading?"

"To begin with, we need to hold a last sale at the Temple as soon as possible. We need gold. We've got to offload as much merchandise as we can from the storehouses and get rid of all the slaves."

Pierre's good eye narrowed. "A last sale?"

"Yes. The Temple's too big a target, and keeping slaves on Isle Dernière would be a nightmare. We'll inform all our buyers that in future we'll take private, individual orders only." He caught the antagonism in Dominique's eyes and added, "At double the price, of course."

His elder brother frowned. "You want to phase slaving out, don't you? I know who we have to thank for this."

"You have Claiborne to thank for it," Jean said. "If he thought we were going to carry on importing firebrands for insurrection, it might tip the balance in favor of invading us. If he thought we'd dropped smuggling blacks for the rest of the year, he might throw his weight elsewhere instead."

"What do you mean?" Pierre said straight to Dominique.

Silence fell. Jean pushed the box of cigars over to Oncle Renato and then sat back in his chair. He took a long drag on his corona, tilted his head back and blew the smoke at the ceiling.

They had no idea he had sent her away, for their sake and hers. They could not know how she resented him for it. But if they were going to bring up her name they must take the consequences.

It was Oncle Renato who, working on instinct, switched back to the practical. "It's more than forty miles to Isle Dernière. We'd better choose what's going to be moved there and what's not."

They made a lot of decisions on that winter afternoon, some of them less intelligent than others. The worst, as it transpired much later, was electing Curtis as the contact in Havana.

By January 1814, Albert Gallatin was still waiting for an audience with the czar of Russia. He had admired all the masterpieces of the imperial palaces that he was allowed to see and had tasted a great deal of St. Petersburg cuisine and hospitality—which had been nowhere near luxurious enough to tempt him to a longer stay. Besides, the other American commissioners who had arrived were not amusing. It was easy to persuade Bayard to accompany him to London, where they could at least establish whether the British were ever likely to consent to meet the czar. Bidding the other commissioners farewell, they departed in separate carriages.

In the fourth week of January the Baratarians cleared their barracoons of 415 slaves. Walking along the jetty at dawn, watching them file onto the boats that would take them to the Temple, Jean weighed up their value. They had been well fed and housed on Grande Terre and Grande Isle and were in superb condition; there was no reason why the able-bodied men should not fetch up to a thousand dollars each. Rapidly he estimated all over again the costs they had represented, in terms of capture, equipment, food, clothing, transport and the printing of the handbills that had been scattered around New Orleans to announce the auction. Whichever way he looked at it, the margin of profit was colossal. A wave of doubt hit him; perhaps he should let Pierre build more than one makeshift prison on Isle Dernière when the time came. Léonore's begging him to give up this trade was like asking President Madison to give up the White House.

Then he ran his eye over the blacks again. Quite simply, from now on they were the wrong kind of merchandise. The times were too uncertain for him to be moving volatile people about the Territory. This was a crisis, whether his brothers were prepared to admit it or not, and he would prefer to come out of it without risky encumbrances.

The rest of the goods promised well: linens, woolens, leather and lace; plenty of silver and china; comestibles including Spanish and not a little French wine. There was some fine jewelry, too, amongst which were some pearls that he had been extremely tempted by. But it would provoke Pierre and Dominique if they ever saw her wearing them.

Dominique went ahead with fifty men to make sure the Temple was clear, while he and Pierre followed with the flotilla. They had discussed the likelihood of a reception party, and decided that this time there should be no hesitation about jumping them. Before the incident at the Bayou Lunaire, he had forbidden anyone to use firearms against revenue officers and ordered surrender if numbers were overwhelming. Such restraint was now a thing of the past. If the United States Collector of Customs had assigned anyone to try to confiscate merchandise from the Temple, let them beware.

He and Pierre headed the flotilla and they had another armed party in the rear. They all heard the shots well before they got to the Temple; he refrained from looking at Pierre and they pushed on with caution, waiting for a signal. It came: two shots at the shortest of intervals, from the swivel gun mounted on the bow of Dominique's longboat.

It was all over by the time they got there. Dominique was waiting for them on the pontoon jetty, his hands behind his back. Near the shore stood a small group of prisoners guarded by men with muskets and rifles, and three bodies had been laid out on the bank of shells at the waterside.

Jean stood up in the boat to get a better view as they approached, and raised his voice. "No more? You've checked?"

"This is the lot," Dominique replied.

Jean stepped onto the swaying half logs. "You've put sentries on the northern shore?"

"Yes. Come and have a look."

Jean signaled for the unloading to begin and went first to the wounded men. The oldest was dead; two clean shots to the chest. One of the others, a youngster, was unconscious; a bandage had been tied across the shoulder to stop the bleeding from a wound near the neck, but he had a bluish pallor and a very feeble pulse. With his fingers still on the wrist Jean looked at the other—a thickset man of about thirty with a chest wound that must have punctured the lung. He was breathing with difficulty and could not speak, though his eyes begged for help.

Jean touched him lightly on the shoulder and rose. "We'll get the surgeon to you soon, never fear." He said to Dominique, "Find blankets and have someone watch with them—they won't do like this." He moved off, saying low, "Who are they?"

"The dead one was the commander, appointed as a revenue inspector just the other day. The rest are new recruits too, for all I know; I never saw a bunch less eager to fight. They're mad as hops."

Jean ran his eye over the nine captives. "Are you surprised?"

"No, I mean they're furious about this assignment. Claiborne wanted a decent force of regulars and the army told him to go fish—he's barely got seven hundred men in the whole Territory and they're not coming down this way to run the governor's errands."

"Which would you prefer, to escort this lot back to Grande Terre for the next couple of days or stay here and let Pierre do it?"

"Stay."

"Fair enough. I don't think Pierre will object to wining and dining them and affording them a taste of good living for a while. The Red Saloon will do. Pierre can dispatch the surgeon to these poor devils as soon as he touches Grande Terre."

Pierre strolled up. "I heard that! What else did you have in mind for them, laurel wreaths and a gold medal each?"

Jean grinned. "I leave the parting gifts to you. Just treat them kindly until our business is done, and then let them sally forth like princes. We'll see what New Orleans has to say about us after that."

"They'll love us," Pierre said. "Like always."

*   *   *

In the last days of March, the troops of Europe's Quadruple Alliance entered Paris, and on April 6 Napoleon Bonaparte abdicated and prepared to go into exile. Viscount Wellington mopped up the French army in the south and reached Paris himself at the beginning of May. The victory parade he led on the fifth was one of the most glittering in history, and he had the honor of having been named duke the day before. The stage was set for a serious offensive against America: England could now select a seasoned force from amongst Wellington's veterans and dispatch them across the Atlantic.

In June the commander of the British forces in Canada received unequivocal instructions to invade the United States. Meanwhile the blockading fleet would continue its employment on the eastern seaboard and await the arrival of reinforcements of ships and men from Europe, which might open the way to a strike at the very heart of America. A fourth division, all experienced veterans led by Major General Robert Ross, embarked on British warships and sailed from the Garonne.

In July the division reached Bermuda, where it received the addition of a regiment of fusiliers before setting sail for Chesapeake Bay, preceded by an eighty-gun flagship bearing Admiral Sir Alexander Cochrane. Cochrane's orders to the officers of his fleet were "to destroy and lay waste such towns and cities upon the coast as you may find assailable."

In those first months of summer Jean was obliged to continue traveling in the region and leave Pierre in Barataria, while Oncle Renato remained at sea and Dominique too made the occasional foray. The hindrances to commerce were no worse than they had been at the beginning of the year; there was another revenue platoon patrolling disconsolately about the city, lake and swampland, but they proved even less competent than their predecessors. By contrast he himself was much more cautious than ever before, and tried to ensure that he was recognized only by those with whom he had business. In June he headed for Donaldsonville again, but near Berwick's Bay on the Bayou La Fourche he ran

into a gentleman whom he had rescued from a shipwreck
the year before, so he claimed from him the favor of
taking the messages upstream instead.

Avoiding the town himself did nothing to stop him
thinking of the two nights he had spent with Léonore at
the Old Oak. Afterwards they had joked together at
having lived them as man and wife, right down to bick-
ering over breakfast. And even as they laughed he had
seen in her eyes the flash of feeling that she could not
hide, and the same tug at his heart had driven him into
her arms again to demand a kiss as final as any husband
might claim.

There was no certain meeting to look forward to, and
he could not even be sure that she understood why they
must stay apart for now. Nor had he written, for whenever he picked up a pen he remembered the first message he had ever addressed to her—the demand that she
come to him at once, to which she had yielded in her
own devastating way. If he wrote, it would be in similar
language and with the same dangerous desire, stated
or implicit.

Meanwhile she had not contacted him in any way
whatsoever. He had not expected her to write; in fact
they had agreed it was safer if she did not which did
not prevent him from hoping that she would, somehow.
In mid-May, Oncle Renato happened upon the frigate
Hero in the Yucatan Channel; he recognized it by the
Roncival pennant, even before they ran out the U.S.
ensign in friendly signal to the privateer. The maître was
not onboard, but news was exchanged, which by the time
Oncle Renato put into harbor again had concentrated
itself into a few terse sentences. So all Jean knew was
that in May she had been alive and well. She had entrusted no letter to her captain to be handed over in the
event of a contact in a port or at sea. He tried not to
care that she had not thought of it.

Each time he came back to Barataria these days he
had to steel himself against two things: no word from
her, and some new disaster on the home front. On this
return, late one July night, he was too exhausted to
properly separate the first from the second, so he met

the sailors from Grande Terre with an obscure feeling of dread, and gained no comfort from their assurance that all was quiet on the islands.

Sure enough, they melted away once the boat reached the shore of the anchorage, and a moment later Alexandre—Dominique—walked out from behind an old fisherman's hut and came down onto the sand, his pointer, Belair, stepping delicately behind him. Jean stumbled as he went forward but concealed it by stopping to greet his brother.

"Well met by moonlight, my dear Monsieur You. You can say it: what have the gentlemen of the Legislature conjured up for us this time?"

Dominique gave no answering smile, just reached out and clipped his shoulder quickly with his palm before turning to go back up the beach. "It's Pierre." He was avoiding his eye.

Dead. No, not with an announcement like this. He sucked in a breath. "He's ill? Where are we going? Stand still, damn it."

"They got him today, in the Place d'Armes." Dominique, talking over his shoulder, slowed down. "Taken in by the dragoons, delivered to the city marshal, charged and in the Cabildo."

Jean took him by the upper arm, swung him round. "What the bloody hell was he doing there?"

"Praying at Saint Louis? *Foutre,* I don't know!" He looked at Jean properly for the first time and softened his voice. "There was no way to stop him going to see Marie. She's pregnant, for God's sake. He was probably being just as cautious as usual, but the fact is he was in the Place d'Armes at the wrong cursed moment and someone in the military recognized him. I got the news half an hour ago. I'd have gone up straightaway to see what I could find out, but I was hoping you'd get back. You look as though you could do with a cognac."

Jean concentrated on getting across the island to the house without a word to anyone on the way, then listening to all the details Dominique had been able to glean, while he sat, devoid of thirst, hunger or the slightest mental agility, staring through the open French doors to the black sea beyond.

At last he said, "I'll go tonight."

"No you won't—get some rest. Sauvinet should be able to get him out. It'll be like last time."

Jean shook his head and pushed away the untouched glass of cognac. "No. The whole thing's coming to pieces. It's been obvious for months; I just wish I could gauge the pace of it better." He sought the right phrase in his mind, then gave up and said, "Nothing is ever going to be like last time again." He managed to get to his feet and look ironically into his brother's puzzled gray eyes. "You can start planning for Isle Dernière while I'm gone."

It took a week for him to believe in the truth of his own prediction. He saw absolutely everyone, and no one had any solutions. A grand jury had been convened a little while before, made up of merchants and bankers sympathetic to Claiborne, and they had drawn up indictments against himself and Pierre, and also against Dominique and Oncle Renato under two ludicrous pseudonyms. Pierre was in a worse cell than before, and in chains. Pierre, shackled and fettered. Bail was denied, and every protest about the manner in which he was held, all concerns about the illness that would assail him in such conditions, were rejected.

It was insane to linger in the city when the avenues were closed, but Jean hung on. When he finally returned to Barataria it was to prepare for visits by both Edward Livingston and District Attorney Randolph Grymes, now a covert supporter, and to ensure that they departed with spectacular gains that they could later claim to have won at table after a series of equally spectacular suppers—if anyone were impolite enough to question them on their engagements.

When Jean was back in New Orleans in August, Grymes paid him a visit at Marie's cottage and during an otherwise entertaining evening regaled him with the story of how he had lost most of his windfall at card parties on the way home through the plantations. It did not seem to strike him that he found the whole thing a great deal funnier than Jean did. Jean even had the thought that Grymes might be angling for more funds.

Livingston on a similar occasion was easier to take. He arrived impromptu with no arrogant assumption that he would be asked to stay, refrained from leering at the women, and conversed with his usual animation and acuity, without insisting on topics that Jean had no taste for. The lawyer was already contriving all he could on Pierre's behalf without having to be begged to do so.

Late in the evening Livingston said contemplatively, "I have a theory about William Charles Coles Claiborne no one else seems to agree with. I'd be interested in your opinion." He stretched out his legs and leaned back in his chair, a half smile on his face. "It's my view that he's the ideal governor for this state. Look at Louisiana— the oddest intermingling of problems you could point to in the whole country. Most of them we owe to history; the rest spring up every day like mangrove shoots from the Mississippi mud. Now, what would be the result if you had some white-hot man of decision scorching about the place telling everyone what to do? What you'd have is open conflict. More chaos than we have now."

"Whereas we need the governorship of doubt and tergiversation?"

"For the nonce, yes. Leaving New Orleans to govern itself. Which it does, more or less successfully."

"And when the war reaches here?"

"In the time of crisis we'll call on General Andrew Jackson and he can swashbuckle into our midst to his heart's content. His decisions will be accepted where Claiborne's never would."

"So you think we need a great man in war and a little one for peace." He laughed. "I'm not surprised you've met disagreement! You can scarcely bring it up at the governor's table, and there are precious few other houses it would be acceptable in."

Livingston smiled back. "I sometimes wonder, though, whether the governor's wife would not secretly agree with me. She has a great knack for navigating through

the shoals of opinion. She is loyal to him without pub-
licly condoning every one of his initiatives. She is the
most accomplished hostess ever to welcome me to her
table."

Vivid and cruel to Jean's mind came the only encounter he had had with her. His throat contracted.

Livingston continued. "If there's a dispute threatening, she never comes out strong on her own side. She
elicits support from someone else instead and then sits
back and controls the outcome in the most benevolent
manner. I noticed it at a supper the other night: someone
brought up the name of an old friend of hers and there
were a few insinuations made. She had her quiet say on
the subject and then enlisted young Sylvain Audubert
for the defense. Pretty eloquent he was too—he's obviously still smitten, though the lady herself has not been
seen in New Orleans for a long while. Madame Claiborne told me later that she is the reason Audubert has
not yet married. He is still hoping she will return."

"Who?" Jean's question cut keenly through the warm
air of the room.

Livingston glanced up in surprise, then looked embarrassed. "I didn't join in the discussion myself, and I have
never met the lady. You have, I know, but I've never
considered that any business of mine."

Jean kept his eyebrows raised and his gaze steady.

Livingston shifted uncomfortably and said at last,
"Mademoiselle Eléonore de Rochambeau."

Jean rose and went towards the door. "Can I offer
you some more coffee?"

"No, thank you, don't bother the ladies. I should be
going."

Jean came back into the room and stood before the
fireplace. "So you think we'll one day felicitate the demoiselle on her marriage into one of the oldest families
in Louisiana?"

Livingston shook his head. "I have no idea. It's
complicated."

"Certainly. You've heard she has a touch of the tar
brush in her background?"

"Really!" Livingston got to his feet, a tinge of disappointment in his expression. "I'd never have guessed, with that magnificent coloring. When it comes to that, however, so has Audubert. Though the society of New Orleans is good enough to overlook the fact."

It felt near enough to a reprimand, but he accepted it with a smile and bade Livingston a friendly farewell.

The women came in to clear away and he sat before the fireplace and stared into the empty grate, sick at what he had just said. The thought of her being spoken of at the governor's, the mere suggestion of her marrying, were so abhorrent that he had reacted with a betrayal of her confidence that was even more vile. Livingston was probably too scrupulous a gentleman to pass the comment on, so it had been useless, in addition to contemptible, as a means of destroying any marriage prospects she might have.

He ran one hand over his face, and jealousy and desolation washed over him again. Marie paused by the table.

"It's too hot in here." he said, "Why doesn't that window open?"

"I keep telling Pierre it's stuck. And since we ain't got Marius no more . . . You want me to have another go at it?" She moved across the room, agile and graceful despite the fullness of her belly.

"Good God no, leave it be. Better still, get to bed. I've kept you up long enough. Let your sister finish it."

Marie dropped her eyes and obeyed. He knew why she was still up—she hated going to bed alone. She had confided that to him once, with a mixture of artlessness and flirtation, and he had replied, with a laugh, that she was better fitted in that case to be someone's wife.

She had said softly, "I'd as soon wait for Pierre half the year than spend three hundred and sixty-five nights with a lesser man."

He rested his forehead on his palm. In what state would Pierre be returned to her? Sapped by a confinement that he loathed and feared, after being chained to cold stone where just to breathe, eat or sleep became trials of the damned. Where he received no medical attention for the ills that had plagued him since the seizure, and could raise no barriers against the terror of another one occurring while he crouched helpless and alone.

The sister finished clearing away and went to the kitchen while he stayed in the chair, too far gone to move, his face resting in both hands. For a second he felt all Marie's horror of an empty bed, and banished it only by conjuring up his own in the big house on Grande Terre, where Léonore had spent one night. One night worth a thousand others. But he could no longer picture her on the sheets, and they lay deserted and surrounded by darkness, strangely illuminated, like a drift of pure snow under moonlight.

The sister had come back. She was standing very close by his chair, as she sometimes did, waiting for the dismissal he never failed to give. At this moment, however, there was a burden across his shoulders like a length of chain and he could not raise his head.

He did not move when she leaned closer, and he felt one cool, smooth arm slide around his neck and the other hand curl under his chin to cup his cheek. The first deep throb of misery came from the recognition of what this was not and of who this could never be—but a moment later all coherence was gone, and he let her gather him in and offer him the relief that he had once, with equal pity but much less sweetness, extended to her.

CHAPTER TWENTY-EIGHT

❧

Treasure

When Jean returned to Barataria he was told that a cutter from Cuba had called in with a packet of two letters before sailing eastwards. Judging by the mode of delivery he rather expected to read a misspelled communiqué from Curtis, but when he unfolded the covering letter he found it written in a firm elegant hand that he did not recognize.

It held no superscription or greeting, but there was a signature. His heart gave a jolt, and he read it at once without moving from where he stood, in the full sun on the terrace with a breeze from the Gulf tugging at the pages.

You should receive this from the hand of an American captain who set out from Cuba on August 9. He carries a dispatch from an American agent in Cuba, addressed to General Jackson, setting out the strength of British ships, arms and forces now gathering in Jamaica and those in harbor in Havana. I have requested that he make a copy of the dispatch and give it to you also.

This is the first time in months that I have been absent from home. All is well there, but I found myself wanting employment, so came on a cruise in the brigantine, during which we fell in with the cutter. I invited the captain aboard, and something about the sight of the brigantine's armament and crew prompted him to be frank about his mission and to be thankful that we wished him well. Something in his eyes when your name was mentioned convinced me he would find it possible to sail a trifling distance out of his way and make the delivery.

In case the dispatch itself does not reach your hands, however, be advised that the British are preparing to mount an attack from the sea, east of New Orleans at Mobile, which they hope will rally the Creeks who have taken refuge in Pensacola, and also find support from rebellious slaves in the Territory. All this is preparatory to a later, combined assault on New Orleans, using shallow-draft vessels to transport troops and artillery over waters such as the Mississippi Sound. So far there is only a small squadron available for this task, commanded by a Captain Percy, but the plan seems to be Admiral Cochrane's and there is no way of knowing how many vessels and troops he may send south from the Atlantic fleet—or even what reinforcements may arrive from England in the next few weeks. Havana has just received confirmation that a British expeditionary force left France at the beginning of June, bound for the East Coast of America, and yet another convoy is expected to leave Plymouth as I write.

You may wonder why I send you news so vital to the Americans—but I hope you do not. I hope you see this instead as a sign of my trust, and of the pledges we made, that have nothing to do with "your" country or "mine." Only you can know how much I longed to bring this message to you myself. Only you fully believe that I must not. All that prevents me are three words that you once wrote to me and that I now send to you with my heart. This is love.

Sida Al Hurra

*   *   *

On the day Jean read the letter, Léonore reached Haiti
and paid a visit to the property on La Gonave where she
usually bought sisal. This time there were no purchases to
be made, and after a brief consultation with the owners
she and Mirliton rode inland on borrowed horses.

Beyond the plantation was a strip of jungle, where the
broad-leafed trees were festooned with lianas and only
a narrow track allowed access to the other side of the
hills. They rode in single file, Mirliton in front with his
favorite Ferguson rifle across his knees, his forage cap
pushed back off his brow. Flamingo plants grew in damp,
steamy hollows amongst the undergrowth, and in places
the jungle canopy was so dense the flowers hovered in
the gloom like the red eyes of prowling beasts. Here
and there, orange-and-yellow beacon plants strung their
shark's-tooth necklaces over the thickets and Léonore
would catch sight of a gleaming blackbird, or the furry
face of a shy little anole, disturbed in the hunt for insects
in the foliage above.

When they reached the top of the ridge the heat
crashed down through thinner cover, and vipers that had
been sunning themselves on the path slithered off
amongst dry grass. They rode on under patchy banana
trees left over from plantings that had once extended
down the hill and over the narrow strip of plantation
beyond. Now this corner of the property was turning
back to jungle, occupied only by a couple of former
slaves who had scratched a farm out of a tiny valley
below. Their children had moved on long since, but the
old people still lived in their emerald haven, in the company of dogs, chickens, and a donkey that Léonore remembered being allowed to ride on when she had visited
the place with her father, only once, at the age of nine.

As the sure-footed horses began to pick their way
down the other side of the hill, she said to Mirliton's
bent back, "You know where we're going?"

He did not even bother to turn. "Nope."

She sniffed in the disbelieving way he sometimes did.
"To fetch Roncival's treasure." There was no reaction,
so she continued. "It's time I took it back to San Stefan."

He gave a quick glance over his shoulder. "Why?"

"Because we don't need the myth of it as security anymore. You know what's happening at home—we've gotten to the point I've been aiming at for years. From now on we can sustain ourselves from the income we get from cordage. We can be planters and manufacturers at last, not privateers. When we get back, I want everyone to know exactly where we stand, so they can make some choices. Most of the men will want to leave—I understand that. I'm hoping enough people will remain to tend the agave and the gardens, and make the ropes and sail the brigantine and all the rest."

He pulled the white mare's head around so she was sidling down the path, and looked at her more directly. "They'll hate this. What about the frigate?"

"I vote we sell her to the Navy Department of the United States, at an attractive price. Good heavens, any price will be attractive, the way they're placed."

"Is the *Hero* worth more or less than the treasure?"

"You'll see."

She waved him on, and after a second or two he pulled the mare's head forward again. She was thus able to continue talking to his back. "There's gold, and my mother's jewels. When she sailed to Martinique she left behind all the things my father had ever given her. He couldn't bear them to be on San Stefan, and he would never sell them, so he brought them here."

He flung over his shoulder: "They're a fortune in themselves. Don't you remember the things she used to wear?"

She said nothing. For Mirliton, everything about her mother had been dazzling.

The dogs heard them first and came racing up the slope, annoying the horses but keeping their teeth to themselves. After a while they consented, grumbling now and then, to escort the riders down a well-beaten section of the track. Farther on Léonore could smell wood smoke and wafts of healthy odors from the byre and the henhouse. The hut, when it became visible through the trees, proved to be surrounded on three sides by rickety sheds and the remains of a corral fence, to which was tied another horse, wearing a sidesaddle.

"Odd," Mirliton said, with a note of alarm. "Whoever she is, she didn't come in our way." Otherwise they would have seen the fresh hoof marks on the track.

The old man appeared at that moment, darting out with an alacrity extraordinary for his age. He was short, bowlegged, with close-cropped white hair and large, rheumy eyes; possibly his sight was impaired, for although she and Mirliton were only about twenty yards from him as they rode out from the trees, he made no attempt at a greeting. A moment later he turned and disappeared as quickly as he had come.

Léonore said as they dismounted, "They'd have no visitors from one year's end to the next. Two lots on the same day has probably frightened the living daylights out of them."

Mirliton looked no more reassured than she felt. "Shall I come in with you?"

"Thank you, no. Sit here on the rail and hold on to that rifle."

As she approached the hut she could hear a sound inside—the reedy, querulous voice of the old man. There was no porch or verandah, just a step made of a smooth, flattish river stone under a wooden door bleached silver-gray by the sun. She put her hand on the finely scarred surface and leaned forward to listen.

Another voice within said, "I see no problem. Simply ask them to wait, if you please."

It was a supple, melodious voice that would always be pleasing to listen to, no matter how ordinary or disobliging the speaker's words might be.

She ceased to breathe.

A third person, the old woman, said, "Where, madame?"

"There are two riders, you say? Invite them to water their horses down at the stream. While they are there, I shall leave."

Yes, there could be no mistake. It was the voice she recognized with her whole being, the voice of her childhood, reeled up from the depths of time to reveal itself here in this sunny place—warm, musical and intensely alive.

It was the child who responded, flinging open the door and stepping at once across the threshold into the low, lightless room.

It was the child who gazed at the beloved mouth and eyes, the red-gold hair undimmed by the years, the white, unlined brow. And met the gaze beneath it, china-blue and petrified.

In the next second, she came to herself and recognized Mathilde de Oleron y Siqueiros.

The wrench was so sudden the breath was driven from her lungs. The group on the other side of the room—two somber shapes with a glowing figure before them—shuddered and blurred. She tottered and was caught, then was lowered into a seat by cool, steadying hands. There was a remembered fragrance, the touch of smooth skin, a pale oval swimming in the air beside her, accented by diamonds, circled by gold.

Her senses returned painfully. She was on a bench by the door. She leaned back, unaided now; the señora was sitting beside her, her fingers locked together in her lap.

"Leave us."

The two shadows detached themselves from the opposite wall and faded out the other door.

After a very long time the beautiful voice spoke again. "You would rather I had drowned."

It was not a question, therefore required no answer. She looked straight before her. "You left us. You planned it."

"No. It was desperation."

"You hated him." *And me.*

On a table was an iron box with the lid tilted back. An oilskin spread on the tabletop glittered as though someone had splashed water over the gems piled upon it.

"No. I hated that place, that hell on earth he wanted me to live through."

"Why come back, then?"

The woman rose from beside her, took two rapid steps, raised both hands and swept the jewels into the air so that they spun and flickered and then showered onto the earth floor like raindrops. "Is that what you think?" She went on bitterly. "Take them. I was going to put them in my husband's hands—but he might not have accepted them anyway. No matter. Nothing I give him can equal his goodness to me."

Léonore gave a choking cry. "What about your true husband? You took everything from him!" *And from me.*

The woman swung to face her, hands clasped once again, white-knuckled against her midriff. "I had no choice. Judge me. You have the right. But don't expect me to explain. You will never understand."

"You did not love my father."

"Yes I did." She grimaced, bent over, put one hand on the tabletop. "I did. Love."

"And Don Julio?"

The golden head came up. "That is my affair!"

Léonore rose and leaned her back against the door. Her voice cut like a razor. "You made it my affair when you brought him to the Caribbean. Can you deny what you two have done to me? You are right. I will never understand. But by God, neither of us leaves here until I have an explanation."

The blue eyes widened. "Can you not guess? I came back because my husband wished to come. Everything else, ever since, I have done for you."

Léonore gave an incredulous laugh, then said, "You might have told me the truth long ago."

"So I could face the hatred I see now?" She turned, walked to the fireplace, flung over her shoulder, "I knew I would do less harm to you dead. But when Julio brought me here, and I learned what was happening to you, I could not just stand by and watch." She faced Léonore, her eyes glittering. "Julio is devoted to me; he agreed to everything I asked. He is the only person in the world who knows what I have done. Yet he has never ceased to love me and support me and help me."

"And you have repaid him as you repaid my father!" She took a breath, appalled. "He even knows about Jean?"

Her mother's face went white. She stammered out, "My God, no. No. But everything else—"

"I am still waiting to hear you explain."

Her mother sank onto a stool by the fireplace. "As soon as I came back I could not help making inquiries about you. It was not difficult; your father's old contacts are everywhere. I learned you had been educated in New Orleans. I heard that you had moved in the best society. I hoped against hope you had married and were safe somewhere. But no. I found you were still on San Stefan. Worse, you were carrying on where Roncival left off. Worst of all, there was an alliance with Laffite. I was beside myself. Julio swore to help me.

"First, we contrived the letter, to drive you away from San Stefan, from that abominable trade. Then you visited New Orleans and I sent Julio to spend an evening with you, so he could tell me—" Her voice faltered, and she put her hands over her face, but she lowered them again and clasped them in her lap, looking at the floor. "I had to see you. The carriage. All he had said was true. How you spoke, how you looked . . . But I had you watched afterwards, and I found out you were still seeing Laffite. Since then I have done everything I could think of to get you away." She lunged to her feet, her voice filled with savagery. "Just what do I need to explain? You are my daughter. You grew up with Roncival. You grew up with him, endured that vile place, that brutal life. When I ran away with him he promised me paradise. And look where I ended up! Could I stand by and see you shackled to just such a man, doomed to just that kind of existence?"

Léonore pushed herself away from the door, took a step forward. "I was a child. You could have stayed and protected me. But you didn't love either of us enough for that."

She said wildly, "Love? It is the greatest torture life can deal out. God save you from love. It has destroyed me." She stepped forward and her hands brushed Léonore's arms, then fell to her side. Her eyes sparkled with sudden tears. "You will not understand me. But promise me you will remember this. It is possible to walk away from someone you deeply, absolutely love. You *can* leave the love of your life. If it is the right thing to do."

Léonore said into her face, "I could never walk away from a child."

Her mother flinched, then held her gaze, her mouth contorted but her words very clear. "Yes, I failed you, then and now. We are going back to Spain; it is free at last, and we have lost everything here. Julio wants to build a new life in the ruins. We sail tomorrow."

Léonore made herself turn aside, glance contemptuously at the dirt floor, sewn here and there with startling points of radiance. "And you would like him to go with your respect and devotion and a fistful of gems. What husband could ask for more?"

Out of the corner of her eye Léonore saw her break then, so that she was bending stiffly over, propped with rigid arms on the table. There was a muffled cry. "You are cruel."

Tears stung. "I am your daughter." Then she turned and looked at her for the last time, seeing the fall of hair that had come unpinned and that partly masked her face, the slender curve of her hips under the fine silk dress, her fists clenched on the tabletop. She burst out, "I can never forget how you were and how I was. You are wrong—I remember you laughing. I remember you crying. I remember everything. I shall never forget you."

Her mother turned, the blue eyes imploring within the veil of hair. "Nor forgive."

"We are beyond that. We are far beyond that." She heard Mirliton's voice outside, with the others, approaching. She put her hand on the latch of the door. "Adieu."

The sun blinded her for a moment as she pulled the door closed behind her, and she nearly tripped on the step. Then Mirliton's face appeared before her, gray and unnatural. She said, "We are leaving."

He stood motionless so she pushed past him, ignoring the others, and went to the horses. Mirliton still did not move, so she mounted unaided, using the rickety fence, and set her horse at the hill. A sick horror came over her, as though there were something reaching out, trying to suck her back down into the deep little valley. She dug her heels into the horse's side, her breath issuing in

sobs as she urged it on. She looked behind when she got
to the top, but there was nothing to see other than trees.
And no one following.

Once across the crest the forest closed in, with twisted
creepers and pools of darkness. The horse followed the
path on its own. It took a long time for Mirliton to catch
up. He crashed past her and took the lead again, the
rifle slung over his shoulder.

She said, "You should have come when I asked you."

"I couldn't. She was crying so."

Only a little farther on she saw the marker tree, with
a blaze on the trunk and a narrow overgrown path behind it. She said harshly, "Down there, to the right."

She recognized the little glade when they reached it,
hushed and overarched by lianas. The reddish earth was
turned back where the farmer had dug out the jewel
chest, and his shovel lay beside the hole. She dismounted
and looked down—the old man had not exposed the
next layer, not quite knowing as yet which Roncival it
might be safest to yield to.

She began to dig, while Mirliton opened the saddlebags hanging over the cruppers of their horses. The
earth was dry and fine here near the top of the hill,
forming a soft blanket over what had once lain trapped
in the rocks of San Stefan.

She heard a muted exclamation from Mirliton when
the shovel exposed a streak of gold, glowing like a pale
line of flame in the ground. She stepped back.

"Get them all out and we'll see how many we can
take."

He lifted the ingots one by one and laid them beside
the hole. Protected only by the earth, they were easy to
prize loose and brush clean. There were more than she
had expected, but not too many to divide amongst the
saddlebags.

Her birthright, and her burden. Roncival's treasure,
that even in her own mind had had the power and the
menace of myth. It had been dug from the bowels of
San Stefan at the cost of men's lives, and there was no
more to be had unless she let her freebooters run that
risk again. Now there was no need. With the gold as

security, her plans for their island home could be fulfilled.

Before they left, she threw a bag of Spanish coins into the hole for the old people to find. They had been steadfast, in their way.

They had to lead the horses, and Mirliton went in front as before. Léonore stumbled now and then, but he only looked back once and they could not meet each other's gaze.

She was crying so.

Now Léonore did too, in silent floods. The forest blurred and ran. The tempests lasted for days, ceasing only when she got home.

CHAPTER TWENTY-NINE

Patriot

The great heat of the summer of 1814 had a debilitating effect on the expeditionary force led to America by Major General Robert Ross: four thousand men whom he could launch, if he pleased, at Washington. After transporting his men some way up the Patuxent River, Ross marched them alongside it in steamy, excessive heat. A small American naval force awaited them, but faced with the three mighty brigades on land and with a British squadron advancing up the river, they burned all their boats and withdrew.

President Madison and Secretary of State James Monroe received the news of the British landing on August 18. Even given the deliberate pace of Ross's advance, there was less than a week to secure Washington against attack. The British must cross a waterway to reach the city, and there were only two bridges. One, at the American navy yard, was defended by artillery and naval forces. The other bridge was at Bladensburg, five miles from the yard. The American commander elected to defend the navy yard, though remained open to other suggestions. On the morning of August 24, therefore, when Ross marched his army towards Bladensburg, there was only one brigade of militia overlooking the bridge from high ground on the opposite bank. The president, the cabinet and the secretary of state were at the yard when a scout sounded the alert, whereupon they began stream-

ing across the countryside on horseback, closely followed
by the rest of their army.

The inconceivable was about to happen—a mighty
strike at Washington, for the first time in history. When
the enemy's light infantry began to push across the
bridge, the assembled American force stood at seven
thousand, so they were superior in numbers, but they
were mostly militia rather than regulars, and inexperi-
enced at that. British rocket fire took them by surprise
and sowed panic in the ranks. Thereafter it was a stumbling retreat down the road towards Washington, covered only by a naval commander, Commodore Joshua
Barney, who without orders had brought four field
pieces and four hundred marines across country from
the navy yard. He did not surrender until wounded,
whereupon he was treated by his captors "with the most
marked attention, respect and politeness, as if I was a
brother."

The British brought no such fraternal courtesy to
Washington itself when they advanced into the semides-
erted city at eight o'clock that evening. Their orders
were to destroy every public building, including the seat
of government and the president's mansion, as well as
blowing up military targets such as the bridge over the
Potomac and all the stores, arsenals, barracks and magazines. Explosions, fires and collapsing masonry killed ci-
vilians and even British troops. Many citizens had fled,
including the president himself, bound for Virginia; his
wife had also escaped, somewhat encumbered by the
family silver. The dinner table at the White House was
found laid for forty, and the food still on the plates was
consumed by the soldiers before they set fire to the
building.

The sack of Washington continued until the following
midday, by which time the parliamentary records and
other archives of the United States were in ashes.
Whereupon a hurricane roared through the city, flinging
the roofs from houses, burying around thirty British soldiers in collapsing buildings, illuminating the shattered
streets with bolts of lightning and releasing cataracts of
rain to douse the fires. The British withdrew the way

they had come, across the fields of battle still littered
with corpses, to rejoin their fleet, unmolested.

It was not hard to guess where this terrifying force
would strike next. The Gulf of Mexico.

At a very late hour on the night of August 24, the
five American commissioners for peace were gathered
around a table in the Hôtel d'Alcantara in Ghent, East
Flanders, trying to complete two difficult compositions:
a report to their president and secretary of state—both,
had the party but known it, then under siege—and a
reply to detailed instructions that had been delivered to
them by the British peace commission.

Albert Gallatin had arrived at this point in his lively
diplomatic career after a series of uncomfortable though
not unrewarding journeys. He had no cause to regret the
detour to London. It had given him the chance to observe the city in the full flush of the celebrations following England's triumph over Napoleon. It had also
afforded him a few insights into British military policy
and, paradoxically, an audience at last with Czar Alexander I, who had since returned to Russia without having
been of any personal or diplomatic assistance to either
side.

His four fellow commissioners were rather less happy
about zigzagging through Europe over the last few
weeks, and the encounters with the British representatives gathered in Ghent had been equally unpleasant.
Gallatin's expectations of the first meeting had not been
high, but even he could not help feeling some of the
consternation that turned Senator Bayard's handsome
face as pale as his well-groomed mane of silver hair.
Since then it had been almost impossible to find anything
that could be put on the table for discussion.

There were some topics over which a certain amount
of wrangling did take place, such as the American fishermen's traditional right to dry their catches along the
banks of the St. Lawrence River. Gallatin heard rather
more about dried cod than he had bargained on, during
both the official meetings and the informal social gatherings.

By this point in a rather acrimonious night, however, the Americans had finally agreed on their reply to a sweeping list of terms from the English.

Gallatin said to Bayard, "Just about all their instructions would cede territory to the English. Their mood is acquisitive, even more so than I came to suspect when we were in London."

Bayard glanced at him nervously. He too had been shocked by the rumor that twenty-five thousand British troops were being prepared for the invasion of the United States, and he would probably not have disagreed with Gallatin's private letter to Madison, which included his opinion that a principal British objective was the city of New Orleans.

The senator growled, "They want to go back to the Treaty of 1795. And whatever that turns out to include, I'm prepared to bet it names a few more slices of our northern territory as Canadian." He sighed. "What in the name of fortune can we discuss? We go round in circles without ever getting even a toe on the ground!"

"A valid point," Gallatin said smoothly, and took a breath. "I think if the English are going to throw in areas like the banks of the St. Lawrence, we might introduce a few minor territorial issues of our own. As a way into fuller dialogue." He shrugged. "The island of San Stefan, for instance."

Four weary faces turned his way. "What?" Bayard said.

"The English probably do not know of it, and it may not even be familiar to all of you, gentlemen. It lies in the Caribbean, at an equal distance from Cuba, Haiti and Jamaica. Its sovereignty is under dispute, and I understand its inhabitants would welcome a closer relationship with the United States. Mentioning it in discussion commits us to nothing, and it may provide a diversion from the issues on which we have such immovable differences. If I have the pleasure of breakfasting with any of you tomorrow, I shall be more than happy to tell you what I know about San Stefan."

On September 3, the British turned up at Barataria. A brig called the *Sophia* arrived off Grande Terre and showed a flag of truce to invite a parley. A four-man tender was preparing to set out from the point and meet the brig's incoming boat when Dominique walked down onto the sand. His pointer, Belair, circled around them as he said quietly to Jean, "You know what you're doing?"

"I know who I'm meeting, at any rate, thanks to the letter."

This was the second reminder that it was Roncival who had told them what the British strength in the region amounted to. Dominique said, irritated, "Why haven't we had the same sort of information from Curtis?"

Jean shrugged. "Do me a favor and check back at quarters while I'm fetching the party. See that everything's going to plan."

"You have one, do you?" Dominique grinned. "All right. I'll make them get out the best plate. As long as I'm to be feted too."

There were three visiting officers: the brig's commander, Captain Nicholas Lockyer, accompanied by a lieutenant, and Captain John McWilliams, commander of marines. Dominique was able to take a good look at them when they arrived at the house, while Jean ushered them in and disposed them about the main room. They were all seated comfortably where they could view the terrace and the waters of the Gulf, framed by two cannon placed at each corner of the parapet.

Jean managed it all with his usual ease, and Dominique wondered what the English officers made of the reception. From their point of view the possible snags were numerous. Their signal might have been ignored, or answered by hostile fire from the shore. On landfall, they might have been attacked instead of just surrounded for fifteen minutes or so by a mob of suspicious rogues. The officers were men shaped by the duties and rigors of a navy from whose steely discipline seamen were constantly deserting, to join the merchantmen and privateers of other nations in the Atlantic and Mediterranean—and especially those of America. They would be fastidious gentlemen, he thought, inwardly arming themselves for a confrontation with *canaille*.

Lockyer had a sensible air: a neatly made man with clear-cut features, he looked people straight in the eye. Dominique asked him one or two questions about the *Sophia* that were answered with rock-hard confidence. Dominique thought he could detect a good captain in Lockyer, and it was always a pleasure to meet a good captain. The lieutenant, a slender young man with fine skin that changed color rather often beneath his long gray eyes, was less relaxed. Dominique could see the purpose of the visit flickering away inside the narrow head; the younger man was impatient for the others to get on with it, and was forcing himself not to feel uneasy in the meantime. There was a certain pleasure in that observation too.

McWilliams looked just what he was. Dominique had always felt a bit sorry for commanders of marines, usually deprived of the glory that might be gained from soldiering on land, condemned at sea to cross swords with the very sailors who kept them afloat and who therefore could not help holding marines somewhat cheap. The officers that he had met all had an outsize ridge of muscle at the point of the jaw—the result, Dominique concluded, of a lifetime spent bawling orders across windswept decks. McWilliams's face had just the square, choleric look that Dominique was used to. There was no hint that he was pulling a different way from Lockyer, however. They seemed molded together, an iron fist in an iron glove. The glove being Lockyer.

There was no lack of conversation. Jean asked Lockyer where they had sailed from, and they were more than happy to natter on about what they had been doing over in the east around Pensacola, which was at present held by a certain Colonel Nicholls, whom he and Jean had already heard about from Havana. Dominique wondered, repressing a grin, whether they really figured that sporting a red coat was some kind of guarantee that the nearest Red Stick or black malcontent would leap instantly into their laps. They also spoke about that part of the Gulf as though it were swarming with British navy blue; they did not seem to realize that he and Jean knew, thanks indeed to certain letters, that their force ran to precisely four ships.

Jean also spoke, to Dominique's own surprise and admiration, of New Orleans. To hear him, you would never have thought that the characters he was naming were the very same who had thrown Pierre in the Cabildo. He made a kind of theater of the city in the mind's eye, with the streets and the grand events and the people lit up with a bright glow as though they were parading past footlights.

It came round to business in the end. They were cool, no doubt about it, for he was sure that they must sense as well as he did the brooding quiet that had descended over the island. You did not need to be tenderly acquainted with banditti to catch the menace all around them.

At Jean's polite invitation, there was a bit of a speech, and some documents were handed over. Jean read each one twice, in silence, while they all smoked their cigars, and then handed them in turn to Dominique. A copy of a proclamation from Colonel Nicholls, released in Pensacola six days before, saying pretty much what he had been spouting in Havana already, about how everyone in Louisiana now had a fine chance to gather together and fling off the yoke of the United States. A letter addressed to Jean setting out what the commander of the local squadron expected Lockyer to seize at once from Barataria on behalf of the British navy—their Spanish prizes, if you please, and command of all their vessels. Plus restitution of all past damage to English ships! Lockyer hauled out another piece of paper too, which contained his own orders. Both demanding the same alliance against the Americans and offering the same rewards—thirty thousand U.S. dollars and a captaincy in the Royal Navy for Jean, plus Pierre's release.

Dominique had trouble keeping his eyes on the papers when he saw the threats they contained, but he was supposed to look as though he was pondering everything, to give Jean time. What really sank in was what the British required Lockyer to do in the case of refusal: "to destroy to his utmost every vessel there as well as to carry destruction over the whole place." To maintain any appearance of peace of mind, Dominique had to swiftly conjure up a big picture of their own scores of ships at anchor in the Lake, and compare it to the visitors' piddling flotilla, none bigger than a frigate, and scattered who knew where.

Jean said, "Allow me to pour you gentlemen another cognac. You'll excuse me, I hope, if I take a moment to consult one of my relatives, whose interest in the matter is important. My apologies."

Outside, as they stood on the back verandah, faces materialized in the foliage. Dominique said, "Oncle Renato's still out. The *Spy*'s not due back until—"

"No. I don't like their cursed smugness. I want them stuck here, thinking this thing through, right down to the bone." He drew Dominique out into the sun, a hand under his elbow. "We need Gambi. He'll love it."

Jean found the rest of the Englishmen's visit moderately entertaining. They had had enough wine to give them an inclination to stay put for a while, and very soon there was more than enough noise around the house to keep them inside. When the Italians and a select rabble began their vociferations in the garden, he placed four guards on the terrace and apologized to his guests; anti-English sentiment amongst the Baratarians was inevitable but harmless. Later, when the rattling began at the windows, he sent Dominique out with a reprimand and drew all the curtains. The proceedings of the next few hours had an angry choral accompaniment, founded on the basso continuo of Gambi's Calabrian snarl and accented by pistol shots from the direction of the Red Saloon. In the end he extended his hospitality to the three of them for the night, reassuring them that the sailors who had rowed them in were being held in safe custody at the landing place, and each officer would have a bedroom to himself.

Breakfast the next morning was early and quiet, but the tumult was building again by the time he accorded the officers a gracious release, and guards were required

again to escort them to the beach. They were so keen to
rejoin the *Sophia* that they made no objection to waiting
onboard another hour or two until he sent out his considered reply.

He enjoyed writing the letters, all of them in English,
and it was a rare treat to allow himself the expressions
he got into the first one. A messenger had just come in
from New Orleans, but after a quick exchange he sent
him off to have a meal, fearful of distraction. The choice
of correspondent for the first letter was not difficult: he
needed to be a respected member of the Legislature who
would be guaranteed to show the documents to Claiborne. Jean Blanque, the gentleman he selected, was
also the secret owner of a few Baratarian vessels; one
could imagine his face when he read the British demands
and registered the immediate threats to his precious
Marie-Louise and *Vengeance*.

Jean wrote a second letter, for Claiborne, and made
up a packet containing both letters, plus everything
Lockyer had handed to him and the copy of the American agent's letter to Jackson, sent to him by Léonore.
He could not resist rereading her own message, which
he did not include. Sida Al Hurra. He remembered their
first hateful dialogue about pirates, during the meal on
San Stefan. Then the candlelit supper on the *Mélusine*.
Often, watching the English officers dine at his table, he
had imagined what it would be like if she were sitting
there beside him. He pictured Lockyer's astonishment,
McWilliams's fascination, awkwardness descending on
the sly lieutenant. She would have relished the fact that
the vintage claret the officers had so praised was from
stock he had lifted off the *Hero*.

He examined the letter to Blanque critically before he
sealed the packet. There was one paragraph at least in
a style that she would approve.

*In short, monsieur, I make you the depository of
the secret on which perhaps depends the tranquillity
of our country. Please to make such use of it as
your judgment may direct. I might expatiate on this
proof of patriotism, but I let the fact speak for itself.*

The third letter, to Lockyer, took very little effort to compose. Dominique came in as he was folding it, and said, "What have you told the English?"

"I've apologized again. I've told them we need time to sort out a few troublemakers before I can pledge our support. They're to come back in two weeks' time for a rendezvous off the point, and we'll give them our answer."

"Do you think they'll be happy with that?"

"Well, they could always sail in right away, slap bang between the two batteries, and see what our troublemakers can achieve with the twenty-four-pounders." He pushed the letter across. "Maurice can ferry that out to the *Sophia*. And I want Ranchier to run this packet through to Jean Blanque as fast as he can go."

"What are you telling Blanque?"

"Everything. It couldn't be clearer. Louisiana leaves us alone, Claiborne releases Pierre, and in return we decline to cooperate with the English."

Dominique sat down heavily. "We've got two weeks, then."

Jean shook his head. "I've just had word from New Orleans. It would seem the governor's prayers have been answered. He's mustered enough forces to throw at us: troops from the forty-fourth regiment and six gunboats under Daniel Patterson, plus a schooner, fully armed."

Dominique narrowed his eyes. "Is it serious? How soon will they move?"

"As soon as Claiborne's stopped rubbing his hands in glee."

"What's the size of the force exactly? We can group—"

"Bloody hell, Alexandre, can you see us firing on them, when I've just given us the best flaming American credentials this side of Mexico?"

His brother got up, making the fine legs of the chair screech across the polished floorboards. "What, then?"

"We've no choice. We'll have to shift. To Isle Dernière."

CHAPTER THIRTY

Suitor

In November, Léonore received a letter brought back by Rigaud from Port-au-Prince. By now everything was in place on San Stefan. Those who had elected to stay had coalesced into three efficient teams that maintained the agave plantations, the rope manufacture and the day-to-day running of island life. Those with aims elsewhere were content to wait for the sale of the *Hero* before dispersing with the gains.

The seamen were not in any particular hurry to give up the old existence, mainly because of the increased shipping that began to pass tantalizingly close to home, through the Windward Passage. At one point Rigaud and a scratch crew ran across units of a British convoy— undoubtedly part of Cochrane's long-awaited fleet, on its way to Jamaica. Rigaud hailed a vessel named the *Helen*, found it to be only a transport, and went for another called the *Volcano*. The number of marines on-board proved to be alarming, however, and he sent the fast-sailing *Fantôme* veering away a few seconds after she touched—leaving a score of his crew clinging to the *Volcano*'s bowsprit. These men all had to drop smartly into the water and wait to be picked up. It was not the most glorious episode in the career of Antonin Rigaud, but it left his men with a strong urge to confront the English once again at close quarters and give a truer account of themselves.

Léonore read her letter, sitting in a cane chair under the colonnade, while out in the lagoon the midmorning sun sparkled along the flank of the *Fantôme* and bounced gold flashes of light off the decks of the *Hero*, where a whole watch were polishing up the brightwork to marketable splendor.

> *My dear Eléonore,*
>
> *Is it discretion that has prevented you from dropping me a line since we last saw each other? I cannot believe it to be lack of friendship and affection, since you know that they persist in my bosom exactly as of old. For the present, let us have done with discretion, for it is a virtue of peace, and more sterling qualities must shortly come into action. What would you wish me to include in a bulletin from the United States? What can I tell you that you do not already know, by one or another of your secret means?*
>
> *News from overseas: I have not heard a word from our Swiss acquaintance since April last year, written on the eve of his departure. He and the others will have their work cut out to extract any advantage from the current situation! As itemized below.*
>
> *Washington: no doubt you know the whole sorry story.*
>
> *Baltimore: at least the Americans managed to hold on to that. Repulse of the British, death of their Major General Ross.*
>
> *The North: no change in British fortunes. The United States will never take Canada, but the reverse equally applies. The war has moved South: the British fleet sailed for Jamaica on October 18. Reinforcements reportedly left England in the third week of September, bound our way.*
>
> *New Orleans: it is quite beyond me to describe what goes forward or backward just now in this city, so I shall make a virtue of discretion and refrain from comment in case this message is intercepted. Such things have been known.*

*Barataria: is no more. The prisoner Pierre Laffite
escaped from the Cabildo on September 6 and has
not been seen since. A $1000 reward is offered. On
September 16 troops, gunboats and a warship were
sent to demolish the stronghold of the Laffites. The
Baratarians, apparently a few hundred in number,
offered no resistance; as the forces closed in they set
fire to all their stores, warehouses and vessels and
attempted to withdraw. Eighty men were taken prisoner, including one of their leaders, Dominique
You. They are in chains in the Cabildo, charged
with piracy. The troops took possession of twenty-
six vessels and loaded them with captured goods,
all of which are impounded.*

*Legal proceedings are underway. The com-
mander of the expedition, Commodore Daniel Patterson, has lodged a claim for prize money. The
United States Collector of Customs has filed for
possession of the contraband. The Laffites demand
the return of the vessels and restitution of the cargo,
which they claim to be the property of the Republic
of Cartagena, under whose flag they operate as
privateers.*

*Correspondence has been received from Jean
Laffite, but he has not been seen in or near New
Orleans for over a year. It is understood he was not
in Barataria when it was attacked.*

*Eléonore, you are aware that I sometimes have
premonitions about you. I had the strongest impression today that your thoughts are turning our way.
Hence this letter, which is a warning: banish those
thoughts if you have them—there could not be a
worse place, nor a worse time. Accept instead these
loving wishes from across the ocean. Until better
days, and let us pray they come soon, I am as always your faithful and devoted S.*

When she had read the letter, Léonore sat for an hour
with it open on her lap. The words burned deep. *Barataria is no more.* Claiborne, after his years of struggle
against the apathy, corruption and venality of New Or-

leans, and his long vendetta against Jean Laffite, had finally been given enough guns to win the battle. Never again would Jean's fleet gather in the silver lake. Never again would his men rest secure amongst the rough luxuries of their unique island life. Never again would those places of refuge and dark violence be the same: Bayou Lunaire, the Temple.

Claiborne had brought an era to an end. And just as he tasted victory, the city for which he took such paternal care was about to be invaded in its turn.

Sophronie, despite the cool confidence of her letter to Eléonore, spent every day in a kind of incredulous panic. But as the governor's wife she could never permit herself to show it, even to the governor himself.

On the first day of December, Andrew Jackson was due to ride into New Orleans with a small group of officers. Knowing that he was coming on horseback all the way from Mobile, Sophronie worried about the state he would be in on arrival, and the kind of reception that the city planned to give him. Soon after dawn, therefore, she was standing in the doorway of the large room that overlooked the courtyard at Toulouse Street, gazing at her husband's unresponsive back as he sat at his desk under one of the tall fan-light windows, penning yet another dispatch.

"I'm not sure anyone realizes how ill the general has been. His health is still undermined by the injuries he received in a duel. He has had months of dysentery, he suffers from shocking bouts of malaria, and he is coming here! It may be as much as we can do to prevent his falling out of the saddle on arrival."

Her husband lifted his head but did not turn. "Kilty Smith is giving him breakfast at his plantation on the ride in. He'll saunter into our midst like a proper well-fed gentleman. He's not meeting us all until later in the day, so he'll have time to settle. And the house on the rue Royale couldn't be more comfortable. But by all means offer his wife your help and advice, my dear, whenever she arrives."

"Who are these *all*?"

He did turn then, with a smile that was meant to be
just tolerant, but set his lips into what she called, privately, his perfect cupid's bow. "Myself, Commodore
Patterson, Grymes, Livingston and Monsieur le Maire."

"The mayor does not speak English. And the general
does not speak French."

The cupid's bow was briefly drawn, then released to
display its most sweeping curves. "We will manage. This
is Andrew Jackson, upright or prone, sound or with the
staggers, dapper or covered in dust. Today we welcome
the hope of New Orleans."

For Sophronie, it was a day of many surprises, one of
which was a shy but beautifully expressed invitation to
a supper at the Livingstons, which she accepted.

Andrew Jackson duly arrived in town, looking gaunt,
shabbily dressed and weary, but after an amiable meeting with the dignitaries he spurred about the city inspecting the militia, such as they were, and dispensing
energy and encouragement wherever he went. He
wasted no time in making Edward Livingston a militia
colonel and appointing him as his military secretary,
which gave Mrs. Livingston the courage to suggest the
supper. The thought of the poor general having to sit
down to solitary meals in a cold house appalled Louise
Livingston, and she was sure she could gather together
a group of people who would demonstrate the spontane-
ity and warmth awaiting him in the grateful households
of New Orleans.

Sophronie suspected that she herself had been the last
person to receive an invitation, but she understood why
the hostess had wavered. It was an informal occasion,
soon to be overshadowed by the great receptions at
which the governor and his wife would both be present.
The focus tonight could not be Madame Claiborne, and
the general himself was invited not out of social preten-
sion but simple-hearted kindness.

Sophronie had really been asked because she happened to be at the home of the Chotards when Mademoiselle Eliza Chotard received her own invitation to
the supper. She had been asked also because of her connection with Mademoiselle Eliza's unexpected guest,

who had arrived in New Orleans only the day before. So she went, without fanfare, without William, and with the liveliest expectations of the evening.

Like the rest of the company, she was enchanted. The general was arrayed not in threadbare fatigues and mud-spattered high boots but in an impeccable new dress uniform that became his tall, spare form. Although the French speakers assembled by his Creole hostess far outnumbered those able to stammer a little American, from the first introductions he found the right tone and at table kept up the flow of talk with adroit courtesies. He had Louise Livingston on the one side, who was as clever and as fluent as her husband, and on the other Mademoiselle Chotard, who was positively learned in English. And directly opposite him he had Mademoiselle de Rochambeau, who was captivating in any language.

Sophronie had assigned herself the modest role of interpreter but, being seldom called upon, had leisure to observe her friend. Eléonore's beauty had a completeness that had been maturing in the last years and that seemed, to Sophronie's perceptive eye, to come from a radiance within. There was a vitality, a sureness in the turn of her lips and the sparkle of her extraordinary eyes that derived of course from youth—but that could only attain this brilliance in a woman who had already experienced a rich, full life. From her expressive face it was clear that whatever joy or pain she had passed through, it had burnished rather than dimmed her spirit.

Sophronie also noticed that Sylvain Audubert, seated on Eléonore's left, could scarcely take his eyes off her. He was so attuned that if her cheeks changed color while she spoke, his did too. It was disturbing to watch, as Sophronie did not know whether to hold out hopes for him or not.

Eléonore had dressed for supper in her old boudoir at the governor's mansion—for when Sophronie came upon her at Eliza Chotard's that afternoon she was so delighted that she insisted she come to stay. Thus it happened that the friends had been together, considering the choice of evening dresses, when a bouquet was delivered for Mademoiselle de Rochambeau. It was in a box wrapped in gold tissue and packed with fresh moss. On the dark lining lay three white flowers, the glossy leaves and petals looking as though they had been carved from separate pieces of jade.

Eléonore had exclaimed, "Gardenias!" Her fingers probed gently beneath them for a message, but found none.

Sophronie leaned close, thinking instantly of Audubert. "In this season? Even he— No, these are camellias. Exquisite. You'll wear them, of course."

Eléonore had gently lifted out one stem, a line of crimson visible along one cheek as she bent over the bloom. "You're right, they have no scent." She laid it back in the box, still looking down. "And so fragile—I am sure the petals would fall if I tried to pin them on."

"Then you will simply have to thank the sender when you see him."

The blush spread and intensified. Eléonore met Sophronie's eyes with uncertainty, almost with fear. "Who do you think it is?"

"Sylvain Audubert. He knows you have returned, and he knows he will see you tonight. Eléonore, he lives for nothing but you. I am telling you this because I am devoted to both of you. I shall not say more. You will do with his tributes as you think fit."

If General Jackson noticed Audubert's admiration of Mademoiselle de Rochambeau that evening, he did not let it interfere with the pleasure of speaking to her himself. He said at one point, "I understand you have journeyed even farther than I to grace this delightful occasion, mademoiselle. You are not a native of New Orleans?"

"No. I come from the island of San Stefan, in the Caribbean."

"A courageous journey, if I may say so—across troubled waters and in dangerous times. You must have had very strong reasons."

She smiled. "I think you will understand them, sir, since they resemble your own. In a very humble way, of course. I came here bringing reinforcements."

The general lifted his chin with a start. To Sophronie,

glancing at him in profile, he resembled for a moment a rangy old warhorse, his gray mane swept back from a sharply alert face. "You have defeated me already, mademoiselle. I am at a loss. Reinforcements?"

"In harbor at San Stefan we had a navy frigate called the *Hero*—it was once English, stationed in Jamaica. It seemed the right time to offer it for purchase to the Navy Department of the United States. Our overtures were kindly received and the *Hero* is moored below Fort St. Philip, while the exchange is being negotiated. In the meantime most of her crew have signed onto the United States ship *Carolina*, which was sadly undermanned until we arrived. The *Hero* will give a good account of herself if the fort is threatened. I arrived here yesterday in our brigantine, with two gifts for the city of New Orleans. Governor Claiborne has already done me the honor of accepting them on your behalf."

"*My* behalf?"

"Two cannon. Thirty-two-pounders." Aiming her turquoise smile straight into the stunned eyes of the general, she continued. "As a matter of fact, they were once the property of a man named Dominique You, of whom you may have heard. I have seldom had the privilege of meeting Monsieur You, but I can confide two things, sir, that I believe absolutely. He is as proud and fond a citizen of New Orleans as you could ever hope to find. And if he knew where his cannon were now bestowed, he would applaud the gift—with all his heart."

Later in the evening, when the gentlemen had rejoined the ladies for coffee in the salon, Sophronie was able to speak a little apart with Audubert.

She smiled and said softly, "Now you know. And by tomorrow, so will the rest of New Orleans."

"What she is? It only adds to her splendor. And if the general receives her so—did you see, he kissed her hands? If she had let him, he would have embraced her! You cannot expect me to aim for less."

She looked at his fine-drawn face as he gazed across the room at Eléonore. "Your flowers were accepted with—a blush of feeling. She has mentioned them?"

He turned at once. "No! That is—" His own cheeks colored painfully. "I sent no flowers."

"Oh!" It sounded cross, which was what she felt with herself.

He said in an urgent undertone, "There is someone else. Who?"

She opened frank eyes on his. "I have not the slightest idea. Does it matter? When she was at once convinced they came from you?'

"How long does she stay?"

"Indefinitely. She tells me she has come here to be of use, and she has sent her ship back downriver, to the fort. The prospect of staying in a city under siege seems not to perturb her in the least. Of course, she is welcome to remain our guest for as long as she pleases; I have never loved her more."

Audubert turned to look at Eléonore again. "Perhaps I should wait, then. But no. I can't. I won't. It must be tonight. Will you permit me to escort you home? I should like the opportunity to speak to Mademoiselle de Rochambeau alone for a few moments, before she enters your door."

Very much later, Léonore lay in bed in the governor's mansion, unable to sleep. She felt feverish, which sometimes happened to her at the end of her month, now due. In retrospect, the evening she had just spent seemed crowded and glaring. Everything she had done and said had been in accordance with her plans, which were now complete, and she had ensured for herself the support of both the governor and the defender of Louisiana. She was safe—at least until the British arrived and threw everyone's lives into question. But she had yet to accustom herself to society again, and the sensations of being tamed and hedged about were too new to be easily endured. Then she relived the highly charged dialogue with Audubert in the carriage, and the discomfort grew so stifling she pushed the coverlet right back.

When she first heard the sound she thought it was the result of a log shifting in the fire. Then it became insistent: fingers tapping on the jalousies.

She rose quickly. The blood pounded in her ears the way it did sometimes in dreams, as she tugged away the curtains and undid the windows.

There was no serenade this time, no whispered debate, no insouciance about rousing the mansion. A silent shadow stepped across the threshold and gathered her in, and she clung tight-folded against his chest, which rose and fell as though he had scaled a mountain to reach her. The pulse in his throat beat strongly against her forehead, and she felt heat flow up into her skin, as though her face and hands could burn him where they touched.

His whisper penetrated. "You're shaking. Come here." He drew her to a chair by the fireplace and returned to shut the windows. Then he padded quickly over to lock the door and came back, collecting candles on the way to light in the embers. He put three on the mantelpiece and one on each side of the hearth. It struck her that it was like sitting in a shrine, and he completed the impression by kneeling in front of her, his hands on each arm of her chair.

He stayed there and looked at her, his breathing not yet under control; the pulse was now in his eyes, which flashed and darted into hers. "What is it? Something has happened."

"Yes. I met General Jackson tonight, and—"

"I know all that," he said impatiently. "From Livingston. I know it. I don't mean that. There's something else, something you don't want to tell me."

Until that moment she had come to no conscious decision about what had happened in Haiti. She had not been able to imagine telling him that her mother was alive, and who she was—yet it had seemed inevitable that the truth would somehow surge up between them, wounding, dividing, perhaps destroying. Now she looked at him and the moment itself divided, alternating like the fever, cold and hot. For one split second the handsome face before her had the eyes and mouth of an inquisitor; then it changed, became vulnerable, and the flickers of expression in the dark eyes, the warm color in the lips made her want to fling herself forward and kiss him. It came to her, on a swift breath, that she would not tell him the secret. It belonged to her, and she had the strength to close it in her heart where it could not hurt them.

She shook her head and caressed his cheek. "There is nothing."

He closed his eyes, until she slowly took her hand away. Then he opened them and said, "If Sylvain Audubert were to propose to you, *mi amor,* what would be your answer?"

It was like a buffet in the chest that rocked her back in the chair. It seemed insane that they could have been inches apart, yet thinking of such different things. It seemed unreal to hear Audubert's name on Jean's lips. But she collected herself and held his gaze. "I would thank him for the honor he did me. And tell him that marriage between us was impossible."

"And if he asked you why? If he kept you in the carriage, outside this house, until you explained?"

She looked at him in consternation. "I would tell him the truth about myself." A pause, and she succumbed. "I owed him that."

He flinched. "And did he take no for an answer?"

"He . . ." Her neck and face were on fire. "He told me I should not consider my past as an obstacle. And it happens that he has some power with the Church. The bishop is his uncle. So I was forced to state that my affections are already engaged." Her voice trembled. "I should not be telling you this. It is not fair to him—it is like hurting him twice."

"What do you think it does to me?" He rose and walked away, to the table beside the bed, back to the hearth, then again to the table, on which was an open box, resting on gold tissue.

"Where are the flowers?"

She went across to stand beside him. "Look." They lay on the pillow next to hers like sumptuous embroidery, white-and-green knot work embossed on white linen. She slid between him and the bed, hooked an arm around his neck. "I have not thanked you for them."

His lips softly joined hers and his arms clasped her

and laid her down on the cool sheets, and then he crouched beside the bed, one hand smoothing her hair down over her shoulder and breast. He watched his fingers as they traveled over her skin.

At last he said, "You have just refused one of the most eligible bachelors in Louisiana. What would you say if a homeless bankrupt were to ask you?"

She stared at him, dazed.

He went on. "Audubert has the bishop in his pocket; bankrupt or not, I must see what sort of a priest I can find in mine. As soon as this is over, we would go to Isle Dernière to be married. Or San Stefan." He caught one of her hands.

She whispered, "Why do you ask me now?"

"Because I have neither country nor fortune and I have nothing to offer you, not even lies. You will never have reason to tell me you were deceived. You know everything about me." He took both her hands in a strong grip and transferred his weight to his knees so he could lean close. "I am yours, to the deepest thought and the last impulse. My brothers and I no longer deal in slaves. There are none on Isle Dernière and there never will be. Your chosen country is mine—tomorrow I seek out Andrew Jackson."

A shudder of hope and dread went through her, and she raised herself on one elbow to see him better, to read his face in the half-light thrown out by the candles around the fire. In one stroke, he was tearing down all the barriers.

"You would do this for me. Jean, is it right for you?"

"The best of my life is in this city. It is right that I choose to defend it." He put his forehead on her clasped hands. "Say it."

"Yes." She tore her fingers from his, knelt before him in the bed, turned his face up to her. "Yes." And read the shock and wonder in his eyes. "Could you imagine anything else?" She flung herself back on the pillow, pulled him towards her. "Come to me."

He enveloped her, pinning her with his weight, and kissed her again. "I asked you long ago. It has taken you four years to consent."

"Then I must conclude you do not recognize consent. For I have consented, time out of mind. This is consent. And this."

A little later he said, "Tell me again."

And long after, while the wordless answer possessed their bodies, he said as though with his last breath, "Are you mine?"

"Yes," she said. "Yes."

CHAPTER THIRTY-ONE

Siege

After that night of bliss in her arms, he expected everything else to be easy. It was not.

The tenderness they found together was so overwhelming it almost destroyed his resolve to part, even though it was crucial to leave before dawn, to avoid exposing her and himself. She was unwilling to see that although Madame Claiborne was her friend, she would always be his enemy; there was everything to lose by seeking her complicity.

Nor, it seemed, did he have Livingston's. In the brief conference he had with the lawyer, he was told that it was not an opportune moment. The general was sick, exhausted, but nonetheless determined on assembling a coherent picture of the defenses of New Orleans. He was due to review the city troops and then ride out of the city for several days on reconnaissance. Livingston, who had known the general for years and was almost constantly by his side, believed Jean would have a better chance of a hearing when the city's plight was clearly imprinted on Jackson's mind, for only the acutest sense of emergency was likely to displace his recorded view that the Laffites were "robbers, pirates and hellish banditti."

Jean went next to his friend Bernard de Marigny, one of the leaders of Creole society, but Marigny was sulking, and not in the mood for trying to exert influence on the man who had chosen to make his headquarters at 106 rue Royale instead of the Marigny mansion.

Jean was furious by the time he got to Marie's cottage and sat down to think, mainly because the only possible course of action was already lodged in the back of his mind. He would have to wait. But not in New Orleans; the temptation to see Léonore was too imperious, and he could achieve nothing for Dominique and the rest by hanging about. He must go across country to Berwick's Bay and see whether Pierre was well enough to be moved from hiding.

He spoke to Marie while her sister was out at the markets; the cottage would continue as a clearinghouse for messages, which they knew how to handle. "I have given this address to Léonore Roncival, who goes by the name of Eléonore de Rochambeau when she is in New Orleans. If she needs to contact me you'll receive a sealed note to send on. Until you see me again, the couriers are to take everything to Isle Dernière. You discuss this with no one."

There was an unusual flash of rebellion in her eyes and he said, "Do I make myself clear?"

"She is going to come to this house?"

"No. But I want your word, Marie, that you'll be faithful to instructions."

She looked down and plucked at the end of one sleeve but murmured, "Sure. Just tell me I don't have to deliver no letters to the governor's."

"That's taken care of. Thank you."

He had written Léonore an unsigned note and sent it with another spray of camellias. Their white petals had a tinge of pink at the edges as though they had been picked at dawn, and the flower merchant who arranged the delivery gave a shake of the head as he laid them reverently on the moss.

"A perfect choice in winter, monsieur. They shatter easily, but the ladies find them irresistible."

The word made him think instantly of glass, and he took away with him the impression of crystal shards, worn next to the heart.

*   *   *

Pierre was recovered enough to travel down the Bayou La Fourche to Isle Dernière. They had plenty of time to talk on the way, sitting in the stern of a boat rowed by four oarsmen, on a blustery but fine morning that felt more like spring than winter.

Pierre did not take in at first the significance of Léonore Roncival's gift to the city of New Orleans. Jean explained patiently, "It was a stroke of genius. It did as much for our cause as hers—maybe more. You'll see the effect as soon as I talk to Jackson."

"Dominique has spent five years waiting for you to get those cannon back! Now she's put them out of reach for good. He'll be fit to be tied."

"He'll kiss her feet. If I ever let him that near her."

Pierre said stonily, "So what's the story in New Orleans?"

"Patterson's handy enough, as we too well know, but all he's got is a toy navy. The regular army comes to about five hundred. Claiborne has a few troops that came in lately, and he's sent them out in dribs and drabs along the river."

"And Barataria," Pierre said dryly.

"Indeed. In the city there are five companies of volunteers—all Creole of course except the Irishmen, the Louisiana Blues."

"How many of them?

"I'd be surprised if they come to five hundred altogether. Then there's the Free Men of Color."

"God almighty, what about troops from Mississippi and Tennessee and Kentucky? Where the hell are they?"

"Ask Jackson. I imagine he's sent off for them smartly. God knows how long they'll take to get downriver."

The boat glided out from the shadow of some poplars, and Pierre looked down at the slick water flashing by. "Marie must be terrified."

Jean shook his head. "She's perfectly all right. She and the others make more fuss about the children than anything else, as usual."

"Could we move her to Isle Dernière?" Pierre said wistfully.

Jean shook his head. "With the baby, she's better off where she is. Tell me about the magazines."

They went over the arms and ammunition, the men, stores and vessels they still had available, not all of which were at Isle Dernière. At last Jean said, "And you've no slaves, I trust."

"Yes, Baudard brought a score in not long ago."

"Baudard? He's supposed to be with Oncle Renato."

Pierre shrugged. "I thought you knew—Oncle Renato has lost contact with Curtis. He sent in Baudard, but Curtis seems to have gone to ground. So he gave him a command."

"Damn him." It was idiotic, but he had never been able to shake off his animosity towards Baudard. He was not a bad captain, so he tried to keep him at sea, and out of his sight. "What in perdition can have happened to Curtis?"

"You've always put him forward," Pierre said moodily, "and I've never trusted him. What if he's been warped over in the Spanish direction completely?"

Jean shook his head. "Not enough rewards." He roused himself. "He'll turn up. Meanwhile Baudard can make himself useful and get rid of those slaves. I'm putting out the order as soon as we get there: we've finished with the black trade."

Pierre made a sharp movement and grabbed hold of the gunwale. "*Jésu*, I thought you'd gotten over that bloody nonsense! Just what—"

"Don't." His voice cut harshly across his brother's. "I'm not in the frame of mind."

There was a long, resentful and complicated silence. They never forbade each other to talk, and on the rare occasions when they quarreled, the end of it came when the one who had pushed too hard made a sign of apology, such as a neutral, insignificant statement, and the other offered the same kind of acquiescence. Pierre's next comment, however, was well outside the bounds of either.

"Marie told me different. We reckoned you had your bed well made with the little one. Think about it—you couldn't do better in the end."

"When I want to share your sluts, Pierre, I'll let you know."

It was appalling, like the flash of a naked blade between them. There was an intake of breath, and Pierre turned away as though blinded. Both hands gripped the gunwale now to stop him swinging back with a curse or a blow.

The boat bumped and sashayed through a turbulent stretch of water and their shoulders touched. Pierre, his head bowed, kept on squinting at the surface of the bayou.

Jean spoke with deliberation. "I'm sorry. I didn't say that. Forget it if you can."

The stream ran smooth again and the sun struck down like a shield between them, bright and impenetrable. Without another word they plunged on side by side towards the gulf.

In the happiness following the night with Jean, Léonore felt giddy, and the intoxication lasted, masking every anxiety. He might have left the city, but this time they were not divided by leagues of ocean, and he could be back in little more than a week. He had not gotten through to Jackson yet, but the general's prejudices were sure to be overcome; there was support for the Laffites' offers from a large faction of New Orleans.

Meanwhile he had shown more delicate concern for her affairs than for his own. He did not like her risking the *Fantôme* alongside the *Hero* below Fort St. Philip, and persuaded her to send a message downstream to Rigaud, instructing him to sail to Isle Dernière and await her there. When he arrived himself, he would give orders that her crew were to be welcomed and provided for. Once he was openly back in New Orleans, he would put up at the Hôtel de la Marine and devote himself to being useful to Jackson. There would be no more midnight assignations at the governor's and they must be wary of how they met in public.

When she protested against such sensitive fear of scandal, he had laughed softly. "I am about to take a great deal of trouble to establish a character, my darling—it will scarcely help if I damage yours."

"You don't care a damn about how you are seen. It all hangs on what you are going to be allowed to do."

"True. How mortifying to be penetrated so easily." His head was beside hers on the pillow, his gaze wide open on hers. "But look harder still and you'll get to the real heart of it. If you marry me, I would not have you stoop to do so."

"*When* I marry you."

"And if I do not survive, there is no need for this city to know on whom you were about to throw yourself away."

She reached out and clung to him. "There is no danger. There cannot be. Not now we have come so far."

His voice was shaken but amused. "May I convey that to Jackson? He'll be deeply reassured."

Meanwhile, until he and the general returned, there was a great deal to do. The region was responding to the frantic call for volunteers, and men began to stream into the city. There was a search for barracks and billets and the realization dawned that the hundreds of recruits had also to be armed, clothed and fed. Léonore asked for Claiborne's permission to assist with the last, and she helped some of the army caterers set up a refectory in the ground floor of a half-empty grain store near the Batture. By the end of the first week they had trained a dozen assistants in the business of feeding a rough, hungry multitude in premises around the city.

Out provisioning one day, she almost walked into Adélaïde Maselari at the markets. In her new mood she had no trouble keeping her composure, and she watched to see which expression Adélaïde would adopt.

"Aha." *Satirical.* "What might you be after?"

"Potatoes. Can you recommend anywhere?"

Adélaïde gave a genuine laugh but no other reply. As she passed by, her look changed subtly, and Léonore thought she saw compassion in it. She felt uneasy, then shrugged. Picking her way back through the streets later, with the carter and the load, it occurred to her that ever since her mother disappeared she had in some way been searching for her, even in the disastrously unsuitable person of Adélaïde Maselari. Now she held a secret that Adélaïde would never know: the search was over, and that part of her life was gone.

Léonore also took part in the great shirt-making campaign. A few Cajuns and "Kaintucks" had made it downriver to sign up with the troops, mostly without arms, provisions, a bedroll or even a change of clothes. They looked as grubby as if they had stepped straight out of the fields onto a flatboat, and wore threadbare garments that when the time of battle came would expose them to almost as much risk as their lack of weapons. Thin cotton was no proof against the chill that often fell during damp winter nights in the plantations and swamps— and supplies of tents and coverings were so low it was a certainty most of the new soldiers would be camping sleepless and shivering under the stars. The ladies of New Orleans made it their business to find material and provide shirts for their defenders, and Léonore joined a group who worked in the Chotard house.

She had become a useful member of New Orleans society, and was accepted in the best houses—just. There were times when the conversation would falter or freeze around her. At Madame Porée's one day the most pressing topic came up: from which direction would the English invade? Léonore made a quick map on the floor with spools of thread, to show the Mississippi delta in the middle, the straggle of lakes to the north and northeast of the city, and Lake Barataria below.

A twelve-inch rule darted amongst the colors as she explained. "The main way is of course up the river, but we command it at Fort St. Philip. Lake Barataria"—a hush—"is also covered." The rule slid northeast. "Up here their approach by sea is extremely complicated: their warships and transports cannot come close in because the lakes are so shallow. They would have to off-load their troops and artillery onto smaller boats to bring them ashore."

"And they must contend with Commodore Patterson," a voice said.

Léonore refrained from remarking that Patterson's courage, though already proven, could not make up for his lack of gunboats. "But if they get past Patterson's little fleet, there are so many ways to approach the city from up here—from Lake Borgne, even Lake Pontchartrain if they can get through the narrow passage at the Rigolets. Jackson is strengthening the forts in that direction, but he cannot guard every bayou."

"There is another route you have not mentioned," Madame Porée herself said slyly. "The British could sail past the delta and head west, then up the Bayou La Fourche to the Mississippi, and come downriver to attack us from above."

Léonore laid down the ruler, raised her head and smiled. "To go that way, the fleet could not avoid alerting the Laffites on Isle Dernière. And the English are well aware that they do not have the support of the Laffites."

Madame Porée murmured, "A pity we look to be in the same case," and went back to her sewing.

Next day, however, the Legislature at last decided to clarify that very issue. Bernard de Marigny's persuasion won through and, after a hearing held before a judge, the Baratarians in custody were granted a suspension of all charges for four months. The eighty prisoners were given their freedom on the day General Jackson returned to the city. Whether the pirates would disperse or sign up with either Patterson or the militia was a matter for conjecture; meanwhile Dominique You and the other lieutenants disappeared to report to Jean Laffite, wherever he might be.

The crisis brought the rarest of wonders to New Orleans—a steamboat, the *Enterprise*, sent by the government to be of assistance if need be. Jackson immediately dispatched it back upriver to order down ammunition barges promised from Pittsburgh. On the same day the English fleet was spotted off Lake Borgne, and the whole city felt the edge of panic, knowing that the troops

Jackson so desperately awaited were far away—some at Baton Rouge, and the rest even farther up the Mississippi.

Andrew Jackson had forgotten what it was like not to be ill. Moments of solitude like this, spent shivering on the sofa in a darkened room of the house on the rue Royale, gave him no more relief than his soul-destroying tours of inspection around the hopelessly exposed and indefensible city. He was drawing on his own reserves, with no idea how long they would hold out.

He groaned when he heard a loud rap at the street door—another fearful or tearful citizen—and was annoyed to realize that his man at the entrance had let the fellow into the house. He was outraged when the door to his room opened and the intruder walked straight in.

"Forgive me, sir." The door was shut firmly, restoring the gloom. "Don't get up, please. I shall not disturb you long." The tall form on the other side of the room was still and watchful.

"You'll not disturb me at all." The general swung his feet to the floor. "Get out."

"With pleasure, once you have heard my name and my business." He stepped nearer and bowed. "Jean Laffite. The bandit."

The general did not rise; it was beyond him. "Good God." His soldier's eye ran a quick check, but no weapon could be concealed within the man's clean-cut, elegant clothes, and the deep black gaze that met his held only amusement and sympathy.

"Call for help if you wish, sir, but rest assured I've not come to cause you any discomfort. In fact"—he took up one of the cushions from the end of the sofa—"I suggest you use this to elevate the feet. You suffer from formication in the ankles and calves?" Wisely not waiting for the general's reply, he went on, "Common enough with the condition you endure." Jackson found himself being assisted painlessly into position. "It's a matter of the circulation, sir. You'll find keeping the feet up brings some relief. Also, it's tempting in a bout of the ague to rest close to the fire. That can be injurious, and therefore"—the bandit moved behind the sofa and the general found himself skimming backwards as though in a skiff—"one is better off conserving the heat of the body with a coverlet." Jackson's cloak, twitched off a chair, descended across him like a comforting wave.

"Now." A chair was drawn up, not too close, and the bandit made himself easy on it and crossed his legs. "Listen to what I can offer, and then I'll make myself scarce."

"You've been doing that, I hear, for more than a year!"

"True. But it hasn't stopped me sending a stream of military information about the English to the Legislature. They'll have shown the letters to you. Every detail is accurate, but the stupid bastards declined to believe me—witness their pitiful state of preparedness. Thank Christ you're here."

This was a man of action, and the general had not heard such talk since he arrived in New Orleans. "Go on."

"I think I know what you need, but correct me if I'm wrong. Men, artillery, ammunition, flints for the useless small arms they've scraped up."

"You're not wrong," Jackson said dryly. "But aren't you somewhat in the same case yourself? I'm told most of your blackguards have dispersed to the four winds."

Laffite shook his head, then proceeded to give the general a catalog of the means for war that he had at his disposal. It was lengthy and enthralling, and the most curious thing was that Jackson could tell it was complete. Like a crack reconnaissance officer returned from behind enemy lines, Laffite enumerated everything with detached and patient exactitude.

When it was over Jackson's mind was ringing. "What do you want?"

"Cessation of all legal proceedings except our claim of restitution. Your guarantee of our freedom of movement for as long as you command New Orleans."

"I can't answer for what the Legislature will do when I'm gone."

"Nor can I, damn them for a pack of imbeciles, but

I'm used to dealing with them. Time enough later for hell or high water. On this day, sir, your handshake is enough for me."

The general threw the cloak aside, leaned forward to grip Laffite's strong hand, and saw the bandit smile for the first time.

The English attack on the tiny flotilla on Lake Borgne was led by Captain Lockyer of the *Sophia*, from barges that were laboriously rowed for forty-one hours to the encounter. It was made under courageous and accurate fire from the Americans, who were heavily outnumbered, and it resulted in the capture of all their gunboats and crews, and the schooner *Seahorse*. The English navy could now land troops and guns anywhere they pleased, within twenty miles of New Orleans. Commodore Patterson, then in the city, received the news on December 15. The following day, Andrew Jackson declared martial law.

Next morning it rained. Léonore, sitting with seven other women in the salon upstairs at the Chotards', listened to the shower rattling on the gallery outside and the flat roof close above their heads and felt a sharp impulse for action that did nothing for the accuracy of the seam she was fashioning in yet another worsted shirt. If the weather had been fine, she could at least have mounted to the roof to look about her. In the height of summer, the roofs were a refuge in the evenings, where one could relax, sip cool drinks and watch the sun go down across the Mississippi. In winter, the damp surface of earth, lime, tar and oyster shells with which they were laid was almost as uninviting as the muddy streets below.

Then all at once the shower ended and a broad shaft of sunlight traveled down the thoroughfare, glittering in the raindrops on the ironwork outside, brightening the room and lifting the spirits of the seamstresses.

A few minutes later Mademoiselle Chotard happened to rise and throw open one of the doors onto the gallery, whereupon the others heard her exclaim, "The general!"

As one, they slid their needles into their work and

laid it down. With a whisper of skirts they moved out
to line the rain-washed balcony rail.

A small group of commanders on horseback was
splashing its way down the street. From above, Léonore
recognized them all: General Jackson, his blue Spanish
cloak clinging damply to his arms; Denis de la Ronde,
recently made colonel of militia; Thomas Beale, commander of the new Volunteer Rifles; Arsène Latour, military engineer. And Jean Lafitte.

There was a collective gasp as he came into view.

The first to speak into the astonished silence was Madame Porée, in her driest, most ironic tone. "Trust him
to find a white horse."

It was Spanish bred: short-backed, with a high, dancing step and a gleaming coat in dramatic contrast to its
black-clad rider. Léonore felt like applauding. She felt
like laughing with a joy that must match his own—for
she saw in his eyes, the instant they met hers, a sense
of triumph that overrode even his first intense surprise.

The group were almost below them when the general
looked up. He did not smile or halt, but lifted his hand
to his leather cap in a gallant salute.

Denis de la Ronde, resplendent in gold braid, made
them a deft bow from the saddle and called up as he
passed, "Good day, mesdames, mesdemoiselles."

There was a murmur and a confused wavering of
morning gowns and neatly coiffed heads along the gallery. Léonore remained quite still, one hand on the corner post, the other on the wet iron rail, facing the last
rider.

Jean swept off the wide-brimmed hat and rode by,
smiling into her eyes without a word. The sun glinted in
his hair, which was cropped shorter than usual to frame
the unruffled brow. He was clean shaven, except for an
imperial that was drawn like an exclamation point below
the flashing, unrestrained grin that he aimed straight up
at her.

She could not see whether the full force of his silent
greeting was unleashed upon the rest of the ladies as he
moved onward under their avid gaze, but she rather

thought it was, judging by the response that fluttered in the eyes and cheeks of Mademoiselle Chotard and her friends at the far end of the gallery. She did not begrudge them the frisson of pleasure. Her world shone, round and complete. She wanted no other.

This exultant emotion could never be shared by the women who most feared and abhorred her liaison with Jean—her mother and Sophronie. Her mother was terrified that Léonore would embrace a life like the one on Barataria, where women were nothing, and where children and slaves were treated with either neglect or brutality. Mathilde pictured Léonore living with Jean not as a true wife but as a dependent, unable to change anything but the surface of his former existence. She imagined her subjected to the small deceptions, the hidden circumventions, the secret betrayals, that had eaten away her own trust in Roncival. She dreaded that Léonore would find out in her turn what it meant to be disillusioned and embittered—and, worst of all, what it was like to feel that any power of protecting and nurturing a child had been sapped and destroyed.

Sophronie's horror sprang from more worldly and practical considerations. In her eyes, Léonore stood just now at a social pinnacle, having at last gained a secure place in New Orleans, along with wealth and independence. It was impossible that she should throw herself away on an unreformed criminal, whose status as an American citizen was temporary, whose credentials were a sham, whose every word was a lie, and who would slide back into outlawry and degradation once he had taken full advantage of the opportunities afforded him by the war. It was unthinkable that she should let such a man work his dire influence in her life and sanction his basest activities.

Léonore knew these terrors, without either woman having had to explain them. But she could not feel them, for herself or for any future child. Because Jean had promised that he and she would create a new life together. He had said that no man and no country would divide them—let no woman do so either.

*   *   *

Jean did not manage to speak to her until two days later, though he glimpsed her during the grand review in the Place d'Armes on Sunday, very near the fringe of the crowd and in company with Sophronie Claiborne. She wore a hat like a garden filled with birds-of-paradise, and her eyes shot halcyon darts at him from under the ridiculous brim, each one sweet and true to the target.

The next time he found her entirely by accident: she was outside Feversham's shop when he came flying along Bourbon Street, and the second she saw him she went straight in. He hauled his Spanish gelding to a sparking stop in the side street, paid a boy to hold him and shot round into the lane behind the merchant's, so fast he got there before her. The narrow space was piled with boxes from a delivery and there was just one assistant there, a chubby, middle-aged fellow sitting on a packing case about to fill a pipe. Jean bribed him so lavishly the man leaped to his feet and darted indoors leaving pipe and pouch lying in the sunshine, so when she emerged and he pulled her into his arms the kiss was redolent of gardenia laced with fresh, fine Virginia tobacco.

There was no hat today, just a poke bonnet that he made short work of. Her eyes beckoned like warm coral seas. "I was afraid you had gone."

"Today. I don't know where Jackson's posting me—I hope to God it's somewhere to the northeast."

Her hands tightened on his shoulders. "Is that where they're coming from? Do we know?"

"We don't know a damned thing. Scouts went out to the lake, but they haven't come back. Dominique and Oncle Beluche are assigned up that way, at Fort St. John. Some of our boys are on the Gentilly Road, and there are more downstream on the *Carolina* and the *Louisiana*. Personally I'd be happiest hauling your thirty-two-pounders through the plantations. If only we knew where the hell to set them up."

"They say two thousand men are expected soon. Is it true?"

He put one hand on her neck, his thumb framing the line of her jaw. She was wearing his sapphires. "Yes, they'll be in town by the afternoon. Jackson wrote to the commander: 'You must not sleep until you reach me.' What a man. And we're about to see one hundred and fifty Mississippi Dragoons come in too, thank the Lord for small, brave mercies."

She never minced words. "What made Jackson say yes to you?"

He frowned at her. "Apart from the fact we could double his forces?" Then he relented. "I'd say ammunition, local knowledge, and ammunition. It was a pretty practical meeting."

"Where was it all, down at Isle Dernière?"

"No, buried at Barataria. And we had a cache west of the Temple; seventy-five hundred pistol flints, to be precise. Which just happen to be crucial. Jackson's got it all now: arms, ordnance, the lot."

"Is Pierre all right?"

He stroked her cheek, looking deep into her eyes. It was generous of her to think of Pierre. "He's fit—he's with de la Ronde." He slid his hand and arm over her shoulder, held her against his chest. "Two or three days, no more. I don't think there's much chance for us, my darling, unless they bog themselves down and sink under their own weaponry. What will you do if they wade over us and march right in?"

"I'll stay put and wait for you."

"I'll come, hell or high water." He kissed her, seeing through half-closed eyelids her tousled hair glowing guinea-gold in the sunlight.

He managed to step back, smooth his hands down each side of her waist, create a few inches of distance. He even managed to smile. "You remember the first time we met here?"

She nodded. She was pulling on her gloves. Her fingers were trembling.

"You can tell me now—were you carrying a pistol in that muff?"

She shook her head, stepped back into the shadow of the back entrance, her eyes wide and steady on his.

He had meant to offer her advice, mention final dispositions, at least say good-bye. But the pitiful words were

all tumbled in his head, like butterflies dashing themselves against stone. All he could do was walk away.

Sophronie Claiborne was extremely grateful for the
company of Eléonore de Rochambeau over the next few
days. She discovered to her shame that she had been
suffering from self-delusion: she had simply not been
able to grasp that if one's husband were an honorary
commander of militia, he was in no less danger from
gunfire than a regular one. The truth called for addi-
tional courage, which he possessed but she did not.

Eléonore was a great support. Madame Porée was inspired by the notion that their little group of ladies
should spend this time of crisis in a patriotic huddle at
her house on the corner of Dumaine Street, but Eléonore had other ideas. They remained instead at the
residence, and while the news—all bad—arrived in in-
stallments, they swapped life stories and played cards.
Sophronie hardly knew which to gape at more, the details of Eléonore's island existence or the rules of play,
many of which she had never heard of before and none
of which she could quite see herself being able to employ
over again, anywhere.

They both managed to stay moderately calm. Eléonore
had been looking thinner and somehow more bright-eyed
lately, but this was understandable, and in fact became
her. She got up and left the room more often and more
abruptly than was quite normal, sometimes in the middle
of a game, but one could scarcely blame her for being
unsettled, however one might deplore the cause. The
name Laffite, however, was never mentioned between
them.

It happened that the British spent a great deal of this
time rowing men and arms from their fleet, right across
Lake Borgne and from there into bayous in the northeast. They then surprised and occupied the Villeré and
de la Ronde plantations—but 106 rue Royale did not
receive confirmation of this until noon on the twenty-
third. The alarm gun was fired in the city, and Jackson
readied the army to meet the English that very night.
They were only eight miles from New Orleans.

Tennessean reserves marched into the city, while other troops were sent downriver. Commodore Patterson, joined by Edward Livingston, boarded the *Carolina,* which prepared to slip down and position itself to fire on the English camp from the Mississippi. Jackson directed further troops to reinforce those facing the English in the plantations—including soldiers from Fort St. John, who ran ten miles to reach the front in time.

The British were eating their evening meal in the quiet of their encampment when the *Carolina* was sighted offshore in the dark. Though they received no reply when it was hailed, they believed it must be a vessel of Admiral Cochrane's squadron, brought upriver in reserve. Then the grapeshot began, fired in seven-gun broadsides expertly directed by the Baratarian artillerymen onboard. And the American advance began on land, in an unbroken line that extended across a plantation and through cypress swamps towards the British flank.

The chaos on the English side lasted until three o'clock in the morning, when they found some sort of formation by moving back towards the Villeré mansion. Jackson, unwilling to become too heavily committed, also withdrew around four o'clock, and established a new line. The American casualties numbered more than two hundred. The British were already bringing up reinforcements from the rear, the number of which was impossible to estimate; but the American line was firm, though closer to the city than it had been in the afternoon.

A messenger from William Claiborne arrived with a version of this news before dawn, and Sophronie's overwhelming relief on her husband's account got the better of whatever military acumen she might have developed in her long conversations with Eléonore. New Orleans was still under siege, but it was holding off the invaders.

The second messenger to arrive was a young black corporal sent into the city with dispatches, who came by the governor's residence with a verbal message from Jean Laffite. Running down to meet him in the vestibule, Léonore called him by his name—Dani—and embraced him, which was ghastly, but the encounter was seen only by one of the servants, whose discretion could be counted on. Laffite and his closest associates were unscathed, it seemed. Thereafter the household at last settled down for a few hours' sleep.

Breakfast was late, but Sophronie had a constitutional objection to eating it on her own. When Eléonore failed to make an appearance, she mounted the stairs and found Eléonore walking along the landing. She was pale and looked as though she had dressed hastily, but Sophronie gave her a warm smile.

"I was persuaded you would come down after all. It is nothing short of a miracle, but things go forward quite as normal in the kitchen. Let me recommend a coddled egg."

Eléonore turned suddenly whiter than before, spun round and beat a quick retreat into her bedroom. The door was half-open and Sophronie, after a brief and compassionate interval, entered the room. Eléonore was bent over a ewer on the corner table, still in the throes, and when they were over she leaned against the wall, her eyes shut.

Sophronie advanced, her skin prickling with sudden cold, and paused by the bed. There was an immense silence, during which Eléonore opened her eyes and wiped her face with a hand towel.

Sophronie took a shallow breath. "Your courses are overdue?"

Eléonore nodded, her eyes huge.

"You expected them when?"

"At the end of last month."

"And you are usually regular?"

There was another careful nod, and Sophronie sank down on the edge of the bed. "Oh, God in heaven." She put her face in her hands. "Eléonore."

"Do you think so?" Sophronie looked up to see a face suffused with joy. "It seemed too good to be true." The blue eyes sparkled like gems against the extreme pallor of her face. "I think I needed someone to tell me."

Sophronie gasped. "You are *happy* about this?"

There was a shaky laugh. "You have no idea how much."

"In that case I have absolutely no idea about anything." Full of pity and despair, she struggled for words. "Unless you would care to explain."

The eyes glistened with unshed tears. "What is there to explain? It is the most beautiful thing in the world."

CHAPTER THIRTY-TWO

Duels

In Ghent, a mixture of relief and foreboding occupied the mind of Albert Gallatin during the week before Christmas. The two commissions had together reached the point of drafting a treaty between England and the United States. In the weary months of negotiation, every condition for peace that he and his fellows had brought to Ghent had proved to be unattainable, and none of the stated reasons for which their country went to war would be mentioned in the treaty itself. But Gallatin's struggle for vigilance and for patience with his colleagues had carried him through to a single resolution; it was time go back to their country with an agreement.

The rest, however, were all dissatisfied with what they were about to achieve, and blamed the others for it. On the evening of December 22, the Americans met to agree on the clauses they would propose for the draft of the treaty the next day. Once both sides had checked over the document it could be signed on the day after that, Christmas Eve.

It was then, at the eleventh hour, that yet another commissioner abandoned control. He leaped to his feet and thumped the table. He spat contempt at the whole shabby pack of negotiators and their miserable bargains, and the meeting room in the hotel erupted once more. All at once, it was too much for Gallatin. For the first and last time in his long-suffering years as a diplomat, he told one of his colleagues to shut up. Then he rose, and into the shocked silence delivered a cutting summary of the responsibilities they undertook for their country. He reiterated point by point the form of the treaty they were about to adopt. It was to their credit that they had been able to thrash it out with the English after months of argument. They would have the privilege of returning to America having signed an honorable peace with England.

Only he knew how much fury trembled below his measured words, but he was shatteringly relieved to see how they all responded. The meeting was brought to a calm conclusion and they all departed, a little subdued, to gather their resources for the morrow.

Except Bayard. Sitting exhausted at the table, staring at the polished surface, Gallatin was aware of the senator poised heavily on the other side.

The voice was conciliatory. "I admire your résumés. It all seems pretty clear to me each night when I go to bed, but every morning I wake up and it looks so damned complicated all over again." A pause. "The letters from the president don't help. I got one today that's full of islands. He's very exercised about the Passamaquoddys. But we're not including them in the treaty."

Gallatin summoned patience again, with an effort. "They're to be settled by commission later on."

"And San Stefan. He's really set on having San Stefan. But we've handed it to the English!"

Gallatin raised his head and faced the resentful glare. The senator had badly wanted San Stefan too, and made that very obvious to the English, which had caused them to covet it even more. Gallatin remembered, and dug in his pocket for a piece of paper, which he smoothed out and slid across the table. His hands had stopped shaking. "Here's a map of the island, if you'd care to take a look."

The senator glanced up suspiciously. "You never showed us this!" Gallatin did not reply, and Bayard bent his head again to examine the map. There was a key at the bottom showing the scale of distance, which Gallatin had taken some trouble over the night before.

After less than a minute, to Gallatin's silent applause, Bayard's head snapped up. "Ye Gods," he roared, "it's a pimple! It probably goes under at high tide! No wonder it's not on any blessed charts."

"Indeed. The English seem to be unaware how small it is."

"They wouldn't want it if they could see this!"

"No, I should think they'd be very happy to concede it to us."

Bayard pushed the map back at him contemptuously. "Well, I don't want it either, now."

Gallatin considered him. "No? But I thought you said the president did."

"What's that got to do with it?"

Gallatin placed his elbows on the table and his fingertips together. "As you pointed out, the issues here are deeply complicated. We may think we are leaving them behind when we go back to America, but on our return we will face endless questions. We will be forced to justify choices. The president himself will engage us in dialogues about what we have and have not managed to do. My dear senator, think how rewarding it will be to have some positive achievements to present; things that lie close to his heart and to yours. Think how useful it would be for you to be able to reply, to some awkward remark: 'But Mr. President, we do have San Stefan.'"

Bayard was staring at him, entranced. "How?"

"Arrange for the English to make a concession of it tomorrow. They will enjoy appearing to do us an immense favor, whilst knowing it's worthless. Quite apart from anything else, it will put them in an amiable mood for the meeting."

"How will you do it?"

"We must leave ourselves entirely in your hands for this, Senator. The English, I fear, rather mistrust me. Whereas you have been far too subtle for them." Astonishingly, Bayard smiled. "You are breakfasting with one of them tomorrow morning—Henry Goulburn?"

A rapid nod.

"I shall arrange for the map to be delivered to you at the table, as part of a small dispatch. You will give it a cursory but satisfied glance, allowing Goulburn a peek as you do so, then lay it down with the rest of the papers."

"And I'll leave the dining room before him," Bayard said with an even broader grin, "and I'll forget to pick it up from the table!"

"A remarkable ploy, Senator. I couldn't have conceived it better myself."

They rose and went off to their rooms, on better terms with each other than they had ever been, or ever would be again.

The meeting on the morrow went smoothly, the document was ratified by both sides without delay, and the Treaty of Ghent was signed on Christmas Eve. It was later declared, by commission, that England abandoned any claim to the Caribbean island of San Stefan, in favor of the United States of America.

Christmas passed in New Orleans to the sound of artillery fire, and both sides went on consolidating their gun positions. The English army had thrown a rampart up on the Lacoste plantation, and their most powerful cannon emplacement was on the levee, a threat to the *Carolina* and *Louisiana* as the two schooners raked the riverside. Meanwhile, in the rear, the English struggled with the leviathan task of bringing men, arms, ordnance and supplies across seventy miles of shallow water from their fleet, and then through the bayous and swamps, to turn stalemate into the most favorable opportunity for the capture of New Orleans.

The Americans' line of defense, lying half a mile from the nearest British positions, began at an advance redoubt on the levee and extended across the Chalmette plantation to within 150 yards of a wood, where a V-shaped earthworks was built to shelter the left flank from crossfire. The rampart would have ended there, had not Jean Laffite said that the line should be maintained right through the wood to the impassable cypress swamp beyond, then curved back to provide complete protection on the left. Advised of this by Livingston, Jackson quickly had it put into effect.

The winter days brought rain and chilly mists to the

low-lying fields along the river, and there were frosts at
night. At the fringes of the conflicting armies, attacks
flared and crumpled. On Christmas Day, American
troops succeeded in cutting a breach in the levee to flood
the English positions and force a retreat, but it proved
too far downstream to be effective. On the twenty-sixth,
American cavalry flung themselves at the British forward
positions and set fire to canebrakes in an attempt to
flush out the occupiers of the Lacoste mansion, but the
invaders stayed put. On the twenty-seventh, the British
gunners on the levee pinned the *Carolina* within close
range and opened up on her with red-hot shot. Unable
to maneuver the schooner out of danger, the crew abandoned ship and rowed to the opposite shore. Shortly
afterwards the *Carolina* blew up with a shattering roar
and a great bloom of flames and acrid smoke drifted
away down the Mississippi.

On the same day, representatives from the Legislature
rode out to view Jackson's ramparts at Chalmette and
raced back again to voice anguished doubts about the
pitiful line of defense they had just inspected—in places
it was only waist high and the excavated mud was still
damp and too soft to support even a rifle barrel. There
were suggestions that New Orleans should be surrendered at the first sign of a reverse, to save its being looted
and burned by victorious British troops. Any such decision was preempted by the British themselves, who
chose that very day to begin their advance.

The brothers Jean and Dominique, in the center of
the deafening conflagration of the next few days, came
to a joint conclusion from which they never wavered:
this was an artillery duel, and the Americans could win
it. There was plenty of evidence to the contrary, amongst
it being the superbly handled British nine-pounders, six-
pounders and heavy howitzers on the levee. Then there
were the rockets and light mortars brought up along the
edge of the swamp on the first day of attack. The
eighteen-pounders that the enemy managed to drag forward in the dark and set up in a field battery virtually
under their noses. The naval carronades they had lugged

carriageless from their fleet and planted snugly in the center of six more eighteen-pounders arrayed across a road in the center.

But there were gaps in the barrage, long intervals between the flashes from cannon that were too far away to be properly assessed, which put more and more confidence on Dominique's tired, blackened, joyous face.

"They keep running out of ammunition. Then they bring more up from the rear. But they have to scrape the bottom for some time, so we hold them off until they do."

Jean was helping Oncle Renato's artillerymen heave the latest load of powder off a dray. On this battery, commanded by Dominique, most of the men were Baratarians. "I can't understand why they haven't sent a squadron to bring some up the river."

Dominique shrugged, his eyes never leaving the boys who toiled around his favorite twenty-four-pounder. "Maybe they've had a go already. But they'd have their work cut out to get past the *Hero* and the fort."

There was a shout from one of the gunners. "They're coming up!"

For a moment they could see nothing between their gun and where the man pointed; but then the screen of smoke began to dissolve. Through it they could see redcoats, a bristle of barrels at the ready, a group of moving shakos tightly bunched together.

"Are they crazy?" Jean snatched up his rifle and knelt at the very edge of the rampart, eyes raking the ground ahead. The enemy were almost within range. "Damnation," he said, "they're toting up another piece!"

Half a dozen of them were hauling something, backs bent, while the men around them concealed their effort for as long as possible.

Dominique, by Jean's side, cursed more elaborately. He had no hope of bringing his big gun down to bear at this close distance, while the English, who were no doubt drawing a carronade, had every chance of setting it up and firing from a neat, devastating angle within the next few minutes.

Dominique leaped to his feet and roared at his gunners to leave off and load their own weapons. A runner shot back towards the nearest platoon of riflemen.

Still on his knees, Jean steadied the long Pennsylvania rifle in his hands and waited. The old piece was a thing of beauty, bought from a Tennessean. It dated from the Revolutionary War, when the Pennsylvania Dutch put their minds to fashioning a weapon to outdo the British Brown Bess. It was mistrusted at first, but in the hands of the buckskin-clad Virginia riflemen it had become the deadliest secret the Americans possessed. At this range, it still was.

"I'm sorry," he said to the man who had come back to his side. "You hate this kind of turkey shoot."

Dominique, fiercely ramming the charge into an ancient musket, just growled.

There was a high call from amongst the redcoats, and the front line knelt and shouldered their weapons. Simultaneously the second rank leveled theirs above them, almost masking the frantic activity behind as the British artillerymen began to set up the carronade.

Jean waited no longer. His Pennsylvania rifle cracked and a soldier in the middle of the second line crumpled out of sight. The center closed; then Dominique fired and one of the kneeling men pitched forward. The other Baratarians whooped and fired as one, in a volley that sliced into the redcoats like a scythe.

Jean was reloading, his actions smooth, requiring no thought; he had been doing this all day, at different parts of the line. When the redcoats below managed to reform and fire off their riposte, he scarcely noticed. They were a solid mass, determined to stay put and get the carronade established. Each time, he aimed for the point where white lace crossed a man's chest. The rifle kept on performing like magic, worth everything he had given for it. Cash being miserably short in New Orleans, he had paid for it in pearls, pulling them from his pocket and tipping them into the man's hand. The Tennessean had looked up, bemused, then said, "You're Jean Laffite!"

He was recognized everywhere now, on the instant; the New Orleanians acted as if he had never been away, and the recruits and veterans from the north knew him from the very first hours they spent in the city and the field. No wonder—he was visible enough. As he went from position to position under Jackson's orders or on reconnaissance of his own, he never troubled to stay out of sight. At one point, over near the woods, an American cannon had taken a direct hit and burst, and everyone else ducked as shrapnel spun out of the heart of the explosion, churning up the ground, smashing into tree trunks and unprotected flesh; but with his usual delayed reaction he kept walking through the hail of metal. He was already being called a hero. It was good for the Baratarians' reputation, and it protected their freedom if the battle was won, so he kept the joke to himself. They thought him fearless, but he was simply slow to accept the notion of death. The devil keep him alive, for as long as he had Léonore. And his brothers. And the hundreds more who depended on him.

There were other riflemen with them now, returning fire. Meanwhile English bullets landed with dull thuds in the earthworks and pinged off the barrel of the big gun behind. Amongst the whine and whistle of flying lead he heard now and then a scream or groan as it hit home amongst their own haphazard ranks.

Jean heard an angry noise, for all the world like a bee caught in his hair, and felt something pass across his ear. He cursed, missed his shot and put his fingers to the side of his face. They came away bloody and he glanced interrogatively at Dominique.

"It's a nick, nothing to pay any mind to. But watch out you don't catch another—you think she'll still have you if you go back maimed?"

Jean was reloading. "What do you think?"

Dominique turned to look at the English and let out a crow of triumph. "That's it! They're leaving the baby to us!"

Sure enough, the remnants of the English were retiring in order, abandoning the carronade and ammunition boxes but maintaining fire as they went.

Jean shouldered the rifle again. The men here would have to keep careful watch during the night, in case English artillerymen crawled back to reclaim the position.

Then he grinned, thinking about Dominique's precious thirty-two-pounders, which his brother had nobly donated to the *Louisiana,* not without a smacking kiss on each barrel. He recalled the wry admiration in his brother's voice as he watched them being hauled out of his sight for the second time.

"You can tell her, when next you see her, she's a pearl beyond price. And I never thought I'd hear myself say it."

On the evening of January 7, Sophronie Claiborne answered a plea from Madame Porée to spend the night at her house on the rue Dumaine. Léonore went unwillingly, for it seemed doubtful that even their competent and witty hostess would be able to prevent the little group of ladies from giving way to alarm.

The advance attempted by the British the previous week had been repulsed, and the New Orleans defensive line had been strengthened in the interval, but the pitched battle was now upon them.

Jackson could do no more. All the troops he could call upon had long been mustered. The rampart at Chalmette, in places twenty feet thick, was dominated by four batteries. The general had placed another sixteen-gun battery on the west bank, under the command of David Morgan, to fire across the river into the approach to the right flank. Jackson's forces, many of them new recruits, came to four thousand. The troops they faced were superior in numbers, training and experience, and a large number of these seasoned veterans had already had the pleasure of sacking the city of Washington.

Léonore found the atmosphere at Madame Porée's almost unendurable. The grand parlors were packed with dozens of women, and the hostess's resources were overstretched. Léonore was divided from Sophronie much of the time, as her friend was constantly approached for advice and comfort. She ended up in a small room that contained a sofa, two chairs and five women, only one of whom had chosen the sensible option of falling asleep on cushions on the floor. Two of the others prayed over their rosaries.

At dawn the cannonades began, causing much shrieking and swooning and giving Léonore something to do,
for Sophronie had come prepared with smelling salts.
The morning dragged on with no news and no movement in the streets outside; to the frightened faces peep-
ing through the jalousies, New Orleans looked as bleak
as a churchyard.

The hostess rustled up a midday meal, which a few
ladies managed to eat. Not long after that, a packet came
for Léonore, brought from the governor's mansion by
one of the grooms, who waited downstairs in the kitchen
afterwards, reluctant to ride back again through the
empty streets. Léonore joined him to read the letter
without the others clustering round.

It was not a note from within the city, nor could it
have been sent from the battlefield; the outside sheet
was creased and stained, and the series of directions
scribbled on it were nearly illegible. The letter had traveled far, through many hands and by devious routes,
over a considerable time. It could only be a report from
San Stefan. Holding her breath, she broke the seal and
unfolded it.

It was not from home. It had been sent from Haiti,
the day after she herself sailed from Port-au-Prince for
the last time. The letter that had been following her
about for months was from Mathilde de Oleron y
Siqueiros.

> *My dear daughter,*
>   *There is something you should know. Yesterday,
> on the eve of our departure for Spain, I decided
> that I owed it to my husband to tell him the whole
> truth about the wife whom he wished to establish in
> his ancestral home. My encounter with you, what-
> ever pain it may have caused you, has had at least
> this effect upon me.*
>   *All along, my husband has been aware of what I
> tried to do for you, and helped me selflessly where
> he could. He knew that I had approached Laffite in
> the hope of driving him away from you—but he did
> not know the means I used. I know not what he*

*may have suspected deep in his heart, but I was
never challenged. I will spare you the recital of how
the truth pierced him. I do not write to tell you how
he reacted, and how once again he forgave me. I
must warn you of what he then did.*

*He confessed to it this morning. He has hired
Manrique Curtis to kill Jean Laffite.*

*Curtis entered our employ some time ago, and
captained the ship that brought us here to Haiti. He
left Port-au-Prince this morning, on a vessel bound
for the Gulf, having received an initial payment
from my husband. The rest of the fee he will collect
from an agent after the death of Laffite has been
reported. The money is all we have left in the bank
in New Orleans, but my husband considers it little
enough to pay for the just vengeance that is due
to him.*

*Curtis will carry this out. He resents all the Laf-
fites, especially Jean. He is even inclined to see this
as a blow for Spain. War and invasion are ideal
covers for such an assassination.*

*By the time you get this, it may be too late. I am
not sure how you are likely to act if Laffite is still
alive when you receive it. I know you so little. I
have deprived myself forever of the chance to learn
your thoughts and your heart.*

*I disdain to write to Lafitte; I have no interest in
whether he lives or dies. But I care about you. Make
of this information what you will—it is sent with
the love I once snatched away from you and that
you scorn to receive from my hands.*

*I shall take the liberty, nonetheless, of writing to
you when we reach Andalusia.*

Your mother, Marianne

Léonore looked up at the groom on the other side of
the kitchen table. "Thank you for bringing this."

He was examining her face. "Is it . . . news from the
battlefield, mademoiselle?"

She got to her feet. "You rode here?" When he nodded, she said, "Wait," and quickly left the room.

Madame Porée was upstairs, chivvying a servant about coffee. She was taken aback by Léonore's request but, ever obliging, took her into her dressing room to examine a chest of clothes.

"I do not ride, but my elder sister had an excellent riding habit that should still be here. It's ten years old, I'm afraid, but I doubt it's fallen apart quite yet."

They found it: in classic dark blue ratteen, and the right fit, if a little full about the waist. Madame Porée assigned a maid to help Léonore on with it and went off, unbidden, to fetch Sophronie.

Her friend caught up with her in the courtyard, where she was already mounted, perched sideways on the saddle before the groom, whose reluctance to set off through the streets again had vanished at the idea of providing her with such close support.

"Where are you going?"

"To find Jean Laffite. Someone is out to kill him."

Sophronie gave a shrill, incredulous laugh. "He is scarcely an exception in that regard!"

"Let's go." The groom swung the pony towards the porte cochere and Léonore twisted to call over her shoulder, "When I get back I'll go straight to the residence. Will you bring my cambric for me?"

Outraged, Sophronie shrieked to the groom, "Reynolds! I forbid you to leave!"

They clattered off the cobbles, into the dusty street and away.

She went to the old ramparts first, for she knew Pierre's address by heart, and the groom reckoned he could find the cottage for her. It was the clearinghouse for all the Laffites' messages; even if she could not locate Jean or any of the others at the front line, the warning would go out—to any Baratarians in the city, and to those on the river and eventually on Isle Dernière.

The groom found the cottage by rousing a few householders in a bare, narrow street. Outside the front door he slipped from the pony and lifted Léonore down. He held the reins while she knocked loudly.

It took a minute of hammering before anyone would

answer. Then the door opened a crack and she saw a dark face and one terrified eye looking out at her.

"I am Léonore Roncival. I have a message for Marie Villars."

The young woman pulled the door slowly back and Léonore strode in to face her. "Are you Marie Villars?"

The young woman shook her head. She was beautiful, with a fine-boned fragility that lent luster to her large, honey-colored eyes. For a second she gazed at Léonore; then with a movement of the birdlike shoulders she seemed to shrink into herself. Without a word she ran back out of the room.

Léonore stood alone in the little parlor and wished suddenly that she had not come. It was one thing to know where Jean ate and slept when he came into New Orleans with Pierre; it was another to have a glimpse of this household. It made her feel like an intruder, or a spy. Or worse—someone who could inflict unbearable pain.

Moments like this, when she felt the reality of Jean's life close in around her, were frightening. She sensed the force of all the choices he had made so far, to gather together and direct hundreds of people for so many years. He governed a world of his own making: whatever impulsive promises he might utter for love, could the work of his own hands allow him to keep them?

She fixed her eyes on the far door, straining to hear what was going on in the back rooms. Then she heard soft footsteps approaching, and another woman glided into the room, carrying a little baby in the crook of her arm. A slight disarrangement of the swathed bodice of her dress suggested she had been nursing.

"You are Marie Villars?"

There was a nod.

She took a breath. "I have a message for everyone in the Laffite company. Manrique Curtis has been hired by the Spanish to assassinate Jean Laffite. There is no shadow of doubt—he is being well paid to do it. Warn them all, by whatever means you have. Tell them to lay hands on Curtis if they see him. They have to warn Jean Laffite."

The woman's face quivered and she clutched her child to her. "Jean's in the field! So's Pierre! What can we do?"

"You stay here and do as I say. I'm going to find Jean." She took a step back towards the doorway.

The baby hiccupped, and the woman laid it against her shoulder, patting its back with one hand. "You really doing that? You believe you can?"

Léonore's soothing voice sounded like someone else's. "I'll do my best. I'm going right now. Try not to fret."

The other woman came swiftly forward and put a hand on her wrist. She was smaller than Léonore, but her hands were large and strong. Léonore was about to pull away, but tears sprang up and trembled in the dark eyes. The hair around the pretty face was soft, and the skin smelled of orange blossom and warm milk.

After a silent moment full of anguish, Marie Villars released her. She said, "No matter what happened, I always thought he would come home to my sister. Now I seen you, I know different. Thank you. But it ain't no use telling her not to fret."

CHAPTER THIRTY-THREE

Battle

The chestnut pony galloped along the levee road. Though not powerfully built, it was supple and dexterous and seemed to have stamina. Now that Léonore had left the groom behind in the city she had to ride astride, which was unfamiliar but gave her more control.

For the first time since leaving Dumaine Street, she thought about her condition, which Sophronie also had been too shocked to remember. She searched her mind and body, but there was no fear in either for the tiny beginning of life that she sheltered. On the contrary, over the last days it had given her a stronger, deeper sense of well-being than she had ever known. There had even been a release from morning sickness, as swift as its early onset. Sophronie was envious, on top of her horror and disapprobation.

She could feel no danger to her baby. The other perils pressed too close. She would keep the fierce, secret joy down inside, invisible and safe. She must thrust her mind forward, into all the battles to come. Towards Jean.

The noises were always there: the crump of falling shells, the tearing roar of the cannon on this side, the ominous sound of mortars and rifles firing at the Americans from across the river—whatever had happened to David Morgan's battery?

Then the smoke came, drifting along the water on her right, through the trees on her left, and onto the road, where the sparse traffic from the city met carts and wagons and men on horseback coming the other way. There were wounded, and soldiers walking, but no stragglers. A few shouted to her, but no one had any chance of stopping her, and she flashed by dazed faces that looked up as though she were a visitation.

She passed Jackson's second line, placed to offer a position for retreat. There was scarcely anyone there; the reserves had been moved up. The distant men on picket duty turned, incredulous; she rode on, weaving amongst ammunition carts that were trundling her way, and the pony whinnied at other horses as it passed.

The last copse faded away on her left and she could see it all, spread out under the gray sky: hundreds of men in tattered groups looming through the acrid haze. A line of shifting colors, stabbed at ragged intervals in the east by the red darts of cannon fire, and before her by black, boiling smoke.

She slowed the pony to a canter, then a trot. Far to her left was a troop of cavalry, bunched together, and held in reserve hundreds of yards behind the line. Closer to her was the mansion Jackson was using as headquarters, flanked by two rows of trees. Littered across the bare plantation around it were piles of equipment, dismantled tents, shallow dugouts with a foot or so of parapet piled up. Everywhere else was flattened, crushed, every stick of crops or vegetation ground down to the clay.

The pony stumbled but walked on. Léonore could not see the great rampart thrown across the Chalmette fields. She could scarcely make out the gunners and the riflemen who succeeded each other, group after group, in the shifting smoke. But she could see enough in that bleak and confused landscape to know that the line had held. Then a hand grabbed the pony's bridle and brought it to a halt.

"What the hell?"

She looked down. He was a Tennessean, a Dirty Shirt, with dust embedded in his skin and his clothes.

"Beg pardon, ma'am, you cain't go on!"

"Then I'll wait here. I've come to find someone. Can you fetch him for me?"

"I druther set a whup to this hoss and chase him back the way you come! What in tarnation are you doing?"

For answer, she slid out of the saddle and took the reins out of his hand. "Sir, I have come with a message for Jean Lafitte. If you can find him for me, you may name your price."

He said something under his breath, then turned and said, "Here, quick." He led her some way off the road to the nearest makeshift piece of shelter, where two carts, tipped on their sides, protected a pile of supplies, camping equipment, cauldrons and tripods.

He caught the reins from her again and looped them around an axle. "I'll find him for nothing, and welcome. I wouldn't do this if'n we hadn't whupped them. But we have. They'll never come through now. You got half an hour. If I cain't find him and I cain't get back by then, I'll make it someone's business to send you on your way. That clear?"

She gasped and then cried out, "You're sure. You've stopped them?"

"Dead, ma'am. Dead." He turned to go.

"You know Jean Lafitte?"

"Who don't?"

Jean went wherever Jackson considered he was most needed, and this time it was over the Mississippi to David Morgan's position, which the American artillery commander was losing. Jean soon saw that he must countermand Morgan if the emplacement was to be held, and went about things in his usual way, walking openly along the line of guns, giving calm advice to the crews, making them concentrate so solidly on range and accuracy that they managed not to regard the lines of redcoats that the English had miraculously brought across the river to attack them.

But on they came, nearer and nearer, breaking up and using cover in a way that was more like an American maneuver, so that finally Jean led a charge to flush out the closest. It became hand-to-hand fighting amongst the trees, and he had left his rifle on the far side, so it was his sword against bayonets until he tore a musket from a man he had just killed and began to use it as a lance. There was blood in his nostrils and the clash of steel in his head, but he heard triumphant shouts as the English swooped onto the height and took the big guns, and he roared at the lads to withdraw.

It was gut-wrenching, hiding in the woods, stealthily gathering them together and all the while hearing their own cannon being used to blast their own troops across the river. They argued about options, one of them being to wait and bring in reinforcements under General Humbert, who had come to the fray with all his medals on his chest and his old saber sharp and gleaming. But a fierce flame of impatience seethed up in Jean and they made the counterattack with just the remnants of their force, screaming out of cover with such violence that the English spiked the guns and ran.

When it was over he was expected back, so he swam across, plunging in far enough upstream for the river to deposit him inside the Chalmette rampart on the other side. The Mississippi was laced with stinging smoke that altered even the taste of the muddy water as he swam. With no boots and no weapons and the cold tug of the current he moved fast, despite the fact that the sleepless activity of the last days had taken a toll on his body.

Amusingly, there was even a reception committee of sorts, a tall, solitary Kentuckian pacing the shore with two pistols at the ready, scanning the water. Jean was too exhausted to wave, but when he came out of the smoke a few yards from shore he was seen all right, and recognized. The man gave a grunt, raised one of the pistols and fired straight at Jean's head.

The wait seemed like hours. Léonore crouched behind the cart, well out of sight but able to look through a gap in the boards and see the road and the distant soldiers. Her thoughts were like the broken jigsaw that she glimpsed now and then through the barrier at her shoulder. Nothing could be fit together amidst the crash of the guns, the shudder of the ground under her knees, the sharp smell of sulphur sneaking back across the trampled earth.

But she loved Jean, come hell or high water. She wanted him with the core of her being, in a way that words and fears could not alter.

Her mother's face appeared in her mind, half-hidden by bright, falling hair. The blue gaze, lit from within by bitter pain. *It is possible to walk away from someone you deeply, absolutely love. You can leave the love of your life. If it is the right thing to do.*

The sister of Maric Villars, slight as a stricken child, holding on to the edge of the door as though she were about to crumple to the stone floor.

The fleeting compassion in the eyes of Adélaïde Masclari. The despair in Sophronie's.

She leaned her head against the rough wood beside her and the surroundings faded. There was no discomfort, just a numbness caused by lack of sleep.

The bullet was so close Jean felt it pass into the water under his chin, and in the same shocking instant he recognized the man in Kentucky uniform. Curtis. Bloody turncoat, back from wherever he had been skulking, on the hunt. And he was swapping the second pistol to his good hand to fire again. Jean glanced behind with an impulse to dash back into the smoke, but it was drifting away downstream towards the reed-lined shore, leaving him exposed. Instinctively he twisted, against the force of the river, and felt the second bullet punch through the roiling water and graze his belt at the back.

He gasped, spat, took in a great burning column of air and dived. Curtis would reload both pistols like lightning, as he always did, despite the crippled hand. Jean's only hope was that the hound thought he was battling upstream. He spiraled, plunged deep, fed his body to the current and thrust downstream towards the shore. If he could reach the reeds before the river sucked the breath out of him . . .

Curtis might have thought the second bullet had touched him before he dived but could not be sure of its finishing him. He would be watching every eddy in the river. Jean's eyes were open in the dirty water, looking for matted roots in the mud bottom. Nothing. His lungs were on fire and insane little white dots danced in his vision.

Then a drowned log loomed ahead; he caught a branch, braced his feet against the trunk and shot forward into the reed bed. There was a splash as he broke the surface, but it was masked by a roar from the American cannon on the rampart. He expelled air and then drew it in hoarsely, shaking the hair from his eyes.

Curtis was ten paces away, standing in the shallows, scanning the water like a cursed gun dog. Jean gathered his legs under him, found a purchase, gripped bunches of stiff reeds with his hands so he could haul himself from the crouch when the moment came. Assuming Curtis did not swivel his way and give him both barrels.

Curtis glanced upstream and Jean leaped forward and broke into a crouching run, with mud and stones spurting up behind him—and the din of cannon stopped. Curtis turned, snarled and fired, as Jean dived low for his legs. The pistol in the left hand bucked and flew out of Curtis's fingers, shooting wide. The right held a truer line, but Jean just got under it, connecting like a battering ram and bringing Curtis down over him. Jean twisted and grabbed for the pistol, the only remaining weapon between them, but couldn't see it—it must have gone wide too when Curtis fell. The hiatus was crucial, giving the other man time to go for Jean's throat.

They were in the mud on the water's edge, the Spaniard with one knee in Jean's stomach and the other pinning both his legs, thumbs on the windpipe, arms ramrod straight with Curtis's considerable weight bearing relentlessly down. The man was fresh, fit and full of hatred, and Jean saw triumph in the olive green eyes. He brought his arms up with the intent of breaking the fingers of the good hand. Maybe the man guessed, for he shifted his grip, altering his balance slightly and Jean took advantage, with a mighty heave that reversed their positions and rolled them farther into the water. They fought for purchase, limbs writhing, too close to get in a blow, wrestling like tigers with teeth bared, wordless

and desperate. They went for the eyes, the crushing grip
around the ribs, the brutal pressure that could dislocate
a shoulder, breaking one hold only to succumb to
another—and Jean could feel himself tiring. Time and
again he would take Curtis on his weak left side, but the
Spaniard would manage to unlock the grip and pounce
with renewed force. They were right in the water now,
and each time Jean went down it closed over his head.

They were face-to-face on their sides, flailing to get a
purchase, and there came a moment when Jean flung
away the damaged left hand but opened a space between
them, wide enough for Curtis to jackknife quickly and
slide his good hand into his boot. Jean saw the gleam of
a blade in the water, and a burst of rage threw him into
savage action. Before Curtis could unbend he grabbed
the shoulder, heaved the upper body towards him and
drove it facedown into the mud with the last of his
strength, trapping hand and knife beneath.

The legs jerked, stirring the murky water, and the
body convulsed. Jean saw blood well out from under,
sprang into a crouch and with both hands on the back
of Curtis's neck and a knee in the small of his back bore
down until bubbles began to rise, frothing pink on the
dirty surface. Bile rose into Jean's throat and he retched
and spat, maintaining the pressure.

It took him a long time to believe it was over, to
release the torpid body and see it rock in the rippling
water, the arms floating gently out from the sides, the
hands pale and empty.

He could have rolled his former captain over and had
a look at the dead face, but he shuddered at the thought.
Instead he let him drift headfirst downstream, and
tugged against the current to pull off his high boots. As
Jean emptied them out on the bank, the body shifted
off groggily into the stream. He yanked on the boots
and walked away.

Léonore did not see the two men approach, nor hear
them until they were quite near and she could make out
their boots crunching across the open ground and hear
their voices against the continued battering of the guns.

She heard Jean say, in reply to a growl from the Tennessean: "Don't talk to me about sodding Morgan. Someone should have rearranged his guts for him at birth."

She rose, with a clatter of tripods and cooking pots, and they rounded the end of the cart and stopped.

The Tennessean grinned, his teeth flashing white in his filthy face. "You're danged fort'nate no one had a mind to grab that hoss."

"Thank you." Her throat was filled with smoke. She was looking at Jean.

He was soaked to the skin. His hair, plastered to his head, had collected a sparkling film of dust. His shirt clung to his chest and he was breathing deeply as though he had been running.

The Tennessean walked away, and Jean took another step towards her. "I couldn't believe it. Then I thought about it and of course I could." He kicked away saucepans and a corner of tarpaulin and reached her, his arms like a vise, his cheekbone grinding against hers. "You idiot. You idiot. What possessed you?"

She thought instantly of the baby, the child he did not know about, held at this moment within his arms. She clung as though they were both drowning.

She could speak, however. "Curtis is out to kill you."

He started to laugh then, in a ragged, exhausted fashion, but it made her cry, so he stopped. He smoothed his hands over her shoulders. "*Mi amor,* Curtis is dead." He looked away from her, towards the smoke, then said with a kind of contained disgust, "Someone told me he was caught by shrapnel when one of the guns blew up, over by the woods. He had a pistol in his hand. I did wonder; the British were nowhere to be seen at the time."

Léonore put her hands on each side of his neck and pressed her forehead against him and forced back the tears.

He continued to stroke her gently. "Dominique said to tell you, you are a pearl beyond price. Little does he know. Lionheart."

She drew away a little, leaned against the cart and

wiped her face with her dusty hands. "Is everyone all right?"

He propped himself with a hand against the boards, inches away. "Yes. I just walked the line. I just got back. Jackson sent me over the river to knock some strategy into Morgan, but we lost the position. It was a bloody shambles. Then, the devil be thanked, the English ran. I had to swim back. Hence." He hardly knew what he was saying. He was devouring her instead with black, disbelieving eyes.

There was a concentrated roar of fire from the nearest cannon. Into the next lull, he said, "Who told you Curtis was after me?"

"My mother."

He went white under the dirt, a greenish white so sudden she thought he would faint. He put a hand over his mouth and shut his eyes.

She did not understand how she could have said it. But she understood at once what his reaction meant and examined him with desolation until he opened his eyes again. She said, "How long have you known?"

He took a step back, supported himself against the wheel of the cart. His voice was thin and unrecognizable. "Since you mentioned to me. About the hummingbird. She still has it."

She thought back. The hummingbird locket had come up when they were together on the voyage aboard Dominique You's *Tigre*, after Havana. "You knew. You could have told me my mother was alive."

"No, I couldn't." He was not looking at her. He was not seeing anything; his ugly, blank gaze was directed towards the fields beyond her shoulder. "What are you going to do?"

"What do you think? Shoot you?"

"It's an option, since Curtis didn't manage."

It was unbearable. She stepped forward, twisted a hand into his shirt to make him look at her. "Jean. Tell me what's happened."

He flinched and looked at her in absolute bafflement.

"The battle. Is it over? Have we won?"

He nodded. "They tried hard. They nearly had the

redoubt there, below us, but we took it back. Then assault after assault, but we kept mowing them down. It makes you sick to look at them. Jackson will have the guns going for hours, to keep driving them back, but we won't see them again. One of them brought the white flag. We're starting to take the wounded to the barracks, and they're all theirs. Heap upon heap of redcoats." His voice ran out.

She flung her arms around him and kissed his face, willing him to enclose her in turn. He did so, with a sound like a gasp of pain.

She said frantically, "It's all right. I don't care. It's over. We're safe."

His arms tightened and they stood locked together without moving for a long moment, caught in a small haven of stillness, within the boom and reverberation of the guns.

"You came to me." His voice was low and almost steady. "Now you must be off, my darling."

He loosened her arms, gently put her away from him. She tried to read his face, but he was looking beyond her, towards the levee. He took a step out from the cart, and she glanced over her shoulder at the trail of men, horses and vehicles on the road.

He shouted. "Dani!"

A head turned, an uncertain figure detached itself to stand on the edge of the field. Jean beckoned with an upraised arm and the soldier began to walk towards them.

"He's escorting the wounded. Go with them, please. I can't let you go alone."

"And you can't come with me?"

He laughed softly. "What do you think? It will be hours yet. I'll find you."

"Yes," she said, and joined her lips to his for the first time. It was a brief, hard collision and it was she who pulled away, half turning towards Dani, who was not far off. "As soon as you can. I have something to tell you."

"You just did," he said stupidly, then ran a hand over his face.

"It's all right. Not now. Later." She took a step away. The pony lifted its head.

"What?" He took one stride, gripped her arm. "Tell me." His eyes bored into hers and his fingers hurt. "You're not going to marry me."

She could not let Jean go back to the guns with that look on his face, with that error consuming him. She put her free arm across his shoulder, curled her fingers into his damp hair, made him see the hidden joy surge up into her eyes. "I am. I will marry you. I will have your child."

Because it came on top of everything else, he took it like a blow. But she was close enough to see every nuance of change in the black eyes. Wonder. Then something like a flash of sunlight over dark water. Then dismay.

"You're worn out. You *rode* here. You just spent an hour crouched in a hole on a battlefield. My God. You don't want to keep it."

Both hands were on his shoulders now, and she shook him a little. It was easy, he had no defenses left. "I came here for you! I do want it. More than anything."

He looked at her as he never had before, his eyes raking her whole body, as though he were relearning it. Then he drew her in and held her with the same tenderness they had found together on the night she had conceived.

He let her go. "Corporal."

"Yes, sir," said Dani from three paces away.

"You'll escort Mademoiselle Roncival to the governor's residence."

"Yes, sir."

He untied the pony's reins and put them into Dani's fingers. "You'll find a place for her on one of the carts." He patted him on the shoulder. "And look after her."

"With my life, sir."

Jean looked at him properly then, and saw the fine-drawn face and trembling jaw. "Then you'll report to barracks. It's over. You've done a fine job."

He came to her side, turned her towards the levee,

one hand in the small of her back. "Promise me you won't ride." She looked up at him and smiled and he brushed her lips with his. "On your way now."

He watched them across the field and onto the road. When Dani had stopped a cart and helped her up to sit on the edge, she looked back and saw Jean raise his hand and then lope back towards the guns.

The cart ride was bone shaking, and torture for the men lying upon it. She did what she could for them and dismounted to walk with Dani, who had hoisted two of the wounded onto the pony's back.

As they passed Jackson's second line of retreat, Dani said, "I went looking for Amirou. He's not there. He's not there."

He started to cry, she reached out and they walked on hand in hand.

The wounded from the battle of New Orleans were taken to the city and cared for at the barracks, the hospitals and in people's homes. Nearly all of them were English, for the British forces had lost 1,186 injured and 484 taken prisoner. The advance brigades sacrificed two-thirds of their number to the American guns and rifles, and when the British sounded the retreat they left nearly three hundred bodies sprawled across the plantation below Jackson's rampart. They lost three of their generals, including the commander, Major General Sir Edward Pakenham, brother-in-law to the Duke of Wellington.

By the time the British had withdrawn their shattered forces and the skirmishing was over, the total of Americans killed, wounded or missing would amount to seventy-one. Amongst the dead were Sylvain Audubert, only son, the last of an old Louisiana line; and Amirou, family name unknown, of the Battalion of the Free Men of Color.

CHAPTER THIRTY-FOUR

Home

Jean found her the next day at one of the hospitals, where she had gone early in the morning with Sophronie Claiborne, taking supplies of food, linen and bandages. He managed to avoid the governor's wife and to persuade Léonore to come away, back to the residence. He had five days' leave; then he had to return to Jackson and stay in New Orleans at the general's disposal. He knew what he wanted to do in the interval; to his unspeakable relief, she wanted the same.

He waited downstairs in the deserted residence while they helped her to pack up in the bedroom that he would never see again, where his child had been conceived. Before going up the stairs she had written a note for Madame Claiborne and put it on the marble table in the vestibule. He strolled over and picked it up, under the scandalized gaze of the majordomo who was standing at the foot of the staircase, and read it.

> *Dearest Sophronie,*
> *I know what you have tried to do for me. One of these days I hope to prove to you how wrong you are. But never never can that alter my deepest friendship and gratitude. With love, Eléonore*

He laid it down, blinded by a rage against the governor and his wife and the whole place that was so powerful he could have smashed it all apart. Then she was coming down the stairs, with a maid and groom behind her carrying her baggage, and a look in her eyes that caught him and pinned him to the spot, disarmed and trembling.

"Dare I assume you are ready, madame?"

She smiled. "Did I take that long?"

He stepped forward to lead her to the door. She was wearing soft gloves of York tan that hardly seemed to touch him. The majordomo was there before them, bowing deeply to her and giving Jean a glance as he passed that would have felled an ox. Or a sensitive ox, at any rate. Jean restrained the impulse to kick him across the steps.

She turned beside the waiting cab and pressed a gold coin into the hands of the majordomo and the maid. The majordomo blushed when he took his, and gave a clumsy bow.

"Christ," Jean growled as he handed her in.

She looked at him innocently as he took his seat and the vehicle moved off. "One never knows with the paper dollar. I prefer to give them something solid."

She did not look back at the mansion as they drove away. He shifted into her line of sight and took her hands.

She said, "How did you get this cab? It must be the only one in New Orleans."

"I commandeered it. You're not too tired to travel?"

She shook her head. "I can't wait. How shall we do it?"

He ran his fingertips over her smooth cheek and under her chin. "By boat across the river." Then he grinned at the spark of amusement in her eyes. "Boat, yes, surprise surprise. All right. By pony to the bayous. If you're sure. If you're absolutely sure."

"I am. I went to see the healer. She told me I am totally fit. There is no danger about riding—it's only falling off that might be a problem. And I have no intention of falling off. This riding habit was only finished this morning and consequently it's the most expensive thing I have ever had made."

"Then I hasten to remark it's adorable. After that we

go by pirogue most of the way. The priest is in a little town below Berwick's Bay—we'll race down the Bayou La Fourche from there and take him with us. I've sent Pierre on ahead to get everything ready. I wish Dominique could have made it too; he actually wants to see us married, would you believe."

"Adorable of him," she murmured. "Do you?"

He went so cold he shivered. "God, what are you saying?"

She turned her lips into his palm and closed her eyes. "Just checking." She took his hand and rested it softly in her lap, then went on, not looking at him. "So you've been to Pierre's cottage today?"

"No. Why?" At the same moment, he knew.

"I did, yesterday, to warn them. Before I came to see you. I met Marie Villars and her sister." She was still not looking up.

He said deliberately, before she could go on, "There is nothing for you to ask. The little one was a virgin when she came to us. She still is."

She gave a gasp and tried to pull her fingers away, but he would not let her. Then she did look up, with defiance. "I'm not sure I meant anything quite so particular."

"Never mind. Now you know."

They traveled faster even than he had hoped. They did not speak a great deal during the day, for they were both tired, but he watched her, and saw the new self-containment she had acquired, and he realized he had never seen her resilience and beauty so clearly before, nor ached so at the thought of the times when he might have lost her beyond recall.

They spoke more at night, lying clasped together before they fell asleep. They did not make love; not because of caution or weariness, but because he could feel in her skin the quiver of anticipation and awe that preceded their wedding. The benign fever that coursed through them reduced their conversation to the simplest of practical exchanges, or companionable silences, or childish laughter. It was almost like being married already.

She said once, "It's so wonderful to be with you, going the same way. You know, don't you, why my path had to be different from yours? I had to save San Stefan, My island home. Now it's yours too, whenever you want, however you want."

"And Isle Dernière is yours."

"I know," she said softly. "You promised. The island of free men."

Then they reached the village on Bayou La Fourche.

They made a stop there so he could lay hold of the priest, and he left her to rest at an inn. Pierre had been through on the heels of the news from New Orleans and had gotten a tremendous reception. Jean was glad for Pierre and hoped it would not distract him from his purpose. He sent a silent prayer up that his brother would adhere to every instruction about Isle Dernière—house, men, protocol, the lot.

He went to see the priest, expecting the sweetest of sailing, and ran aground at once. From the first few words, the man named a sum so huge that Jean was stunned into silence, wondering whether Pierre had imagined for one crazy second that he was softening up the bishop at Saint Louis.

But he could bear no delay. He smiled and said, "By all means. We would like to help you towards the new chancel. As soon as we arrive at the island, I shall put the sum in your hands. Can you be ready within the hour?"

The old man looked up at him, genuinely startled. "I made no offer to travel to your . . . to your headquarters. No. That was not the arrangement."

"Here, then."

The other man rose. There was a kind of false timidity in his manner that invited strangulation. "You will appreciate, my son, that I am the father of a little community. I must take care that the actions of its priest, and those he associates with, are above reproach."

Jean ground his teeth. "You want payment in advance."

"I . . ." Not a flicker in the face, but a deprecatory wave of the hand. "The Church honors your wish to contribute to God's work. The manner of your donation is immaterial. But for me to feel secure, as the pastor of this tiny flock, I must say I would prefer such a guarantee as you suggest. In fact, if you were prepared to add one hundred dollars to the full sum, and have it delivered to me tomorrow, I would make the voyage, and perform the ceremony the day after, on the island. Your marriage in this holy place is a spectacle that certain of our worshippers might wish to be spared."

Jean had to turn on his heel and remember that he was in a church to contain himself.

A year before, even a few months before, despite the disasters, he would never have had to endure it. It showed how close his reputation was to being destroyed.

Afterwards, walking along the bank to the inn, he slowed, nauseated, and had to stop and pretend to watch the water running by, glinting beyond the reeds. It was the first humiliation of the many that were waiting to break upon him in an endless stream. He was free no longer, for he had begun to buy allies, first Jackson, next it would be the governor and the merchants, then the tinpot townspeople of Louisiana. In the past they had resented or feared him, but they had paid up, and handsomely, for what he had to offer. Now they believed they held the whip hand. It would not be long before they decided to wield it.

At the inn, Léonore was stretched out on the comfortable bed, daydreaming. For the first time in her life her energy had begun to fail her, but she told herself this was nothing like failure; it was more like luxury, since the very changes in her body were a precious sign of the miraculous new direction she was taking. After struggling so long with danger and uncertainty, she could at last look forward to rest and peace. Until now, becoming tangled in Jean's life would always have meant surrendering San Stefan—and that she could not do. She had held on to her island, for the sake of what her forebears had created, for the sake of what her parents had sacrificed, and to keep the islanders safe. San Stefan was home, in the profoundest sense, and if she had abandoned it she would have become a lesser person than the woman Jean loved.

Finally the dread and confusion were over, and she was ready to "throw herself away," as Sophronie would say—not into oblivion, but into Jean's arms. Now she could dream of giving her whole self, and losing nothing. Jean had promised, so there was no risk to her and her child. She was not destined for the kind of marriage that had crushed and warped her mother; this would be a union based on a man's unbreakable oath, chosen with open eyes and open heart, a marriage to be lived freely, sheltered by love. Jean was not Roncival. He and she had met in the midst of violence, fear and mistrust, but over the years love had brought them together. He had lied to her in the past, but that was over. He accepted her principles and her belief in their future. He would tell no lies to her now; nor would he fail the child she carried close to her heart.

She rose from the bed and began walking languidly around the room, wrapped in the sweetest thoughts. They could divide their time between his enterprises and hers, and if Isle Dernière became unsafe they could live on San Stefan. Her people would accept that situation, once they knew she had not betrayed them by marrying Jean. He had said he would never run slaves again, and by making that one fundamental promise he pledged to honor all the rest. The island community she had fostered would remain intact.

When he came back from the interview with the priest he looked as though he were brooding about something, but she chose not to question him. The hour alone with her dreams had taught her a new patience.

He said nothing about the call at the church, and explained instead about the pirogues that would take them down the bayou. There would be two men in each to do the paddling, with himself in the back of the first pirogue and herself in the second.

"Why are we separate?"

"Your baggage, my darling. It has to be evenly distributed. And if you fall out of the canoe behind me I can hook you out as you float by."

"I can swim, remember?" All at once she wanted to arouse the look in his eyes that had been there so often before. At the first hot encounter in the coral cove on San Stefan. Or during the dangerous, half-naked descent into the black ocean, from the prison ship off Havana.

He wrapped his fingers around her wrist and put her hand against his chest. They were by the window that overlooked the jetty, where sunshine leaped off the water and cast a glow right under the eaves, lighting up his crisp white shirt. He looked like a bridegroom already.

He said, "You don't mind waiting until tomorrow?"

She shook her head. Then she ventured, "Did the père say why he can't come today?"

"He's tied up. You do mind."

"No. We are married, if you recall. We have already sworn."

"Lionheart, then you were marrying a man. Not an American."

She was so taken aback she laughed. "Either or both." Her fingers dug into his chest.

With his other hand he drew her head in against his shoulder. "I wish I could take you home."

"You are."

He did not say more, just held her in the rigid clasp that told her as little of his body as it did of his mind. But his arms enclosed their child as well—the baby for whose sake she craved his utmost tenderness.

Along the bayou, there were no frosts or fog like those by the Mississippi, in the fields of slaughter. Warmth from the Gulf, in a coil of sea breezes, reached in and tugged them south. The sky was washed blue, promising stars over Isle Dernière for the first night— which it would be, wedding or no wedding, for Jean wanted her more than in all their years together. Together or apart.

Near the coast, the stream tossed them in its bright grip. She did not ride behind him for long, for she saw turbulence ahead and with a quiet word to the brutes he had hired she had them streaking past and into the tumbling water before he caught on. She turned and laughed at him when she reached the bend, with drops from the paddles flashing and dancing behind her head.

Baratarians were waiting with a pinnace and they put to sea before dusk, so Léonore was able to watch Isle Dernière approach. She stood with her back against the mast, as she used to do when her father was alive, when a vessel was someone else's responsibility, not hers. She watched Jean direct the seamen and marveled at how he did it without speaking.

He told her that he and his men had been at Isle Dernière so little time they had not even fixed on which anchorage to use. For now, the vessels were all moored in a bay looking out on the Gulf, instead of on the lee side, for they had not yet charted all the shoals there.

"It's still chaos. The house is bearable, but you won't like the rest of it. We'll honeymoon indoors."

"You know just what I like—being with you. I want to see everything."

As they came around the last point, he stood beside her with one arm around the mast, his fingers just touching her waist. She caught sight of a few low, thatched roofs, and fewer trees than on Barataria. There was a stiff breeze raking the coastline and as they came into the offing it whipped through her hair. She put one hand up to capture it, and suddenly saw all the ships bouncing in the bay.

"The *Fantôme*!"

"I should damned well hope so."

"Look at the lights. They must be all onboard."

"Not keen to share the huts at night, I suppose. We'll teach them manners tomorrow."

She turned to stand in front of him, struggling with her flying hair. "I want to go by and greet them."

"It's getting dark."

"So?"

He walked away and gave the order, then came back. "Turn around." He undid her hair, then pulled it back and plaited it. The action was smooth, deft, and caused her not a twinge of discomfort. Then he told her to face

him, and adjusted the top of the lace that was ruched
across her breasts. He removed from it and then re-
pinned the diamond that had been stripped from him at
San Stefan.

"You're cold." He had a heavier cape brought and put
it across her shoulders, and this time his touch lingered.
Suddenly, just before the pinnace glided within hailing
distance of the *Fantôme*, he wrapped his arms around
her from behind, and caught her breasts, and pressed his
lips hard to her neck.

He kept his arms around her until she was announced
and Rigaud and all the rest came crowding to the rails.
The pinnace was maneuvered in next to the brigantine
and held off the *Fantôme* while she stepped out of Jean's
arms and yelled up greetings and told them about New
Orleans. She could not say anything about the wedding.
It was not something you bawled across the ocean in
the dark.

Jean appeared at her elbow. "Go aboard, why don't
you. Then they can bring you down to the jetty, at the
back of the bay, you see? They know where to come."

"I'd like to. I'll be ten minutes."

"As long as you want."

He helped her up the ladder they unrolled down the
side, but did not speak to Rigaud. Then he leaped down
into the pinnace and stood by the mast, watching her as
it pulled away towards the jetty in the distance.

It was like a celebration onboard the *Fantôme*, so she
stayed longer than she intended, and some time had
gone by before she realized her crew were under a
misapprehension—they were expecting to sail for San
Stefan the next day. Pierre Laffite, who had arrived a
few hours before, had clearly said nothing about the
wedding. And her men, it transpired, always spent the
night onboard. The old truce with the Baratarians had
not yet progressed to their living cheek by jowl with
them.

Rigaud partly explained as two others rowed them
straight in to the shore. "With the Laffites and Curtis
away, that Baudard acts like a king. The rest of them
can't stand it and nor can we. If we beach the dinghy just

up ahead here, I can take you through the settlement so you can see the lay of the land. Not that there's much to it."

From the waterside she could not see the rest of the bay, which was concealed by a promontory of jagged rocks. The ride in on the dinghy was swift, as the sailors matched the sweeps of the oars to the lines of breakers. When the prow hit the sand, the last wave gave them a strong nudge and creamy foam swept out before them in a giant fan, shells rolling at its edge. She got her shoes and hems wet as she jumped out and ran up the incline.

"Come," she said to Rigaud. "Show me the way."

The others sat down in the leathery grass at the edge of the dune to wait and she and Rigaud trudged up over the sand, along a path edged with lupins and onto dry land where the settlement began.

"What's this place like?" she said to the shadow beside her, before they got to the huts.

"Don't ask, Maître." When she looked quickly at his grim face he avoided her gaze. Then, knowing she would not give up the question he ground out one word: "Rough."

There was a smell of fish as they walked past the first shanty, and she noticed a plank on barrels at the side, where someone must have been cleaning a catch earlier in the day. All of a sudden there was a rush of wings, and a seagull slashed through the air in front of them with a squeal of protest.

"How many are they?"

"A dozen vessels, a couple of hundred people. The lamps are out: they must all be down welcoming Laffite. Pity there's no moon."

She listened, but heard only the sea breeze in the stunted trees. This was a lonely place. Beyond the huts she hesitated and looked around amongst the low bushes, then said to Rigaud, "Shouldn't we go that way instead? The path looks wider and there's a light up there."

"No, that's just the barracoon. Best way is straight ahead. Wait, I'll grab someone and ask for a lantern."

She stayed where she was. *Barracoon.* She tried to catch her breath. "What is that building for?"

He peered at her in the darkness. "Slaves. What else?"

She stepped closer, searching his face. "But there are none."

"That's news to me. There were yesterday."

"They have orders . . ." Her voice shuddered and stopped and she tried again. "They have orders to take no slaves."

He shook his head.

"I don't believe you!" She shouted it into his face, then turned and ran. Up the slope to the building on the hill, where slivers of light flickered and leaped in the palmetto thatch of the roof and walls as she came near.

"Maître!" Rigaud was not far behind her, his boots thudding on the path.

She reached the end of the building. The door was just a panel of palmetto laced to branches. She gave one crashing blow to it with her fist and it opened at once, inward.

"Hey!" It was Pierre Laffite, alarmed and annoyed. He took one step back when he recognized her, then another when Rigaud reached the edge of the doorway. Pierre's face in the slanting light of the lantern above the door looked twisted and deformed. Behind him were two armed guards.

Beyond, huddled on the earth floor or leaning against the dry, leafy walls, were a score of people, some motionless, some just opening their eyes. There was a lad lying just a few paces away, his oval face resting on one coral-pink palm. His mouth twitched once in his sleep, then was still.

All Jean's fears about Isle Dernière crowded in on him as he strode into the so-called village and sent people scurrying as he came. Pierre was nowhere to be seen—not surprisingly, since he would have no mind to answer for the state the place was in. Even in the dark Jean could tell it was a shambles—but at least he had provided himself with an interval to put a few things to rights, before Léonore got into the jetty.

As it happened, his own house was not too appalling. It was well lit, and spotless. There was a meal in train. The rooms had the swept, empty feeling that told him no one had been making free with them in his absence.

He went out on the verandah and Dominique's pointer, Belair, came loping around the house, then whined in disappointment and dropped to his haunches. The men collected, and when the usual rapid hush fell over them he brought them up to date. Except about the wedding, which Pierre was supposed to have hinted at but not confirmed. He caught a few gazes as he raked the assembly and he got the whiff of a certain slackness and uncertainty that riled him. But it could all wait until tomorrow.

At the end he said to Maurice, who was standing in the dirt just beyond the verandah post, "How's the saloon coming along?"

"Grand, Bos."

"Have you lost any of your taste for whiskey since the *Tigre* went down?"

"No, Bos."

"Anyone else?"

A chorus of expletives.

"Then you can leave me in peace and get over there for the night. Baudard is cracking the barrels open now."

He went straight back inside, then out the back to the lean-to kitchen. "Where's my brother?"

The cook looked up from the fireplace. "Over at the barracoon, Bos. There was a bit of trouble there this morning. He said he sure didn't want any tonight. Should be back soon."

The firelight flared out, hurting Jean's eyes and turning the man's face into a bulbous mask surrounded by an orange haze. "You're telling me we've got slaves?"

"Not many, Bos, more's the pity. But—"

He darted away as though the kitchen had exploded and the fire was roaring and chasing him through the deserted lanes of the village. He ran as though a volcano were spewing lava up behind him and the huts on each side were about to be smashed flat and engulfed. He tore towards the barracoon on the hill, with a rage so fierce inside his chest that he was afraid he would burst before he got there and disappear like a gout of flame from a gun barrel.

He got there. He was at the door. He crashed his fists into it and it cracked and swung inwards crookedly on one hinge. Pierre was just inside, with the guards. The slaves were cowering behind them, all awake, their eyes gleaming with hostility and fear.

"I said no blacks."

"I know, but Baudard—"

"No, it's you. It's you!" He slammed his hand against his forehead.

"She didn't say anything. She didn't look angry, as far as I could see." Jean raised his head, took a long, panting breath. Pierre's voice gained a note of appeal. "She just walked off. I reckon you could explain."

"She was *here*?" The whole place, full of eyes, shadows and faces, began to burn and crumple at the edges. "When, you bastard? When?"

Pierre's mouth twisted. "Half an hour, maybe."

Jean hit Pierre in the face, so hard he flew back over the table, to the wall and then to the floor.

Then he turned and ran again, into a darkness as dense as granite, as cold as the black side of the moon.

Léonore sat in the dunes, looking at the sea, her knees drawn up to her chin and her arms around them. Her head and chest were like blocks of ice, in which the impulses of thought and feeling had congealed and almost ceased. But the wind blew on her right cheek. Westerly. Favorable. The small perceptions were painful, like heat on frostbite. Soon she would have to admit more pain, walk back over the hill and into the village, confront Jean.

Down at the dim edge of the waves, Rigaud waited with the crew of the little boat, uncertain but patient. She must make a move soon. Then she heard a sound to her right, from the direction of the barracoon, and turned her head.

Jean came towards her, a tall figure against the gray sandhills, walking as steadily as the footing permitted, until he drew close and she could see his chest was heaving, his breath deep, as though he had broken through barriers to reach her. For a moment he stood silent, within arm's reach but very upright, as if he were some kind of totem planted on the deserted beach to warn of danger. Then he dropped to the ground and sat beside her, his gaze penetrating, his face composed into a stone-like severity.

He said, "You found them."

"Yes."

"Now you know."

"What?" she said, and terrible fear made her voice shake.

He looked down and pounded his fist into the sand between them. "You know. How. Far. My power goes." He looked up again, desperate fury in his eyes. "And it's only as far as I go. If I'm not by, I can't answer for anything they do."

"That's not true!" she cried.

"Yes, it is. But you won't accept it. *Jésu*, I wish I didn't have to face it myself. But I'm bound to them, and they to me."

"Congratulations," she said, and anger catapulted her to her feet. "That's a fine loyalty you espouse."

He stayed where he was. "You've a home to go to. In what does that consist?" His voice sounded venomous, alien, as he answered for her. "A family, of sorts." Her heart went cold. *Of sorts.* Was he speaking of their child, of himself? She looked at him in bafflement, but he went on in the same tone, "An island paradise—self-sufficient and impregnable, as I too well know. A community fostered through generations." She tried to interrupt him, but he forged on. "Fragile, but nonetheless whole. Thanks to you." A pause. "You also have America on your side. Don't deny it."

"So do you!"

He gave a short, incredulous laugh. "For just as long as Jackson stays around to savor the triumph. Then we'll be hunted as never before. It began with Barataria and

it won't stop now. We've been outlaws and hellish banditti a long time. Now we're fugitives as well. This is our
last island in name only—it is no refuge, and soon we'll
be off to find another."

"But you've been given the chance to change everything."

He shook his head, and for a moment, by a flexion of
his straight shoulders, she saw his despair. "You're de-
luded. *I* have changed, for you and with you. But everything else remains the same; the battle never ends. No
man can alter what's been given to him. And I shall stay
the course. What I hold, I hold."

"Oh yes? So that means *them* too?" Her whole body
shook, and her arm trembled as she thrust it out in the
darkness, pointing towards the barracoon on the hill.

He rose to his feet, so quickly that she took an involuntary step back. "The slaves were captured against my
orders. I knew nothing about them until I saw Pierre
tonight, and—" He stopped, controlled his voice. "They
are free. That is my wedding present to you. Do with it
what you will."

She turned away, in shock and confusion, unable to
thank him and knowing he did not expect her to. He
threw her this gift savagely, without generosity or tenderness, because he felt compelled to. How had they
come to such a pass, on the very eve of their marriage?
She burst out, "This is not how I imagined things."

His voice behind her was falsely calm. "No? I'm surprised to find your imagination so much at fault. You
are one for home truths, Lionheart. Can't you face them
here?" She felt his hand on her cheek and he turned
her head to him. "I led my brothers and these men to
this point. And whatever their fate is, I will not abandon
them. I *will not* see them go to prison again. You know
how much I've done for you; you know me better even
than my own kin. I will never let you down, nor them.
That is a promise, not a guarantee. I can offer you only
myself, and my resolve. If you can't accept that, tell me."

A surge of strange emotion shook her, and he withdrew his hand. She stared at him, seized by the injustice
of it—that he should make her see the flaws in her

dream of security, that he and she should be forced once again to reshape their lives. In that dreadful second, she resented him for it, and he caught the flash in her eyes.

His voice, dark and bitter, pierced the gloom and echoed in her chest. "I would take you even if we stood at the gates of hell. You must take me equally, with all our imperfections on our heads."

And she came to a swift realization, as though the light from the nearest star had darted into her mind. Their marriage was not a safe conclusion, but a beginning. If they were to be together, face everything together, then they must *always* be reinventing and reshaping their lives—for ahead lay joys and trials that they could not possibly predict. There were certainties in her future nonetheless—San Stefan and the island home that Jean envied, the place he had sworn to sail to as her partner. And foremost among those certainties was this man she had chosen, who stood before her now in all his uncompromising strength and beauty. The man she loved, whom she wanted with a raw passion that urged her into their union, clear-eyed and unafraid. She had only to take one step across the soft sand, place her hand in his.

"Come," she said.

They walked down the beach in silence and she gripped his fingers as hard as she could, willing him to give her time to decide what came next. She did not speak until they reached the boat.

"Monsieur Rigaud, the *Fantôme* is putting to sea. We need one watch onboard. The other will spend the night ashore." Rigaud threw her a worried glance. She said firmly, "Tomorrow Monsieur Laffite and I will be married on this island. And henceforth his men are brothers in arms to those of San Stefan." With the gaze of all the sailors riveted on her, she said, "This is an alliance, Monsieur Rigaud. And we will honor every part of it."

He hid his expression for a moment by looking out towards the *Fantôme,* then said with dignity, "When do we sail for home, Maître?"

"Soon. Time enough to talk of that tomorrow."

*   *   *

When the brigantine's sails caught the wind, it scooped her at once towards the open sea. For a time the lights at the back of the bay were visible. Two in the foreground, on the jetty—lanterns on poles. A few more beyond, amongst clustered dwellings and sparse trees. Tomorrow Léonore would step with Jean across the threshold of his new, invisible, temporary house. Tonight they rode the waves.

Above decks, the faithful watch melted into the shadows; it was as though her ship were sailed by benevolent ghosts. Below, she found the *Fantôme* well stocked, so she cooked Jean a meal for the very first time. Simple and flavorsome: ackee rice, salt pork with fresh greens, and sweet Spanish wine. They ate little, though, and found themselves sitting face-to-face, trapped in superabundance like creatures caught in honey, until she laughed at him and said, "Suffer some more to pass your lips, monsieur. You have sat at my table only twice before, both times as my enemy. This will not do."

He looked up. "Will this?" Their glasses met across the board, above the old chart table over which she had labored so long to outplan and outwit him, and through the gemlike glow of the wine she saw his lips curve in a tantalizing smile.

Later he helped her unfold her bunk from the wall, and he courteously admired the ingenuity of the arrangement, while she stood and looked at it, overwhelmed by the memory of his own mighty Empire bed in which they had voyaged in the past, and its contrast with the crisp, narrow whiteness of this one, which looked bridal—almost virginal. She sat down on it, her fists closed in her lap, and he resumed his chair by the table, fixing her with his black, questioning gaze.

"Do you remember the blindfold game you made me play, that night on the *Mélusine*?"

He nodded.

"Then close your eyes." There was a moment while she poised herself in hope, letting all her love and resolution pulse through her. "Now. What do you see?"

He opened his eyes and said at once, "My love."

Warmth flooded her face and shoulders and she lowered her head. "You have all of me. As my present to you."

He sat for a long time with his head bent and his elbows on his knees, looking down into his cupped hands. One tear fell into them, but he crushed it between his palms. Then he leaned forward and folded his fingers around hers so that they pressed against her stomach, their warmth penetrating the fabric, enveloping beneath it the small scrap of life that would be his child.

She said softly, "If it's a daughter, I hope she has your eyes."

"If it's a boy, I pray he has your heart."

After a while she said, "Come on deck, and let's see if we have left the land behind."

It was as she desired: the *Fantôme* was alone on the ocean. They stood in the stern and Léonore looked up at the mizzen, dark blue canvas against the velvet sky. From each corner of the sails, the hidden coral beckoned her to her island, and high above the Roncival pennant flapped across the stars, making them look as though they danced along its thorned edges. *My darling child,* she said silently, with infinite tenderness, *soon we are going home.*

Jean meanwhile was looking north, raking the barely perceptible horizon.

"Searching for prizes, Monsieur Laffite?"

"I have them," he said, turning quickly to put one arm around her and set his back against the rail. "All I want."

She leaned close so that her body was aligned along his, then felt a prickle against her breastbone where the diamond brooch pressed into her skin.

She drew back a little, looked down and plucked it from the lace beneath her throat.

"Do you recall how I got this?"

"How could I not?"

As she held it up, it sparked in her fingers, as though catching light from his mocking glance.

She said, "I stole it from you when we were enemies. Now that we are one, its time is over."

She raised her bare arms and put them on his shoullers, against his neck. He shivered, as though at the sudden coolness against his hot skin, then tugged her to him.

The *Fantôme* glided on, a lone ship with indigo sails, far from land. The man and woman on her deck clung to each other in a kiss so profound that it was as if they were drowning, oblivious, in the vast midnight ocean and the fathomless sky. Unseen except by the stars, a single diamond dropped over the stern, flickered once in the waves and went out.

Historical Note

Anyone writing about Jean Laffite must do so in awe of the storytelling abilities of the man himself, yet this novel is based more upon fact than legend, and most of the characters were real people, from William and Sophronie Claiborne, Andrew Jackson and Edward Livingston, to less public figures like Adélaïde Maselari, Marie Villars and her little sister.

It seemed natural to follow the exact events of Jean's life for those six turbulent years up to the siege of New Orleans. Barataria, the auctions at the Temple, the association with General Humbert, Jean's profitable dealings with the citizens of New Orleans, his long contest with the governor—all these form a vital part of the history of the Deep South. Jean's handling of the English flotilla, the Laffites' war with the customs officers and the Legislature of Louisiana, the sack of Barataria and the bargain with Andrew Jackson were all precursors to the siege of New Orleans over Christmas–New Year's 1814–15. And those who meet Jean Laffite (now usually spelled Lafitte) here for the first time will not be astonished to know that in battle he behaved with the gift for strategy, the coolness and courage he displays within the pages of this book.

And then there are those incidents at the margins of history, recounted by men and women in his lifetime and begging to be retold—the child brought to Grande Terre to cut the cards, the brutal confrontation with the

alians, the surprise encounter with Sophronie Claiborne in a château beside the Mississippi, Livingston on
gambling spree in the bayous with Laffite money . . .

Though San Stefan and its mistress are fictions, history
provided a scaffolding on which to build Léonore Roncival's dream of islands. Adélaïde Maselari did indeed
have a child by Pierre Laffite in New Orleans in October
1810—why should she not have earlier been the mistress
of another pirate, in another place? The wreck of the
Barbadoes has yet to be salvaged from the Shoals of
Heniagoe, but perhaps one day when treasure hunters
reach her, they may find that others have been there
before them. Andrea Santo did not lie when he said the
Library Society of Charleston once had to ransom a
cargo of books from a Guadeloupe privateer. Jean Laffite certainly kept a rendezvous with someone in Donaldsonville when Léonore was there in 1813. An
American agent did indeed write a dispatch from Cuba
on August 8, 1814, setting out the English plans to invade Louisiana: history cannot tell us who got a copy
through to Barataria, but I attribute the deed to Léonore
Roncival. When the English fleet appeared in the Caribbean on its way to Jamaica in November 1814, two of
its vessels, the *Helen* and the *Volcano,* were attacked by
unknown pirates; in this account I have named them as
Léonore's. And why shouldn't the Secretary of the U.S.
Treasury, Albert Gallatin, have come home from Europe with at least one small diplomatic triumph?

Despite the wealth of known facts, Jean Laffite remains elusive. His origins and his family, his ultimate
endeavors, are still as ambiguous as he made them, even
to Léonore. Despite nearly two centuries of research, no
one knows when, where or how he finally disappeared.
Which allows us to dream that perhaps one day he found
safe harbor on an uncharted island, where he was known
but not feared, a hunter no longer, and a prey only to
love.

Acknowledgments

For insights into the history of the countries of the Caribbean and the Mexican Gulf I am indebted to many scholars, amongst whom I pay special tribute to an English historian, Robin Reilly, for his brilliant account of the New Orleans campaign in the War of 1812, *The British at the Gates*. I greatly appreciate the dedicated research of the Jean Laffite Society of Galveston, Texas, whose investigations constantly discover new aspects of the pirate of the Gulf—and debunk just as many false claims. Special thanks are due to Don Marler and to Laffite Society historian Jean Epperson, who kindly read the manuscript for historical accuracy.

The two stanzas quoted in Chapter Twenty-four are from an occasional poem by Lord Byron, "Remind me not, remind me not," written in 1809. The exploits of Jean Laffite (known to history as Lafitte) provided the initial idea for Byron's "The Corsair," written in 1813, from which I drew the epigraph to this book.

I am most grateful to Anne Bohner and New American Library for the warm welcome they have given to the story of Léonore Roncival and Jean Laffite, and deep appreciation goes to my wonderful agent Kristin Nelson, who made it all happen.

My thanks go as always to my husband for his inspired dispensations of counsel or champagne. I am also grateful to friends who have contributed much encouragement in

ifferent ways, especially to Isolde Martyn for the ideas
nd laughter we've shared, and to Ken Shearman for
ending me his ears and his remarkable eyes.

The story of Ayisha, the grandmother of Léonore
Roncival, is told in my first novel, *La Créole*.

In her first years, New Zealander **Cheryl Sawyer** lived just a few steps from the sea, and her favorite places are still within sight and sound of an ocean, whether they be Caribbean islands or coastal towns on the Pacific rim. She has two master's degrees with honors in French and English literature, and her early years of teaching included a university tutorship in French. After living and working in England, France, Italy and Switzerland, she returned to the South Pacific to pursue a career in publishing and writing. She has had two previous historical novels published, *La Créole* and *Rebel,* and is the author of a children's book and an academic translation of the journals of explorer Jean-François-Marie de Surville. She currently lives in a penthouse with views of the harbor city of Sydney, Australia. Her Web site is www.cherylsawyer.com.

Don't miss Cheryl Sawyer's next
gripping historical romance filled with
war, treachery and sensual desire.

The Chase
June 2005

A love story where the most dangerous
battle of all is fought within the
stronghold of the heart.

Read on for an exciting sneak peek. . . .

Sophia told Harry a horse story when she tucked him into bed that night, about a chestnut mare who came safely to a green field after incredible adventures and had foals that ran swift as the wind, and always the very swiftest on the home stretch. She knew from his satisfied smile that after she left the bedchamber he would conjure up a dream about Scheherezade dancing down to Clifton.

She spent the next hour in her room, but it was impossible to think. She fiddled about, perching on the edge of the bed, staring blankly at the curtained windows, then getting up and going to rearrange the items on the desktop near the door.

The event that her father had asked her to reconsider could not be analyzed. Only relived with a vividness that always caught her by surprise.

The revelation that came upon her that day outside Sydney Town, far away on the other side of the world, had torn away barriers, and she could put nothing up again in their place.

Mrs. Macquarie, the governor's wife, had made the horse available, a big hack that Sophia had ridden before. She would have loved to go out alone, as she used to do at home on the Sussex downs, but an escort was indispensable here, so she was accompanied by Lieutenant Jones of Governor Macquarie's regiment. Instead of galloping free, tasting the sense of risk and adventure that she could never indulge in except on horseback, she put the hack to a sedate trot alongside the lieutenant and they went up the rutted streets of the settlement and onto the eastern ridge where a new, wider road was being constructed by convict laborers.

She was already familiar with the route, so she recognized the giant red gum tree at the fork, the strip of open ground that led to a track she had not yet explored. She had been told that it ran to a lookout point at the far end from which one could see the vast, beautiful harbor spread out below. Lieutenant Jones left her to make the short detour while he rode ahead to the work party. There could be no danger here, no watchers in the woods—the road makers and the soldiers supervising them were too close by. The invisible cordon around the area was as secure as the fetters around the convicts' ankles. She was riding through redcoat country.

Above her, silver gum trees reached up like supplicants to the cobalt midsummer sky, insects shrilling in their high crowns. The hack flicked its ears back and forth, stepping gingerly, wary of snakes and big lizards in the knee-high undergrowth. It should have picked up the presence of the man behind the dense foliage at the turn of the track, but it did not.

Suddenly he was there. A tall, broad figure, with feet firmly planted, arms outstretched, palms open, he blocked off the track like a gate slamming in her way—yet without a sound, for at that very instant all the insects on the ridge stopped singing. As the silence crashed down she took in an impression of his face: a lock of thick, sun-bleached hair over his forehead, deep-set gray eyes smoldering in shadow.

Then the horse shuddered under her and flung its head sideways with a whinny that was like a strangled scream. It reared and plunged into deep leaves to the left of the path, hooves trampling the ground.

She managed to stay on, gripping the pommel of the sidesaddle so hard that she bruised the inside of her knee. She lost one rein as she grabbed for the horse's mane.

The man growled something that might have been a curse, then stepped forward, despite the animal's dangerous panic, and spoke to it very low. Sophia righted herself but could feel the massive body beneath her tense and gather, ready to rear again.

The soldier put his hand over the top of the horse's neck, directly behind the ears. Four heavy thumps resounded through the glade as the creature brought its hooves one by one to the ground and kept them there. The big head stopped tossing, and the body stilled. Sophia could feel the sides of the neck quiver under her fingers, but the horse remained immobile, poised on the edge of violence but momentarily subdued by the man's voice and touch.

The soldier stroked one hand down the horse's nose, talking in French, soft words that she could not catch. Once his hand was on the bridle he met her gaze again.

If he had spoken to her at once, she might have been able to cope, to ignore his eyes, to mask her own response. But he looked startled, as though she had taken him unawares instead of the other way around. His eyes were wide now, and a lighter gray than they had seemed at first, the color of rain clouds just beginning to gather. He gave her a look that was somewhere between politeness and impudence: naked, frank and demanding in a manner she could not define. But she could feel it, as though he had laid a hand on her in the tender, authoritative way that he had touched the horse.

It was a sensation of pleasure so acute that it shocked her, and her voice shook as she said, "How dare you!"

"Excuse me." His open gaze did not change.

"What, pray, do you think you're doing?"

There was the faintest access of color across his cheekbones. Was he embarrassed? To mask her own confusion she leaned quickly forward and scooped up the dangling rein, her hand coming so near his that he gave an involuntary movement. The hack shook its head and stamped its forelegs uneasily.

"Excuse me," he said again. His voice had a caressing timbre that seemed too gentle for his big frame, and he spoke with a slight French accent. She realized he was one of the Chasseurs and by rights should be up by the roadway, on duty. But she could not dismiss him; she had no authority to do so. And could not summon the will.

He said, "You must not continue in this direction. The ground is unstable—rain has washed away the side of the path and it's not safe to go near the edge. This horse is not bred for the terrain—you are risking an accident."

"An accident? You very nearly caused one!"

"Forgive me." He let go of the bridle and stepped nearer, running his hand smoothly down the side of the horse's neck. *"Tiens, mon brave, ça va mieux?"* Then he looked up at her as though she had already granted the forgiveness he asked for so confidently. "I heard you approaching, but I did not realize you were close. I was too hasty. But you are a superb rider, and there is no harm done. After all."

There was a smile in his eyes now, a warm, complicit smile that seemed about to spread to his expressive mouth. His fingers were tangled in the horse's mane, inches away from hers, and he was standing too close for courtesy. He looked at her as though he knew her but had been longing to know her better, as though this were the most fortunate of circumstances, a meeting in the woods between new friends. Friends who might so very easily become something more to each other. That was what the glint in his eyes said, and the half smile that now touched his full lips and the tilt of his head as he looked up at her. He was letting her see into him with a bold candor that she could not resist, despite all her will and training. She simply looked back without protest.

She had never been so shaken, so thrilled, by a man's sheer presence. She had never been in this kind of delicious danger, where one look was like a touch, one word an intimate caress. It was as though all her life she had been a stranger herself, and it had taken this stranger to break down the barriers to her own desire.

He frightened her. But it was not his glorious, inviting smile or the closeness of his strong body that caused this panic in her; it was the depth of her own reaction.

Then Lieutenant Jones rode into the glade, and she recognized that the sound of hooves had been approaching for some time. She glanced back toward the lieutenant and tapped a rein against her horse's neck to send it smoothly out to the side, farther still off the track.

The soldier remained looking at her, unmoving, as she brought the horse to a halt and faced the two men. She was trembling inside. She could hardly meet the lieutenant's gaze, as though he might discover her shameful secret if he looked at her too hard.

He said, "Lady Hamilton, are you all right?"

"Yes, thank you."

"I thought I heard a cry." When she did not reply, Jones said impatiently, "Decernay. What are you hanging about here for? Report back to duty, at the double."

The soldier saluted—not to the lieutenant but to her. His face was solemn now, the eyes opaque as gunmetal.

It was absurd: he wanted to stay. And, even more absurdly, she needed him to. Her body rebelled at his going, while her mind struggled to encompass what was happening, to understand whom she had become in this extraordinary encounter.

She had a ridiculous impulse to say some word of farewell, but it was too late; he turned and sprang away, and seconds later he disappeared through the trees.

Lieutenant Jones said, "Would you like me to accompany you to the point, your ladyship?"

"Thank you, no." She put the hack in motion. Her heart was pounding, but her voice obeyed her. "I'll return to the road. It's safer. I find my mount is not very sure-footed over this ground."

As they rode back up to the crest, he said, "Private Decernay was not making a nuisance of himself, I hope?"

"Not at all. He warned me about the track."

At the top, they put their horses to a trot. She tried to concentrate on their progress, on her surroundings. To quell the tumult inside.

The road, built by the infantry only a couple of years before, had neither paving nor gravel, but it had been

cleared of outcrops and stumps and the holes filled in
with broken pieces of the sandstone that formed the
bedrock of the ridge. The surface was firm if not very
level, a shallow layer of sandy soil. It was compacted by
the traffic of carts, horses and people on foot who went
as far as the lighthouse at South Head, eager for news
of incoming ships, or for recreation, in a colony where
choices were limited and the fresh sea breezes along the
ridge could be counted as a blessing.

Then suddenly they rounded a bend and overtook Private Decernay jogging along by the shallow ditch at the
side. He had a vigorous action, and his boots thudded
purposefully, the sound accompanied by the rattle of a
short sword in a scabbard that jolted against his thigh.

Lieutenant Jones took no notice of him, but Sophia
looked down irresistibly. As the Chasseur ran, his bright
hair and his high, well defined cheekbones caught the
sunlight. He had the hard, rugged strength of a common
foot soldier, but his features—the generous brows, the
straight nose and chiseled lips—suggested a character
formed for other pursuits, another kind of life. The
range of expression in his face and his beautifully modu-
lated voice had astonished and compelled her, and in
their sudden meeting he had revealed emotions that no
other man had ever offered her so freely. Just now, his
face was alive and intense as a beacon, and through that
one incandescent glance she took in the knowledge that
he wanted her. And knew that she wanted him.

She passed on.

When she got back to the house in town it was late
afternoon. She checked on Harry; Nurse said he was still
having his nap. She went to her chamber, closed the
door, stripped down to her shift and lay on the white
satin counterpane of the smooth bed, waiting for the
cool of the evening, while the heat flicked around her
like a rough, silent tongue.

Simply looking at Decernay, inhabiting the same space
as he did for a few snatched moments, had aroused her
in a way she had never known before—except in the
dark, in the bedchamber, safe in the arms of the husband
who loved her.

This was lust. This was betrayal. If she had ever thought herself capable of such intensity of feeling she might have guarded against it, but it was as unfamiliar as being struck by lightning, swept away in a flood. Even now, when the man's remembered presence overtook her senses and filled her imagination, she felt a throb of sweetness. And loss. For he was forbidden to her.

Decernay was a Chasseur, a captured soldier who had turned coat to join the lowest ranks of the English army. He was French, of the race that killed Andrew. He was her enemy.